WHITE MAN'S LESSON

The plate clattered to the ground again, and Silver watched numbly as his right hand reached toward her. It slid under her hair to wrap around the back of her neck. Her heart tripped and she could not breathe, could not think what to do—but she swallowed, it did not matter; her feet were stuck to the ground anyway!

Walker's voice was soft, like rain on wet leaves. "I was wondering if . . . you'd ever been kissed by a white eyes."

"Me not know this 'kiss,' " she whispered.

He tugged, and she took a stumbling step. He put his lips to hers and they lingered, moved until hers parted; they slid against her teeth, pressed the corner of her mouth, grabbed her lower lip.

She drew back with a gasp. "Me not like this k-kiss!"

He pulled her to him. "Then let me show you again." He folded her against him.

COMANCHE LOVE SONG

CHERYL BLACK

ZEBRA BOOKS
KENSINGTON PUBLISHING CORP.

To my husband, Harrison—for being my cheering squad, my babysitter, my financier, and the romantic hero who puts all the rest to shame.

Forever and always . . .
Cheryl

From The Author

J. Emmor Harston made Comanche history a lifetime study. He lived among them, sat with the old chiefs, and spoke their language. No other tribe in Indian history fought so long or defended its home as valiantly, against such odds, as did the Comanche. Harston's book, *Comanche Land*, was an effort to correct many erroneous facts recorded about them, and is considered among authorities to be one of a kind. Most of the research for this historical romance was taken from his work, which was uncompleted at his death.

As a geology graduate, Mr. Harston's civil engineering work took him into the heart of the Comanche land of his youth, and in later life he was determined to record the side of the story that was never told and spent those years laboring to bring his particular understanding and first-hand knowledge about the tribe to light. The Comanches called him Nad-e-mah Tao (Little Trader Boy), for his father was an Indian trader and he grew up living among them, near the army post in Fort Sills, Oklahoma. Perhaps Harston alone of his peers had such a thorough history of the Comanches — as told directly by them.

When the tribe who later became Comanches* separated from the mother tribe of Shoshoni in present day Idaho, they were Co-cho Te-ich-as, or Buffalo Eaters. They came into southeast Colorado, Kansas, New Mexico, and Texas, driving out the Apaches who had previously driven out the Shoshoni to occupy the area for a brief time (the cause for the bad blood between Apache and Comanche). Many historians have written that the Comanches came to Texas screaming their savage war cries and driving out the peaceful Tejas Indians, never understanding that the Te-ichas (Spanish spelling, Tejas) Indians and the Comanche were one and the same tribe. Mr. Harston found that the earliest records of a tribe calling themselves Buffalo Eaters had entered the area as far back as 900 A.D. when they first broke off from the mother Shoshoni tribe.

It sometimes seems that we Americans are always finding yet another skeleton in our closet. But let it be said that no nation has ever turned to magnify its errors or give glory where it was due to those we have wrongly persecuted as much as this one. In that light, I have once again chosen to interweave some of the colorful, though tragic, Comanche history into this love story. I would be very pleased if it is remembered as a small tribute to the tribe who lost fifty-seven of their number for every single white person killed in Texas by all Indians combined. To that tribe who has been more maligned and more hated than any in history. Who gave up their only orginal name — as well as the land itself — to us: *Te-ich-as . . . TEXAS!*

Cheryl Black

*The name *Comanche*, or Caum-onses, was originally brought to the Teichas tribe of Buffalo Eaters by another band broken away from the mother Shoshoni tribe. It means Bald Heads. The Shoshoni nickname was applied because that particular band taunted their enemies by shaving their heads and leaving only a scalplock, which said to their enemies: "Come and get it if you can!" But use of the nickname later spread to include the other three tribes which sprang from them, namely the Antelope Eaters, Fish Eaters, and Dog Eaters. According to the chief of the Wichitas, speaking of the whole of the Teichas tribe, Tawakana Jim said they were unfortunately stuck with a misnomer, for ". . . there is not a baldheaded Indian in the tribe." Later the name Caum-onses was corrupted to Comanches by the Tex-Mexicans who poured into Texas from 1810 to 1840. Thus it was doubly a nickname that every Teichas hated, for the "che" ending meant Horrible. The name to them was: *Baldheads Horrible*. However that, like other indignities imposed upon them by the white man, was here to stay.

To my Friends and Neighbors in Nacogdoches:

According to the folks at Stephen F. Austin University

Library, the Old Stone Fort was a store, and once a saloon. It was never a fort in the traditional military sense, although early settlers did flee there from raiding Indians in the early 1800's. Please accept my apologies for using literary license so I could have my fort in Nacogdoches.

Cheryl Black
Alto, Texas

Author's Note: Gray Shadows is a ficticious house not in any way connected to the many antebellum homes still in existence in southern Louisiana.

Part I

Chapter 1

"Jamie, you better get out and feed the livestock. Papa's been in the fields since dawn."

She smiled to herself as the ten-year-old scooted his plate back without a grumble, grabbed his dusty cap from the door peg, and ambled out. When they'd first come west, she argued that frontier life was too hard on the young ones, but she had since changed her mind as she watched the strain of becoming a man put a spring in the boy's step, turn the baby fat to stringy muscles, and sharpen his mind and reflexes until he could drop a deer from a hundred yards in one shot.

She stood at the cabin door drying her hands on her apron, and surveyed their kingdom of short sturdy oaks, one cleared field, a lean-to for the livestock, a rail pen for the milk cow.

Her hands were so rough that the skin snagged the dish towel, and she glanced at them ruefully. The baby had been just one year old when they moved from southern Louisiana, where the pines and oaks were giants, the undergrowth more like jungle than forest; and they had laughed at the stubbly little oaks that flourished on the plains — before they tried to clear them. She had grown callouses as large and hard as Will's in the process.

A little misty-eyed, she turned back inside long enough to swing the baby to her hip. She had a sudden urge to be outside, and grabbed the walking stick beside the door as she headed for the chicken pen. She took a special joy in her laying hens, but the old white rooster had become a thorn in her side. He got meaner everyday. One of these fine mornings she was going to swing the stick a little harder and serve up some fresh chicken and dumplings!

Before she rounded the corner of the cabin she glanced toward the fields where Will was straining behind the mule. They had turned up more twenty-five percent more acreage, and if weather held again this year, they could expect another bumper crop of cotton. There would be enough money to make a new suit for Jamie. The first school in Sandy Creek would open next fall; she intended, in spite of opposition from both Will and Jamie, that her firstborn be enrolled.

She stood the baby by the feed shed and scooped out a bucket of feed. Then she pointed at the shed and told her daughter, "No, no. The shed is dirty. You stay right here till Mama gets back."

With an already dirty thumb hooked in her mouth, the two-year-old smiled and drooled, and as soon as her mother headed for the chicken pen, promptly crawled in among the dusty, spider-ridden sacks of grain. A sudden breeze caught the heavy door and pushed it closed upon her, but she didn't cry.

Martha slung the stick to ward off the rooster until she could empty the feed in the trough. While the chickens were busy at that, she went to the roost house to check the nests.

She gathered the eggs in her apron, her fingers lingering on a warm brown one just laid. But an inner prompting urged her to hurry. Her daughter lacked a natural fear of either crawling things or the wild varmints that strayed in from the woods; also, she was not as inclined toward obedience as her brother.

Martha pulled her apron tight against her belly and turned.

For one instant her eyes sprang wide, stunned, and perplexed. But the mask of horror never formed before a tomahawk plunged into the center of her forehead.

* * *

Yellow Bear spoke in rapid Comanche.

"We will be blamed!"

"We will be blamed anyway," replied Horse Back. "I am going to see how many *tivo* they have killed. You can go or stay."

Horse Back was reputed for knowing exactly what he would do and when he would do it. It was one of the traits that had made him big chief of the Quo-hadie Te-ich-as, or Antelope Eaters, tribe of Comanche. He was sixty-five years old, straight as an arrow, and stood over six feet tall, carrying himself like a warrior in his prime.

Although Comanche raids were as bloody and ruthless as purported, they were never carried out wantonly. They were well planned and executed according to the law by which the Indian had learned to live: Kill or be killed.

The raid on the Daniel's farm was not of their doing.

"Kiowas?" asked Yellow Bear, looking at the dead man whose scalp had already been taken. A mule was grazing at the edge of the woods, still dragging the plow behind him.

Horse Back's answer was tinged with bitterness.

"It is sad day when we let Kiowas stay in our land to help kill white eyes. They enjoy their work too much. But it could be white eyes who kill for sport and then blame us." His face hardened. "No difference. We will be blamed, so we will be sure to be guilty. When we kill enough *tivo*, they will leave our land." He spat in the dirt.

The two warriors studied the dead man in silence, each occupied with his own thoughts. Then they mounted their horses and rode slowly toward the farmhouse.

After a short search, they found Martha Daniels where she had been struck down. Dismounting, they walked among the squawking chickens to the body.

"There are no children for captives," noted Yellow Bear.

Horse Back sighed, swallowing a faint nausea as he looked at the corpse. No captives. Nothing to barter for food and supplies. The slaughter was useless but for the fear it might inspire.

He turned away. *"To-quet.* We take supplies and the mule, and go."

"Cah-boon!" Yellow Bear pointed.

Beside the feed shed stood the two-year-old, sucking her thumb and brushing the cobwebs from her dress with quick, uncoordinated movements. Her legs were sturdy and plump, her hair a pale shining silver against her sun-browned face.

As they walked to the child, Yellow Bear took out his knife. It was sharp enough to slit the jugular vein in one painless stroke.

The child was still brushing herself clumsily when they stopped in front of her. But when she spied the moccasined feet, her face clouded. The shed was, after all, very dark. Her mother did not come to get her out, and only after pushing a long time did she get the door open. She was ready to go to the house, and very thirsty.

Her luminous gray eyes lifted to Horse Back. Then her chubby arms raised, her chin trembling only slightly as she opened and closed her fists in the age-old gesture of infant need.

It was a grave error not to proceed immediately. Yellow Bear glanced quickly at his companion.

Horse Back's face was pained as he looked at the child, so Yellow Bear said, "I will do it."

Horse Back's gaze left the child and turned upon him. "Why?" His dark eyes were sharp and accusing. "Why?" he repeated. "The deed will be ours before Father Sun has slept anyway. Our purpose will have been served by the hand of others."

"Then we take a captive and this is good," said Yellow Bear.

Horse Back regarded him a moment before speaking with unaccustomed vehemence. "Only *tivo sata* kills for no reason. You are not *white man dog,* I am not *white man dog!*" He stared hard at Yellow Bear, then bent and took the child in his arms.

June, 1872

Layers of scarlet, orange, and yellow simmered low on the western skyline as the small entourage with Maj. Gen. Walker Grayson followed the Red River, now a wide ribbon

16

of molten color that mirrored the sunset. They had followed the river that separates Texas and Oklahoma until they reached Cooke County, and would now head south and east for the rolling, pine-covered hills of East Texas.

Under orders from Washington, the twenty-eight-year-old major general had just completed a week of meetings with six other officers at Wichita Falls where, under the direction of Gen. Nelson A. Miles, they had planned the extermination of all Comanche Indians, particularly some of the old diehards like Horse Back, Lone Wolf, and young Quannah Parker, a group who for the last several years had been a source of considerable embarrassment to the army. On his way to those meetings, Walker had overheard a civilian remark that Horse Back and a handful of savages against the U.S. Army sounded like a pretty even match to him.

"Looks like more soldiers," said Phillip Martin.

Major Grayson eyed the bedraggled group. "So I see."

If there was a note of despair in his quiet reply, only Phillip Martin would have noticed. He had been under Grayson's command for the past five years, a record by military standards. He could anticipate an order by the merest lift of an eyebrow or pick out the flicker of anger in a pair of cool, gray-green eyes. Perhaps he alone understood the cause of Walker's black mood when, in fact, their meetings in Wichita Falls had been an unparalleled success.

Before the birth of Columbus, Comanche Land had embraced southeastern Colorado, the eastern two-thirds of New Mexico, the western portion of Oklahoma, and all of Texas. It was a big job for a hundred thousand Comanches to police such a vast domain. Now, thanks to Major Grayson and others like him, their holdings had been reduced to reservation lands, a few mountain strongholds in New Mexico and Colorado, and the present hot spot, the Texas Plains. Palo Duro Canyon lay just south of Amarillo, and from that natural fortress the last and most defiant Comanche headmen lead raids on unsuspecting settlers in the hopes of regaining some of their former homeland.

But according to the illustrious officers at Wichita Falls,

the days of Texas Indian troubles were at a close. Under the direction of General Miles, Walker Grayson and Col. Ronald Mackenzie would lead a Kansas-styled "rabbit hunt." With the recent installation of telegraph lines by Signal Corp, the army could be directed en masse against the Comanches. They were to be shot down in a drag wire of army militia.

The camped soldiers sat watching the approach of Grayson's men in silence until one of them let out a low whistle. "Lordy, look at all that brass!"

Their weary lethargy gave way to a flurry of movement. They scrambled to their feet, fell into a crooked line, and stiffened to their best attention just as the entourage of officers drew up and dismounted.

"At ease, men. I'm Major Grayson from Fort Nacogdoches," said the tall, leggy officer whose rank of insignia had first caught their eye.

A young man stepped forward and saluted.

"I'm Corporal Wainwright of the Fifth Infantry, major sir. We took part in some Indian fighting a few days ago, and we're headed home, sir."

Walker managed a tired smile then turned to his aide de camp. "Let's get settled in. We could use some extra sleep."

As the men from the Fifth Infantry scurried to make room for their guests, Lester McCaleb elbowed his companion.

"Look alive, you fool. Don't you know who that is?" Lester turned to stare openly at the major. "Imagine us stumblin' into somebody like that out here in the middle of nowhere." He wagged his head in wonder. "It's him and old Mackenzie's that's gonna show them Comanches what for."

"I've heard of him all right, but don't expect me to be doin' a jig over it." Lester shook out his bedroll. "My back a-killin' me, my feet are swelled big as five-pound cantaloupes," the other soldier muttered. "It's gonna be a long enough night without havin' to set stiff as a three-day corpse and smile till your jaws ache as bad as your tailbone—just so's we can entertain some big brass from Washington."

18

Lester looked as though his companion had blasphemed.

"Well, that's a hell-uv-an attitude. How many times in your life you think you're gonna rub shoulders with somebody like that? Did you know that he ain't thirty years old yet and he's already been decorated twice't?" His voice dropped and he jerked his head over his shoulder. "You can't tell so much in the dark, but they say he's a real looker. His daddy's rich as King Midas, too."

"He looks wet behind the ears to me." The soldier stood and grabbed his middle back with both hands, and glared when Lester elbowed him again.

"Maybe you're just a mite jealous," Lester cackled, his voice touched with the strain known as battle fatigue. "Why, they say women stick to him like flies and he don't even pay 'em a never-mind. Got a real lady back home — Miss Camelia Rhinehart. Her daddy's a congressman, you know."

The other man leaned in Lester's face and nudged back roughly. "Could be they're fallin' all over them brass medals and his daddy's money." He spit a plug of tobacco in his hand and tossed it away. "I thought you said you had a little whiskey left," he frowned, "an' half's mine 'cause you owe me. So go get it. I'll need it if I'm gonna have to smile like a bloomin' idiot all night."

Thirty minutes later the same soldier sat listening, nodding and laughing at correct intervals — and finding it inexplicably pleasant to do so. Major General Grayson sat in their loose circle about the fire, cross-legged on a blanket spread on the ground. Lester was right — Grayson did have looks: a tall rangy frame and wide shoulders, yet he moved with the kind of negligent grace women seemed to admire; his rugged features were browned and lined by the sun; his dusky blond hair curled rakishly around his temples and ears, and his gray-green eyes, trimmed by thick gold lashes, had a peculiar way of looking vaguely misty when his face was sober, and sparkling like jewels when he laughed. He was so perfect it was a wonder the rest of them didn't hate his guts, yet there they sat — bunched around him like kids listening to the schoolmaster.

19

The soldier grinned as he stretched out his legs, feeling as cozy and lighthearted as if their camp had been visited by a warm and smiling god. Well, he mused, some had it and some didn't.

"The 'gator measured fifteen feet. He was the largest to come out of the swamp behind my house," finished Walker.

A young soldier fresh from the glory of his first battle was so enamored by the personal glimpse into the life of a living legend that he mustered enough courage to ask, "Major Grayson, sir, is it true that you went to war when you were only fifteen and just a year later you were decorated?"

The warm currents changed course, and everybody felt it.

"Yes," said Walker after a pause. "I ran away from home to join the Confederate Army in '62."

"I believe your daddy's a West Point graduate, ain't he?" said Lester McCaleb. "I guess he wuz real proud when you won all them medals for bravery—"

"I'm sure he was." The major interrupted smoothly, then seemed to glance at each individual in one sweeping look. "But the fact is, my father had forbidden me to join the army because I was so young. Having been to war himself, he knew it's not the path to glory but a trail of blood and horror no man should ever have to travel."

The gentle rebuke provoked an uncomfortable but thoughtful silence, and during the lull Walker saw one of the soldiers peer over his shoulder into the darkness and utter a gruff command in Comanche.

Walker understood only enough to recognize the language, but he gazed uneasily beyond the men. It was very dark now, and he saw nothing.

The soldiers from the Fifth Infantry were so eager to air their recent exploit that they soon forgot the major's remarks on the nature of war. With an inward groan, Walker smiled politely as Corporal Wainwright began a lengthy and gruesome description of their last Indian battle.

Walker tried to listen attentively but soon found himself slipping into the same black mood that had haunted him for the past few months. He was sick of soldiers, he thought suddenly. Sick of Indians and sick of war—especially this one. The corporal's words evoked images that were somehow more terrible than real-life experience, for in the heat of battle the mind functioned on instinct, following a course predetermined by hours of planning strategy and repeating skills, blocking out those things which might distract—like horror and revulsion—those glimpses of reality that could mean instant death.

His thoughts wandered tiredly, groping for something to keep him occupied until Wainwright wound down, and he had even begun to feel a little drowsy, when there was a soft metallic *clink* from somewhere behind the soldiers.

He shifted his gaze covertly and stared into the darkness. Though once more he saw nothing, a spray of gooseflesh streaked down his arms. With the amount of Indian blood flowing lately, he would have expected seasoned soldiers to come to their feet at the slightest rustle.

He shook himself and tried to relax. It was hard to trust one's senses when they were keyed so high. He desperately needed a good night's sleep. No, he thought despondently; what he needed was a leave of absence—not an order to slaughter more Indians.

Walker stiffened. He definitely saw something just beyond the circle of soldiers, a form just a shade lighter than darkness that moved with a strange *clink*.

As it glided along behind the seated soldiers, Walker's mouth opened and he started to point—but then the vague shape seemed to turn and fade to blackness again.

Corporal Wainwright had not missed a beat in his tale, and as Walker looked at the other men of the Fifth Infantry, he found no acknowledgment in a single face that something had just passed close enough to slit their throats. They paid no more attention to the noise than to a camp dog sneaking scraps.

For a moment he engaged in a piercing scrutiny of each of the soldiers of the Fifth Infantry, his years of training ever alert for nuances of the out-of-place; his eyes and ears were like a dolphin's sonar, cued to overturned rocks, broken twigs, the call of an owl that was a little off-key.

21

Then he slumped again and rubbed the back of his neck; his bones felt like the marrow was being drawn out with a needle, and he stared with grim malice at the long-winded Wainwright, thinking with fresh longing of that leave he'd promised himself before the campaign against the Comanches started in September.

Then several things happened at once. One of the soldiers had gone to look for something in his bedroll and lit a lantern. The light flared bright and for a millisecond Walker saw an outline in black relief. Then the soldier miscalculated by backing the wick down too far, dousing the light again.

Walker was on one knee, straining his eyes into the darkness. The illumination had lasted no longer than a flash of lightning freezing scurrying night creatures before dropping a black shroud again; yet the silhouette was imprinted in his mind vividly, an impression of long hair and its graceful forward swing, long shapely legs that could belong to no man.

The sound was fading now as the figure slipped further into the cover of night, but Walker knew what the haunting sound was and why the figure leaned as though facing a strong wind.

When he came to his feet in a single leap, Wainwright's climactic battle scene slid to an abrupt halt.

The corporal's gaze darted up in surprise.

"Er . . . is something wrong, sir?" he asked, feeling a sudden urge to get his own feet under him, though he did so with the same slow caution of a man trying to stand on ice.

The major's voice was soft as the swish of a skirt, as lethal as the sound of a coiled rattler.

"Is there a girl in this camp?"

No one answered, and no one moved.

Walker repeated the question very slowly, not raising his voice. "Is there a girl in this camp?"

Corporal Wainwright was on his feet now. He stared blindly ahead and dragged the words from his throat: "Er . . . yes sir."

The major approached him leisurely; — Wainwright

watched with field vision, for he dared not move his eyes,—and then peered at him from very close.

"Would you like to rephrase that answer, corporal?"

Wainwright whipped himself to attention and shouted, "Yes sir, major sir!"

"Thank you," murmured Walker, and clasped his hands behind his back and began to pace slowly.

The campfire hissed and crackled for several moments before Walker stopped beside the corporal again.

"Am I mistaken, corporal, or is that girl in chains?"

Wainwright thought for a horrified moment that nothing would escape his parched throat. He was shocked to hear his voice ringing out in a girlish squeal: "Y-y-yes sir, major sir—but I can explain!"

The men of the Fifth Infantry made as little noise as possible as they found a perpendicular position. The smiling god was gone and what was left was major general to the soles of his boots. They had been lulled by his charisma into forgetting that the secret they carried within each of them could be viewed in a different light once they were off this godforsaken prairie.

The major raked the tattered line of soldiers with a look that stood their neck hairs on end, and turned back to Wainwright.

He pointed to the ground. "I want her *here*. In front of me. You have two minutes to obey this order."

Wainwright wheeled, beads of sweat blinding him so that he stumbled—and there in front of him were his men, staring at him pathetically.

Walker's eyes darted from the hesitating officer to the men of the Fifth Infantry. "Do you have a problem with that order, corporal?"

Wainwright pivoted, tromping one foot in beside the other.

"Er . . . yes sir. I mean, no sir. Well, what I mean is . . . is . . ."

Walker crossed his arms with the patience of a leopard waiting for its prey to slip up.

"The girl is . . . well, I was thinking that if I had some help, . . . yes, if I had some help, there'd be less chance of

23

injuring her. I sure wouldn't want to do that, sir."

Walker lifted one brow. "I see." Clearly he saw more than he needed to. "Okay, take whomever you wish. Just get her here."

Wainwright motioned a man named Wiley Holcomb toward him, and both men had started off when a quiet voice checked their stride like a noose dropped suddenly about their necks:

"One of your two minutes is already gone."

The wait seemed interminable for the men of the Fifth Infantry. They shifted from foot to foot, coughed, stretched their necks and looked into the darkness beyond the campfire; but not once did the major general speak or soften the hard line of his jaw as he paced back and forth, his steps as hypnotic and nerve-grating as dripping water: step . . . step . . . step . . .

Phillip Martin had watched his superior indulge in the habit until it had been honed to an art; now he recognized it as a ploy to heighten tension, but it was working so well on his own nerves that he stepped to Walker's side.

"What do you think's going on here?" He spoke under his breath.

Walker stopped to stare briefly into the darkness. "I don't know but I'm going to find out if we stand here till dawn."

The wait drew out to five minutes, seven, nine, and the line of pacing had shrunk to a mere five feet, so that Walker pivoted more frequently and his movements seemed more agitated.

He was beginning to wonder if his statement had been prophetic when there was a strangled noise, perhaps a cough cut off abruptly by pain.

Walker glanced at the corporal's men, ever alert to catch any unguarded expression, but all were straining anxiously in the direction from whence the other two of their group had gone.

There was a profound silence broken only by the approach of boots thumping against hard-packed ground.

And so they came, two men and no girl.

They walked into the ring of light, and Walker stared. Wiley Holcomb was bent like a hunchback yet he attempted to assist the corporal along, who was himself walking quite well except that he held one wrist in the other hand like a doctor just scrubbed for surgery.

Suddenly one of Major Grayson's men called upon his Creator in a hoarse voice. Walker's eyes widened, and he stepped forward to take the corporal's hand carefully.

"I-I'm sorry, major sir," said Wainwright. Then, finding no other words, he repeated, "I'm sorry."

Walker recovered. "Ben! Farley! Get your medical bags quickly—this man's fingers are almost severed!"

He looked at Wiley Holcomb. "What are your injuries?"

Holcomb craned his neck so as not to straighten his body too much. "Bruised shins, sir. *Badly* bruised shins and a—" He flushed. "A groin injury."

The major contemplated something in the darkness, then came back to himself and barked, "Damn you, Ben. Hurry before this man bleeds to death!"

Chapter 2

Someone brought a bedroll and Corporal Wainwright was eased down upon it. When the blood was cleaned away there appeared to be no broken bones, but the more he moaned the more sympathy he got from his men. Walker interrupted the cycle by kneeling beside him.

"This girl is Comanche, I assume. I heard one of the men speak to her earlier."

"Yes . . . but sir, what do you think about my hand? I mean, do you think I could lose these fingers?"

Walker frowned as he examined the injury again. "This isn't a knife wound, is it?"

"No sir," said the corporal sullenly. "She *bit* me. They say a human bite is worse than one from a wild animal — there's danger of infection, you know."

Walker smiled briefly. "So I've heard. But with all due concern for your injury, corporal, I have trouble with the idea of two soldiers — Indian fighters, no less — being overcome by a girl in chains. Perhaps you would like to explain."

Wainwright leaned back and closed his eyes. "It was . . . well, when she . . ." He peeped through his lashes, then closed them again. "She doesn't take to being touched and when we laid hands on her . . . well, like I said, we wouldn't want to hurt her, sir. She's a woman, after all."

Walker's expression changed suddenly and he stood up so quickly that Wainwright dodged. "So you said, corporal."

Phillip stepped closer and spoke quietly over the sickbed. "What does it look like, sir?"

Walker continued to look down at Wainwright, the mus-

26

cles in his jaws as hard as kernels under the skin. "The worst human bite I've ever seen, but he's going to think it was a pinprick when I get through with him."

While the wounded were being attended, the rest stood in a crooked line talking in hushed tones. When Major Grayson began to speak, they became as quiet as church mice.

"As you are all well aware, you could be facing serious consequences for what I've found here. Keeping this girl in chains is unconscionable and inexcusable. However, I'm willing to accept that there might be mitigating circumstances. These are hard times—nobody knows that better than I do. Now. How long has the girl been with you?"

Encouraged by the major's reasonable tone, one of the soldiers stepped out slowly. "Best I can remember, sir, 'bout two months."

"Why do you have her? Where did you find her and why is she chained?"

A different soldier spoke up. "Sir, I reckon Lester McCaleb can tell you more than anybody. He's the biggest gossip in three states."

There were awkward attempts at laughter. Acting on fourteen years of experience, Walker allowed himself a faint smile of encouragement as Lester glared at his companion and shuffled out from the ranks.

He stood up very straight. "Well, as you can see, sir, she's a mite hard to handle. She don't speak no English a'tol so we couldn't tell we were gonna let her go. If we could have, she mighta let somebody get close enough to do it."

"Are you saying that the girl was wearing a ball and chain when you found her?"

"Yes sir. We got her from another detachment we met up with."

"Do you have any idea how long she's been like this?"

Lester rolled his eyes at the men behind him. The jig was up. Their best bet was to throw themselves on the major's mercy and hope that somewhere beneath that predatory

27

expression lay the smiling god of an hour before.

Pulling at the neck of his shirt, Lester took a deep breath and went on. "We just know what those other soldiers told us, sir. And I swear I don't even know what regiment they were from. Anyway, some of them Tonkawa scouts the army uses found the girl at an Apache hideout. You know, there's still a few Apaches around, and there's bad blood between them and the Comanches."

"Keep to the point, soldier."

"Yes sir. Well, them Tonkawas are a purty sorry lot, and they wanted the slave girl. She was in chains even then, I understand. So they stole some horses from those Apaches and then traded them their own horses back for the girl. But . . ." His voice fell a little. "There's more. One of them Tonkawa scouts said the Apaches robbed her from Horse Back. He's the Comanche's big war chief now—well, I guess you know all about Horse Back."

"Unfortunately," replied Walker, and began to pace again. "So you're saying she was originally taken from the Comanches by Apaches, who then traded her to the Tonkawa scouts, who then traded her to the soldiers you met up with. Now." He stopped and looked up. "So. How did your group gain possession of her?"

Lester noticed that his fellow soldiers were studying the mystery of the ground, and he felt like a man alone on a limb that was being sawed off at the trunk.

His Adam's apple pumped as he whispered, "We bought her."

Something burned deep in the major's eyes, and it was a moment before he spoke. When he did, the words were soft and carefully separated. "For . . . what . . . purpose?"

Lester's eyes bulged. "Beggin' your pardon, major, but you're dead wrong! We ain't used that girl nary a time! I mean, none of us ever saw anything like her before an' I ain't saying we weren't thinking like that at the first. But when we found out she killed two soldiers from the other group, we thunk twice't about it, I can tell you fer sure."

The major's intimidating frown slipped completely.

"She *what?*"

"It's true, sir," said Lester quickly. "Ask anybody."

The others nodded vigorously, and Walker looked back to Lester. "Was it murder or was she . . . defending herself?"

Lester's defiance wavered until he had to drop his gaze. "They tried to rape her."

"Then why the hell — " Walker stopped to lower his voice. "Why is she still restrained? Assuming, of course, that thirteen soldiers could hold her down long enough to cut the chain?" he added caustically.

Lester tried to meet the major's flinty gaze but failed.

"She claims to be Chief Horse Back's daughter, sir. We thought the army might be glad to get hold of her and she would bring a good . . ." He glanced at his comrades apologetically. "A good price."

The major stood looking at them and saying nothing. Lester found that he preferred the former expression to the one he saw now.

"Sir," he said quietly, "I know it looks bad — soldiers blackmailing their own army an' all. But I'm a farmer. I been burned out by the Injuns so many times that my kids are starvin'. I signed up for six months, now I been in two years. I guess . . . none of us wuz thinkin' straight." He did not look up again.

Walker turned away to pace again, and Phillip Martin was the only one to recognize the weariness beneath the veneer of calm.

The major stopped for the last time and straightened his shoulders before he spoke.

"There's been enough confusion for one night. We'll leave things as they are. Apparently the girl has a strong constitution and can survive one more night in chains." Then his gaze penetrated each of them before he went on. "In any case, let it be known that the girl will be released from those chains first thing in the morning if it takes the entire Fifth Infantry to accomplish it. Then I'll let you know if any of you will be following me to Nacogdoches for questioning."

He turned suddenly and left them.

Long after the camp was asleep, Walker lay looking at the night sky. Decent family men changed to slave traders for a few dollars — one of the invisible battle scars, the kind that took the longest to heal. Or did men ever go back to what they were?

He tried to remember the world of quiet paths winding through moss-hung oaks, the sound of a paddlewheeler rolling up Bayou Teche at sunset; a world of ivy-grown mansions ruled the aristocracy where a woman's most pressing problem was which bonnet to wear shopping. A world a million miles from this one.

When he finally dozed off, his dreams shifted from one to the other, from the gray stone mansion in Louisiana to the tawny plains of the Texas Panhandle. From big Sunday dinners after church to burying the hairless corpse of a friend. He knew each shade of night — from darkest pitch to the gray fog creeping over the camp at first light.

Near dawn a sound awoke him. Ever cautious of unexplained rustles, he slitted his eyes open.

What he saw made him realize that he was not awake at all. From the early morning mist a vision materialized: A girl came toward the fire with a kettle and hung it over the flames, then she turned to look at him. And he knew he was dreaming because no flesh-and-blood woman ever looked like this one. This exotic beauty could only be conjured from the depths of a man who'd known months of abstinence. So he settled back with a sigh and watched from under his hat brim, lying very still and studying every detail.

The roots of her hair were smoky, but the outer layers were streaked with pale silver; a wispy, weightless veil that hung straight, past her shoulders. Then the ends curled up like vine tips. Its platinum shimmer set off dark skin and turned her clear gray eyes to a translucence he could only describe as silver. Her face was somewhat narrow with dark slanted brows, high cheekbones, a slim straight nose, and a square jaw. Her mouth was small, a tender little slash that turned neither up nor down at the corners.

She wore what might have once been a gray muslin dress with sprigs of flowers on it, but for this special vision she

30

had slashed out one shoulder and ripped the hem into jagged edges that came halfway to her thighs. Her breasts were, of course, disproportionately large for her slender build, their taut nipples straining at the worn fabric—for she would naturally be wearing nothing under the dress.

She was moving toward him now, her large silver eyes wide with apprehension, and he knew that if he dared move she would bolt like a frightened fawn into the mists from which she had come.

Suddenly he was choking for air. The blood started to pound in his ears yet he could do nothing but hold his breath because her hand was reaching for his hat. He made little obscene sucking noises as he tried to breathe undetected, and then he thought what a strange phenomenon dreams were; how you heard and saw and felt with such heightened perception.

Her hand stopped short, for she was, of course, shy. A pure untouched virgin created solely for this special moment.

Yet dream or no dream, there was a fire in his groin. She was there to give him relief. Of course. He understood now.

Lunging up, he caught her by the shoulders.

The girl knew her part well, indeed. Her lips parted with feigned surprise, and Walker wasted no time before he took them in a searing kiss.

Fingernails slashed his arms, then he was knocked back to his bedroll by a right hook that left his ears ringing. By the time his head ceased to spin, he saw nothing but the flash of a bare foot disappearing into a nearby stand of willow trees.

He shook his head a little, for he could still hear the sound of her chain as she moved through the brush; and then he lay back staring at the dull gray sky overhead, his strange dreams of the night before adding to his befuddlement.

But slowly and then more quickly, blood poured into his numb brain, and he realized at last that she was not a dream.

His heart raced with anxiety. He remembered everything:

31

how she had come out with the kettle, been curious about him; and for her timid interest been practically assaulted by the commander in charge.

He propped himself on an elbow to survey the camp. Fortunately there had been no witnesses. Plumping his pillow brutally, he flopped down and tried to sleep.

Her skin was like cool satin, the taste of her mouth like brandy and honey, and her eyes . . . those disturbing orbs with the silver translucence of mists shimmering under the moon . . .

His bedroll felt like a rack of nails, and he flung the top covering back to stand up and shake himself like a horse stepping from the water. His shirt was plastered with sweat, and he stripped it off, tossing it aside.

After working clumsily on the fire for several minutes, he got it going and pulled up a log to sit and wait for the others to wake.

He tried to picture Camelia. It had been perhaps four months since he'd seen her. He had been reluctant to give in to family pressure and let her set the wedding date, but afterward he had begun to look forward to the married state. He was tired of corn pone for breakfast, tired of the whirlwind of debutantes who celebrated every leave—tired of the dowagers who stalked him like some prize stud at the county fair. What he needed was a woman at his side. A *good* one. One whose father was a congressman—an indispensable attribute if one considered politics after retirement.

He had known Camelia forever it seemed, and while he had distinct misgivings about their emotional compatibility, there was a great deal of affection between them. It didn't hurt any that she was beautiful, of course.

But thinking of Camelia made him more uncomfortable. In fact, plain disgruntled.

He got to his feet with an urge to glower at the camp of sleeping soldiers—which he did. Then he stalked toward the cigar-shaped mound that was Phillip Martin. After the business of those wretched chains, they would push on to Nacogdoches. Maybe he would take a leave of absence quicker than he planned. He needed to see Camelia again, to remember what it was like to touch that creamy white skin, that cute little dimple in her chin, and look into those wide, silver-gray eyes.

He squinted thoughtfully at the air. No, Camelia's eyes were blue. Yes, blue. Or possibly green. Blue-green—they were blue-green. They could possibly be hazel, but he didn't think so.

The image slipped from his grasp suddenly and completely, and swimming before him was a pair of lustrous gray orbs in a sun-browned face.

He bent down and pounded on Phillip Martin with a gusto that brought the usually calm aide to his feet with a squawk of terror.

When the girl appeared again, Walker was grooming his horse and the others were beginning to stir from their beds.

He watched from the corner of his eye as she dipped coffee grounds into the boiling kettle, looking neither left nor right. The soldiers studiously ignored her, but Walker could feel a tension in the air: She was no longer chattel but possibly the catalyst for their imminent incarceration.

He tried not to be obvious in staring after her, but he was looking enough to see that when she finished at the fire, she vanished into the willows again.

He stopped a passing soldier. "Where does the girl go? Where does she sleep?"

"Well, the supply wagon's hid out in them willows yonder on account of thievin' Injuns. But the girl sleeps with the horses. Nobody *makes* her or anything," he put in hastily. "She just prefers it, I guess. And that's another reason why we have to keep that ball and chain on her, you see. If she ever got a leg over a horse, she'd be gone like the wind." He added nobly, "We give her her own bedroll."

The ground mist had lifted by the time the soldiers gathered about the fire. Although there was a thin overcast to the sky, it was a temporary condition that would burn off all too soon.

Presently the girl came again, dragging the heavy ball behind her. As she lifted the kettle from the hook and poured coffee around the circle of men, Walker's attractively sculptured lips curled with disgust. She seemed to take her condition as much for granted as the soldiers did.

Walker leaned aside to Lester McCaleb. "She hardly seems to have the destruction of the Fifth Infantry on her mind this morning. As a matter of fact, I don't think I've ever seen a more willing slave. How do you account for that?" he demanded suspiciously.

Lester kept his voice low. "Sir, I can see what you're hintin' at, but I swear I ain't ever laid a hand on that girl. There's only two men that will do that."

Walker's eyes followed the girl. "I'm listening. How is she controlled?"

Lester squirmed his bony buttocks against the hard log. "Well, if she don't tend camp duties, one of the men—a particular one—sets a guard on the supply wagon and don't let her eat," he ventured, eyeing the major to see how the information was settling. He went further. "One time, at the first, she went three days without food and water, and keeled over. Corporal Wainwright got real mad and wanted to take the chains off her while she was unconscious—he's a right nice young officer—but these other two talked him out of it. One of them joined up in the army with the corporal—they wuz childhood friends, you see. The other one's a stepbrother to the first, and he ain't much more'n a halfwit but that's why the army let in, 'cause there weren't nobody to see after him when the older one joined up. But anyways, after that the girl always did her work."

Walker looked surprised. "So she accepted her fate after that?"

Lester couldn't hide his shock at the major's ignorance. "Sir, she's been raised a Comanche and Comanches don't buckle under till they're dead. You should know that, sir. Anyways, you oughta see her when she goes on a bender—bitin' and snarlin' and sometimes jumpin' on one of the men with a knife. Them two I'm talkin' about . . ." He hesitated but found no course but to finish. "They use a whip on her."

The girl was approaching them now and the men fell

silent.

As Walker held out his cup, he gazed intently at the top of her bowed head, hoping she would raise her eyes. She didn't look up, but he noticed that the kettle weaved and the coffee sloshed rather than poured into his cup. He couldn't keep his eyes off of her as she limped away into the willow trees.

Lester offered cheerfully, "She's a purty good cook. I reckon she's about got breakfast fixed by now."

Walker stood up so abruptly that Lester started. "There won't be time for that—I want those chains off *now*." He glanced down at Lester McCaleb, who was making every effort to get his feet under him in order to offset the major's towering height. "I don't guess you know if the girl has a name," inquired Walker icily.

Lester brushed his seat off, not speaking until he could attend his superior in an upright position. "One of the men speaks a little Comanche and says she calls herself Pow-he-wa-te Nau-be. It means Silver Dawn but the men call her Silver when they call her anything at . . . all . . ." His voice trailed away at Walker's expression.

"If you know what's good for you," said Walker softly, "you'll give me the names of the two men who've beaten her. In fact, you can think of it as their necks or yours."

Lester spoke without hesitation. "Buck Santos and George Greelee."

"Thank you." Walker turned to stride away toward Phillip Martin.

Major Grayson and Phillip Martin stood in the center of two ranks, their small corp of officers to their left, and the men of the Fifth Infantry on their right.

The latter group wore expressions of anxiety. After some discussion, they had concluded that the swift and unexpected change in their new idol was due to the fact that the slave girl was white. If she had been the real daughter of Horse Back, the major could have looked the other way. Lester McCaleb said there was talk in the major's home state of a political career, perhaps even the governorship.

35

The major enjoyed an outstanding reputation both as a gentleman and an officer, but his position guaranteed him enemies. There would be those motivated by jealousy or imagined injustices who'd be happy to leak the word back to Washington that he had blatantly ignored the plight of a white woman. On the other hand, having the return of an Indian captive to his credit could surely do no harm.

The major had been pacing for some time. Now he stopped and faced the line of soldiers on his right.

"I would like to speak to George Greelee and Mike Santos."

The men stood for a moment, then looked blankly around them when no one stepped forward. Corporal Wainwright moved out of the ranks to survey his men.

"I'm afraid they're not here, sir. One is real tall, the other's fat so you can't miss 'em."

"Send somebody to check the horses," ordered Walker impatiently. When the corporal just stood there, he snapped, "Move it!"

Two men hustled off and returned shortly.

"They're gone all right," panted one of the soldiers. "Leastways their horses are. Looks like they left in a hurry, too. They didn't take any extra water or food, I checked the supply wagon as I went by it. I guess their not AWOL since we're on leave, but we could go after 'em if you want."

Walker thought a minute, then turned to Lester and spoke sharply. "Private McCaleb, you will see to it that a complete description of the men is given to my aide here, Phillip Martin. Corporal Wainwright, I'll see you in private before we leave. As for the rest of you, I'm going to let you go on home. But keep this in mind. If I find out later that any of you have been brutal to the girl beyond keeping her in chains, I will personally see every last one of you brought to trial if I have to hunt you down myself. Is that clear?" The men nodded their full understanding. "Now," said Walker, surveying the tattered ranks with a hard gleam in his eyes, "how many men do you think it will take to bring the girl here?"

Corporal Wainwright spoke up with authority. "It'll take more than two, Major Sir!"

"Do you suppose *four* will do?" Walker gave him a long-suffering smile.

"Well, I don't rightly know," the corporal deliberated, missing the barb and causing Walker's lazy smile to desert him suddenly.

Wresting the decision from the simpleton, he ordered four of his own men — the highest ranking officers — to get the girl, restating emphatically that she was not to be injured.

Once again the group waited in silence.

Presently there came a noise from the willow trees, and Walker started. The sound was the scream of a panther, and he knew no healthy cat would wander this close to a camp of soldiers.

As he touched the butt of his pistol, the Fifth Infantry swung their collective heads toward the brush where the racket was steadily increasing in volume.

Walker's jaw slowly sagged as he listened to the frenzied screams and guttural snarls with an alarm that grew in direct proportion to his discomfort, for he now understood what the sounds were. He began to pace with supreme confidence, raising his head occasionally to smile into the distance. What these men needed was a little demonstration in the art of handling a woman. The trick was to be kind yet firm — to show genuine concern for the girl's welfare so she would realize she was safe from more torture.

No great time had passed before the clamorous commotion drew nearer. Limbs cracked and snapped with the fury of an approaching brushfire and finally the men emerged from the willows, backs first. A man on each side held her arms, another her bare feet, and the fourth man followed along to carry the metal ball. They were all missing their hats and bore bloody slashes on their faces and hands.

Corporal Wainwright was not the only one to note that there was not a man left to spare. He shot the major a triumphant look, but Walker firmly refused to meet his gaze.

The girl kicked and bit and clawed anyone she could reach, addressing her captors in shrieks and moans. From time to time the strange tongue erupted into a high-pitched

37

caterwauling, which, in turn, ended in a *"yip-yip-yip."* Lieutenant Armstrong's face was streaming with blood, Sergeant Miller's right eye was swollen shut, and Captain Thornberg's torso was hunched over the girl's feet in a posture of agony.

Walker stared fixedly at the ground until they reached the spot he had so firmly pointed out, and he was forced to look up.

Walker inhaled sharply. Gone was the dream girl and back was the savage. He did not doubt that she would claw him to shreds if possible.

For some time Silver continued her vicious resistance, but she had occasion to get brief glimpses of the major's face, which was calm and quiet on the surface. He looked at her as though he intended to wait all day for her to come to her senses.

Under this new chief's steady and somehow soft regard, Silver felt her rage losing momentum. Gradually she ceased to resist and hung suspended by the soldiers' hands. She was winded, disheveled, and wild with fear, but she had learned not to exhaust herself. It was a favorite white eyes trick to hold her down until she could struggle no longer, then attempt to mount her like dogs. She had killed one Apache and four soldiers defending herself after they had beaten her almost senseless. Fortunately, she had fashioned another knife the night before. They were animals not men, and she had never once felt remorse for killing them; only relief that they had not been able to plunge their reeking flesh inside her.

At first she had thought the Apaches would kill her for her deed. But that brave was hated among his own people for incest with his daughter, and after the incident she enjoyed some notoriety and better treatment in the Apache camp.

With the white eyes soldiers it had been different. They seemed only too anxious to hush up the entire episode. White eyes! she thought. Murderers of old men and children—rapers of women! A bloody people who took what was not theirs and left behind death and fear and their dreaded diseases.

38

Her blazing defiance faltered imperceptibly as the white eyes chief stared back. Then suddenly her gaze circled and zoomed up to the sun, not squinting but wide-eyed, and she prayed that the gods might return her to Horse Back — supplicating, whining, intoning the ancient incantations that thus far had failed to sway the gods. When the prayer ended, her face contorted and her mouth opened with a long mournful wail so piercing that several stunned onlookers grabbed their ears.

That done, she bared her pearly teeth like wolf fangs and looked again at the cause of her misery, her eyes smoldering like white-hot crystals.

Her entire audience had frozen, their faces like those in a parody of some tragic drama, petrified in all sorts of unbecoming grimaces. Walker let out his breath and the sound seemed to signal the others to rustle back to life.

"Well," he said, as though that one word were sufficient. Hearing the crack in his voice, he repeated a little louder, "Well. I . . . guess you should . . . well, why don't you just try to set her feet on the ground — and very gently, like you were helping a lady from a carriage."

Though the soldiers exchanged doubtful glances, they lowered her feet to the ground, stood her upright, then took their hands away like men who had built a tower of blocks, their outstretched arms waiting for its collapse.

The girl stood very still, her shoulders slumped, arms hanging limply, head tucked low as she glowered at Walker from under fiercely slanting brows.

Taking a deep breath to steady him, Walker pulled his eyes away and reached for the hatchet in Phillip's hand, motioning one of the men to put a rock under the chain. As he bent with deliberate slowness, he could feel her eyes boring into the top of his head, so he brought the hatchet down swiftly.

The tool split the iron chain and simultaneously Walker heard a *whop* as an elbow slammed down on the back of his neck.

He staggered forward and the next thing he knew Phillip Martin was holding his elbow to keep him from toppling. "Major? Are you all right, major?"

Walker threw away his hand and blinked at the bare ground in front of him, and there was a different but still placating voice: "Don't worry none, sir. We'll get her back in a jiffy."

Walker straightened weavingly and his gaze shifted sideways until it had settled on the one who had spoken.

"Get her?" he inquired through his teeth. "Did you say *get* her? Maybe you could tell me how in the hell you lost her in the first place—did she melt perhaps? Run like water between your fingers? Or maybe—" His face darkened. In seventeen years he'd never lost control of his temper in front of his men—and certainly he had never embarrassed them in front of their subordinates. He couldn't believe he had done it.

So he started over again, unaware that his voice gradually began to crescendo and somehow the malicious words exploded from him anyway.

"I left Nacogdoches with a corps of commissioned officers. What were they trained to do?" he asked. Then he answered himself, his voice shaking and thundering, *"They were trained to fight Indians.* Indians—do you understand, you dim-witted—"

"Major!" Phillip put a hand on his arm, and Walker bestowed a single glance that removed it. Then his gaze swung back to the four men.

"Bring . . . her . . . *back!"*

The girl had not gone far and she was returned shortly, in the same manner as before, with the exception that no chains restricted her movements. The soldiers scrambled about, some on the ground and others standing, but none able to immobilize her. Walker was certain she was going to break something if he could not come up with a tactic besides brute force.

He scanned the group. "Where is the one who speaks Comanche? You—here!" He snapped his fingers and the man hastened to fill the indicated spot.

Walker shouted over the girl's racket. "Try to tell her we'll let her go if she won't run away."

While the soldier complied, the others hung on each strange word like thieves waiting for the right combination

40

to pop a padlock. But they waited in vain. The girl fought like a demon until the phrase had been repeated three times. Then she raised a smoldering gaze to Walker's face and out of her mouth came a stream of savage intonations that kept the translating soldier flinching with every word. She finished by spitting defiantly in Walker's direction, and it was only due to his quick reflexes that the spittle fell short of its mark.

"Well?" he demanded quickly. "What is it? What did she say?"

A flush stained the interpreter's cheekbones. He stood to attention and looked straight ahead.

"Er . . . if I get the gist of it, sir, she says that all white eyes chiefs are . . ."

"Yes?" Walker urged tensely.

The soldier stretched his neck inside his collar. "Are . . . er, liars and filthy swine, sir. And that white eyes would mount dogs if they—the dogs, that is—would allow it, sir."

Walker's tan deepened. So hard were his jaws clamped that they ached, and he spoke again between his clenched teeth.

"Tell her *I* said that until she behaves she will wear chains." He held the girl's gaze. "Her journey will be three hundred miles—*in chains,*" he emphasized. Ears pricked forward as his voice dropped low. "And tell her there is a white eyes saying: The more savage the beast, the sweeter his surrender."

With a fuller flush, the soldier began, and Walker's eyes locked with the girl's as the interpretation was made, which, had he only known it, carried a very literal connotation in the Comanche language.

Thinking the red line creeping up the girl's face was a sign of repentance, Walker gave her a mocking bow. "Now I think we understand each other." He pulled on his gloves with professional brusqueness and turned to Phillip. "Put her on the horse with her hands and legs tied to the saddle. We leave in ten minutes."

The men who were left holding the girl looked at each other and raised their eyebrows ominously, for they had seen the malignant gaze that followed his exit.

41

Chapter 3

Sergeant Miller loped from behind the stand of willows yelling. "She got loose, major! I don't know how, she just — "

Walker took off in a dead run, passed him up and disappeared behind the trees.

Two others had waited by the staked horses.

"What happened?" Walker demanded.

Their faces were sheepish and exasperated. "She just got loose, sir. She kicked Henry in the groin. He fell and knocked me off balance and she was just gone. She ran over that little rise there. You still see her, Hank?

"Just barely," called Hank. "The ground and the sky's the same damned color what with the cloud cover. But I see her and she's still a-runnin'."

"Won't be no chance of losin' her on this godforsaken prairie, major," Sergeant Miller assured him.

Walker looked thoughtfully toward the rise. "She's got no food or water. As a matter of fact . . ." He stared at the small knoll, then started walking toward it.

Topping the incline, he stood looking across the treeless, brownish-gray terrain. He could see her hair trailing behind her, her legs sprinting with the grace of Olympus.

Phillip halted beside him, panting. "I came as quick as I could. I'll saddle up and go get her."

Others were streaming toward them, and Corporal Wainwright had caught up, relieved it was not his soldiers who had let her escape. "I'll send one of my men, too," he offered.

Walker said nothing. There was a catch in his throat as he watched her run.

He turned abruptly and started back down toward the

horses. As the others hurried to catch up, there was hope in their voices. "You gonna let her go, major? I wouldn't blame you a bit. None of us would."

"For now," said Walker, not slowing. "The exercise won't hurt her after being confined so long, and being alone in that wasteland for a while might do her good. I'll take my horse and follow at a distance until I think she's learned her lesson."

Behind him, glances darted among the soldiers, but each looked ahead again quickly, unwilling to confirm his disappointment openly.

Her bare feet flew, scarcely feeling rocks and thorny brush. Except for a few young warriors, she had been the fastest runner in her village. Now that the stupid white eyes had cut her hands loose, she had no problem keeping her balance.

There was no place for cover except a line of mesquite trees a mile in the distance. Her heart pounded heavily, but she had to get there. They would have already spotted her from the horizon by now. If she could get to the brush, she would have half a chance to escape, for she could head in either direction along the line of trees.

She ran soundlessly and reached the timbered creek in four and a half minutes flat. Her lungs were ready to burst, but without slowing she plowed into the brush.

"What the hell—"

The man's voice broke off as a body slammed into him. He sprawled in a tangle of skinny arms and legs while his companion, whose weight hindered him substantially, lumbered to his feet from the stump where he had been sitting.

The pair had left hurriedly before dawn, but once clear of the camp, took their time to stop and water the horses. No one would care about their absence anyway—except the major, and most likely he wouldn't take the time to pursue them. After all, they were on leave; where they went was their own business.

The heavy man, Buck Santos, wore only his pants. His cone-shaped head was bald and shiny, and sloped radically to encompass huge jaws covered by layers of flesh. In his childhood he had been called Pinhead.

Gripping his big belly as though its burden must be lifted, he rose to his feet, his small eyes sunken into fleshy sockets, giving him the squinty look of a mole as he stared down at the girl's uncovered buttocks. Her skirt had flipped forward when she fell.

George Greelee raised his six-foot, hide-and-bone frame from the dust and saw what had hit him. "The devil take us! It's the slave girl!"

Buck grunted, his eyes glinting dully. A drop of saliva hung perpetually from his pendulous lower lip.

George's gaze was also glued to the girl's exposed posterior. "Never did see such a female undergarment, did you, Bucky?"

For a moment, Buck's bloated body quivered. Then he fell to his knees and crawled to the girl's feet, shoving them aside to wedge himself between her thighs. He fumbled with unaccustomed dexterity at his fly and grabbed his flaccid member in one hand while slipping the other under the girl's belly, pulling her hips upon his lap.

"Damn you, you *idiot!*" George danced around more agilely than he had in years, pounding the kneeling brute on the back. "Git up, you slobbering fool! Don't you know that girl probably woke the whole camp? The major will come after her—you saw how he looked at her. Now git up! We gotta git outa here quick."

"A minute," Buck panted, clumsily trying to reach his mark with an insufficient length. "Gimme justa minute . . ."

George grabbed him around the neck. "Not . . . now!" he snarled, tugging with all his might. "If you'll git the hell up, we'll take her with us. Then you can play with her all you want to."

Buck cocked his head like an orangutan. "I kin?"

"Yes! Yes, you can do anything you want and there'll be nobody to stop you like before. But you gotta hurry, Buck. Listen! They're comin'." He put a hand to his ear and pretended to hear something. "If you don't hurry they're gonna catch us. They'll lock you up in a hole and you'll never have any fun with her, you hear me?"

44

Reluctantly, Buck stuffed himself back inside his pants and struggled to his feet.

"Dead?" he queried, looking at the girl with disappointment.

"I don't know," George mumbled. "It'd be a helluva lot easier for me if she wuz. Come on."

They had no supplies to pack. George threw his stepbrother's shirt to him, then lifted the girl, bracing her rump against his hip like a mother carries a stubborn child; her arms and head flopped forward as he hurried to his horse.

The dull gray sky was a little lighter now, and by riding slowly Walker was able to see the girl's tracks heading for the timberline, which he knew would be near water.

He was only half watching the ground. He had relaxed since he left the others behind, and was still glad he had brought none of them with him. He found it very difficult to watch the men with their hands all over her sleek young body — though their motives might be, like his own, to insure she didn't injure herself trying to fight them. But he was repulsed by the sight, like he might have been watching an adult molest a child. At least, that was as far as he cared to analyze the subject.

Walker pulled up his horse, looking toward the brush in surprise. He listened and heard a thrashing, then the sound of hooves. His brow knitted. Horses?

He looked down and noticed for the first time that there were two sets of hoof prints alongside the girl's, heading for the treeline. In a blinding flash he realized who had made them, and cursed his failure to see them before.

He laid his crop to the big sorrel gelding and rode like a madman until he reached the timberline, then plunged into the brush.

While the two ahead of him blundered like elephants through the trees, Walker gave his veteran battle horse free rein, and the animal picked its way through the brush with little more than a graceful sidestep to avoid collisions.

Though he was gaining rapidly, he could see the girl's arms and legs and upper torso flopping from the side of a horse like a boneless dummy's. The sight made his heart thunder harder.

Buck's horse was tiring under its burden and floundered, its rear legs buckling from the battering of stumps and snags in its path. George screeched over his shoulder, "He's coming! Hurry!" Buck whipped his horse furiously but the poor beast could do no more; his back knee gave way and both of them crashed to the ground, breaking saplings as they went.

George did not stop. Either the obstacle would slow the major or he could lead their pursuer on and give Buck a chance to get mounted again.

But Walker barely wasted a glance at the thrashing pair. He was closing on the rider with the girl. Finally he stopped long enough to pull out his pistol and fire over George's head.

George wheeled his horse, fumbling for his gun.

"Drop it."

"She came chargin' into me, I wuz just—"

"Shut up," said Walker softly. "Shut up and drop the gun before I put a bullet between your eyes."

George stared at the end of the Remington Army .44 and didn't feel the girl stirring against him. "I don't want her," he tried again. "You can have her, I—"

He stopped as he looked at the advancing pair. The red horse was prancing, foaming at the mouth, and striking his hooves against the ground. When George met the rider's eyes, he knew he was looking at a man who would enjoy killing him. He tossed his pistol on the ground.

Walker urged the sorrel closer.

"Dismount," he instructed in the same soft tone. "Hold the girl carefully and when you're down, lay her gently on the ground."

George obeyed.

Silver had come to twice, but had been knocked unconscious again by the passing trees banging her head. She lay still with her face pressed into the grass, smelling the earth and remembering the prairie after a rain. She had died and gone to the happy hunting ground. Now she was safe forever.

Walker raised his gun and fired twice more in the air to bring help. He could not be sure the girl was still alive after the battering her head had taken; she had not

Then he remembered the second man. Nudging
with his heels and pulling on the reins, he was back
horse so he could see in both directions at once. But be re
he had a chance to look around, there was a loud cracking
sound and a whip coiled about his neck, its tip slashing
brutally across his cheek as he was ripped from the saddle.

Buck pulled his victim along on the ground, grinning like
a child playing tug-of-war with a puppy while Walker clawed
at his throat.

George's gratitude turned quickly to anger when he saw
the stupid look on Buck's face. He lunged at him and
knocked the whip from his hand.

"You bloody bastard, you've caused enough trouble! The
whole damn army'll be down on us in a minute. You take my
horse since you've 'bout killed yours. Get on old Pepper
there and ride like hell. I'll be right behind you." Buck stared
at him blankly, and George gave him a hard shove.

Silver had gotten upon her knees and now she raised her
head. She saw the tall back of George Greelee and knew to
whom it belonged, though she couldn't remember where she
was or how she had come to be there. She neither felt pain
nor saw the man strangling to death on the ground. Her eyes
looked down a tunnel and the only thing at the end of it was
George Greelee's back. She got to her feet soundlessly.

George blocked Buck's view so neither man saw her until
they heard a shrill scream. Silver sprinted forward and
leaped on George's back, locking her legs about his waist.
She looped one arm about his neck and raked her fingernails
at his face with the other.

George danced in a circle, believing that the thing on his
back was a mountain lion.

Buck drooled and cackled as he rocked toward the pair,
seeing nothing of George's bloody face, only the flash of the
girl's bare legs. He got behind and grabbed her around the
waist, greedily feeling her breasts and between her thighs
before she could be snatched away from him again.

George was in a blind panic; their time was running out.
He wiped the blood from his eyes, picked up his gun, and
pointed it at his stepbrother. "Put her down, Bucky. I'm

warnin' ya, put her down!"

Buck sullenly dropped his burden and this time Silver lay still. She remembered that the fat one was slow-witted, and once it had required several soldiers to break his hold on her neck. He had only been trying to touch her and didn't seem aware he was slowly killing her.

She lay unmoving on her back and watched the rolls of fat on Buck's back as he waddled away behind the lanky one. In a moment she heard their sounds fade completely.

Only a few minutes had passed since Walker was pulled from his horse. Now his struggles to claw away the death at his neck had ceased. He was not moving at all.

Silver noticed him for the first time and recognized the white eyes chief. His handsome features were strangely harsh, his lips blue. She crawled to him on her belly.

Places in the whip were wet, making the leather stick to itself. Though she used every ounce of strength in her fingers, she lost more precious seconds trying to loosen the whip's hold before she could finally press her ear to his chest.

The first beats were dull and heavy, but after a moment his heartbeat surged wild and frantic, and she whispered in Comanche, "He lives," and her eyes rolled back in her head.

The sorrel flinched as a saddle was slapped on his back and his master's voice stung the air like a willow switch. "If I'm well enough to eat that garbage you called breakfast, then I'm well enough to travel." Walker stopped to frown suspiciously at his aide. "You're sure about this? I mean, there's no doubt in your mind that she's well enough to travel."

"Yes sir," repeated Phillip for the tenth time. "Didn't take her half as long as . . ." He corrected hastily, "What I meant was—"

But Walker leveled him with a jaundiced eye and Phillip knew he could not recover the slip.

Walker yanked at the cinch belt, giving the animal more cause to flinch, and finished his task in silence. He had been assured that the girl was completely recovered, a fact that had settled like water on a hot iron, for while relaying this surprising information, his men had kept him flat on his back for a day and a night by refusing to make a crutch for him — for his own good, of course. The medic pointed out that a sprained ankle needed at least twenty-four hours of rest, not to mention the trauma his whole body had undergone during near suffocation.

The girl, however, was reportedly so recovered that it had been necessary to restrain her again and post an armed guard. No other recourse could be found without resorting to the ball and chain again.

Walker scarcely suppressed his emotions, and the horse's eyes flared in alarm when he tossed the reins over its head. It was not enough that she had disrupted his life — not enough that he had lost almost two days of travel time and endured considerable pain for his efforts, or even that he had risked his own life to save hers. Apparently gratitude was beyond the little hellion's comprehension.

He spoke to Phillip in clipped tones. "Have the girl on a horse exactly as I instructed before, hands and legs tied to her mount with a lead rope attached to my saddle. We pull out in twenty minutes."

Phillip sighed — a very small but detectable sound. "Yes sir. Whatever you say."

When the departing men were ready to leave and the girl's mount had been secured by a rope to Walker's saddle, Lester McCaleb stepped up to him.

"Major sir, I just wanted to thank you for lettin' us go on home."

"You don't have to worry about charges, but I hope all of you have learned something," replied Walker. "I'm posting a warrant for the arrest of George Greelee and Buck Santos when I get to the fort. I'll check the records of Indian captives to see if her age seems to match any of them. She needs to be returned to her own people, not sent to rot away on a reservation." Appeased that at least some people knew the meaning of gratitude, Walker smiled. "Who knows, maybe someday the girl will have reason to thank you."

"Speaking of the girl, sir . . ." Lester threw his head in Silver's direction and moved closer. "There's a few things I oughta warn you about."

He had Walker's attention. "Pray go on, I'm all ears."

Lester lowered his voice. "She's always got a knife. Don't matter how many times you take it away, she can make another one out of bone, rock, wood. You keep an eye on her if you prize your throat. And one other thing: Don't let her get to a horse. She's like all Comanches — she rides sideways, backwards, and under the horse's belly. We learned the hard way. If she hadna tried to jump that roan over a ravine and lamed him, we'd a never caught her."

With a faint look of awe, Walker nodded. "I'll keep that in mind."

Lester moved back and they were ready to leave. The men of the Fifth Infantry stood in a line, all saluting at once, Walker returned the gesture, smiling more freely as he thought of leaving the desert to the vultures and getting a good night's sleep, a hot bath, and crawling between clean sheets at the fort.

But as he turned in the saddle to check the ranks behind him, his mouth hardened: His captive's gaze was fixed upon him, and if looks could kill, he would have been a corpse.

Facing ahead again, he saw Phillip smiling reassuringly at the girl, and gritted under his breath, "Stop grinning like a fool and move these men out!"

For a time Silver rode with her eyes glued to her captor's back. She called upon every deity within her knowledge to curse his soul, his body — the very horse he rode. She even waited several miles to see if the gods would strike him down. They did not, and after a while she tried to relax in the uncomfortable saddle. It did not matter. He could do no worse to her than others had already done.

Yet she glanced back over her shoulder anxiously. They were heading south and east, their trail taking them farther from the Eckhoft Pahehona, the river called Red by the white eyes. In almost eighteen months of captivity she had never been more than two days' ride from Horse Back's numerous camps and not so great a distance from the reservation itself. Fear stirred inside her, snuffing at the hope that had kept her alive and sane. How far would they take her?

Turning back, she settled herself for the ride. The more white eyes came, the bolder Horse Back grew. She heard more and more often of his raids. Eventually she would escape. And later, when they had driven the white eyes from their buffalo grounds, she and her father and brothers would ride the plains again, happy and free!

As she noted the proud grace with which the white eyes chief sat his horse, she felt an odd sense of disappointment. Though he had kissed her boldly, his touch did not hurt like the others but was restrained, almost tender. His beauty fascinated her and his eyes had been kind and good like her father's. When she was first brought to him, she had thought he looked beyond her face and saw her soul. Later, his soft eyes seemed to twinkle when others were not looking, as though he felt warm and happy when their gazes touched. She had felt a drowning sensation not altogether unpleasant.

She scowled. But that was before. If she had not pulled the whip from his dying throat, he would not even be alive now, yet he repaid her like this! His influence over the other white eyes was great. He could have released her and no one would have dared to stop him.

For a moment her eyes lingered on the tawny hair curling at the back of his neck, and her face grew warm. Then she tossed her head. White eyes! They could not even ride a horse without their squaw blankets and sharp spikes on their boots! She must remember to make another knife tonight. Perhaps she would use her remaining one to take back the life she had given, when she escaped.

Throughout the long day's ride, Walker grew increasingly resentful of his new responsibilities, a feeling that was fueled by an unaccustomed lack of mobility and the fact that as night drew on, the girl had not altered her resolve to fight him tooth and nail—in the most literal ways imaginable.

That his heroic efforts in her behalf had not improved her plight augmented his already black mood—when he allowed himself to remember it. He preferred to recall that in spite of everything he had done for her, she would tear off to Horse Back the first instant she was free. And even with no grasp of English, she could have picked up some ideas about military movements from the soldiers. That, if no other reason, kept his hands tied; he couldn't possibly release her.

Phillip gave the order to camp, then turned to Walker.

"Shall I try to get the girl untied and off the horse? You know, she's been mounted for almost six hours. We men have a way of taking care of certain things, but the girl . . ." He paused delicately.

Walker paled. How many miles had she ridden in silent discomfort, unable and unwilling to voice such a request?

"No, she's my responsibility," he said stubbornly. "You see that camp is set up."

Walker went to her horse and stood looking up at her. Although she stared stonily ahead, Silver felt her heart set up a peculiar rhythm. This one seemed to see too much.

Their stopping place offered the blessing of a few trees. His mouth pressed in a hard line, Walker led her horse to the stoutest one and tied it. Then he reached up to untie the leather thong that held her left leg to the stirrup strap.

The sun was setting and its reddish glow gleamed on her dark thigh. Walker's hands were seized with clumsiness and he couldn't untie the knot. With a few unintelligible words, he gave up and reached for his knife.

The girl's head whirled about, her expression horrified. Walker gestured quickly that he meant no harm and slowly moved in to snip the leather with the knife tip. The strap had left a deep indention across her thigh. With a grimace, he moved swiftly to the other side of the horse and snipped that strap without touching her. He was so preoccupied with the tendency of his eyes to stray over her brown flesh that he forgot the nature of his captive. He cut the single strap that held her bound hands to the saddle horn. They were badly swollen. Staring at her hands, he also forgot his frequent observation that profanity was a sign of an inadequate vocabulary. "Hell and damnation!" he muttered savagely.

Silver stiffened. He sounded angry, and his hands were coming up. She glanced at the reins and calculated the consequences of kicking the horse's ribs. But then the large hands were around her waist, pulling her from the saddle. Her wrists were still bound and she could do nothing to stop the dreaded touch of his hands.

But his touch proved to be warm and somehow comforting. She couldn't seem to move, only hang limp as her back slid down his chest and belly, her buttocks resting briefly against hard thighs. When her feet were on the ground, he stood her upright.

Then she was free of his touch and the lethargy vanished. She sprang away from him with the speed of a cat.

There were soldiers everywhere but though she ducked the first few successfully, two of them finally intercepted her.

She was fighting ferociously when Walker reached them, and grabbing her around the waist from behind, he grunted as she used her bare heels against his shins.

"Quick!" he ordered. "Get some of that small-gauge rope from my saddlebags!"

After a prolonged battle, the men stepped back, and Walker surveyed their work with a pained expression. They had secured a loop around her waist, tied by a hard knot; the five-foot end of the rope was in his hand. The leash would work perhaps if only . . .

"She's got a knife," he whispered breathlessly, sweat popping from every pore as he realized how close they had come to disaster.

The faces of the men drained. "We'll hold her while you search her, sir," one offered through dry lips.

Walker's brows dropped. "I'll hold her and *you* search her," he snapped childishly, then changed his mind when he saw the sly expression come to their faces. "No!" he barked. "I mean . . . I'll do it." Another look passed between the men, but it was of the briefest duration; their commander had keen eyesight.

Her hands were still tied and her arms were hooked between two well-muscled biceps. Walker's hands felt huge and heavy as they lifted and then settled on either side of her waist.

That he found nothing but a lean and shapely torso gave his face a look of undue strain. Drawing a deep quiet breath, he felt her hips, no longer aware of the killing rage in her eyes. Then he moved his hands down, over thighs that seemed to go on forever.

Phillip leaned over and whispered discreetly. "Er . . . sir, we could see a knife if it were strapped to her leg."

Walker jerked his hands back and scowled fiercely. "I was checking for injuries," he said indignantly. The other two soldiers were staring at him, causing him to fairly shout in their faces. "Don't just stand there like two dunces; turn her around!"

After being presented with three backs, Walker found it easier to breathe. Beginning at her waist again, he moved up under her armpits until he felt the curve of her breasts. He stopped to wipe his brow with his sleeve. "Nothing. I guess I was wrong."

"Sometimes they hide 'em under their hair, sir," offered one of the men over his shoulder, struggling a little as the girl squirmed.

Walker touched the wispy filaments and they were like corn silk in his hand. He lifted her hair in one hand and stared at the dark sheen of her shoulders before he moved his other hand down her spine, at last touching something hard. The chill that ran down his back helped to clear his senses.

He held up a small, perfectly formed knife made of bone that had a needle-sharp point. He let out his held breath. "Now we know, don't we?"

The others said nothing.

After sending the assisting soldiers to other duties, Walker told Phillip, "I'm going to take her a little way from the camp. You stay with the men. If I'm not back in a reasonable length of time, suppose the worst."

"Yes sir. Just yell if you need me. "

Nodding grimly, Walker waited until Phillip was out of earshot before he turned to the girl.

For a long moment they stared, unable to converse or transfer any of what each was thinking. Something passed between their eyes, but neither could be certain the messages transmitted and received were correct. Walker tugged on the rope, turned and frowned over his shoulder, then took one step and tugged again.

Silver let her eyes blaze with hate to cover her fear and confusion. This one was too cunning: One moment his gaze was warm, the next he was watching her slyly, planning some evil behind his two-colored eyes. She did not like his hands touching her. They made her weak; above all she had to stay strong and alert so she could protect herself.

Walker tugged again, their gazes interlocked.

Silver twisted her body to return the favor, tossing her head defiantly.

Walker's eyes narrowed and he yanked harder.

Silver maintained her fierce expression but she knew resistance would accomplish nothing unless it was a good beating. He was taking her out alone to try breeding with her like the others. So, she would go meekly. Then when he was dull-witted with lust and there were no others around to help him, she would escape. Only this time she would make it.

She veiled her eyes with her lashes and stepped forward.

With the girl at his back, the hair on Walker's neck rose on end and stayed that way. She seemed to follow entirely too willingly to suit him. He glanced threateningly over his shoulder from time to time to remind her he'd as soon dangle a steak before a starving wolf than offer her his blind side.

When he found a group of trees growing concavely around a rock, he pointed to the spot and nodded in what he hoped was an encouraging manner.

She looked at him, then to the place he had indicated.

Seeing her bewildered look, Walker leaned back against the rock, crossed his arms, and stared idly into the distance. After a time, he felt movement on the rope and gripped it tighter in case she tried jerk it from his hand. But he did not turn around.

Silver crept cautiously behind the rock, hoping against hope that she was getting a true message. The first white soldiers had never once offered her such a moment of relief. They slipped away to see to their own bodily functions, afterward seeming to leer and watch her for signs of discomfort. She gave them none. She waited until they were asleep,

55

no matter how horribly her belly ached. For that one cruelty she hated them almost as much as for her beatings.

A snide smile touched Walker's lips. Six hours in the saddle seemed to have wrought a remarkable improvement in the girl's ability to comprehend his intentions. There was a popular concept that some women required a harsh, unrelenting hand, but he had never believed it; he had been taught from the cradle to hold women in the highest regard, and because he adored and admired his own mother, he followed that dictum faithfully. Yet despite the fact that he had risked more for this one alone than for any woman he'd ever known, he had incurred nothing but her resentment and defiance. His head nodded thoughtfully; it was a mistake to dismiss popular concepts without first trying them.

Walker sensed that she was standing in the open again, and turned his head. Her face was no longer twisted with hatred, though, as always, she held his gaze fearlessly. But beyond that, he could not determine that she had suddenly acquired the virtue of gratitude.

He set his jaw, stood away from the rock, and started walking. There was no resistance on the rope.

Silver gave in to the urge to tremble. He seemed to be taking them back to the camp and he had done nothing but offer her a kindness no other stupid white eyes had ever thought of. The feeble hope that he would not assault her was enough to bring tears to her eyes. Maybe at last she had found a white eyes who had no stone for a heart.

The ground blurred suddenly, and she failed to see the rock before she had tripped. She stumbled forward several steps trying to catch her balance, and Walker swung around in a fighting stance, his hands in the air.

Silver's gaze leaped fearfully to his face, and she stood very still, her cheeks growing warm when she could not pull her eyes away.

He stared at her for a long moment. At last he turned and started walking, giving the rope a small jerk when she did not respond immediately.

Silver heard her breath making too much noise in the air, and the cause was not exertion.

White eyes! she gritted silently. She would not trust one to give water to his dying grandmother. This one seemed to have done her a kindness. But then they were not back to the camp yet.

Chapter 4

As darkness drew on, the corps of officers discussed their superior whenever it was possible to do so without incurring his sharp-eyed gaze. Since they had taken the girl on, his temper had grown short, his eyebrows were prone to remain at a threatening angle, and he found little to say.

They were sitting around the campfire. Walker tried unsuccessfully to lose himself in the light banter of his men as they roasted a rabbit over the fire. Though his ankle was much improved, it still caused him some pain, especially toward the end of the day.

His brows knitted and slowly, covertly, he shifted his gaze to the two bare feet in the sand, which were not far away because he had come up with no satisfactory alternative to keeping her tied to him by the length rope. And there were definite drawbacks even to this solution. It was like being haunted by a shadow: He turned, she turned; he walked fast, she walked fast. He glanced at her feet again. They were brown and smooth and strangely sensual. He noticed the ring of callouses around her right ankle, a token of her months of slavery.

Downing the rest of his coffee, he stared moodily at the fire, not really listening to the conversation until he heard Sergeant Miller say, "It sure seems like you've done what a passel of others couldn't, Major. She's lookin' tamer all the time, don't you think?"

"Yeah," another voice chimed in, "maybe that was all she needed; just somebody to show her a little kindness."

Walker's reply was a sustained, morose silence. If their remarks were sincere then they were blind men and fools. Maybe he should order one of them to lay hands on her and demonstrate the validity of their kindness-works-wonders theory.

"You know," said Sergeant Miller, "that old Horse Back musta stolen her years ago, and that's why she's not like a real white woman." Miller chuckled. "They say that old bastard's a wily cuss. I been hearin' he was the smartest Injun west of the Mississippi since I was a kid. He must be pretty old—"

"Seventy-five years," Walker said, snipping off the sergeant's words.

Eyes rolled askance and lips closed firmly. But young Lieutenant Armstrong somehow missed the blunt ending of the subject.

"Well, it's not right," he said indignantly, "him living to a ripe old age after all the decent white folks he's slaughtered. Women and children, too!"

Walker felt a tension on the rope and looked over his shoulder, but the girl did not appear to have moved. She was still hugging her knees and staring into the distance.

Walker's eyes dropped lower. With her knees drawn up, the bare backs of her thighs were visible—and more too, he guessed, from where the others sat.

When he indeed found several sets of eyes glued to that very spot, his pulse raged as he glanced from the men to their object of focus, finding no way to indicate discreetly to the girl that she should change her position. He glowered at her for an extended time but she would not respond.

"Sir, what do you think about tonight? You gonna stake her out and set a guard, or just keep her tied to you?"

"I suppose I don't have any other choice unless . . . there are volunteers to keep watch . . . I didn't think so. Yes, I'll keep her on the rope," he finished dryly.

Phillip Martin made down three beds: one for himself, the next for the major, and the last one for the girl. The arrangement was his own idea, for Major Grayson seemed unaware of the gossip already being circulated about his dogged determination to keep the girl. Wouldn't it be simpler, the question went, to let her go and good riddance?

When they were all bedded down, Walker lay awake for a

long time listening to the prairie wind and wishing he could breathe pine and the scent of brackish water in a river bottom.

He looked at the girl's back and felt sure she had gone straight to sleep. He relaxed for the first time in hours. Thinking of her resting peacefully made him feel like the time he had put a wounded war-horse out of its misery.

Their days ran together like muddy water, indistinguishable and inseparable, a ceaseless toil under the sun followed by sweltering, uneasy nights. Although they were leaving the hottest spots of Indian trouble, there was always the chance of encountering an isolated band of Comanches — or worse, being surrounded during their sleep. Horse Back could have somehow discovered the new owners of his adopted daughter; he had a way of being in several places at once.

Their sleeping arrangements remained the same. As long as the girl was left strictly alone she caused no trouble, and their lives settled to a routine.

Silver no longer had the drudgery of tending camp, a chore made excruciatingly painful when she had worn the ball and chain. There had been a never-ending need for firewood, hauling water for the pots and pans, and cooking — and that without being allowed the use of a knife or any sharp utensil. She could not deny a sense of gratitude toward her new captor, yet she was not fooled into complacency. If there was one thing for which one could depend upon a white eyes, it was deceit, and to that philosophy she strictly adhered.

The ordeal of dragging his shadow about day and night did not improve Walker's mood. Since the girl made no effort to make things easier, mounting for the day's travel took over fifteen minutes. She either remained completely limp — a dead weight difficult to handle — or she fought them like a wildcat.

Several days into their journey, Walker began to stake her out in the middle of their campsite. It allowed him a moment of freedom and yet he was not forced to impose on others to guard her. With all eyes available for that purpose, he was able to take short walks to try and unwind without wondering if a knife was winging its way toward his back.

He continued to see that she had privacy when they stopped for breaks along the trail. Stands of timber were easier to find now and made the task somewhat less of a strain on both of them. If the fact that the private matter attended by him at all times, grieved her, the girl did not show it beyond her already visible contempt and hatred. As a reward for her good behavior, Walker started tying her to a tree then walking a short distance away while she tended to herself. But he only stayed for what he considered a minimum amount of time. Thus Silver learned that what she must do, she must do quickly.

The land began to gently roll as they came into the section of the state known as the Piney Woods. When they camped this particular night, spirits were high; they were only seventy miles from the fort in Nacogdoches.

Walker had not come to accept his role as taskmaster with any more grace, nor with any less irritation to his conscience: He was the evil tyrant, she the tormented slave. And she stubbornly refused to cooperate in any way that might allow him to change that status.

Further, their constant close contact did not create a more familiar—and therefore less acute—relationship. He was intensely aware of her and under constant siege by her scanty clothing. It was rare in those days for a man to get such an eyeful of flesh. Now he was bombarded by shapely legs, breasts that were free to sway enticingly with every movement, and the peeping curve of trim, taut buttocks when she stooped. The others enjoyed the view as well, but their temptation was mitigated by distance and the firm conviction that closing it would substantially endanger their scalps.

An irritant of almost equal consequence was the faint wild scent that clung to her; it drove him to distraction and he had begun to suspect it had come off on his own clothing as well. He knew an old trader once who had lived among the tribe for years and said that full-blooded Comanches had poorly developed sweat glands and absolutely no body odor of any kind except that the women chewed spicewood leaves, spitting them on their clothing or rubbing the leaves in their hair. As Walker pondered the scent—definitely somewhere on his person—he reflected again on how thoroughly the girl had grafted Comanche ways.

They camped on the banks of the Sabine River. Ever since the low mountains had emerged and the huge stands of pine, oak, and gum had walled them in, Walker had seen the girl grow more distant and more skittish. Perhaps she realized the distance between her and her home was now great, and growing.

Unable to force himself into confinement with her again so soon, Walker prolonged his freedom by leaving her staked throughout the evening meal. She never ate in front of them; they left her untouched plate beside her bedroll, and the next morning some but not all would be gone. He worried that she was not eating enough.

The soldiers had developed more sympathy for her since she'd been behaving herself, and while Walker was eating his supper and watching her, the cook handed a plate to Corporal Rose, who in turn went to the girl.

But as he leaned over to offer the plate, the girl came to life with a savage snarl, springing at him and backhanding the tin plate to send it sailing into the underbrush.

During the stunned silence that followed she lunged at the end of her rope, gesticulating and threatening with her hands while the heathen babble—the intent of which was clear—spewed from her mouth.

If intimidation was her game, it worked. There was a settling back into shadows, an electrified hush where there had been talk and laughter. Presently she sat down again, folded herself up, and stared. Shortly thereafter the soldiers seemed to tire and begin to make their beds, talking only in hushed tones.

Walker was too tense to sleep and lay for a while looking at the girl's implacable back stretched out a few feet away, feeling the weight of his new responsibility as never before. It was beginning to seem as though he had hung a millstone about his own neck.

Silver's heart beat with short, hard throbs. She was very far from home now; it would take hours to put any distance at all between her and her enemies, let alone reach the flat plains. They had taken her to a strange land where the sky was only a window above and she could see no moon to guide her. *So many trees!* She imagined her tortuous flight through strangling vines and underbrush that had grown wild and ferocious.

And this river awed her. She had seen one of the soldiers try to test its deepness by pushing a long pole down in it. The pole did not ever reach the bottom! And the water was stirred with an evil spirit—it swirled angrily, grabbing the pole and almost twisting it from the soldier's hand. She could not cross it without a horse, yet she must cross it to go north. She did not remember crossing any rivers coming down, but they must have. Yes, they must have.

The past few days were a fog of terrors as she was passed to yet another group of white eyes. Her senses swam with memories, horrible hands crawling over her body, trees banging into her head; and then waking to find the white eyes chief, his face blue as the whip drained his life. She pushed her knuckles against her lips until she tasted blood, but she could not remember crossing this river before.

Rolling to her back, she turned to look at the white chief. Moonlight softened his craggy brows and sharp cheekbones; it hurt to look at him and remember that he had tried to be kind, if only in his stupid white eyes' way. He had never once tricked her like the others. When he took her off from the camp, it was apparently because he was trying to make her journey easier. The thought made her eyes sting, for not a single soul in the past months had shown her so much as the kindness one would offer a dog. She felt unable to explain a feeling of sympathy for him. He seemed a victim like herself, and his face was often hurt and bewildered, as though he could not understand the injustice heaped upon him.

She turned away. He did not deserve her sympathy. He was the most dreaded of all Comanche enemies, a white eyes chief. They were shrewd, evil, capable of subtle and ingenious tortures—what need had he of her pity? What need had he of anything, for he had only to crook his finger and the others jumped. If he wanted to see his family then he did; if he wanted to sleep then he slept; if he wanted to eat then he did that—and all in the order that suited him.

She clenched her teeth when she thought of it. She had nothing but the ragged cloth on her back. She had no horse, no weapons but the crude little knives she could fashion in the dark, and no food but the slop left over from the soldiers' meals. All she had before was hope and now that was dwindling. The land had changed and she felt utterly desolate, a babe in a hostile womb. She was estranged not only from her father but the earth, who was her mother. For the land sang with strange voices, the night air was sweet and heavy, and the forest palpitated with unknown terrors.

She fought off the thoughts before they overcame her with hopelessness. Only one thing mattered: She had made a blood oath to return to her father—and the daughter of Horse Back was not like white eyes whose words meant nothing!

She curled her body over and began to chew on the rope.

Walker took command.

"Spread out. You only have four lanterns among you, so split into two groups. Phillip and I are taking a lantern each. Yell when you spot her and don't do anything until I get there."

"But don't you reckon the girl's long gone by now, Major?" asked Sergeant Miller hopefully.

"No. She couldn't have been gone more than a few seconds or she would have already made off with one of the horses. I checked; they're all there. Now try to remember that you are dealing with a white woman. Her safety comes first."

After motioning Phillip into the woods, Walker started his own search where the horses were tied, heading in a northwesterly direction. The moon was just barely visible overhead, but it would be enough to guide her toward her precious Horse Back.

Using his saber like a machete, he hacked impatiently at tangled vines and kept one ear tuned for the cry of his men in case they found her first. In a matter of minutes his shirt was soaked through to the skin. He paused, wiped the sweat from his brow, and leaned against the trunk of a large red oak to catch his breath.

Only a flurry of falling leaves alerted him to something in the tree above him. He shoved away from the trunk and held the lantern up, and in a moment he could just make out a hunched form on the overhanging limb fifteen feet above his head.

His held the lantern higher and the light shimmered in her eyes, making them look almost white.

"What am I going to do with you?" he said quietly. "I can't leave you there, you know that."

She inched further out the limb, but Walker could see her eyes shining through the leafy branches like those of a treed animal, and he spoke quietly, knowing she could not understand his words anyway. "Please—by some miracle of God come down without a fight. I don't want to have to hurt you."

Her eyes seemed to glitter more brightly but she scooted a little further along the limb.

"Major, is that your light?" someone shouted.

"Yes," Walker answered dully, "it's my light."

Miller puffed as he tore through the underbrush, then stopped to look up. "Granny's drawers, major. She looks mad enough to eat us alive, don't she?"

Walker sighed and said without conviction, "Maybe she'll come peaceably this time."

Miller looked at him quizzically before he turned to shout at the others. Then he began clearing a spot beneath the tree, which was filled with other soldiers in a remarkably short time.

Walker handed his lantern to Phillip and surprised no one at all by announcing he would go up the tree himself.

He leaped nimbly to the first branches, crawled as far as he could, and finally straddled the limb. Glancing down, he saw a sea of expectantly rounded eyes and gaping mouths, and thought dryly that he couldn't blame them. After all, they had come to expect a certain quality of performance in this particular act.

He made no attempt at trickery, holding her gaze with a gleam of determination in his own. He talked as much to calm himself as her, for his pulse was racing madly. "Just hold out your hand. I won't hurt you."

Silver had reached the outer extremity of her retreat and Walker closed in swiftly with a lunge, managing to catch her wrist. For a moment they tottered precariously while she attacked him with her free arm, and he was certain he would lose her, causing her to fall in the process. But he clamped his legs tighter about the limb, took a good hold on her wrist, and overpowered her enough to shove her over the side of the limb. He thought he felt her shoulder slip out of place, but he hung on. She kicked wildly, making contact with several noses and chins as the others tried to catch her feet.

"Okay, Major, we got her!" Walker let her drop.

It took a moment for him to climb down. By the time he reached them his face was black with fury, for his men were accomplishing nothing except to engage the girl in an increasingly violent tussle, in which the aim seemed to be seeing how many places they could put their hands.

"Get back, I'll handle it from here," he shouted, taking her by the wrist again and setting off at a merciless pace, ignoring her catlike attacks on his arm. He used whatever force was necessary to march victoriously ahead, his eyes squinted as he reviewed a previously considered alternative: that of turning her over his knee and blistering her backside!

The camp eventually settled back to a restless quiet. Walker lay awake, glaring at the girl occasionally. She refused to do anything but sit with her knees drawn up under her arms. Since she had chewed the end of the rope, it was very short, but he was too tired to go to the horses and search for more.

He noticed that her right ankle had begun to swell and that she rubbed it sometimes. He winced and looked away. She had probably turned it when he was dragging her through the woods.

But now that he thought about it, his own ankle — forgotten and maltreated during the excitement — hurt considerably. Which reminded him that neither injury would have occurred if she hadn't acted like a little heathen.

He flopped over and fought with demons until sleep came.

Walker awoke to a low whimper beside him. Jerking awake, he saw the girl was lying in a fetal position, her back to him. He leaned over.

"Silver?" She didn't respond, and when he touched her shoulder there was not even a flinch.

Ever leery of a trick, he untied the rope from his belt, not taking his eyes from her. There was still no response when he leaned over her again and repeated her name, so he struck a match and held it above her.

He gasped. Her right ankle was discolored and the swelling so severe it had risen up her calf and thence over half her thigh.

With a trembling hand, he felt for the lantern and lit it. She did not stir as he examined the purple splotches. And finally he saw the wound: two little pinpricks side by side.

He reached behind him to pound on his companion's shoulder. "Phillip! Phillip, for Godsake, wake up!"

"What is it, sir?" Phillip rolled his eyes at the surrounding brush. He had known it would end like this — their bloody scalps strewn for miles.

"The girl's been bitten by a snake. Get some water boiling quick!"

For the second time in scarcely two hours, Walker's men were roused from their beds. More than a few cursed the dwindling wisdom of their leader in not letting the little spitfire go when he had the chance. Several were sent for buckets of waters, others wearily rearranged their beds and tried to sleep again.

Walker leaned over the wound, his knife sharpened and disinfected.

"It's probably too late for suction to do any good, but we'vc got to try," he said, squinting under the lantern's meager light. He had made dozens of such incisions in his military years, yet his hand froze except for a slight tremor. He shoved the knife at Phillip. "You do it. I can't see a blessed thing the way you're waving that damned light around."

Phillip made a small X between the fang marks, while Walker stared into the darkness, and afterward sat back to look at his commander, whose face was almost as pale as the girl's.

"That's about all I can do, sir. She's gonna be awfully sick. That cottonmouth must have been as thick as my fist, and he got her pretty bad."

Walker stood up abruptly. "I need a little air. I'll be back in a minute."

When he thought Phillip was asleep, Walker untied the rope and slipped it from the girl's waist. She whimpered, and sometimes a hard rigor shook her body. He watched as long as he could stand it, then glanced about the camp to be sure there was no movement beneath the lumps of bedrolls. Pulling the blanket back gingerly, he eased his body down beside hers, lying very still until his frantic heartbeat slowed down. Finally he put his arms around her and held her against him.

She stopped shivering immediately, but when she seemed to snuggle closer, he drew away in alarm. After a second's deliberation, he grabbed a handful of blanket and stuffed it between their bodies before he pulled her close again.

The next thing Walker knew, Phillip Martin was shaking him.

"Sir, wake up! It isn't seemly, sir. You know how the men will talk."

Walker came fully awake to find his legs and arms

68

wrapped about the girl as though he had just bedded her. He remedied the situation like a man disengaging himself from the slimy tentacles of a sea monster, jerking himself to sit some distance away and glare accusingly first at Phillip Martin then at the sleeping girl.

Phillip met his scowl with infuriating patience, and Walker pointed out unnecessarily, "She's still unconscious." Phillip just looked at him. "I was keeping her warm. For the fever," Walker added.

Phillip removed his knowing gaze to the girl. "She's real sick, sir. I don't think she'd last many miles traveling."

"I know. I thought about it a long time last night. I've decided you can take the men on to Nacogdoches and I'll follow along with the girl as soon as she's able."

Phillip drew in the dirt with his finger.

Walker stared through narrowed lids at his aide. "The men want to spend time with their families. They're overdue for a leave and I refuse to ask them to use it up on the girl's account." Phillip did not look up. "Well?" Walker demanded. "What would you have me do, throw her to the wolves? Or maybe we should just put her out of her misery with a bullet through the head!"

Phillip raised his eyes, his face calm and inscrutable. "I'm sure you know what you're doing, and I wouldn't presume to question your right to do it. But . . . don't you think it might be wiser to order one of the others to stay behind with her?"

The gray-green eyes flashed and Phillip feared he'd gone too far.

"As you said, I know what I'm doing," said Walker coldly. "If Horse Back has somehow discovered where the girl is, I don't want it on my head that I left somebody in charge of my duties."

Phillip let the smallest of sighs escape him. "Okay, I'll get the men up and started packing. But what should I tell them at the fort?"

Walker got to his feet and looked down at Phillip. "Sometimes I think we've been together too long. I grow weary of having my thoughts dissected." Phillip dropped his gaze to the ground again, but Walker saw him square his shoulders stubbornly, and said, "Since you know so damn much, I'll let *you* figure out what to tell them at the fort." And he stalked off into the darkness.

Phillip rose wearily. He would have to go break the news to the others, and he was already feeling disagreeably defensive on his superior's behalf.

Chapter 5

It was noon of the second day and the woods were like a
rain forest, the verdant foliage seeming to grow under one's
very eyes. A breeze came up the river, and Walker thought
that if the girl were closer to the bank, she would be much
cooler. As it was, he sat fanning away a few flies and
mosquitoes from her face until his arm ached and he
wanted desperately to take a dip in the river. Instead, he
climbed down the embankment and went to the edge of it
to haul two more buckets of fresh water.

When he topped the bank again, he dropped his buckets
and rushed forward. The girl had raised up on one arm
and was looking about her dazedly.

He knelt beside her.

"Don't be afraid. We're alone." He swept an arm about
the camp. "I've sent the soldiers away. *Vamoose—*" He
pointed. "To Nacogdoches."

She blinked at him and looked about her again, plainly
unable to believe there was not a single soldier in sight.
Then her great silver-gray eyes came back to him and he
saw the shrewd little gleam in them.

Anger made his jaws clench, but he forced the grimace
into a big toothy smile through which he said mildly,
"That's right, you little heathen, it's just you and me.
Thrills your soul, doesn't it? Now there's only one throat to
cut before you go on your merry way."

Her small brows lifted in confusion, and Walker's sense
of revenge faded. Spying his knapsack nearby, he rum-
maged through it until he found a cold biscuit and held it
up.

"Hungry?"

71

Silver eyed the bread but made no move to take it, and suddenly the poison in her ankle caused her to feel a sharp throb and she reached down to rub it. She was accustomed to masking her face against pain — and did so, though it was not an easy thing.

Walker tossed the bread aside and crawled forward, glancing at her face and feeling unaccountably annoyed that it revealed none of the agony she felt. He had seen more than one soldier scream like women in childbirth from the painful venom.

"Snakebite," He explained, making a slithering movement with his arm. "*Suave-ti* snake?"

The demonstration, and the grave concern in his face, were such a boyish contradiction of Silver's former opinion of him that she forgot her pain and threw one hand over her mouth as she giggled.

Walker's brows dipped. But as they stared at each other, his temper cooled. She had actually laughed.

He smiled back experimentally.

Silver's mouth drew up, her brows rushed together, and she eyed him warily. No white eyes ever smiled from the goodness of his heart. How could he when it was only evil?

Walker returned her scowl in double portion before he shoved himself to his feet.

"Somebody around here has to do the work," he muttered, and went to his horse, standing on the opposite side so he could keep a watch on her over the animal's back.

He stroked the horse brush along the muscled spine bone. "Well, Jack, it's been a rough one, hasn't it, old boy? Better enjoy your rest. We'll be heading for Nacogdoches in the morning."

He frowned thoughtfully. The girl had her head tucked low, studying her hand as though she had a splinter. The gesture rang false to him. If he were in her position, he would be straining every nerve in an effort to understand what was happening, yet she seemed suddenly unconcerned about her fate.

An idea grew in his head and he spoke a little louder.

"Better enjoy your rest before we head out after that old scoundrel Horse—" There was no need to go on. The girl's chest was heaving up and down and she was rubbing her ankle like it was on fire.

Walker dropped the brush and strode leisurely to where she was sitting. He hooked his thumbs in his pockets and propped his weight on one foot.

Silver bent her neck as far down as it would go, trying to hide her face from him. Horrible white eyes! Always they had tricks! She smoothed at her too-short skirt and glanced only once at the tall black boots, but no higher, for the hated uniform was gone and he wore nothing but a pair of tight breeches, which only a stupid white eyes would wear. How could he mount a horse when his legs could surely not move!

"Do you need anything, Silver?" Walker drawled. "Perhaps you would like some water. Or a bite to eat. Or maybe you need to take a trip to the woods. I'm at your service." His eyelids dropped. "All you have to do is . . . say the words."

Silver tried to erase the image of the hard, gold-furred chest, which she'd had occasion to see several times before now, but she could not do it. Horrible, horrible white eyes!

"Don't you have anything to say, young lady? Hmm, that surprises me. I thought all women—"

Silver lifted her eyes, the pretty squarish jaws flexing as she rattled off the Comanche's favorite excuse: *"Ka nei mah nah-ich-ka ein!"*

Walker's expression did not change. "Oh, but I think you do. I think you grasp more than a little of our language." He warmed to his subject, biting his words off so hard his teeth snapped together. "Obviously your little game has given you much satisfaction in the past several days, but the jig is up, sweetheart. If you think I'm going to bow and scrape and try to anticipate your every need while all the time I'm being played for a fool—" She was shaking her head as if she didn't understand. "Oh, yes, I know. You may not get every single word, but apparently you get enough." A long, lean finger jabbed the air. "Now listen well, my little white savage. When you want me at your beck and call from now on, you will address me as Walker. Do you hear me? *Wall—kerr.* Then you will very politely make your requests known and if I deem them reasonable, I will accommodate you. But you get nothing unless you ask for it. In English! Do you *suave-ti* that, my dear?"

The crystal gray eyes flashed like strobe lights. *"Ka nei mah nah-ich-ka ein!"*

Walker stared, shaking with fury, and Silver knew he was going to kill her on the spot. "Like hell you don't!" he said, and stalked back toward his horse.

Silver watched him as he took up his position on the far side and began brushing the animal again, glowering at her over the sleek red back.

When it appeared that death was not imminent, she rolled over and tried to push herself up. After a lengthy effort, she got her left leg under her, but the right one extended stiffly to the side. She couldn't keep her face from twisting this time as she staggered and tried to balance on one leg.

Watching, Walker grimaced with her, but the single time she looked his way, her eyes were hot enough to singe his hair. So he turned his attention to a tangle in the horse's mane, watching her only from the corner of his eye.

Off she hopped, dragging the swollen leg behind her. Walker held his breath as she progressed to the nearest tree, fell against it and clung, her face pressed to the rough pine bark. Her body shuddered with the effort to breathe. Yet after a moment, she hopped to the next tree, rested, then to the next.

The horse brush went sailing. "Dammit, dammit, dammit!"

His long legs closed the distance between them before she could move to the next tree, but by that time, Silver had bitten her lips to keep from screaming. He lifted her without ado and took her back to the bedroll.

As the pain began to ebb, she peeped through her lashes. He was leaning over her, his gray-green eyes intense and pained. A fine film of sweat covered his face and naked chest.

"This is your pain. *You* caused it!"

"Me daughter of Horse Back, War Chief of Quohadie Teichas! Me princess of Antelope Eaters and me no need

74

white eyes words. Me need go home!" She pounded her chest and said the last word in an agonized wail.

Walker sat back on his heels. "I-I know you want to go home, and I really wish you could do that. But it's . . . it's just impossible."

The girl rubbed her forehead, shading her eyes from him. "Me no can go, me *slave*. Slave of white eyes chief!"

Walker paled. "You are most certainly not," he said indignantly. "You may be a slave of circumstance and ages of injustice, but you are no slave of mine."

"Me go where you go, eat when you say — me slave!"

"If I let you go, you'll run straight to Horse Back. The Comanches will soon be whipped for good and there'll be no place for you except the reservation. Is that what you want, to live out your years with a pack of heathens on a reservation? Is it?" He reached to move her hand from her face, but she beat him to it.

"Me never go reservation!" She glared defiantly, and when Walker kept looking at her, she jerked her face away. "Me hungry," she demanded petulantly.

Walker studied her and after a moment smiled slyly.

"Okay, princess. There's more than one way to skin a Comanche."

Silver looked sideways at him and Walker smiled broadly. "That's an old white eyes saying." He stood up and grinned at the top of her head. "The princess has given a command. She wants to eat. So as soon as I finish with my horse, I'll fix you something. And then bring it to you. I'll even feed you." He could not tell how much of his satire she comprehended, only that her neck hunched lower between her shoulders and her fingers curled into claws.

He chuckled as he sauntered off to stake his horse.

Walker whistled as he boiled coffee, sliced some bread and cheese, and opened a jar of beans. Silver maintained a brooding silence and watched him suspiciously, but he defied her to find reason to continue her stubborn resistance. A man tamed the savage beast with kindness, not cruelty. He had almost forgotten that.

After propping one of the saddles behind her back, he handed her a generous plate and took a seat across from her.

To his relief, she began to eat quite heartily. Voraciously, in fact, using her fingers to do it. He saw the spoon lying beside her leg.

She started to sip from the cup, then screwed her face up and turned away.

"What's the matter?"

"Me no drink *to-oh-pah*."

"How's that?"

"To-oh-pah," she said impatiently. Black water. Me no drink."

"With a name like that I'm not surprised, but you'd better drink it anyway. It will make you feel better. Very much stronger." As an afterthought, he flexed one bicep.

Silver ducked her face behind her hand and laughed.

Walker frowned fiercely. "And eat with that," he commanded, pointing at the spoon. "Your mouth is covered with beans and so is your nose."

His tone wiped away any inclination Silver might have had to try the spoon. She slitted her eyes and inspected his furry chest.

"Paph is for head, not body," she explained smugly. "If it grow on body, it is—" She searched for the word. "It is shame. Braves pull out all *paph*."

Walker's left brow leaped up at an angle and the right one dropped as he looked down, expecting to find bean juice dribbling down his chest. He remained unenlightened until she pointed boldly at his chest.

"A true warrior, he would pull *paph* out, for his skin to sure enough shine like sun." Walker looked up and she nodded at him wisely. *"Mah-cou-ah* . . . that is, wo-man, she also do this. All True People do this."

Walker bristled, but he was also fascinated.

"You do this?"

She answered with a superior nod. "Me Quohadie Teich—"

"No, that is wrong. You should say, *I* am Quohadie Teichas."

76

She lifted her chin. *"I* am Quohadie Teichas. *I* am The People. Hair, as you say, goes on your head or it is shame. I take out." She drew her hand slowly along her good leg, and Walker's eyes went there. *"Ca boon?* There is none."

Walker's face heated as she stroked her dark, silky leg with pleasure. Then she glanced up puzzled, as though she had failed to make him understand the benefits of this marvelous technique.

"See? It is good. You touch."

Walker searched her face but found it guileless. He dropped his eyes again as she pulled the tattered edge of her skirt up so that her whole thigh gleamed darkly at him.

Smiling patiently, she placed his hand on her shin and began to pull it along to demonstrate the creamy texture of her skin.

But a trail of chill bumps raised in the wake of his fingers and Silver gasped, flinging his hand away like a spider. She stared at the ground for a moment to let her heart slow down, then she threw her head back to gaze down her nose.

"This is good, no?"

Walker stared at her leg. "Yes . . . very good."

"That . . ." She pointed at his chest. "Is no good. Yes?"

Walker came to himself, and scowled. "It is very good— it grows there, doesn't it?" Before she could jerk her hand away, he grabbed it and pressed her palm against his chest.

Silver felt animal-like fur—felt the quick strokes of his heart against her palm, and it seemed her own would burst before she could snatch her hand free.

She curled it to her and looked at the ground.

Walker grinned. "This is good, yes?"

She would not look up. "Me . . . that is, I, am thirsty now."

"Sure, princess. Whatever you say." He was still smiling as he went to get the canteen.

Evening saw an increase in Silver's fever again, and several hours of delirium. Walker kept up a steady stream of buckets from the river, first covering her with wet towels and then wrapping her in a blanket. Her temperature continued to climb.

As a last resort, he carried her to the river in his arms and waded out deep enough for the water to cover them both to the neck, holding her while she trembled convulsively, her head rolling against his chest. He talked to her, told her his life history in an unpunctuated stream. Finally her moaning ceased and she slept in his arms.

He stayed in the water until her burning flesh had cooled completely, then trudged up the steep bank, laid her gently on the bedroll and stretched out beside her. When she began to shiver again, he lay close to her, pulling the blanket around them both.

Silver slept the entire night through, and Walker left her side only long enough to eat or relieve himself. By morning he was bleary-eyed from lack of sleep and had two days' stubble on his face. But he arose early, bathed, shaved, and dressed in his uniform. He had hot coffee and breakfast ready when she awoke.

Although she was very weak, her skin pallid and her eyes smudged with dark circles, he was fully prepared for a volatile mood swing. He wasn't fool enough to think she had given up escaping, but he did hope she had abandoned the idea of cutting his throat.

He handed her a cup of coffee.

"Drink this. Try to think of it as medicine."

Surprisingly, she obeyed, her eyes following him as he walked to the kettle and poured his own. He sat down on a log close to the fire, for the mists rolling off the river were chilly.

Silver's memory was foggy, but she could recall strong arms holding her, hands that brought cool relief to her burning face and neck. Her instinct to mistrust and hate warred with an overwhelming sense of debt. Perhaps he had only saved her life for some evil purpose yet to be revealed, but she could never lift her hand against him now.

Her nose wrinkled at the foul-tasting brew but she

78

drained every drop. It would be more difficult to escape now that she could not take his life. She would have to hit his head to make him sleep, although she flinched within herself at the thought of bringing hurt to one who had kept her from death. She rubbed her swollen leg, taking comfort from the fact that she could not escape until her leg was better, and that might be some time. So she didn't have to think about escape at all right now.

She smiled faintly. "Black water sure enough horrible."

"That's because it's good for you." He looked down. "I think your leg is not so swollen now. I mean it's not so —" He gestured with his hands again. "Big."

Silver giggled. "Me know swol-len."

"Oh."

They drank in silence.

"I think we can move on by tomorrow," said Walker presently.

"This day. Me can — I can ride *this* day. I am Quohadie Teichas." She lifted her shoulders proudly.

After a pause, Walker said, "You are not Comanche, you are white eyes."

Her eyes flared, seeming to turn almost white. "Me Quohadie Teichas. My father Horse Back — me can ride *this* day!"

Walker looked at her without blinking. "We travel tomorrow."

Regardless of her improvement or the blemish of her past record, Walker made up his mind that he would not tie her again, although he decided it was wise not to mention the fact and give her time to make plans.

They sat at the fire eating breakfast.

He went back to their previous conversation, speaking as casually as he would of the weather.

"Your hair and skin are not Comanche." He took a bite, chewed with studied thoroughness. He could see anger flickering beneath her eyes, but she seemed to be holding it in check.

"Me — I — was born on Father Sun's birthday. He

79

touched my skin and hair. Horse Back told me."

"Your nose, your mouth, and your cheeks are not Comanche." He mumbled through his food, gazing with interest toward a tall pine.

Silver weighed him for a moment, then copied his mien by biting off a large chunk of bread and chewing it leisurely.

"You are Comanche, not white eyes," she said mildly.

Walker looked at her. "That's ridiculous. I am white eyes."

She smiled demurely. "You say you white eyes. Me say me Comanche."

Walker's startled look faded to an answering grin. Living with savages had not dulled her wits. He ate in silence, letting her think she had won, then he struck suddenly.

"So. Why do you hate me?"

Silver set her bowl down with deliberate calm. He had tried to catch her off guard but she would not let him know he had succeeded.

"When . . . *I*, was only six suns, I rode before my father, Horse Back — not left in the village to work like others. I was yet six suns and my father gave me horse." She gazed into the distance and spoke softly. "There was much meat in our village and the old women sang, the *mah-tao-yo* laughed and played games. The People moved as the wind, following the buffalo to sweet grasses." She looked at him and her eyes had begun to smolder. "But white eyes come. They kill many buffalo. Soon The People cannot eat. We move to more buffalo. The white eyes come more. We move. Now there is no more buffalo for The Eaters, the *Teichas*. White eyes bring bad sickness. My mother cannot get up. She breathe blood and cannot eat. She die. Many papoose die for no *ner-be-ahr's* milk. White eyes come when warriors are gone, kill little ones and old men." Silver felt a knot rising in her throat so she spat on the ground. "Horrible white eyes! Horrible!"

Walker studied his bowl of mush with revulsion. "Not all white eyes are bad," he said quietly, "and not all Comanches are good."

Silver regarded him thoughtfully for a moment. "Both

80

bad and good as you say. But only one path is straight and true. White eyes speak with two tongues. He say he come to live in peace and we give land. He want more, we give more. Now he wants all and he kills even babies to get it."

Walker could say nothing for the heavy stone in his chest, pushing up until it choked off his breath. He looked down, and the heavy silence was strung so tight between them that he felt he could reach out and pluck it.

But as he watched, he sensed she was alleviating the tension for him, playing the savage to his fullest expectations by scooping her fingers around the bowl of mush and slowly licking them clean one at a time. She glanced up slyly and he wondered if he was supposed to laugh; but he was afraid to set her off again so he just looked at her solemnly.

And she must have known there was a dab of mush on the end of her nose, for though she didn't smile, her eyes danced.

Not wanting their supplies to run short and force them to push on too rapidly, Walker left the girl alone late in the evening and shot two rabbits. He left her unrestrained, slipping back occasionally to check on her. She did not roam from the camp.

Another mealtime came upon them and, as usual, the settling of darkness made the girl jumpy. Their roasted rabbit was eaten in silence.

Watching her eat, Walker felt a distinct reluctance to push on for the fort tomorrow. He was enjoying a kind of possession of her—this wild creature he had caught. There were no soldiers, no Horse Back. The strain between them had most definitely lessened.

Silver was quick to note that her captor did not intend to restrain her when he made down his bedroll a little apart from hers. She watched with fascination as his tall, lean body danced, a graceful stoop, a sidestep. Only the hated blue uniform marred her pleasure. She liked to dance very much.

Walker stripped down to his trousers to crawl under the

81

blanket, and from the shadows Silver reaffirmed that her new owner was indeed a strong and capable man. Which was a mixed blessing: He would be hard to trick yet offered good protection.

She discovered she was able to block out the haunting forest voices and doze a little. Her leg ached steadily but it was easy to ignore when there was so much else to think about.

She was still awake when she detected the steady rhythm of his breathing; she waited a little longer, then stood up to test her leg.

At each Comanche camp there were several baths made of rocks and surrounded by hide-draped poles for privacy. When a fire was built inside and water poured over the heated rocks, a vapor was produced. For Silver, months of slavery had permitted no more than a quick and fearful dip in whatever water was available; but always she remembered poor Quannah's efforts to rid himself of his tainted "white" smell. That a faint yet similar odor sometimes clung to her own body made her desperate enough to risk anything when such infrequent opportunities presented themselves. She searched the supply bag for cloth and soap, and headed for the river.

The dangerous eddies were crystal rings under the bright moon, and Silver shivered to think of them sucking her under. Walking to the end of a sandbar, she pulled her dress over her head and stood naked but for her sole undergarment, a triangular cloth similar to a warrior's G-string that just covered her womanhood in front and, after passing between her legs, split into two straps that formed a V, the ends of which tied to the band around her waist, leaving her buttocks bare.

She sat down with difficulty, letting only her legs rest in the evil-spirit water, and began to scrub herself from head to toe.

Walker awoke with a jolt and knew she was gone without looking. He scrambled to his feet and began searching for the rest of his clothes, considering no alternative but to saddle up and trie to find her tracks.

Then he heard the splash. Buttoning his pants, he

started toward the riverbank, furious that she would risk her life to escape him. Without his boots, every twig caused him to wince, slowing him at last to a frantic hobble.

He stopped dead as he looked below.

She stood in the moonlight on an arm of land, her slender nude body doubled into a graceful upside-down U as she bent over to squeeze the water from her hair. He could make out the paleness of her breasts sagging toward the water. Then she straightened and flipped her hair back in one movement, pausing to let the water drip down her back. The moon defined everything, from the slim hips to the full, tip-tilted breasts, and as she raised her hands to push her hair back, her breasts tightened and rose upward.

Walker's throat went as dry as the Kalahari Desert; he tried to call out to her, but the words were stuck there.

After shaking out her hair, she started to dry herself with the friction heat from her hands, and Walker felt a fire spreading through him.

Her hands moved to her breast, rubbing quickly, jiggling every ounce of ripe, cool flesh, and Walker started down the embankment.

Silver spun about with a start. The moon glittered in his eyes and his look was all too familiar. She wheeled and plunged into the water.

Walker's senses cleared quickly. "You stupid little fool, you can't swim with that leg," he shouted, half falling down the slope in his haste.

Although an excellent swimmer, Silver was paralyzed with pain. The touch of land fell away and her leg would not push her up. She floundered, clawing at the wet death that swathed her face, and gasping for air.

Walker overtook her in a single dive, circling her waist with one arm and bringing them back to touching the clay bottom again with only a couple of strokes.

But Silver struggled wildly; she could feel his hairy chest against her bare back, the touch of his skin hot beneath the cool water. Her breasts were pushed up by his forearm like two balloons ready to burst.

The most venomous Comanche word she knew was *Ki-*

owa, scoundrel; *che* was the superlative of bad, and by attaching the vilest title of all, *tivo,* she stumbled upon a satisfying mouthful: *"Kio-wa-che tivo! Kio-wa-che tivo!!"*

Walker gripped her tighter as they stood, dripping, on the shoreline, and began to laugh, for he heard only "Wa-che!"

"Of course, I watched," he hooted. "I never claimed to be a priest!" But suddenly her kicking thrust him backward and she came down on top him.

The shock of his skin — so hot beneath the chilly water — and the feel of his hairy chest against her back, sent Silver into the frenzy of mortal combat, and though she was hampered with her back to his belly, she fought so well that Walker considered the possibility she could do him in if he lost his grip. He raised his knees and clamped her hips between them, trying to immobilize her; but his hand accidentally touched a rigid nipple, and both of them went still.

Walker jerked his hand back as though he had touched a viper, and for many seconds there was nothing except the noise of their panting.

"Let me go, *tivo sata,*" she whispered.

"Don't move." His voice was oddly strained. "Please, just don't move." Then his hand lowered slowly and she saw it coming but couldn't move. And finally he had cupped the taut, chill-ridden mound gently in his hand.

Silver went weak, for the steel pallet beneath her suddenly softened, became a stirring lover's embrace. A warm, delicious, satin-and-down bed for her cold back. And his boldness seemed to paralyze her; she could not move one muscle as his fingertip traced a slow circle around her nipple while the other palm slid down wet skin to rest lightly on her belly.

"Silver," he breathed in her ear, nuzzling it lightly, touching it with his tongue, and she shivered all over.

"Tivo sata," she cursed him, but the sound was that of a desperate plea, and she lifted one arm over her head to grasp his thick hair. Walker felt her breast spread under his fingertips; and his body curled up around her like a bloom folding at dusk, and he caught the nape of her neck with

84

his teeth.

"Silver . . . Silver, let me love you. Now—please now!"

The words sped through her veins, making her heart race, and she seemed to be melting away—into him; her legs seeped like hot wax into his thighs, her back sank into the mold of his chest. Somewhere in her head she could observe from a distance and she thought with wonder that everything was going, everything but her breasts, rigid, pointing skyward, straining after his touch like little birds when the mother shakes the nest.

Walker clutched her to him savagely, groaning deep in his throat as his hands moved down to the mound, covered only by her strange undergarment.

The drugged mist blew away and Silver went stiff, seeing the pale faces leering above her, their hands grabbing, hurting, humiliating—and she snarled like a panther, jabbing her elbows into his ribs. "You like others! You will *not* do, me *kill* you!" She levered her arm up, bringing Walker's forearm close enough that he felt the sharpness of her teeth just in time to snatch it away.

But it was what she said that doused his passion like ice water.

He pushed her aside to get out from under her and propped on one elbow.

"It wasn't like that," he said breathlessly. "I wouldn't do anything to hurt you. I—"

Silver covered her face, and deep sobs tore up through her throat. He tried to pull her hands away, but she jerked violently when he touched her.

"I-I'm sorry. Everything happened so fast, so naturally. But I—for Godsake, don't cry! It's not the end of the world."

She kept her face covered. "Me Comanche, me not cry like papoose!"

"Shh, I know, I know . . ." He wanted to hold her but dared not try. "Look, it's over now. I won't touch you again. All I wanted was to see if I could find your . . . I mean, I wanted to return you to your people."

Silver peeped through her fingers. "You t-t-take me t-to Horse B-Back?" she blubbered.

85

Walker did not have to pretend that more important matters pressed him. He stood up quickly. "I've got to get you back up to the camp before you take pneumonia."

As he lifted her, Silver folded her arms to keep her breasts from rubbing against him. Walker's mouth twisted. Too little too late!

Her back scraped against his arms and when he realized it was embedded with gravel, he fairly leaped up the steep bank and hurried to the blanket, lowering her gently.

"Just sit here a minute —" He knelt behind her, fumbling in the darkness. "I know there's a towel somewhere — here it is."

He brushed but the gravel stuck tight. Tossing the towel aside, he leaned and squinted, using his fingertips.

Silver sat very still and after a moment, she began to relax. Indeed she found a certain pleasure in the situation. No Quohadie Teicha ever clucked over a woman like a mother hen.

"Does it hurt?" he asked anxiously.

She shook her head. "No hurt."

He muttered something she could not understand, but no matter. This one *was* different. He could have taken her, for his arms were hard and strong. But he did not. *He did not,* she thought happily, reveling in her discovery.

"Are you cold?" His fingers flicked at the small of her back.

"Not cold," she murmured.

His touch moved lower but stopped before reaching the plump bulge of her upper buttocks, and gradually her pleasure dimmed. Had not three young braves and the son of Lone Wolf offered many horses for her hand in marriage? And had not the white eyes soldiers offered heap many beads, blankets, and even silver if she would come to their beds? Yet this one had thrust her away when he could have had her — when his flesh was burning against hers and she could not get enough air, could not think what to do. Her chin rose as she stared into the darkness, while his fingers flicked softly but moved no lower, and her flesh strained after his touch — but he moved no lower. She had taken ten stripes from the white eyes' whip, and now he

86

worried over a few small rocks!

Affecting a small moan of discomfort, she reached with deliberate helplessness toward the gravel stuck to her behind.

Walker's eyelids drooped as he watched. He hesitated. Was she that hopelessly naive, or was she planning some trick? Just in case, he scooted a little away from her. No woman could be *that* naive. Apparently she was not above a little coquetry when it could be turned against a white eyes.

He grinned faintly.

"Here, let me help you." He slid his hand gently over the cool ripe spheres, brushing away the very few pieces of gravel.

Silver's ego swelled with a sense of power. She was smiling again.

Walker brushed, and waited for her attack. He brushed some more, and still nothing happened. She sat so motionless that his hand slowed, then lingered, then kneaded.

"That's enough," he said abruptly, getting to his feet and staring down at the top of her head. She sat with her arms across her breasts, her fanny shining in the moonlight.

He wheeled away with an unintelligible mutter, pausing only long enough to throw a gruff reminder over his shoulder. "I suggest you get some sleep because we're leaving for Nacogdoches first thing in the morning."

Silver swung her head to watch him until he disappeared into the shadowed woods. Then she let out a quaking breath and pulled the blanket over her without donning her ragged dress, though it was lying conveniently at her side when she distinctly remembered leaving it on the riverbank. Her smile lengthened. Chief White Eyes had thoughtfully brought it with him, but perhaps it was for his own benefit rather than hers.

Chapter 6

Though the woods were still shrouded in mist, Walker practically had their small camp dismantled when Silver awoke. Wearing only his boots and jeans, he was tending the final task of gearing the horses and loading the pack animal.

Silver slipped her dress over her head, no longer feeling like a temptress. Her mouth was dry, her tongue felt swollen, and her skin itched from sleeping naked on the *tivo's* wooly blanket.

Her eyes fixed on her captor's naked back as he worked. He would, of course, be arranging a way to tie her to her horse—a strange sensation interrupted her thoughts: The sensors in her fingers picked up the exact delineation of the broad muscle straps down either side of his spine; every vein and wrinkled knuckle in his hands seemed as if they were part of her—familiar and belonging. She knew their texture, their shape.

She pulled her eyes away and looked about her. Where was her *sen-ge?* Her eyes roved faster. It was down by the water and she would have to go get—but no! Her face twisted. It was not. It was lying just under the edge of the blanket and *he* had brought it!

She snatched it up and, scooting under the cover, slipped her ankles through the straps and wriggled it up over her hips, her heart galloping so fast she couldn't breathe. She must be careful if she bathed again. Perhaps she had been hasty to judge the young maids of her village so harshly. When they sighed and giggled over their men, she sneeringly concluded it was all a bid for attention. They wanted it known they had been "chosen." Those who could lure their betrothed to their beds and begin to produce sons quickly guaranteed themselves a prominent position with their husbands, whether they were First Wife or not. But she knew now why a brave could wiggle his finger and his wife came running like a puppy to the master's feet. It was because she saw him moving about the camp with far less clothing than this white eyes wore, and her heart ran away and her belly turned to porridge. She melted to a formless lump when he touched her.

She did not like *commar-pe*. She would not marry. Not for many winters. Maybe not ever. *Commar-pe* was dangerous; its sweeping fire was like the skittering of the heart when one looked over the walls of the great canyon, Llano Estacado.

Confident that he could overtake her if she escaped on foot, Walker elected not to tie the girl to the saddle, attaching only a lead rope from her mount to his.

They rode the first few miles in silence, Walker glancing back occasionally to see how she was faring. She gave no signs of pain but rode with her back straight, her chin in the air. With more disappointment than he cared to acknowledge, he noticed that her former moroseness was alive and well. She stared often to the north and west. That was fine with him. It was a damned sight better than becoming a victim of lust with a knife in his belly.

He faced ahead to watch the trail, which had grown abruptly narrow and strangled by undergrowth. The horses struggled along for several moments before the thought struck Walker that the girl could reach up for an overhanging limb and disappear silently from the saddle. After that he looked back more often, inviting the snarl of briars around his neck and the stinging slap of limbs across his ears.

They stopped for a break and Walker took her down from the horse to let her stretch her legs, handling her as gingerly as a decrepit old woman. Indeed, he tried to think of her that way, concentrating on her feet to avoid sight of the rest of her. But finding them, also, of a certain seductive nature, he tried not to look at her at all, so that when he reached for her forearm to steady her, the back of his hand brushed her breast. He wheeled away to strike out for the nearest clump of brush, snarling over his shoulder, "Stay right behind me or you'll find yourself wearing another rope!"

He found a place of privacy for her and waited until she was through. When they walked back to the horses and were ready to mount, he offered her a canteen.

She drank thirstily, eyeing him over its cavalry-blue canvas casing. When she had wiped her mouth with the back of her hand, she pointed to him.

"What name?"

"Walker Grayson."

"You Gray's son?"

His smile was condescending. "No, my father's name is Samuel. Samuel Grayson."

"Su-vate? That is all?"

"It's not enough?" he replied stiffly.

"What it mean?"

He crossed his arms. "I don't suppose it *means* anything."

"Funny name. River Walker good. Or Sky Walker or Desert Walker. But you no Gray's son and 'Walker' mean nothing."

He put one hand over his heart. "My deepest regrets."

Gray eyes twinkling, Silver sipped from the canteen again and handed it to him. Then she turned, grabbed the saddle horn, and lifted herself to the horse's back with surprising strength, considering it was only last night that she was too weak to brush the gravel from her shapely behind. Walker was frowning when she looked down from her superior height and smiled faintly.

"Me call you Chief White Eyes. That mean plenty."

St. Martinville, Louisiana

Amanda Grayson tilted her head back and laughed.
"You boys came all the way over here just to tease us!

90

You know perfectly well my parents won't let us go with you unchaperoned, much less to the train depot. Daddy says its a den of thieves and cutthroats."

Paul Bascom leaned boldly forward and whispered in Amanda's ear while the other couple exchanged shy glances. Paul spoke with a mixture of two Louisiana dialects, Cajun and Creole, whereas Amanda Grayson, a transplant of some ten years, intoned only the gentle drawl of the northern part of the state where she was born.

"Meh, I cood talk m'mere into eenythin," he laughed throatily. "She weel l'me en Brahford tek yooh to dee ice cram pahloor."

Amanda squeaked with mock dismay. "How dare you carry on so, you old scallywag. Both ladies in your present company are already obligated. I have seen Mark Whitaker several times in the last month. You must think low of us, indeed."

Paul grinned wickedly. The petite brunette, with her hair parted docilely and drawn into a neat chignon—her soft brown eyes twinkling merrily at him—was certainly no raving beauty like the golden-haired Camelia. But her lively wit and keen intelligence kept a string of male suitors at her door; he meant to be first in line.

Camelia had little to say, and one might have presumed her manner shy. In truth, she was infuriated that Amanda always managed to be the center of attention. It wasn't that she was looking for a man for herself, of course. She had the pick of the litter already in a long-legged major general, six feet four inches tall with eyes that could melt a girl's heart! Nonetheless, her lower lip protruded a little and she swept a sidelong glance at Paul's companion, Bradford Ross. He was as blond as she, and very handsome. Camelia fanned her silk fan with new fervor, knowing that the golden tendrils at her temples and earlobes were dancing.

Kathren, stepmother to Amanda, Walker, and Seth Grayson, strolled through the double french doors onto the front veranda. She was tall, slim, dark, and still a striking woman at forty-eight. Her rich black coiffure showed no signs of gray, and her manner, unlike the Graysons' easy-going ways, was restless and alert. Her dark eyes flitted everywhere at once, and her mouth was usually engaged in speaking. She favored rich hues rather than the subdued colors Amanda wore. "Let not the adorning be the plaiting of hair or putting on of apparel," Amanda often quoted. And with a hearty laugh at her stepmother's reply: "Dress like a dusty old prophet if you want to, my dear, but ruby red is my color. Besides . . ." she would purse her lips playfully and add, "your father simply adores me in red."

If Kathren was exotic and lively—and quite exasperating at times—her difference, from the former mistress of Gray Shadows, was embraced as new blood. Yes, she was flamboyant. (She insisted on using lip paint.) And vain. And vivacious, charming, and intelligent. Samuel Grayson was in love for the second time in his life, and Walker, Amanda, and Seth were willing to overlook a multitude of sins to see a smile on his face again.

Melissa Grayson's passing a year ago had turned the gray stone mansion into a tomb. The servants crept about, and Samuel locked himself away in his room, Walker went back to his post, unable to watch the mutual agony of grief feeding on grief. Amanda roamed the grounds in search of the happy home of her childhood, and Seth, unable to coax any of them with his notorious sense of humor, became a brooding shadow.

Seth finally left the townhouse as well, going to the plantation seven miles southwest of St. Martinville to oversee its phenomenal recovery from Reconstruction. Samuel Grayson, in truth, had a Midas touch. His fleet of cargo barges and warehouses on both the Bayou Teche (pronounced *Tesh* by the Louisiana French) and the Mississippi, along with two pleasure and gambling paddlewheelers in New Orleans, supplemented income until the sugar plantation was in the black again—only two years after Lee surrendered.

It was Kathren who had saved them. Or rather saved Samuel, which was the same thing. Eight months after they laid Melissa Grayson in the family plot, Kathren and Samuel were wed. Their marriage was four months old this week.

"What is this I hear about the ice cream shop?" Kathren smiled knowingly at the young men. "Are you gentlemen trying to seduce these beautiful young women?"

Amanda flushed at Kathren's crude reference to their flirting. Kathren had not been born to the aristocracy but "worked her way up" as she put it, and she was prone to have embarrassing lapses.

"Where's Daddy?" asked Amanda to change the subject.

"Your father is writing a letter to Walker. He hasn't been home since our wedding, you know, and that's over four months. Samuel is starting to grieve like an old hound after the departed 'massah.' "

Amanda blushed again, for she did not consider the analogy appropriate to the loving relationship between her father and her oldest brother.

Kathren's dark eyes came to rest on the low border that lined the walk to the front steps, and she frowned. "That William. He gets lazier every day. Why, look at that. The rose moss is seeding all over the flagstones. It'll be sprouting up through the cracks next year."

"I guess we'll have more flowers than ever then," teased Amanda, trying to steer her from one of her binges, for though Kathren was admittedly never much of a housekeeper before, she had become quite fastidious about the house and grounds since she married Samuel Grayson.

With a parting smile at the young men lounging against the wrought-iron railing, Kathren started to go back inside, then turned back and said firmly, "I don't see a thing wrong with you young people taking the carriage down to the square and enjoying some ice cream. In fact, the girls have hardly been out of the house all summer."

Amanda started to protest but remembered to do so carefully. Samuel was a little defensive of his wife's lack of social register; he would overlook an indiscretion on his daughter's part quicker than he would forgive an insult to Kathren. She glanced at Paul to see what he thought of her liberated stepmother, then opened her mouth to sweetly plead a headache.

Kathren could see the gleam in Amanda's eyes and preempted her stepdaughter's excuse. "You children just go on now and have some fun. There'll be no problem with Samuel, Amanda," she smiled slyly. "You *know* I can handle your father." She lifted her eyebrows meaningfully.

Amanda rolled her eyes. The woman was incorrigible. She fought like a wildcat to carve her place in the aristocracy yet couldn't seem to resist those slightly off-color remarks! But finally Amanda smiled, too, because Kathren was right. She had wheedled favors from the old pontiff that none of the children dared even suggest.

Amanda's eyes met Kathren's evenly. Kathren could handle Samuel all right, but *she* could handle Kathren.

"Kate, don't you think Walker would be just a little upset if Camelia joined us? And I refuse to leave my best friend sitting here alone while I take off with two handsome gentlemen." Walker's name should have a quieting effect; he was the only one Kathren could not cajole with sweet smiles. While he didn't seem to resent his new stepmother and, in fact, seemed mildly fond of her, Kathren's manner became a little more subdued in the eldest son's presence. He saw through her little subtleties and tolerated them only so long as they did not conflict with his own interests. Of course, he could afford a little cynical amusement, thought Amanda—he didn't have to live here. Dimpling her smile, she added demurely, "I know neither Paul nor Bradford is anxious to run afoul of Walker."

The last ploy might have worked wonderfully on their male suitors, but Kathren said suddenly and rather sharply. "Oh, tish, Amanda! What on earth is wrong with a girl having a dip of ice cream with three other young people? Absolutely, sometimes these stuffy genteel ways stick in my—" She stopped and smiled her best. "I will take personal responsibility if either Samuel or Walker disapproves. Camelia, you go ahead, dear. Anyway," she said, shooting a coy glance at the young men, "being engaged doesn't mean you've *died,* for petesakes!"

Camelia came from the wicker chair so quickly that her pale green taffeta gown swished with excitement. Then she recovered herself and spoke gravely.

"Oh, do you really think Walker won't mind, Mrs. Grayson?"

"Certainly not," Kathren giggled, "especially if he doesn't know about it!"

Paul straightened from the balustrade and swept off a stylish, flat-brimmed planter's hat.

"Tenk *you,* M'dame Grahsone!"

Kathren's dark eyes sparkled. "Oh please, Paul, call me . . . Kitty."

Amanda stood up and jammed her bonnet on her head. Only those nearest heard her muttered comment: "That woman!"

Camelia maintained a proper decorum throughout their trip to town. It was on the way home along the bayou road that Walker's affianced bride let her hair down. The two young women had ridden in back of the Graysons' finest open carriage, pulled by two stunning dapple-grays, while the men rode in front. But on the way back, Paul prevailed upon them to pair off—Amanda in front with him and Camelia in back with Bradford Ross.

Camelia's dainty laughter floated to the pair in front with increasing frequency.

Amanda tossed bluntly over her shoulder, "Don't tire yourself, Camelia. You will have missed your nap time this afternoon." Her jibe went unheeded as Camelia laughed gaily and used her Georgia drawl to advantage.

"Oh, I jus' cain't hay-elp myself, Mandy. Bradford is an absolute rogue!"

Amanda turned back around in disgust, and no amount of charm on the part of Paul Bascom could engage her in further conversation.

Later, in Camelia's room upstairs, Amanda chastened her in no uncertain terms.

"You have been living in this house like one of us for the past two months. I expect you to regard this family as your own and thus respect it as we do ourselves."

Camelia tried to look properly repentant, but her blue eyes danced.

"I'm so sorry if I offended you, Mandy." She extended

two soft, flawless palms. "I love you like my own sister, you know that." Now her bottom lip pouted. "It just so hard being away from Walker! I sit like a wallflower at all the parties, and there's no one to escort me shopping or—or anywhere! I'm only seventeen, Amanda, and my goodness, you're already twenty. You can't expect me to be as grown up as you are."

The deliberate reference to her spinsterish age stained Amanda's cheeks. Unwrapping her chignon, she shook out her hair and began to brush it with unwarranted vigor.

"You've never been a wallflower in your life, Camelia," she replied flatly. "Furthermore, it takes absolutely nothing in this town to start tongues a-wagging. I simply don't think you behaved yourself in a way that becomes a woman betrothed. When Walker comes home—"

Camelia cut her off in a mocking voice. "When Walker comes home, when Walker comes home! When—I would like to know—*is* he coming home!" She went to the mirror and pursed her lips at her reflection, tilting her head to admire each angle.

Amanda sat down on the edge of the bed, the hairbrush lying idle in her lap. She looked at Camelia's reflection of perfect doll-like features covered in pale creamy skin, and a line creased her forehead. She loved Camelia—truly she did. They had been friends since childhood and were like sisters now since Camelia had moved into Gray Shadows.

Oh, she was somewhat spoiled and selfish but Samuel and Kathren hadn't helped any. Ever since Camelia had come from Georgia to spend the intervening months before her wedding at the mansion, they had bent over backwards to accommodate her. Their indulgences seemed to bring out the worst in Camelia.

Amanda shook off her treacherous thoughts. Camelia was a lot like Kathren. She needed a firm hand—which she would get when she married Walker Grayson. I guess, thought Amanda, we're lucky she hasn't tried her charm on Ferrell.

The thought of their other recent guest deepened Amanda's frown, for her tolerance did not extend to Ferrell Cassadyne. He had taken up residence in Gray Shadows two weeks earlier, though his great-aunt, Kathren, denied she had extended any such invitation. His manners were impeccable; he was quite good-looking — in fact, he was so graciously and damnably correct in everything he did, it was hard to understand why her flesh crawled when he so much as entered the same room. The only tangible evidence to support her dislike was the fact that he was known to be impatient with the livestock — although the stable hands assured Samuel that the mettlesome thoroughbreds required a beating often enough. Amanda hid her dislike for the sake of peace in the family. Perhaps, after all, it was only his not-too-subtle interest in her that riled her — an interest she most emphatically did not return.

She pulled her thoughts back to the present.

"I hope you're really ready to settle down, Camelia. Walker means a lot to me and I wouldn't want to see him hurt."

Camelia preened a moment more then turned to Amanda with a sour expression.

"You're beginning to sound just like Kitty, Amanda; always so worried about the way things look. I've done absolutely nothing wrong this afternoon — even Kitty approved." She snatched up her straw bonnet with the matching green ribbons and tried it in the mirror, her face still petulant. "Besides, I'm sure I'll learn to make the adjustments of being 'attached' just like everyone else, in spite of the fact that it's going to be particularly hard for me. I don't mean to sound conceited but I'm used to being . . . well . . ." Her lips pouted prettily. "Noticed by the male population, I guess you would say," she finished.

Amanda laughed outright. "So you are. Even I admit that." Her face sobered again. "I really mean it about Walker, though. Love him, Camelia, and always be a good wife to him. He deserves the best."

Camelia grabbed her skirts and did a little pirouette, her face starting to beam again. "Don't you fret, Amanda. I intend to be the most perfect wife this town has ever seen." Her laughter trilled infectiously as she danced round and round the room. "Just you wait and see, Mandy, I'll be as good as gold!"

It was late evening when Walker found a place to camp near a stream. They had left the Sabine River far behind, and he waited to stop until they found a cooler low area. The girl was used to a hot dry climate and he thought she must be suffering considerably under the heavier humidity of East Texas—although when he thought about it, she seemed to hold up under the strain of riding better than some of his men. She never complained, she never slumped in the saddle, nor did she draw any attention to her injury. Her only request came after they had dismounted and Walker was tying the horses.

"Me no want squaw blanket next day," she said, rubbing her backside gingerly.

Walker grinned. "That's fine. I'll just put it on the supply horse."

His amusement faded when she turned and, without a word, sat down on a bare spot of ground, wrapping her arms over her knees. Walker sighed. She could double for an inanimate object—perhaps poor Lot's wife, turned to a pillar of salt. Maybe she was more upset about last night than he thought. But if that was the case she'd have to get over it. It was her own fault for going around half clothed—no, not fair. That wasn't her fault.

Then he scowled, realizing he had misconstrued her motives. She wasn't worrying over last night but lamenting her fate again—planning a way to escape to a home that wouldn't even exist in a few more weeks.

"If I were you, I would concentrate on how I'm going to act when I reach the fort," he said coldly. "People there aren't used to savages anymore. And I'll tell you something else. Not a damned one of them thinks Horse Back is the president of the United States."

She made no reply and while he went about setting up camp, she continued to contemplate spaces. After giving her a reasonable time to grieve, Walker stopped in front of her with an armload of firewood. "At the risk of sounding rude, this is not a roadside inn. I could use some help."

Silver missed the sarcasm but she did understand she

98

should work; hauling wood, after all, was woman's work. She hobbled to him quickly and tried to take some of the wood.

"What the—not *this*, woman!" He glowered, snatching the wood out of reach. "This is man's work. Get over there and sort out some food for supper. And then find some pans to cook it in."

Silver glared. "Me have heap good ears." After giving him a wounded look, she turned away to obey, and in a moment Walker was grinning at her back. Hmm. He must be getting the hang of it now.

The woods pulsed with the sawing of crickets and singing of tree frogs so that Walker's ears rang with the racket. The girl watched the surrounding woods as though she expected a headless horseman to come charging out.

Presently Silver felt her captor's gaze, and looked up. He seemed so disconcerted to have been caught staring that she gave him a very small smile. Walker returned it tentatively, ever wary of any evidence of good humor.

While they ate, the night sounds drummed on the silence between them. The girl sat on a log, her graceful and always bare legs extended toward the fire. After a moment, Walker set his plate aside and clawed at his collar. The first matter he would address when they reached the fort was to get the girl some decent clothing!

Glaring at her profile, he unbuttoned his shirt, for it was very hot. He was surprised to see her gaze slide around to him briefly—and she was not looking at his face. His frown relaxed, and he stripped off the shirt, pausing to stretch his arms and flex his muscles, and her gaze swung around again, flickering over the chest she claimed to find so disgusting. He gave her a devilish grin and she looked away.

"We'll reach Nacogdoches by noon tomorrow," he said. "There are some records of Indian captives there and I'm going to search the records to see if your age matches any of them."

She jerked around, her eyes hard and bright. "Me

99

Quohadie—"

Walker held up his hand. "Please, spare me. I'm just telling you what I'm going to do. If I turn you loose my conscience would never let me rest. You'd run straight into the army's—" He broke off and watched her intently.

But her short narrow forehead was knitted in confusion. "What mean, *con-shush* . . ."

"Conscience?" He bit off a piece of corn pone, finding it a pleasant change to be consulted on an abstract psychological phenomenon. "It's like a voice in your head. It tells you if you're doing something right or wrong."

She looked indignant. "There no one in my head but me!"

Walker's mouth twitched. "I don't mean a real person, just your thoughts reminding you of the things you've been taught to respect, like guidelines or rules. Do you know 'rules'?"

"Laws?"

"Yes, exactly."

"What your law say when he speak in your head?"

Walker's smug look vanished. He stared for a moment, then turned to fumble with his shirt, muttering unintelligibly until he found a cigar, lit it, and leaned back on a stump to inhale deeply.

"What your conshush remind you of when he—"

"Different things," he said tersely. "It's a deep subject and not one we can go into now."

"What things he remind you about?" she insisted, and he glared at her.

"Inordinate lust, infidelity, broken promises—" He stopped off and lowered his gaze, for her face was perplexed. He leaned back and tried to look relaxed as he blew a ring of smoke. "I suppose my conscience tells me I should love and respect my parents because they brought me into the world. I should love and respect my country because it supplies me with food and shelter, a way to make a living, protection from enemies." He glanced at her again and found her looking at him solemnly.

"Me love brothers and Horse Back. Me love wind, land of good grass and many horses. Me go there soon," she

100

said quietly.

Walker looked away to study the stars a moment.

"How old are you?" He changed the subject.

Silver held up ten fingers, then ten again and dropped one.

"Me *samon-eh-samon quits-u-wite.*"

"That's nineteen. White eyes say *nine-teen.*"

"You have wife?"

Walker drew on the cigar thoughtfully. "Not yet. Do you have a man?"

Many," Silver answered with a wry face. "But me no want any they are."

Walker smiled thoughtfully. Maybe he wouldn't tutor her English after all. It would be like trying to touch up a Rembrandt.

He jumped to his feet. She had gathered her tin plate and cup, and stood up unsteadily to carry them to the wash pan.

He was beside her quickly. "Here, let me —" His impulsive hand bumped into hers and the items clattered to the ground.

They smiled awkwardly, bent again, and their heads came together with a thump. They straightened, Walker chuckling softly and Silver laughing behind her hand.

With a courtly bow, he said, "Please. Allow me." And he retrieved them.

"Me wash," offered Silver shyly. "Wash wo-man's work."

Walker stood with the cup and plate in his hand, not moving as he looked at her. Then he held out the plate slowly.

Silver hesitated, her heart beating jerkily at the strange light in his eyes.

Finally she reached out but just as she touched the plate, his other hand came up and caught hers. He turned it and pressed a kiss to her palm, rolling his eyes to watch her expression.

She could not move. The moon shone full on his face, and his gaze trapped her — sapped her bones and muscles as though she had been struck by the tongues of fire from a thundercloud.

The plate clattered to the ground again, and she watched numbly as his other hand moved toward her. It slid between her skin and hair to wrap around the base of her neck. Her heart tripped. She could not breathe, could not think what to do. But it did not matter: Her feet were stuck to the ground anyway!

His voice was soft, like rain on wet leaves. "I was wondering . . . if you'd ever been kissed by a white eyes."

Silver swallowed. "Me not know 'kiss.' "

He tugged until she took a stumbling step, touching her nowhere but on the back of the neck as he put her lips to his. They lingered, moving until hers were parted; they slid against her teeth, pressed the corner of her mouth, grabbed her lower lip. She drew back with a gasp.

"Me no like t-this 'kiss.' "

He pulled her forward. "Let me show you again," And he folded her against him, his body pressing, his hot skin melting the thin cloth that covered her breasts. The hair on his chest was like fur as she put her palms there, hoping at some point they would obey her commands to push him back.

He took them in his and placed them on his shoulders. "Put your arms around my neck, Silver." She obeyed. "This . . . is how we do it."

His head dipped, his mouth slanted across hers, and Silver went limp in his arms, though she made one feeble effort to turn her head away. He only held her closer, his hand caressing and kneading the back of her neck. The taste of firewater on his breath registered with faint alarm, but her arms tightened about his neck; she could not stand if he released her anyway.

His nose slid across her cheek to her ear. His whispered words ran from her earlobe down her neck, from there down her spine. "I could never let another man hold you, Silver . . . or touch you, like this . . ." His lips trailed back to her mouth and, sighing deeply, he kissed her again.

His male scent intoxicated her, and her breath came faster as he nibbled with increasing hunger at her mouth. Her head fell back and she panted, "Y-you are white eyes!"

He pulled her up closely, supporting her neck with his

arm while the other hand removed the single strap from her shoulder. He bent to press his mouth to the rounded top of her breast.

"You are enemy," she croaked, and his mouth stopped more words. Still kissing her, he eased the dress front all the way down, and the cool air touched the newly exposed skin, making her shiver.

She shivered again at the touch of his hand, his fingers cool but his palm warm as he weighed her breast, bent his head, and kissed the cool cushioned flesh before his lips followed its contour to the nipple.

Silver swam in a whirling eddy, floating one minute, sinking the next. "Me have n-no man to . . ." Her strangled plea broke off and she arched toward his mouth, groaning when he stiffened his neck and toyed with devilish purpose at the taut peak. "Me not know how to mate with you!" And she thrust again at the maddening lips.

"You were born for it, sweet love. You will know what to do." He took the nipple between his teeth lightly and Silver gasped, her head falling back so far she could not tell up from down.

Sliding one hand up to brace her neck, he lifted her on his hip and carried her to the bedroll, impatiently stroking the wrinkles that encumbered his movements.

"Raise your hips," he demanded hoarsely, and once again it did not occur to Silver to disobey. He stripped her dress down, tugged at the undergarment that flaunted more than it hid, and looked at her. A quiet moment passed and finally he said softly, "I won't hurt you. I would never hurt you." Then he got up and pulled off his boots, unbuttoned his pants and stepped out of them.

Silver looked in fascination, feeling a mixture of exhilaration and vague apprehension as her gaze rested on his swollen manhood. He was not the first naked man she had seen; the braves wore only a G-string about the camp, and the young girls made every effort to see more whenever possible—usually with success. But surely there was never a warrior more perfectly made than this one! Her body began to tremble as he moved toward her.

Walker's head filled with a deafening roar. He knelt,

103

stretched out, and lowered himself on top of her, spreading her thighs with one knee. He probed gently and felt her stiffen when the alien hardness touched her. He pushed harder, and she struggled more forcefully. "It's only small hurt," he whispered raggedly, bending to kiss her until she relaxed. Then without warning he pushed hard.

A fire exploded through her and she cried out, throwing her forehead into his shoulder.

"It's all right," he urged. "This is a small pain for such a brave one." His mouth swooped down again, kissing her gently, then urgently, then almost brutally. Silver kissed him back, consumed with the budding pleasure inside her, a throbbing fullness that made her feel somehow complete. Their hearts thundered together like stallions across the Great Plains, and then he was lowering his chest against hers. There were more kisses—hotter kisses. She could not stand it. She would faint!

Then he set a rhythm that attacked her senses, a slow thrust followed by a pause. Silver groaned, holding his neck in a vise, arching her body as he first gave then denied. Her legs wound around the back of his knees, her feet hooking with unerring accuracy beneath his shins.

"Don't *do* that, woman!" he gasped, then slipped his hand beneath her hips to hold her to him.

His plea drove Silver to new boldness, and she met his thrusts, glued herself to him and would not let him pull back, until at last he drove forward in a mindless frenzy.

She felt the earth open to swallow her but she did not fall. Instead she shot upward and saw the stars exploding around her as she whizzed past them like a speeding comet, faster and faster until at the final moment she seemed to die. The roaring noise in her head stopped and she floated untethered, encased in the soundless, tranquil, diamond-studded darkness of space—the world beyond, the abode of the gods.

When she felt herself drifting back down, she fought it by curling her arms tighter about his neck, and they held the pose midair until Walker's trembling arms could no longer support them.

He lowered them back to the blanket and Silver heard

sounds again: cricket and frogs sawing the air, and a voice whispering her name over and over. The blanket scratched her back, and suddenly her scattered senses rushed together.

When he moved beside her, she lay like a carcass in the frozen Arctic, her eyes fixed on the night sky from whence she had fallen.

Throwing an arm across her breasts, Walker murmured drowsily, "Tell me I didn't hurt you." His finger brushed a damp strand of hair from her cheek.

She turned away from him, her words choked, uttered like a scream that couldn't break free: *"Habbe-weichet."*

Walker rolled close to her warmth, his senses floundering as sleep overtook him. "English, sweetheart . . . speak English."

Silver pressed the wooly blanket to her face and tried to muffle her sob. *"Habbe we-ich-et! Habbe we-ich-ket!"*

But Walker had sunk into a blissful oblivion, unaware that his lover had been moved to sing the Comanche Death Song in his arms: "I long for death, I long for death."

Chapter 7

Silver opened her eyes to a leafy ceiling, felt the warm body against her—and rolled away, aghast. She stared at the thick gilded lashes, the strong nose and firm lips of the man beside her, and her fingers curled into claws.

It couldn't be. It couldn't be that she—the golden child of Chief Horse Back—had done this thing. It was a dream. It *must* have been a dream.

But the night came flooding back to her. Not only was it real, but he had not taken her by force. If he had—if *only* he had.

She got to her feet and hobbled to the creek where she sat down and splashed water on her face. It was true. Nothing could alter the fact that she had willingly participated in an official and binding wedding ceremony. And she had married not just a white eyes but a chief. She who refused to train the younger boys to mate had brazenly lain with a complete stranger, binding herself to him forever!

She sprawled on the wet sand and pounded it with her fist. As her husband, this Walker Grayson had all rights and power over her. A squaw could go on the rampage and express herself verbally, even abusively, so long as she was waiting obediently when her husband came into her tent!

"*Habbe-weichet,*" she sobbed, beating the ground. She cried for another moment then sat up to splash more water on her face. All the tears in the world would not help anything, only drain her strength. She dried her eyes with the tail of her skirt, blinking at the strange plant life that grew like green mold on the creek. Even the dirt is evil, she thought miserably.

Hiccoughing, she dropped her chin on her knees and stared at the water. She must accept it; it was done. All hopes of returning to her homeland were gone, for she could never disgrace her father by bringing home a white eyes husband. There was very little unfaithfulness among Comanche women because their punishment was severe: The husband carved away half of her nostril, leaving the exposed cartilage to hang over the upper lip. So even if she escaped to her home, she could never marry and bear sons to a true warrior. In fact, Horse Back's honor would force him to return her to her husband, white eyes or not.

She heard a sound and turned. Walker was standing behind her, his face quiet and strangely twisted.

"I want to talk to you."

She looked away.

Walker squatted beside her and they watched the coursing water like spectators intent on the outcome of some event. Walker broke off a piece of creek fern and fingered the leaves.

"I want to apologize. For what happened last night."

She did not look at him. "No *suava-ti apolo* . . . *apolo* . . ."

"It means I'm sorry about what happened. It wasn't your fault. I took what I wanted, with no regard for the consequences." He looked at her profile. "Do you understand what I'm saying?"

Silver glanced at him once and looked away. "Me no *suava-ti* this *soor-ee*," she said sullenly.

"It means to have regret for something you've done." Her face was still blank so he tried again. "Regret means . . . it means you wish you had not done what you have done. It means to be sad. *Suava-ti* sad? Okay, it means to be sad about the way things have turned out and wish that you could change them back to what they were."

Understanding came, and her head swung around, eyes blazing like white-hot crystals.

"Comanche have no such word!" she spat. "He no need

107

that word; he no do horrible things and go back like dog with tail in his legs! Only white eyes have such word and he have heap many times to need it, me think!"

Walker winced. "Perhaps that's true. Still, there's no sense kicking a dead horse. We can't undo it."

She looked at him incredulously. "Me no have dead horse. *Me no have horse any kind!*"

"I'm not talking about horses, I—" He crushed the frond and tossed it in the water. "Look, I understand that you don't have anything to call your own, and I can imagine how bad things must have been for you. But I'm trying to change all that if you'll only let me. Everything will be different when we get to the fort."

Silver looked across the stream at the gnarled roots of a tree clutching the clay bank. At least that much was true. She would be a wife now, not a slave.

She toyed with the pebbles beside her foot, pressing them into the wet sand. "When we come this 'fort,' you would give me horse, yes?"

He looked sideways at her. "I might. Later, when you learn to behave yourself."

She thought a minute. "You would give me heap many blankets?"

"I suppose that could be arranged," he said thoughtfully. "Anything else?"

Her eyes skimmed over him briefly then went back to the face she was making with the gravel. "Meat. Not bad like on reservation. Good meat. Much meat." She lifted her eyes.

The muscles in Walker's face twitched. So she planned to sell her favors like a common whore. To *him!*

"I don't plan on starving you to death," he said, his lip curling.

But she missed his sarcasm. Instead, she seemed to settle back, and he could see her thoughts racing through her brain, out her eyes. "One thing you should understand, though," he said, feeling the crunch of his teeth with every word. "What happened last night won't happen again. So I wouldn't run to the bank just yet."

Silver looked down at the frowning face she had drawn

with the pebbles, her heart hammering against the walls of her chest. So now he would not come to her bed again. He had not even taken another wife and she was already being moved to the last tepee! Or maybe he had lied when he said he had no wife. White eyes loved to tell lies best of all — even more than they liked Indian women.

Her eyes turned smoky but she sat very still to keep from leaping upon him.

"Well," said Walker coolly, standing up to brush himself off, "I'm glad we understand each other. I'll go back and finish packing. We need to get an early start."

He left her sitting there and climbed the creek bank, pausing at the fire to stir the coals. It was just lucky for him that they had this little talk. He could stop beating himself over the head now. She was still a virgin only because she'd been saving herself for the right price. And some price, he thought savagely. A horse, a blanket, and a slab of meat!

A weak flame had burst to life in the smoldering coals but his absentminded and rather vicious stirring snuffed it out again. Well, if she thought she would be making any new sales at the fort, she had another "think" coming. Fortunately he'd had the foresight to bring the ball and chain along.

He looked at the dead fire and swore, then he heard her footsteps and glanced up. She was coming toward him, moving with the sliding grace developed from carrying things on her head. His pulse quickened just watching her, for the unmistakable fitness of taut muscles and strong bones was a new and alluring phenomenon in the world of women's bodies.

Thank God their enforced intimacy was almost at an end. One more taste of the forbidden fruit and she might start to feel possessive. She might even mention the matter at the fort, in which case the ensuing scandal would rock clear to New Orleans.

Her eyes came up and for just an instant Walker thought he saw her old hatred simmering below the surface. Then she lowered her gaze and kept walking.

He drew an uneven breath and decided it was his imagination. After all, what did she have to be upset about? She had named her price and he had agreed to it! And yet . . .

He eyed the twitch in her hips, and a foreboding shivered through him. Maybe it was a good idea to try to see that Silver Dawn Sky entered Fort Nacogdoches in the best possible spirits. His brow wrinkled thoughtfully. Yes, it was definitely a good idea. God help them if her dark side emerged first.

Walker had set up his shaving supplies on a nail keg and hung a mirror on the trunk of a pine. Silver stood a short distance away, watching as her new husband scraped the strange stick over his face. He wore only his uniform pants, with the bright gold stripes down each leg. His movements made the muscles in his back ripple. She couldn't keep from staring a little breathlessly.

Then she saw his face in the mirror, and clenched her teeth. While she had hauled water for the horses, plus an extra bucket to douse the fire, he had spent more time preening than a young maid preparing for her wedding night—and still he did not seem satisfied. Sometimes she remembered the way he had cared for her after the snake-bite, the whispered words of encouragement, cool hands against her brow. But if he'd really cared about her, he would have released her. Then she wouldn't have tried to escape and the snake wouldn't have bitten her and—

She put a stop to her thoughts. Walker Grayson was her husband now, and she could not defy him even if he had refused to come to her bed again. To dishonor one's husband was to dishonor oneself, and she'd had enough of dishonor to last a lifetime. Instead she must revere and obey him. That was the Law of The People.

She lifted her chin and approached him silently, remembering to use her pronouns correctly when she spoke.

"I would wash in the creek."

Walker gave a start and the razor slanted across his jaw.

"Damn, woman!" He flung the soap and blood away as he wheeled around. "Do you have to *sneak* everywhere you go?!"

110

Silver was faintly alarmed at the blood dripping between his fingers. She suggested tactfully, "Pull *paph* out and you no hurt."

Walker's nostrils flared. "I've been shaving myself since I was fourteen—*I don't need instruction on how to do it!*"

Silver looked at him, meek and seemingly frightened.

At that, Walker squinted suspiciously. "Well? What do you want?"

"I would bathe in creek," she murmured.

"Speak up, for petesakes."

"I would bathe in creek," she said, her eyes flaring a little.

Walker glanced in that direction, then turned to look in the mirror at his bloody jaw. "All right, I'll trust you. But I'm warning you, one slipup and I'll tie you again. Do you understand me?" He glared threateningly in the mirror.

Silver nodded and turned around.

Walker watched her humble retreat over his shoulder, one brow raised. He could see the horses, and she couldn't go far on foot because she was still limping.

He went back to his shaving and finished, drawing on his shirt. He might just go check on Miss Meekness.

On second thought, he might find her nude. He went instead to check the gear on the horses. Again.

Although the only official welcome prepared for Major General Grayson was a lineup of the same corp of officers who had accompanied him to Wichita Falls, the fort at Nacogdoches buzzed with activity. Everyone had found a reason to be outdoors to view the major when he arrived. A wire had arrived incognito that a certain major and what appeared to be a half-Indian captive had passed through one of the northern settlements a few hours earlier.

In consideration of their respite from war cries, East Texans could now view the Indian with historic curiosity and kept up religiously with all news that pertained to them. This tidbit was promising indeed. Even a glimpse of a real Indian titillated their imaginations no small amount. The stockade walls had been abandoned many years before, and the white settlers east of the Brazos River had known peace since the ousting of Chief Bowles of the Cherokees in 1839. The fort was maintained solely for the convenience of those militia and officers traveling beyond the frontier line seventy-five miles to the west, where civilization gave way to flatter land, stubbier timber, and the ancient war of red against white.

The town of Nacogdoches, incorporated in 1799, was now a thriving eden of rich farming land and infinite stretches of the finest pine timber in the nation.

The picturesque main office, built of rock and affectionately called the "Old Stone Fort," was flanked with long barracks for the visiting soldiers. With the removal of the stockade wall, the original gristmill, dry goods store, granary, and livery had evolved into something more resembling a village. The fort, as well as the main settlement further down the creek, was shrouded beneath the graceful giants, which had so eloquently bequeathed the name of Piney Woods to the area. With a deep reverence for their natural blessings, the settlers cut little of the timber at the town's heart, or around the fort, boasting that one could walk the length of any street with never a ray of sun to fall upon his shoulders.

A shout heralded the approach of two riders along the road, which entered from the north and was a fact that had pleased one of the riders especially. The more populated town section lay further south, and their approach had offered a small measure of obscurity. Had they been forced to pass through town first, no doubt they would have been trailed by a long line of curiosity seekers. This Walker had come to realize only after they passed through Ponta and left the entire population of sixty souls gaping in the middle of the main street.

The heavy sense of foreboding Walker had experienced earlier settled upon him in the form of a stiffness of posture that flattered an already striking figure. He wore the full regalia of his office: tall black boots that gleamed like ebony in the sun, spotless white kid gauntlets, both his gunbelt and his saber with the gold-embossed handle, his flat-topped cavalry hat, and finally his military coat with

112

its bright gold shoulder braid along with numerous badges and decorations flashing against the navy cloth. His spirited horse pranced, imitating the negligent pride of its rider.

In contrast, Walker had deemed it wise to mount his companion on the less nimble of the other two animals, the packhorse. A skeletal assortment overlaid with roan rawhide, its pale bulging "moon eyes" neither looked to the front nor behind but both ways at once, for neither appeared to be connected to the other by the usual optic ligaments.

This did not concern the beast at all, however, for seeing the approach of danger from either direction would not have caused one foot to deviate from its appointed path nor its emaciated legs to swerve from a singular gait known to no other of its kind: a sliding, shifting slouch, every other step of which appeared to cause its right front knee to buckle.

Upon the nag sat a girl whose skin could not be called white. Her silver-gray eyes had an unsettling effect upon the stoutest heart. Under the added humiliation of being mounted upon an animal who did injustice to the word "beast," her eyes had become frozen glaciers in a face savagely kissed by the sun. At least half of her body was shockingly nude. And not only was her face as swarthy as a pirate's but also the firm legs and arms, one entire shoulder, and the tender flesh of her upper chest where her bodice slanted down under one arm.

Riding through so many miles of lonely forest, Walker had not taken objective notice of their appearance until they passed through Ponta. Now, as he eyed the throngs milling in front of the Old Stone Fort, a fierce frown marred his face and the muscles along his jaw stood at attention. Although he stared straight ahead, his field of vision allowed that Sergeant Miller was first in the line of officers on his right, followed by Phillip Martin, both of whom had whipped an arm up to salute. The others followed suit, staring in front of them at the main building while forming a broad path through which the two riders might pass.

113

The entire assembly of Fort Nacogdoches slowly froze: Hammers were halted midair, arms stopped half raised, and words died on parted lips.

But after a fleeting second, a murmuring stirred the air.

"Sweet Adeline, look at that!" breathed a soldier.

There were other eyes watching, and tongues not so kind.

"God help us!" croaked Mrs. Quattlebaum, and fell back to grab her companion's arm. Somewhere behind the line of officers there was a vaporous sigh and Mrs. Weldon sank to her knees. From the flutter of shocked gasps surrounding her came the raised voice of her husband: "My God! My wife! *Her heart! Get the doctor!*"

Only when a couple of his officers broke rank to assist the ailing woman did Walker favor the group with a withering glance. Then he dismounted and tossed the reins to Sergeant Miller, grating from the side of his mouth, "For God's sake, clear these people out."

"Yes sir, I'll try," said Miller quickly.

Phillip rushed to Walker's side. "She's looking real good, sir," he assured his commander, then winced at that one's black look. "I-I mean her leg, sir. The snakebite."

With a parting glare, Walker wheeled away and went to the nag where Silver was mounted, her whole body rigid as she scanned the crowd about them; and when he reached up to take her down, it remained stiff, making her dismount an awkward and humiliating spectacle as her legs clamped tenaciously about the horse, her fingers tangled like steel coils in the hair on the beast's withers. Walker tried to reassure her under his breath.

"It's okay. Silver, let go of the horse—Silver, dammit, let go of the—"

She let go. Walker staggered backward as her weight fell against him and slid down the front of him—until her skirt hung on his gunbelt and lifted pertly to reveal her bare buttocks pressed intimately against his groin while he, in frantic haste, struggled to free it.

The spectacle was noted by the crowd in one long, unisoned gasp.

Finally freeing himself, Walker snatched his ward by the

114

wrist and made for the front door of the Old Stone Fort. Phillip hurried along behind him.

"Get out of my desk!" Walker bellowed, causing the young sergeant to leap upward, his chair crashing into the wall behind him.

"Yes sir. I was just filling out some reports—" He stopped at Phillip's warning look. "Yes sir, yes sir—I've got to put out the mail, anyway." He departed quickly.

Leaving Silver to stand alone and rub the welt made by his grip, Walker went behind the desk, bending over the strewn papers until he had shuffled them into a single tall stack. "Shut and bolt the door!" he ordered, and Phillip hurried to comply.

"Would you like me to go, too, sir?" asked Phillip hopefully as he slammed the door in Sergeant Miller's face.

"No. I want you to check the room next to my quarters, and see that it's readied for the girl." He looked up at Phillip, chin jutting. "As you can see, she is completely reconciled to her fate and will cause no more trouble."

Phillip dared a small smile at Silver. "Yes sir. I see she's not wearing chains anymore." Walker's face hardened briefly, then he went on while his thoughts were in relative order.

"First of all, she'll need to bathe. Is the tub still in my room? Okay, move it to hers. Order someone to haul water. Do you think one of the women here could be persuaded to lend her a dress? She'll need something immediately, then I suppose I'll have to take her to town to buy her a decent wardrobe. It's apparent that she can't parade around like this."

"That little Millie Whitehead, the cook's wife? She's slender like this one," Phillip suggested. "I don't think she'd mind lending us—"

"Okay, see to that too. In the meantime I'll keep Sil—uh . . . the girl, with me. I want no one in this building but the three of us, is that clear?"

"Uh, yes sir. But Captain Lawrence has a lot of business with you when you can spare the time."

"*When* I can spare the time. For now I want that door bolted every time you go out, and I don't give a damn what

115

explanation you come up with as to why." He held up a warning finger. "Remember, absolutely no civilians . . . wait. I've got to do something about Mrs. Weldon."

Taking a pad from the desk, he scrawled out his exact message: "I regret most deeply the shock to Mrs. Weldon and am gravely concerned for her welfare." Phillip took the paper with relief. It was imperative they maintain good relations with the civilian sector because the post was their only way station to the turbulent West.

When Phillip had gone, Walker crossed the room quickly to lock the door and turned his attention to Silver. She had backed near the corner and looked visibly shaken.

He stared at her for a moment. "I'm sorry if I hurt you."

"No hurt."

Walker looked at her bowed head. Finally, he tossed his hat on the desk and went to her. "Come on. My quarters are in back. You'll have a little privacy there."

Silver followed him through the left one of the two doors behind his desk. A dark hallway ran behind the front office and from it opened several sleeping rooms used by those in command. They turned left and followed the hall to the last door on the right, which Walker held open for her.

His officer's quarters were modest. A double bed shoved in the left corner between two windows, a small desk sitting against the right wall near the door that opened to the adjoining room. There was a horse trough for bathing.

Walker went quickly to the adjoining door and opened it.

"There's another room in here. I'll have the tub moved in there for you. Captains Lawrence and Mackleroy will be moved out to the barracks so the only ones sleeping here then will be me, you, and Phillip Martin." He searched her face. "Is . . . that all right?"

Silver lowered her eyes and nodded. She had no right to feel hurt; he had warned her that he would not take her to his bed again. She should only be grateful that she was not with her people now. Being ousted from a husband's bed either meant she could not make *commar-pe* for some physical reason and would be maintained as a "sister," or that the husband suspected her of infidelity. She could not have borne the shame.

Walker cleared his throat. "Well . . . just see if you can relax, I guess. Maybe you could take a nap. That means to sleep." She shook her head firmly.

"Well, okay, maybe you can just rest. I've got some things to tend to, but I'll see to it that Phillip brings you some lunch."

He went to the door, turned, and held the knob while he spoke. "I'm trusting you not to try to escape. It would be worse than foolish, it would be fatal. Can I trust you to stay without a lock and key?"

Silver nodded again, rubbing her wrist distractedly. Walker noticed, and went back to her.

"I didn't mean to hurt you." He took her wrist and looked at it.

"It no hurt," she assured him, not looking up.

Walker held her wrist gently and looked at the side of her face where the fall of her hair hid all but the end of a slim, straight nose. Silver felt her heart start to pound as he lingered so near, but relief was only a breath away. Walker turned and walked out the door, closing it firmly behind him.

Silver drew a shaky breath and sat down carefully on the bed, testing its feather plumpness with her hands. Her brows were knitted, for she had heard many tales of the surprises encountered when one tried the white eyes inventions. Some of them were only frightening while others could pose a serious threat, like the great iron horse that thundered across the prairie spewing black smoke from its lungs and scattering the mustangs in terror.

The bed did not seem dangerous. She stretched out gingerly, enjoying the softness — until it started to swallow her! Her hands sank into it and the more she tried to get away the more it leaped and tossed. She escaped at last and stood looking at it fearfully. Better to test it later when there was someone to save her.

She went to the back window, which was raised, and pushed her hands at the strange netting that covered the square hole. The woods behind the building were cleared of underbrush, and she could see a path that meandered through the giant trees-with-no- leaves. She watched the shadowed, sun-dappled ground for a long moment, and something stirred in the back of her mind like a memory. But she could not grasp it and soon wandered to Walker's small desk to finger the papers on top, which had white eyes writings upon them. This is his place, she thought, trying to visualize him going about whatever business a white eyes chief went about.

After a moment, she opened the middle drawer. Her eyes widened at the gold-tone photograph of a young girl lying on top of more papers. The girl was about her own age, with saucy curls gathered about her face and an equally saucy smile.

Silver's hand stiffened against an urge to crush the picture in her fist. Carefully she laid it back and shut the drawer. It was surely his sister for he had told her he had no wife and so far, at least, he had not lied. Scorned though she might be from his bed, she was still First Wife.

Her step was slow as she started back to the bed, which seemed so kind to one's bones. She wanted to try it again but she could disappear into its depths and smother before she could scream for help. She must wait and see how Walker approached the matter first, then she would know what to do.

She went instead to the left corner from the door, where there was no bright window, and curled up on the floor to rest.

Shoving the munitions report aside, Phillip swore under his breath. "Damn old battle-axes!" He recognized both voices outside the front door. One belonged to Mrs. Bigby, the plump and dimpled sidekick who could be most jolly when she had her way, and the other to Mrs. Appleby, self-appointed guardian of Nacogdoches virtue. She stood a towering five feet eleven, moved with the grace of a drill sergeant, and possessed a stout Roman nose that found its way into every matter that concerned the military — which, she deemed, was any matter that concerned Nacogdoches at all, for in her opinion the settlement owed its greatness to that branch of government, and also to her devoted husband, Colonel Appleby, commander in charge during Walker's absence.

Phillip stalked to the door. "I'm sorry, ladies, but Major General Grayson gave strict orders. I cannot let you inside."

"Dear Phillip," said Mrs. Bigby, "surely you do not expect us to stand here holding these hot dishes forever, and we most certainly do not intend to leave."

Phillip peered out the window. Both were indeed carrying steaming platters held by quilted potholders.

"We met the major crossing the street and I assure you that opening the door to us is the only thing you *can* do!" stated Mrs. Appleby in her coarse, deep voice.

"He gave you permission?"

The women exchanged sly smiles. "He said—and I quote: 'I'm pleased that you feel so kindly toward the girl.' "

Phillip pondered the statement and decided to crack the door, whereupon a stout foot appeared in the opening. Before he could react, Mrs. Appleby's gargantuan form charged like a battering ram against his arm and she wrested the portal from his grasp.

"Now, ladies, you just wait—"

The matrons headed straight for Walker's quarters. "Thank you so much, Phillip. We won't be but a minute." Phillip hurried to catch up with the broad, retreating posteriors. Mrs. Bigby was clucking, "That poor child! Terrible, just simply *ter*rible!"

At the door to Walker's room, both dowagers turned at once to dismiss him. "We won't be but a moment, dear boy, and thank you so much for allowing this kindness. Major Grayson will be *so* pleased with you."

Phillip's face steamed. But he was first and foremost a gentleman. He wheeled about to leave them, throwing a firm reminder over his shoulder. "Two minutes and that's all, ladies." It was difficult to believe Major Grayson had sent them with his blessing because the pair was known to be ruthless in their search for, and expulsion of, "evil." But the major had become unpredictable lately and furthermore he couldn't dispute the word of the madames without explosive consequences.

Phillip sat down at Walker's desk, ignoring the munitions reports in favor of a short prayer.

Chapter 8

Word reached Walker in the middle of his meeting with the Washington emissary, a Corporal Weissman. There was a discreet but insistent knock on the door, and Walker looked up irritably.

"Come in."

Sergeant Miller poked his head through the door. "Sir, Aide-de-Camp Martin wishes to speak with you at once."

"I'm afraid it'll have to wait. I cannot be interrupted now and I'm sure I told Martin that."

"Er, sir, it's concerning the . . . captive?"

For only a moment Walker froze. Then he came to his feet and barreled around the desk, mumbling to Weissman, "I'll be back as soon as possible."

On their way to the main office Sergeant Miller repeated the tale that had circulated like a grass fire. It seemed that the wives of Colonel Appleby and Lieutenant Colonel Bigby had offered the slave girl kindness in the form of some freshly baked food. They discovered the girl asleep on the floor, and when she awoke to see visitors, it was reported that "her eyes turned to white coals filled with violence." Afterward, she allegedly leaped upon the women and tried to take the food, during the process of which, she threw the dish to the floor and scattered the "exquisite" stroganoff everywhere. Then when Mrs. Appleby hastened to deposit her peach cobbler on a table and make her exit, she could not do so before the girl had fallen upon the dish and proceeded to "devour it like a wild animal."

At the main office, Phillip Martin had been watching the major's approach from the window, and now he un-

121

latched the door and swung it wide.

"Sir, I can explain. I don't think it's at all like those old war-horses told it and—"

Walker brushed past him while Sergeant Miller turned back to lock the door. A large crowd was gathering in front of the building.

Walker hit the door to his quarters like a spring gale, having no time to reckon with the greasy trail of stroganoff. His feet went out from under him and the seat of his immaculate navy-blue trousers landed with a muffled splat on the remains of Mrs. Bigby's cuisine.

Silver, sitting quietly in the corner on the floor, gasped. Then she burst out laughing, clapping her hand over her mouth quickly when she encountered Walker's killing glare.

Although Phillip almost entered the room in the same manner, Sergeant Miller was behind him to break his fall, and upon finding his feet firmly under him again, Phillip bent hastily to assist the major.

"Sir! My God, sir, are you all right?"

Walker threw off the plucking fingers. *"Yes, dammit!"* Phillip stood safely back as Walker lifted himself stiffly and turned on them, his voice starting out low then exploding in a bellow of rage.

"Get out . . . *now* . . . *both of you!"*

As the others departed, Silver could not see for tears of laughter, but Walker's face was black with rage. He grabbed her wrists and yanked her to her feet.

"What the devil have you done this time!" he roared, giving her wrists an extra yank.

Silver met his glower with one of her own as she snatched her hands free.

"Me no do—they do!" She pointed at the floor.

"And I say you *lie,"* gritted Walker. "Those women didn't spend hours cooking that food and then take a fancy to dump it on the floor. What happened was, you returned hatred for kindness—the way you've been taught by that tyrant you call a father!"

Silver clenched her fists and advanced until her nose jutted under his.

122

"Me no see kindness, me see trick. But me take food. Me hungry! They trick!" She spat to the side then looked at him again, a faint tremble at her bottom lip. "Pot burn bad. *Bad.*"

Walker's face drained as she opened her hands. There were twin bars of red blisters across the palms.

"Here, let me see that—"

Silver jerked her hands back and slitted her eyes. "Me hungry. Me eat and they laugh like prairie dogs!"

As the scene rearranged itself in his head, Walker stared.

"I guess I . . . must have misunderstood the situation." He reached for her hand again but she stumbled back toward the wall. "I didn't realize they meant to take the food to you," he said sheepishly. "I would never have allowed that. I thought they would leave it for you." Then his eyes flared again. "But damnation, woman! Can't you see that things like this will keep happening until you learn how to act like a human being instead of a bloodthirsty little savage? I'm breaking my fool neck to teach you the white man's ways, and you're fighting me every step of the way!"

Walker winced at the hatred in her eyes, aware that their angry shouts must be carrying clear to the barracks. But his expression changed back to rage at her next words.

"Me no want white man's ways, me want go *home!*"

"*I,* dammit. *I* want to go home." He reached for her again.

Silver jumped back, her eyes squinted against tears. "You go home when *you* say. Me can no do anything me say. But me make new knife and when white eyes come again—" She made a graphic motion under her chin. "They no come again sure enough!" she finished.

Walker dropped his hands to his sides.

"Well, my dear, you are not going home," he gritted. "Not now and probably not ever!"

He stalked past her to the door but just before it slammed Silver caught a glimpse of the seat of his trousers, and her anger flagged when she realized that his own warriors would see his disgrace. She wanted to say something to remind him of his predicament, but the log walls shuddered from the door's impact, and he was gone.

She dropped her head, her eyes and fists clenching to the same pulses of pain. After a moment, she turned and went to the bed, longing for its softness against her bones. So what if it ate her alive? She had betrayed her people, her father, and now she had even made a fool of her husband. And perhaps his tainted white eyes seed already grew within her. Her children would live as she lived now.

The urge to crawl onto the white eyes contraption and let it suffocate her was very strong. But she could not die yet. She had married this man and unless he sold or traded her away, she was stuck with him. If she died now, it would be with the added shame of having been rejected from even the bed of a white eyes.

Her knees tried to buckle as she made her way to the corner, where she curled up on the floor with her head on her hands.

No, she would not die. She had made her path and she would walk in it. Only she would not walk alone. She would use everything she had ever learned about the art of pleasing a man, and next time it would not be she who lay in a moaning, mindless heap but Chief White Eyes himself!

Mr. Weissman had left an hour before, and Walker had gone to work on his reports again. Phillip was sorting or posting them as they were completed. They had worked in silence.

Walker stood up suddenly. "Here, see what you can do to this mess. I'm going to get some air."

Phillip turned to glare. "I guess you're mad at her."

"At who?"

"Her."

"Is that any concern of yours?"

"Injustice is everybody's affair."

"Injustice? You have the gall to say that to me after all I've done for the little savage?"

"And you have the gall to ask that after you sent the old bags over here in the first place? You send out the bloodhounds then browbeat the hare for getting caught."

Walker jammed his hat on. "I'm going out. You get on that paperwork."

"You'll be back in time for the ball tonight, I presume," Phillip persisted. "You're officer-in-command and they've been planning this thing for months."

"I'll be back in time. You just see that the girl has something to wear." He started for the door.

"But why do you want to make her go in the first place?" Phillip blurted angrily. "Don't you think she's had enough for one day?"

Walker explained with the exaggerated patience of a man holding his temper in check only by supreme effort.

"Keeping her hidden away will only add fuel to the gossip."

"You could say to hell with gossips and do what's best for the girl."

Walker squinted. His voice was low and flinty. "Or I could remind you that Indian captives are official army business and that friendship is no excuse for insubordination."

Phillip sensed he was nearing the end of his rope and resisted until Walker was almost through the door.

"May I respectfully inquire what you'll be doing while Milly and I dress the girl?"

Walker turned slowly, a faint but unpleasant smile on his lips. "Now that I think about it, you should make good use of your time." He nodded thoughtfully. "Yes, and Milly can help you."

Phillip frowned suspiciously. "Help me . . . do what?"

"I'm ordering you to at least attempt to impart some vague comprehension of proper table manners to the girl. It's my opinion that if she would only half try, she could have the town eating out of her hand by the night's end. I think you'll agree that would make both our lives considerably easier."

"I can't believe you're doing this to me."

Walker grinned smugly. "Cheer up. After what happened earlier, maybe she'll be more open to the adage that sugar catches more flies than vinegar."

125

"Git your eyeball away from that window!" George Greelee hissed, slapping a hand over the massive shoulder of his stepbrother. It was almost dusk and the fort's inhabitants were fully occupied with preparations for the ball. The two men had discovered that the fort was absent of the customary stockade walls—which allowed them easy access but offered no cover for clandestine activities.

Having tied their horses deeper in the woods at sunset, they had no trouble working from one gigantic pine to the next through the clean, needle-carpeted woods directly behind the Old Stone Fort. If the girl was here, she would be kept in this structure because it was the commanding officer's quarters. That the major would not let the girl out of his lusting sight was obvious to George Greelee.

Buck drooled when he spoke. "She heah? Don't see nobody but a scrawny soldier at tha desk."

George succeeded in pulling Buck into the shadows. "Well, she's here, I know it. While you wuz wallowin' like a hog in that last stream, I wuz makin' myself useful," he sneered.

It had been surprisingly easy to glean information. Due to the planned offensive against the Comanches in Palo Duro, army uniforms were in such abundance that little notice was paid to the branch or division insignia. Though George spoke to no one, he had been able to find out what he already suspected. In fact, the reward posters had been tacked up before his very eyes.

WANTED
George Greelee—6 foot or more. Thin. Dark eyes.
Buck Santos—Approximately 300 To 350 lbs. bald.
eye color unknown.
Both are soldiers of the Fifth Infantry. Warrants Of
Arrest issued this twentieth day of June, 1876.
Signed: Walker Grayson
Major General, United States Army

Buck had a habit of rocking from foot to foot. George

whispered irritably, "Stop that infernal swayin'! Do you think these pine trees move, or don't you care if somebody spots us!"

"She heah?"

George squinted toward the stone building. "I'll believe it until I'm proved wrong. And if she is here, our work's cut out for us. You hear me, Buck? We got to git 'er. No mistakes this time. Without her they got no witness except the major. What's more, without the girl they ain't even got a victim. So we're gonna git her this time, Bucky. You got to do ever'thing just like I tells ya." George turned to see if his words were sinking in and found Buck's orangutan features glowing from the shadows. He was grinning.

Millie Whitehead and Phillip Martin conversed uneasily in the front office.

Although mildly shocked to learn that the girl understood English, Phillip now counted the fact as one of the few real miracles ever performed for his personal benefit; the girl had followed their instructions and he deemed their venture a smashing success—at least when compared to a number of other possibilities he did not even dare to imagine. Because word of the Indian captive had not spread widely through the town sector and what was known was sketchy, Milly's explanation of a "cousin" was accepted.

Milly attended the fitting personally—answering for the girl when possible—and chose a pale peach gown of watered silk for the night's gathering. The gown's sleek seamless waist hugged Silver's body below a scooped neckline which bared only a modest amount of cleavage; large puffs stood on the shoulders of long, tight-fitting sleeves, and a luscious skirt that was neither full nor straight fell snugly over the hips to gather like a cloud at the girl's feet. To Silver's half-begun replies, Milly had interrupted to explain that her cousin had a speech impediment, which made her difficult to understand.

The first hint of turbulence came when they were back inside the wagon. The girl's tongue was loosened and she complained most vehemently that she could not breathe and that she was very hot and would surely be sick if she had to wear the new garment. During her speech she plucked anxiously at the sleeves of the pale gray muslin Milly had lent her and decried its restrictive nature. It was the lightest, coolest dress Milly owned, and she could think of no way to alleviate the girl's distress.

When they reached the fort and unwrapped the new gown, they discovered that the girl had solved the problem herself. The way she had gone about it was the present topic of discussion between Milly and Phillip.

The door swung open with an abruptness that startled them both, and they moved some distance away as Walker strode around to take his chair behind the desk.

"Well?" he inquired brusquely.

"Oh, everything went smooth as butter, major," Phillip assured him, casting a brief look at Milly.

"And did you find something suitable for tonight?" questioned Walker, sifting through the still formidable mound of papers on his desk.

At Milly's pleading look, Phillip cleared his throat and proceeded like a man stepping through a mine field. His impertinence earlier in the afternoon was uncharacteristic, and after cooling down, he hoped Walker had forgotten the incident; it was a first in their ten-year relationship.

"Well, we did the very best we could, sir. Milly picked out a real pretty dress and had her fitted for several more. Oh, and Milly chose the fabrics herself. Very pretty. Very pretty indeed."

"Good," said Walker, his tone indicating their presence was no longer needed nor desired. When they did not move to vacate the premises, he lifted one brow and asked quietly, "Is there something *else* I should know?"

Milly twisted her hands. "Well, major sir, Silver said she was very hot in the dress and we didn't know what to do about it so . . ." She looked at Phillip again.

"So we didn't do anything," Phillip supplied calmly. "The girl's dressed right now. Why don't we bring her in so you can check everything out?"

"Good idea," Walker muttered, becoming immersed in his paperwork again.

Silver followed Phillip Martin obediently. Although the dress was still like being wrapped for one's burial, she would endure it patiently for now. At her first refusal to cooperate, her husband's face had taken on a gray rage; so she asked meekly if this was truly his wish. His affirmation had been a long stream of words, most of which she could not understand. But in this one thing she was sure to please him a little, for the gown was not unpleasant to look at. The mirror in Walker's room allowed her to see the way the clinging fabric enhanced the slimness of her waist and hips while allowing her proud breasts free movement. Of course, if she had worn the white eyes garment called a "cor-set," the tops of her breasts would have been very pleasingly full; but not even for a husband would she endure that. In fact, her own undergarment with the strap low on her waist had shown an indention that marred the fluid lines of the skirt, so she had abandoned it as well. The sleeves had presented a problem at first, but after a few words with the seamstress when Milly was not looking, she had made her instructions clear, whereupon the woman hastily and with great fervor slashed out both the beautiful sleeves, tears sparkling in her eyes for their loss.

When Silver again tried on the dress at the fort, neither the young white woman nor Walker's slave said anything at all. So the sleeveless effect must have graced well an already graceful garment.

Now, as she presented herself to her husband, he found no words either. He stood up very slowly, his eyes growing strangely still and intense as they slid over her.

"You like?"

Walker's face flushed and he couldn't find the air to reply. Not only were there no sleeves to the garment, leaving her dark shoulders gleaming like wet rocks against the peach blush of silk, but it was obvious she wore not a stitch of underwear. Her nipples, large and well defined, strained against the bodice so that he knew their exact configuration even without carnal knowledge of her body. From there the cloth slithered down the slender column of her torso to press itself revealingly to an almost concave stomach. He could discern twin hipbones pushing forward

129

against the garment and—if one used only a meager amount of imagination—a distinct and enticing pubic mound.

Walker dragged his gaze back to her face.

"Yes, it's very . . . nice." There was a rasping sound that was Phillip clearing his throat, and Walker amended, "I mean, it's pretty."

Silver smiled. "White eyes make cloth very pretty."

"Yes," Walker said again, allowing himself one more lingering scrutiny before he took a deep breath and spoke to Phillip cryptically. "The . . . best you could do?"

Phillip nodded solemnly, relieved that on some occasions the major's recent befuddlement seemed to lift and he was able to see facts of a situation: Any efforts to change or condemn the girl's alterations would simply crush her.

As the moment for an explosion seemed to pass, Phillip hastened to speed the process. "We thought you would be pleased, sir. After all, it a far cry from her other dress."

Walker scanned the faces before him for signs of a conspiracy. Dare he let the vixen attend the dance like this and risk her being assaulted by the entire male population? But his tense perusal revealed only anxious smiles. Perhaps he was overreacting. Indeed, that she lowered herself to wear white eyes clothing was no small miracle.

"Yes," he said slowly, "it is it will do. And I appreciate your efforts on the girl's behalf." He nodded formally at Milly and Phillip.

Silver watched her husband with a dwindling enthusiasm. Must he always speak of her as "the girl"? She lowered her lashes and said haltingly, "I . . . am pleased Walker likes me . . . that is, my . . . my . . . " She faltered then finally remembered, "My dress." Milly had spent the remainder of the afternoon coaching her English, but Silver found the effort still brought a blush to her cheeks.

Likewise, the familiar use of his first name brought one to Walker's. He bent over the desk to rustle his papers.

"Yes, I told you it's nice. But I do have work to do before tonight. So I guess that will be all for now."

Phillip and Milly were glad to make their departure, but

Silver stood her ground. She had searched deep within herself to forgive Walker Grayson for the old squaws who came to her room, and she had gone to much trouble to wear this white eyes gown.

"White eyes dance tonight?"

Walker glanced up, as though he didn't realize she was still there. Then down went his eyes; the papers rustled. "Yes, white eyes dance tonight."

"I dance good."

"I just bet you do," he murmured.

"What say?"

He amended, "I said it's nothing to worry about. If you'd like, I'll come to your room in a little while and show you how white eyes dance. It's different but very easy." His mind skipped forward and he looked up at her. "I noticed you haven't used your room yet. Is there something wrong with it?"

Silver shook her head.

"Well, I distinctly remember leaving orders for someone to draw you a bath, but I guess it was overlooked in the confusion." He held the stack of reports in both hands and tapped the lower edges against the desk until they were so straight even Colonel Appleby would have been envious. "Anyway, if you'll go on back to your room and try to make yourself at home, I'll see that some water is brought in directly."

"What mean di-rect-ly?"

"Soon. It means soon." He laid the reports to rest finally but leaned over the top one studiously.

"I say my English good now."

Walker glanced up briefly, and smiled. "Yes. You said it very good. I mean *well*." Noticing that his position was a backbreaking one, he pulled up his chair and sat down rather harder than he anticipated, bringing a sudden distortion to his smile.

"Not good?"

"I will explain later," he snapped. "That is *if* I ever get to this backlog of paperwork done. Now please. Run along to your room—your *own* room—and I'll be there shortly."

Silver bit her lip then turned away and walked sound-

131

lessly through the darkened doorway. Only when the rustle of silk faded did Walker look up to stare at the empty portal.

Having delayed as long as possible, Walker finally straightened his desk, turned the oil lamp down low, and made his way back to his room.

He knocked at his own door just in case she had not obeyed and he might find her in a state of undress. But inside he saw that a thin line of light came from the adjoining door.

With a sigh of relief, he lit the wick on the wall and crossed to the door, rapping lightly.

"Silver, are you dressed?"

There was no answer.

His voice rose. "Silver, I'm warning you. Answer me right now or I'm coming—"

"Yes, Walker. I am ready."

Inside the next small enclosure sat the tub, and Walker noted with satisfaction that the surrounding floor was wet. He stepped around the tub and when he looked up again, she was standing before the bureau, her hands behind her back like a child waiting to be told what to do.

Walker's gaze slid over her again and his voice sounded stilted.

"Well, I suppose you should come over to my rom and I'll show you a few dance steps. There's no room to move in here."

They stood in the middle of his dimly lit quarters and looked at each other.

"Well, we don't have any music but . . . well, we can just . . ." He moved closer and took her around the waist. Silver jerked back.

"White eyes dance together," he explained, thin lipped. *"Touching."* She eyed him suspiciously as he came closer again, putting an arm about her waist and taking her hand in his. He cleared his throat. "Now it's really very simple; you just take one step at a time in the direction you will feel me move. I'll go like this." He stepped out and Silver followed awkwardly. "Then, like this." He moved back, then out again.

To his relief, she could anticipate his direction. "Very good. Now as the music moves, we'll follow the beat." He began to hum softly, accenting the beats so she could feel the connecting rhythm. He looked at her and smiled. "That's very good."

Silver returned his smile. "I do it good?"

"Very *well*."

"I do it good *and* well."

Walker chuckled softly, "Indeed."

He closed his eyes as they moved. She smelled good enough to eat—nothing like the faded soap he kept in his quarters. He pulled her closer, let his cheek rest against hers as they swayed to his tune: around . . . back . . . forward . . . to the side . . . He could feel the pressure of her breasts against him, and his arms stiffened to keep from pulling her tighter.

"Not so hard, is it?"

"Not hard," she murmured. She seemed to press closer, then there was an explosion in Walker's right ear: *"Yee-ahhhh!"*

Walker staggered back. "My word, I stepped on your foot! I—I'm sorry. Here, let me see—" He bent to lift her skirt, then said a word Silver had never heard before.

"Where are your shoes?" he shrieked.

Silver snatched her skirt from him. "Me no wear white man's shoes! Hurt feet."

Walker straightened, his face twitching. "You-have-to-wear-shoes."

She backed as he advanced. "Me not walk in white man's shoes!"

Walker stopped, for her eyes were beginning to glitter.

"Well, all right," he conceded ungraciously, "but make damned sure your dress stays down, do you hear me? You'll have the whole town laughing at both of us if you don't."

Silver relaxed a little. "Me . . . that is, I, will do. I will dance good and well," she assured him.

Walker heaved a sigh and glanced around the room,

suddenly uncomfortable. "Look, you better go to your own room now. It's not a good idea for us to be caught here alone together."

A look of disbelief swept over Silver's face. "We should not be alone?"

Walker was already at the door, holding it for her. "Certainly not. People would assume . . . well, that we were doing something we should not be."

Her eyes went wider, her jaw slack. "What we be doing?"

Walker stared. "You know damned well *what.*" He snatched the door wider. "Our rooms might be joined but that does not mean . . . Are you going or not?" he glowered threateningly. "I've got to take a bath and dress, and we're already late."

Lifting her skirts, Silver marched past him with slow haughtiness, and the scent from her was so intoxicating that Walker stood on, holding his hand on the knob of his door, and staring blankly.

Silver stopped and turned back when she reached her own door, and looked pointedly at the tub on the floor between them.

"You bathe in this?"

"And where else?" He thought there was a bemused twinkle in her eyes.

"I bathe there."

Walker's words were clipped as close as spring hedge. "I realize that, but there's hardly enough time to draw and heat more, now is there?"

The girl dropped her head, rolled her great silver eyes up so that the tip of the black lashes almost touched her eyebrows. Her expression was innocent yet somehow sly; and it was coming to him—not through innuendo but through a kind of telepathy—that her cryptic mien had something to do with the intimacy of their bathing in the same water.

The gist of her taunt—if indeed it was one—slipped from his grasp when, with a bewitching smile, she stepped backward into her room and closed the door.

Chapter 9

There were no lavish furnishings in the ballroom of the Fredonia Hotel. Lacquered oak planks instead of marble floors, plain white ceiling and upper walls, with the lower portion papered in tailored red, brown, and dark green stripes. There was a single chandelier made of wagon wheels of graduated sizes, and bedecked by candles.

Having arrived after the dancing had begun, Walker, Silver, and Phillip entered from the front lobby unnoticed. Walker led the way straight to the large buffet table and helped himself to a glass of wine, then, belatedly remembering the shadow at his right heel, pulled Silver around in front of him.

"Normally I don't approve of giving firewater to . . . Here, drink this. You may need it." He took another glass and finished it off neatly.

Silver sipped then drew back, her small mouth making outlandish contortions. "Sure enough horrible," she noted. "It is good for to make me strong?"

"Yes," Walker mumbled distractedly, his gaze sweeping around them to anticipate an attack before it arrived.

The fiery liquid slid down Silver's throat easier the second and third time. After the fourth, she wore a beatific, blank smile, and she looked at her husband with pride. She who never had a man to call her own had ended up with this one!

Her eyes glowed as they slid over him. He was like a big tawny puma, all weather-browned skin, burnished

135

hair, and furry gold lashes. His uniform, once intimidating, now took her breath away with its dark crisp cloth and shiny gold buttons.

"Good Lord, here they come!" said Walker.

Toward them marched Mrs. Appleby and Mrs. Bigby, each escorted rather firmly by their husbands. "I handle this," he warned with a pasty smile. "Good evening, ladies. Frank. John," he said coolly, removing his hat.

Colonel John Appleby nodded briefly then grabbed his wife's arm more firmly, leaning to stare into her protruding brown eyes. "Ahem, Ema . . . "

Mrs. Appleby returned her husband's look haughtily, then slowly removed her gaze to Silver.

"My husband feels — *ouch!*" She yanked but could not free her trapped arm, so she turned to Walker, her eyes flashing. "I mean, *I* feel that I . . . that *we,* owe you an . . ." She gave a mighty jerk and hauled her arm free at last. "Apology!"

Walker smiled thinly. "You owe me nothing, Mrs. Appleby. It's Silver to whom you owe an apology." He waited a long tense moment before the older lady dipped her head and mumbled an apology.

Her expression was anything but repentant, and Walker went on. "There, that wasn't so bad. And I'm sure that from now on there'll be no further misunderstandings."

Deeming the climax now past, Mrs. Bigby smiled, her deep-set eyes drawing into half moons. "I, too, am sorry for any misunderstandings, Miss . . ."

"Silver," supplied Walker.

"My, what a lovely name!" Her handkerchief fluttered. "Oh, it's just so unfortunate that we got off to a bad start. But when you came up off the floor so fast like that, we were just frightened to death —"

"Myrtle!"

"I-I mean t-t-that —"

"She means," said Colonel Bigby, "that all's well that ends well. Miss Silver, I'm delighted to make your acquaintance." After bending a snowy head over Silver's hand, he straightened and gave her a warm smile. "You're a very lucky young lady. You know, if Major

Grayson had been a couple of months later in his rescue, I'm afraid—"

"Excuse us, ladies and gentlemen," Walker broke in hastily, "I believe this is a waltz, and Silver has promised the first one to me."

Walker tugged gently at her arm but Silver only tottered stiffly, for she was still beaming warmly at the women. The two old squaws could not hurt her with Walker near, and the man was very kind. She felt too wonderfully warm and giddy to keep anger inside her.

Colonel Bigby cleared his throat, despising those occasions when he was forced to acknowledge the younger man's rank.

"Major . . . uh . . . sir, I do hope you and the young lady enjoy the evening. And once again, we're relieved this little matter has been cleared up in a civilized fashion. I hope you know that we hold no bitterness over the occasion."

"Oh, yes," chimed Mrs. Bigby. "You two make a most striking couple!"

Walker's gaze swung round at her words but before he could splutter a denial that they were any such thing, the foursome had turned to join the waltz in progress. He was still gaping when he felt a small timid hand touch his.

When he saw Silver's face, he said, "Oh, Lord! You're not going to be sick, are you?"

Silver shook her head bravely, tottering slightly to one side. "No. No sick."

Walker was taking no chances. After a quick glance about them, he took her wrist and headed for the front lobby doors. The back garden was far too populated.

The evening air was not brisk but certainly fresher. The entrance walk was lit only by a few dim lanterns.

He took her by the shoulders and turned her to face him.

"Now is this better? I really shouldn't have given you the wine." He found his handkerchief and leaned to blot the perspiration from her upper lip, then her forehead. Her big eyes were shining up at him in the dark.

137

"I know this is hard for you." He brushed a strand of hair from her cheek. "Do the uniforms bother you?" She shook her head, standing closer, it seemed. He looked at the curve of her lips and remembered their taste, their supple, cushiony texture, thesmall tongue teasing his.

He took a sharp breath and leaned back. "Let's go inside now. Your head will clear in a moment, but don't drink any more wine."

When they reached the ballroom, the band was starting up again. It was a slow tune, one she could follow.

"If you feel up to it, we could try the dance," said Walker, smiling into her eyes.

Silver's breath caught, and though her mouth was opened nothing came out. She nodded again.

Walker waited until the dance floor was crowded before he guided them only to the far edge.

The crowd melted away as her boneless warmth came against him. After a moment, his cheek was resting lightly on hers and he was not aware that his eyes were closed. It seemed like they were alone again, the night woods stirring about them, the pines sighing overhead.

When a hand touched his shoulder, Walker snatched himself back so swiftly that his partner, lost in the swirling beauty of the dance, gave a startled squeak.

"I'm sorry, sir!" said Private Anderson. "I didn't mean to slip up on you like that. It's just that we—I mean I— noticed she could dance and I wanted to . . . cut in?"

Walker forced a tight smile. "Of course. This is Silver Dawn. Silver, this is Private Anderson."

But Private Anderson barely let him finish before he had swept Silver against him and whirled off with her. Walker noted sullenly that the girl never missed a step.

Frowning, he went for the buffet table and, after taking another glass of wine, saw Phillip coming toward him, smiling happily. A young blond woman was hanging on his arm.

"She's doin' great, isn't she, sir?" Phillip nodded toward the dance floor.

"Umm, fine," replied Walker, his gaze following the slim column of peach silk. "I just hope she keeps her dress down.

Phillip flushed and glanced at his companion, who was also red-faced.

"Uh, beg your pardon, sir?"

Walker's eyes were fixed. "Nothing," he mumbled. Nothing . . ."

Walker's expression was grim as he watched his ward dance with increasing skill. He tried to think if there was a single man she had not danced with, and decided there wasn't. And that list included both old buffoons, Appleby and Bigby.

Leaning against the buffet, he downed his sixth glass of wine. The table heaved with his weight, making the wineglasses tinkle dangerously.

Phillip eyed the goblet in Walker's hand.

"She's doing so well, why don't we step outside for a breath of air?" he suggested calmly.

"No."

"Well, you're going to have to leave her here alone anyway when you go to Waco, and that's only the day after tomorrow." He spoke reasonably, but his eyes never left the endangered wineglass.

Walker's gaze slid around. "And just who do you suppose is going to be in charge of her while I'm gone?" Phillip looked up. "B-b-but I barely know the girl, and besides—"

Walker smiled unpleasantly. "Then keep your suggestions to yourself." He looked back to the dance floor where three young soldiers were standing on the outer edge of the dance floor, shoving and jostling each other for the next position when the present dance ended.

Walker slammed his glass on the table. "This has gone far enough."

"Sir. Major! *Walker, wait!*"

Walker pried his way rudely through the dancers but managed to loose sight of his prey for a moment. When the way cleared again, Silver and Private Anderson had disappeared.

Walker went back to where Phillip was standing. "I can't believe she's done this." His voice shook.

"I don't understand."

"She's let some young hoodlum talk her into going outside. Come on. I'm going to find her."

They searched the garden and the grounds beyond.

"I can't understand it," puffed Phillip, trying to match Walker's long strides. "It's like they've vanished into thin air. Maybe they went out the front lobby door."

"I don't know how without us seeing them leave," muttered Walker. "Besides, why would they go out the front when there's nothing . . ." He stopped and stared at Phillip for a moment, then ordered briskly, "I'll work back through the ballroom and you go around from the outside. And remember to stay calm even if you find the worst."

Phillip looked at him. "I'll try my best, sir."

After Phillip disappeared into the shadows around the corner, Walker went back through the garden and thence through the double doors.

It was while he was charging ruthlessly through the Jennie Reel that he spotted them. They were standing where he and Phillip had been before, by the buffet table, and it was apparent they had just come through the front lobby doors. The *unlighted* front lobby doors.

Walker was shaking when he stopped in front of the young soldier, but he spoke with deceptive calm.

"Private Anderson, I would have a word with you in the lobby." He preceded them to that locale, not even glancing at Silver.

Phillip was just stepping in the front door, and stopped when he caught sight of the young couple standing slightly behind Walker and looking pitifully guilty.

"I'll handle this alone," said Walker. Phillip nodded and left for the ballroom.

Walker stood in a posture of rigid restraint, looking from girl to soldier, unable to trust himself to speak.

"Sir, I hope you haven't got the wrong idea," began Anderson. "Silver wasn't feeling too well and I thought she needed some air."

Walker looked quickly to the girl and saw that her face was indeed a peculiar shade of gray. Yes, she looked quite ill. His face softened the smallest amount.

"Silver, is this true? Were you ill?"

She said nothing, did not even nod her head. Her eyes were enormous, her face stricken—she was definitely sick, he decided.

Walker frowned to hide his relief. "Private, I think it's best that you leave us alone for a moment. Undoubtedly I have misjudged the situation. The girl is not accustomed to spirits. My apologies."

Private Anderson gave them a brief bow and left, but when Walker took a step, the girl dodged as if he were about to strike her.

"Silver, stop that. This is no time for your frightened savage act. I need to get you outside before you embarrass us both. From now on you should stay away from firewater altogether—apparently you can't take it. Of course, that's no disgrace," he added.

A time passed and she said nothing. In fact, she did not move, but only stared at him in that strange way. "Silver, I—"

"Major, sir, I'm sorry to interrupt but Mr. and Mrs. Weldon have asked to see you," said Phillip, stepping into the lobby. "Mr. Weldon's a merchant in town and his wife was here at the fort the other day when you arrived. She had an attack of some sort, remember?"

Walker kept looking at Silver as he leaned closer to Phillip; her expression had not changed.

"I think she's had too much to drink. She looks like she feels nauseous but I can't get a word out of her. Can you stay with her a minute?"

Walker found the Weldons on the far side of the ballroom, and Mr. Weldon was holding out his hand.

"Ah, Major Grayson, I'm so glad you could see us. I just wanted to let you know that Mildred is fine now. Seems it was only a fainting spell . . ."

Four silk fans swished furiously.

"She's *barefooted*. I saw it with my own eyes!"

"Well, John *made* me apologize. But I'm telling you all, she's as wild as an animal. As dangerous as one—not to mention being a disgrace to the God-fearing ladies of this town!" said Mrs. Appleby, her face quivering with indignation. "You know, I don't believe she's . . . well, I hate to be indelicate, but I don't think she's wearing any *undies!*" The others gasped then rallied to assure Mrs. Appleby.

"I know just what you mean. Did you ever see anything like the way she was dancing with Major Grayson? It was absolutely obscene!"

"This town won't stand for it, I tell you," declared Mrs. Coffman. She was the mayor's wife and not restricted by the complicated entanglements of military protocol. "The fort is nothing more than a convenience we offer to the army—and a mighty expensive one at that. Why must we be subjected to heathen immorality?"

Mrs. Appleby quieted. A breach between the town and the military were ramifications she had not considered.

Mrs. Bigby was not as perceptive. "It looks like to me that she's made a spectacle of herself already. Did you see her dancing with my Frank? Why, she was—oh, I hate to be crude—but she was rubbing herself all over him!"

"Look. There she is now, by the buffet. Look at her eyes. They don't even look human!"

"And that Aide-de-Camp Martin standing over her like a mother hen," sputtered Mrs. Coffman, coming out of her chair and grabbing up her skirts. "I think it's time we had a talk with Major Walker Grayson. If he plans to use this fort at his leisure, then he'd better take this town into consideration."

Phillip had not pried a word from the girl and, helpless to do anything else, followed as she moved like a sleepwalker back into the ballroom. He was looking anxiously at her and didn't see the brigade of matrons as it swung around the edge of the dancers.

"Miss Silver, I don't know how to help you if you won't tell me what's wrong," he urged again. "And if you're looking for the major, I don't expect he wants to be interrupted right now."

The girl went suddenly stiff and Phillip, following her gaze, saw the legion approaching. It was with some relief that he heard Private Anderson's voice.

"Miss Silver, I'm glad to see you're feeling much better." He had come to stand on the other side of the girl.

"I can't get a word out of her," Phillip said, "but for now, don't move from that spot — and that's an order."

Mrs. Coffman brought herself up in front of them.

"Sir, we demand to speak to Major Grayson at once."

Phillip bowed politely. "I'm sorry, ma'am, but the major is busy at the moment. Can I help you?"

"Perhaps you can at that," said Mrs. Coffman. "I believe you are aware of how much time and effort have gone in to this ball, a great deal of it mine. And as the wife of Mayor Coffman, I feel I have more than enough right to demand all guests attend this function properly attired."

Phillip's brows shot up. "Begging your pardon, ma'am, but I was always taught to remove my hat indoors. This is a social occasion, but if that offends you —"

"I am *not* referring to your *hat,* sir! I am referring to this . . . this *girl!*"

Phillip's dark eyes flashed. "Ma'am, I politely advise you to notice that Miss Silver Dawn is by far the most beautiful young lady here — present company not excepted."

Mrs. Coffman's yellow eyes and hair seemed to shimmer with fire.

"Even a *heathen* cannot brazenly march in here wearing no shoes, Aide-de-Camp Martin!" she bellowed. "Not to mention other articles which I could not dare name in mixed company!" She brought her voice to a more lady-like volume but her eyes were like flames. "Just because you people wear uniforms doesn't mean you can tramp on the integrity of the decent folk of this town. If you think you can then you'll soon find out differently!"

Phillip was vaguely aware that the girl seemed to be shrinking around behind him, and when he felt her arm brush his back, he thought for a moment that she was going to grab him for support like a child beset by an enraged adult. To think of her being so frightened made him furious.

"Mrs. Coffman, I have no earthly idea what you are talking about," he replied heatedly.

"This!" Mrs. Coffman screeched. "*This* is what I'm talking about!" And she bent down, reaching to snatch the peach-colored hemline far enough to expose the girl's nude feet. But just as her hand darted out, something hit the top of her head and immediately the bun at her crown became a burning center of pain. Her head was yanked up with a snap she heard in her neck, and her face felt like melting wax when she met a pair of cold, gray-glittering eyes.

Then her gaze dropped and her face screwed up with apoplectic shock, for the savage held in her other hand a small butter knife whose blunt blade had shed all appearance of the harmless instrument it was, and sparkled with wicked slivers of light. She froze.

For a moment Phillip could not move either; he could only stare at the knife, perplexed, remembering it as part of the Rogers silver service with which he had spread a slice of bread. But in the next instant, he saw the way it was held: the blade not pointing from the edge of the hand but jutting between thumb and index finger. One was the grip of a lunatic, the other an expert. He gasped.

Silver had no intention of harming a helpless old woman, even if it was the final indignity to be assaulted when one was a guest of another tribe. Not the most fiendish enemy of the Quohadie Teichas would be harmed while he smoked and ate as a guest.

But white eyes had no honor. Nothing was beyond them—from an unprovoked attack upon a guest to a husband betraying his First Wife with brutal lies!

Before Phillip could react, Silver gave the woman's hair a final twist, meaning to let go then and take up a defensive position, for she deemed the incident closed unless the woman attacked again.

But the old one squawked like a dying chicken, her eyes almost popping from her skull, and the sound carried so well that the music faltered and Silver saw heads turn their way with expressions of horror, as though she had had some embarrassing bodily lapse. The waltz in progress developed small gaps as the musicians also stared.

Then Phillip's delayed reflexes went into action. He lunged and pinned the girl's arms to her sides with a bear hug, the cry breaking from his own throat just as the orchestra ground to a complete halt, so that his voice echoed over the silence in a loud *"Nooooooo."*

Silver stood still, transfixed by the hundred staring faces. But every last rustle fell silent as the guests picked out the knife clenched in her hand.

Beyond them Silver saw a man taller than the rest shoving through the crowd, and her heart beat so fast she thought she would faint. She could not look on his face. She could not!

The arms about her relaxed when she did not move for a moment. It was all the edge she needed. Levering her arms up, she broke Phillip's grasp, ducked and whirled before he could grab her the second time, and headed toward the front lobby doors. Behind her the great hall seemed to explode with confusion, and she could imagine the hordes streaming after her like ants pouring from a disturbed mound.

But her mind never panicked, never stopped turning like the wheels of a chariot roaring into battle; and as she passed the buffet table, she shot one hand out and deftly exchanged the butter knife for a better weapon: a long carving knife.

The lobby was empty and she made the doors, but when she jerked one open, there were two surprised soldiers standing in her path. She immediately wheeled for the staircase to her left, tripping and staggering on the long hem, her bare feet flashing from under its folds as she scrambled for balance.

At the top of the stairs she was forced to turn left again, and found herself on a balcony overlooking the

145

mass confusion of the ballroom. The musicians were trying bravely to start up again but no one was dancing; they were all staring up, their mouths open.

Then there was the thunder of boots on the stairway and Silver ran again, stopping midway on the balcony. For there were other boot sounds, now in front of her—and she saw the trap. A second stairway ascended from the other side of the ballroom. The balcony connected them and the only doors were behind her.

She did not know they were guests rooms and wasted time trying one before she saw Walker rushing onto the balcony from the way she had come.

"Silver, stop! Stop right there! Nobody's going to hurt you!" he shouted. But he knew his message was doomed the moment he saw her face. She was no longer the woman he had held softly in his arms. She was Comanche—the ultimate fighting machine, the most cunning escape artist; blind instinct intertwined with trained reflexes, sinews and bone that became a complex miracle of strength, and the whole of it controlled with a brain honed by centuries of warfare. His mind whirled with frantic despair. He could not imagine what she would do, but he knew what she would *not* do, and that was surrender peaceably.

Only he should have been able to make an educated guess. Her right hand flicked out from the folds of her dress, and he saw the knife.

"Get back!" he ordered as more soldiers poured onto the balcony from the opposite side. "Stop where you are! he shouted again, trying to be heard over the grinding discord that was the orchestra trying to play and watch at the same time. But what measure of tension relaxed when they finally, mercifully, ceased their efforts, increased tenfold in the tomb silence that followed. Walker was acutely aware of the sea of upturned faces below them, and lowered his voice.

"Silver, I don't know what's wrong but we can talk about it. You know I'm not going to let you get away. There's nowhere for you to go. All you have to do is put down the knife and come to me." He tried to sound calm and reasonable.

"Ka nei mah na-ich-ka-ein!" she gritted savagely, gesturing with the knife.

Trying to warn the others back with a glare, Walker took one step forward. "That's an old Comanche excuse for hatred—" He broke off, knowing by her expression that he was moving from quicksand to bottomless pit. "Silver," he said quietly. "Silver, look at me. Look into my eyes. You can trust me. You should know that by now."

Her eyes flared more brightly. *Ka nei mah na-ich-ka ein!"* She bent and began ripping at the tail of her skirt.

The soldiers on the balcony seemed petrified at the spectacle and only watched as Silver whacked mercilessly at the once beautiful gown, her wild gaze darting up from time to time to scan both ends of the balcony.

Walker was bewildered, for now he could not begin to imagine what she was doing unless it was indulging in a temper tantrum designed to set the enemy off balance. Had he only known that she was facilitating her imminent flight, he might have galvanized himself sooner. But he was, like the others, so spellbound that he simply stood and stared.

She was breathing hard by the time she finished scant seconds later, for the knife was small and the silk weave dense and tough. Yet now her skirt hung in tattered streamers about her legs, and she wasted no more time. With a war cry that could have come from a two-ton bull elephant, she bounded lithely toward the balcony railing and leaped upon it.

There was a huge gasp from the crowd as she tottered on the five-inch beam, but in a moment she had balanced herself, arms out, knife clutched tightly in her right hand.

Walker dared not move or breathe. He was praying—promising a blameless life from now to his grave if only the angels could keep her from falling. And for a moment—just a moment—her eyes crept in a slow circle until they rested upon him, and he saw pain like a beacon's flash, so brief that only one tick of time later he could believe he had dreamed it. Then she looked down.

In the brief instant before it happened, Walker knew what she was going to do but it was too late. He saw in slow motion, horror and disbelief molding his face, stretching his eyelids, twisting the heavy gold brows. A scream convulsed his lips but no sound emerged as her arms drew back for the final spring, then whipped forward like a diver's, and the motion propelled her body from the rail into arched flight.

The crowd gasped like those watching a suicide dive as she sailed above them for an instant. For nobody realized there was any other end to her madness until she reached her mark and hit the chain above the chandelier.

As the impetus carried her out in a pendulum swing over the crowd, the force of motion was too much and the chain began to slip rapidly through her hands. She slid down the length of it and her feet aided the remaining candles in toppling, flames and hot wax showering down on those below. The crowd fanned out with horrified screams, thus the center of the floor was empty when she dropped during the next backward swing.

Walker shouted again from the balcony, but his voice was lost in the wave of hysteria. The acrid smell of scorched hair and cloth rose on the air, and amid the scurrying and screaming of those around her, Silver ducked low then weaved and crawled and shoved her way through the frenzied guests.

Then she saw a way of escape. The french doors that led to the garden looked only like a wall of small squares—not much of a barricade to freedom; she could see through it to the garden beyond where tree branches swayed in the light of pole lanterns. Though her limited experience allowed that certain white eyes walls opened, she did not think of that. Only that escape lay beyond the flimsy wall.

There was enough cleared distance to gain speed, and gain it she did. The great wall of squares loomed closer as she ran like a gazelle until the very last moment. Then she leaped on the final step to arch through the air with the other foot extended, the ball of it striking the center of the wall. Glass shattered and spewed like a fountain of sparkling water, but her momentum was such that she never felt the bite of a single shard.

Her speed barely dented, she landed on the extended foot in the very next step, and kept going.

Chapter 10

As Walker dashed down the staircase and began clawing his way toward the garden doors, his mind registered the disaster around him. In their haste to avoid the falling chandelier, some had stumbled against the buffet table. Wine bottles lay broken and gurgling out their contents; whole layers of white cake were smeared across the floor, a vase of flowers lay smashed, chairs were scattered and turned over. He passed a woman who was standing and screaming at the top of her lungs as she looked at the floor, where her hairpiece was burning into a black grisly ball. Pretending not to see her humiliation, he ran on. Phillip was already waiting at the doors.

"Stay and get some help in case I lose her," Walker told him, and squirmed between the splintered wood and jagged glass.

Silver knew no silent urgings to pace herself, had no awareness of physical limitation. Her heart swelled in protest, her feet and hands tingled because her lungs couldn't keep up with her legs, yet she pounded them faster — faster! Beyond lay darkness and freedom, a welcoming black void where she would never have to look on her husband's face again. She would go home to the Llano Estacado and not know or care when he took the new wife — the one who had been promised to him for so many moons that Private Anderson knew every detail of the wedding plans! And if that one knew, the whole fort knew. No wonder the white eyes women laughed at her!

The face-likeness in Walker's room was not his sister. It had a name now, *Cah-meel-ya*. The one who smiled because she had leaned against Walker's hard body, whispered love words to him, touched him intimately. One of his own kind who would come second but always be first—to whom Walker would go to make *commar-pe* while his true First Wife dried into a barren old slave!

Her heart palpitated, the darkness closed in to hide her but she couldn't slow her feet. Never, never, never! Not until she saw the palisades of Llano Estacado. The Law of Many Wives could not be a good law when it brought so much pain, and she would not live by it for her father or anyone else. Even if Horse Back returned her to Walker Grayson, she would escape again and again and again.

Her breathing sounded like a bellows, masking the sound of thumping boots until an arm wrapped around her waist and pulled her down.

The darkness revealed nothing, but Silver did not need light to know her assailant. She knew by the smell of him, the texture of his hands, the layers of hard muscles on the arms. She tried to scrape her nails down his face when he flipped her to her back, and as he deftly avoided her clawing, she tried to lever her knee toward his groin.

Walker grunted as they struggled, saying nothing until he managed to trap her wrists and force them above her head, holding her down with a leg flung over her belly.

"Fight then, you little savage!" he snarled. "Fight and scream all you want to but nobody's going to help you. I'm the only fool who tries to do that!"

She fought him harder, hatred and shame exploding together to give her extraordinary strength. *"Tivo sata!"* she shrieked in his face. *"Nei may-way-kah ein!* Me kill you, you snake!"

Walker held her hands above her head and laughed harshly. "I hardly think you're in a position to make threats, and believe me, I'll know better than to give you the opportunity. I should have left you in chains. I should have turned you back over to the vermin who used a whip on you!"

With all her strength Silver arched her body and jerked her hands, and when the right one slipped free, she brought it across his face as hard as she could.

There was a resounding *slap!* as her open palm struck his cheek. He went suddenly still, and she could feel how badly he wanted to hit her back.

Instead, he brought his face down to hers and kissed her ruthlessly, pinching her bottom lip against her teeth until she tasted the iron tang of blood in her mouth.

For a moment she was stunned at his reaction. But the next instant she was returning his kiss, matching his violence. Always white eyes soldiers wanted to master, to conquer! But she was Quohadie Teichas, who knew courage and its price, who had faced death not once but many times.

When Walker drew back gasping, she laughed at him and hissed in a garbled mixture of Comanche and English, "One battle man always lose to woman. You will lose this one, Walker Gray's Son!" Taking advantage of his surprise, she wriggled until her belly was pressing his, and before he could move away, she raised her head and began kissing him sensually, her tongue darting and probing.

He drew back, grabbing her hair and twisting it in his free hand. "Don't!"

Silver let her body soften against him. He was *her* man. His hard muscles, his sun-browned face, his loyalty and protection and devotion—all rightfully hers! Then she choked back a sob. But only in the dark woods where no one knew. Before his own people he would wear a bright and shining Camelia like a badge of honor.

She felt his body begin to move so that his hips thrust against her, but his voice was more savage than before. "Is this what you wanted from that poor simpleton, Private Anderson? What did he promise you, horses? Food? Rifles for your people so they can slaughter more white eyes?"

"Walker." The knot in her throat made it easy to feign a seductive whisper. "Walker," she said again, looping her legs over the backs of his knees.

Silver felt a shiver go through his body. She imitated his movements, pressing until she could feel his rising hardness.

"Don't do this to me," he said raggedly. Her dress was pushed up around her waist and he released her hands so that his own were free to move down over her naked stomach and thighs, over the mound of her womanhood. Then suddenly he recoiled, raised himself above her.

"And you probably think it was your charm that kept you on the dance floor," he laughed harshly. Then he grabbed her hands again, pushing them flat against the ground and looking down at her. "You don't know how badly I'd like to take you up on your offer," he sneered, "but it's time you learned who's calling the shots here. It's not you and it's damned sure not Horse Back. Comanchero will belong to the United States Army in a few short months and Horse Back — if he's still alive — will be nothing but a legend to tell your children."

Silver's eyes burned at him through the shadows. "When Horse Back come, he kill you. Me go home then, where warriors do not fear to take a woman's body like white eyes, who crawl in the night where no one can see and feel shame when he take a woman!"

He looked at her. "That's all this is to you. A sideshow. A way to humiliate a white eyes chief, a way to show the world how superior you are."

His hands were hurting her wrists. Pain, always they give pain! Only the ultimate insult was left to her and she spat hard at his face, realizing by his indrawn breath that she had hit her mark. His body went rigid; he clamped so tight on her wrists she thought they would break, and this time she knew he would kill her.

He did not draw back to strike her, but when his voice came from the darkness, it was low and shaking with fury. "You win but you don't win. I can play the savage. Any man can. So I'll give you something for comparison. Just do one thing. Remember what it was like before. Remember and weep. It'll never be like that again."

He released her hands and fumbled between their bodies, then without the slightest warning spread her thighs and plunged inside her.

Silver gasped at his power but tried not flinch from it.

He wanted to punish her for making him break his stupid vow. So let him.

She wrapped her legs around his hips and arched to meet each savage thrust. For now she *had* won. This Cah-meel-ya was far away, and there were many long nights ahead to lie in her husband's arms. By the time the second wedding came, Silver Dawn Sky would be his sure enough First Wife—his most beloved wife!

In spite of his threats, she could tell he was restraining himself, not quite unleashing the primitive power that shook his body. And in a few moments she knew he was also holding back the explosion of pleasure until he felt her mounting with him. As it should be with husbands and wives. *As it should be* . . .

Then her thoughts broke up into small airy bubbles as she rose up to ride the night sky with Walker Gray's Son.

Though it was only ten o'clock, Phillip presumed the ball had been terminated in chaos. As he watched Walker throw his clothes into a finely crafted leather bag, he waited for the right opening, for although his companion's expression hardly invited friendly advice, he knew all good leaders adhered to the proverb of wisdom in an abundance of council. Walker Grayson was such a leader and in a quieter moment, he would consider the idea carefully.

"When you're gone and the girl's had time to quiet down, I could let her come back here and stay in your room," he offered tentatively.

Without looking up, Walker tossed the last shirt in the suitcase, snapped the gold catches, and began to pull on his gauntlets. Phillip went another step. "I don't suppose you would even think about sending her to Horse Back."

Walker held out the bag and looked at him. "I don't want to think about her, period."

Phillip followed with the suitcase until they were at the front door, then instead of opening it, he cut off Walker's exit, dropped the bag down with a splat, and crossed his arms.

"Sir, in view of the fact that you're leaving me responsible, I think I have the right to —"

"You have no rights but to follow orders," Walker reminded him tersely, and Phillip responded just as swiftly.

"As I always have!"

Unaccustomed to being challenged, Walker drew back in surprise and Phillip pressed his advantage. "Let's forget our official relationship for just a moment — no, let's consider it. You've been a little unreasonable about the girl — please let me finish. I know she's asked for trouble but think about it a minute. It's like putting a prisoner in solitary for a minor infraction. Think how far she's come since we found her. Maybe it's time to reward her good behavior as well as punish the bad."

Walker turned abruptly and went to the window, staring into its black panes as though there were a sunny landscape beyond.

After a long pause he said, "She'll run off now. I know she will." His words were so indistinct it was a moment before Phillip could reconstruct them.

"Is that such a bad idea?" Walker wheeled about angrily but Phillip demanded, "Well? Is it?"

"Do you have any idea what this meeting is about?" said Walker, looking at him as though amazed at his stupidity.

"Yes sir. I know exactly what it's about," answered Phillip quietly.

Walker stared at him a moment, then marched across the room to snatch up his bag and open the door for himself. "Contrary to what you might think, it would give me enormous pleasure to do what you suggest. I would move heaven and earth if I could do it. But I'd be sending her to her death. Maybe you can do that but I can't." He stared intently into Phillip's eyes and repeated, *I . . . can't.*"

After Walker stormed out the door, Phillip paused to let his pulse slow down, then followed outside to wait until Walker had thrown his bag up to the driver. He opened the carriage door, standing too close to be easily avoided.

"I'm going to say my piece unless you stop me by force, and I know you won't do that." The hunted look in Walker's eyes almost stopped him, but he took another breath and went on. "We make pets out of wild things and tell ourselves how lucky the beasts are for having food and shelter. But they're not lucky; they're prisoners, living from one breath to the next for freedom—"

Walker moved toward him, a bright shard of light dancing in his eyes. "Come September there's going to be a massacre in that canyon. She can turn this fort upside down, she can scream and tear her hair out, and you can say it's all my fault. But not by my hand. She will not die by my hand! Now I'm warning you. Step aside."

"I think I know what's wrong with her. What's wrong with you. Furthermore, I know why she went crazy like that. She found out from Private Anderson that you—"

Rage washed over Walker's face at the mention of Anderson, and Phillip stopped mid-sentence.

"You go too far, my friend," said Walker coldly. "If you value our friendship at all, you'll get out of my way. And if you value your career, you'd better see that my orders are carried out to the letter." His eyes glittered. "Is that clear, Aide-de-Camp Martin?"

Phillip stiffened and saluted, and his voice was a sneer.

"*Quite* clear, major sir."

The grind of the wagon wheels was scarcely out of earshot when Phillip had reached The Stocks, a musty cell which had housed too few inmates of late to be kept in good condition. He muttered a colorful phrase when he found that Walker had posted an armed guard by the door.

"Good evening, Sergeant Miller," he said. "I'm sure Major Grayson informed you that I'd be responsible for the girl in his absence."

"Yes sir, he sure did."

Phillip looked him in the eye. "Then as you can see, sergeant, your services are no longer needed."

156

Miffed by Martin's tone, Miller hauled himself away from the wall and shrugged. "Suits me. I could use the sleep after a night like this." He slung his rifle over his shoulder and slouched away.

The single square slab cell was located at the end of the westerly line of barracks, and had housed in past days of glory such notables as Davy Crockett, Jim Bowie, and Stephen Austin; thus it was a natural fortress of mud and log with a single window covered in bars that formerly kept out marauding redskins. Because of its thick walls it was not cold, but the small cot was covered by a musty blanket. The floors were dusty, and there was no light inside, just a lantern on the outside wall. Phillip took the keys and unlocked the door, grabbing the lantern from its hook as the heavy door swung open.

"Miss Silver, it's me, Phillip." He heard a rustling and held up the lantern.

The girl was not on the cot but huddled in the corner on the floor. Her arms were hooked over her knees, her bare toes peeping from beneath one of the cotton frocks Milly had lent her.

The gray eyes that lifted to his were dull and haunted by shadows. He spoke gently. "You're coming with me, Miss Silver. I'm going to take you back to your old room next to Walker's, and when you've got all tidied up I'll fix you some good hot soup. Nobody will bother you there."

He took her hand and helped her to her feet, repeating himself several times. "I can promise you that. Nobody will bother you there . . ."

Sergeant Miller had not gone to sleep. He was burning with curiosity and went to the main office a few moments later.

But the door to the main office was unbolted before he even knocked, and a piece of paper was jabbed through the crack at him.

"See that these orders are carried out posthaste, sergeant. And remember that I'm acting on behalf of Major

Grayson." The door slammed.

When Miller reappeared, it was almost midnight. He drew back a fist and attacked the door. By the time Phillip had turned up the wick on Walker's desk and rushed to the noisy portal, Miller's frustration was enjoying a little appeasement.

Phillip snatched the door just wide enough to grab the jug of hot soup and sack of crackers, but as he started to shut it, a hand darted out to catch the edge.

"What the hell's going on in there, Martin?" demanded the sergeant. "The whole fort is in an uproar and everybody's sayin' the major's left town." He tried to peer inside. "Where is that girl? You got her in there?"

"Yes, she's in here! Now I suggest you get some sleep, sergeant. We're having inspection in the morning at seven-thirty sharp."

Miller lost his hold on the door and it shut barely a hair's breadth from his nose.

Silver sipped only enough of the soup to soothe her flaming, hollow stomach before she crawled to the corner of her room to wait. She was surprised to find that she had dozed off when she heard the door to Walker's room open. She looked up fearfully.

Phillip did not comment on her preference for corners as he went to sit on the edge of the bed.

"Walker had to go away for a few days," he said, and stopped when her face swung toward the wall. "It's a meeting with other white chiefs, and he had to go. He told me to look after you real good and . . . and he said he was sorry about that other room but he was afraid you'd try to run away again." She hugged her knees tighter, rocked back and forth. "He told me to tell you how sorry he was . . ." The improvisation faltered and after a moment changed course. "He locked you away because he thought you would try to escape. But I don't believe that. And I'm not going to put you back in that damned cell." Her head came around, big gray eyes trusting. "That's right. If you need anything, all you have to do is holler at that door. I'm going to stay in Walker's room all night so nobody can get in here to bother you." He gestured expansively. "I've got this place locked up tighter than a drum."

At the door, he paused to smile reassuringly. "I'm just going in the other room now and get some sleep. But remember, all you have to do is knock on this door." The girl nodded bravely and Phillip said the words only in his head: That bloody, hardheaded bastard. And he closed the door.

During the next half hour Silver crossed the small bathing room several times and opened the door to Walker's room with deliberate clatter, but the slender young man on the bed did not stir.

Her breath came easier as she inspected the deserted building. In the front office there was a lamp burning low on the desk. Her eyes went to the heavy door that led outside, especially to the bolt across it. Though the endless hours in between seemed like years, she remembered that when Walker brought her through it — only just this morning — the bolt had lifted upward and when something was done to the metal hooks below it, the wood partition opened.

She lifted the bar, fumbled at the metal hook, and jumped back when the door swung open with a loud creak.

Adrenaline quickened through her veins as she closed it, dropped the bolt quietly, and looked about her. Not only had her new master accommodated her escape, but there were weapons hanging all around on the walls. There were long guns, which Horse Back said were responsible for *tivo* conquering so much of Comanchero, but she was terrified of them and would not know how to use one anyway.

She went to the wall and instead took down a knife that was so long it reached from her waist to the floor. It was very heavy and its blade ran on both sides so it could pierce a man's body with one stroke! The thought

of killing again made her shamefully ill. But she squared
her shoulders. She was Quohadie Teichas. If no *tivo* tried
to stop her, he would live. Otherwise he brought on his
own death.

She took the heavy blade with her when she opened
the door again and stepped onto the wide porch that ran
the length of the building. The yellow lamplight flooded
from the doorway to mar the purity of the night, so she
closed it quickly.

There was not a sound abroad in the stillness. The
moon had not quite sunk below the jagged timber tops
and she could see well after her eyes adjusted. She went
to the edge of the front steps to let the moonbeams wash
her face, closing her eyes until the hush filled her spirit
and she felt stronger. But now she must go.

She moved back into the shadows and walked slowly
along the porch until she came to the last window, and
her legs stopped. After a moment her head turned
against her will.

The low burning wick on the desk cast flickering
shadows about the room; she could see him sitting there
so plainly, his craggy brows furrowed over his endless
papers.

"*Su-va-te*, Walker Gray's Son," she whispered, and as a
sob gripped her chest, she hurried on to the end of the
porch.

They had waited for so long that Buck sank into a
stupor. George had napped intermittently but was awak-
ened when groups of soldiers straggled back from the
ball prematurely.

He was starting to nod again when the hair on his
neck prickled. He bolted up just in time to see a form
glide swiftly through trees. He waited.

The second time, it passed through one of the ribbons
of moonlight that wove through the lacy ground
shadows. No other woman would be out at such an
hour—and it was a woman all right, one with pale silver
hair who moved like a cat.

He cursed as he reached for Buck's shoulder. Fate had

again handed them a mixed blessing, for though he wouldn't have to risk going inside the stone building, he hadn't planned to move so soon; there still might be men returning late from wherever they had gone in town.

He waited until the girl was out of earshot then pounded Buck again.

"Buck! Buck, the girl's loose. Go wait with the horses till I catch her and meet you there. And by damn I'll skin your hide if you mess up again!"

His warning fell on deaf ears. In the end, he left Buck staggering in a semi-conscious state with only a frail hope that the idiot would make it to the creek in time.

His long thin legs ate up the ground, and he didn't even worry when she heard him and picked up her speed; no woman could match his stride, not even a savage.

He was wrong. It would have taken some time to overtake her if she hadn't tripped over a root and sprawled headlong on the ground. George skidded to a halt and loomed over her for a minute, enjoying her fear. "Yep, it's me again," he cackled, then reached for her.

Silver moved too soon and the saber was too heavy. Spotting its silent arch, George deflected it with his arm and knocked it to the ground. When he had yanked the girl to her feet, he pressed a knife to her throat. "You let out a peep and you're done fer. *Done fer,* you got that?" The fetid breath in Silver's face struck a chord of familiar terror and she tried to hit the evil face.

George Greelee drew back his hand and smashed it into the girl's face. He had learned what several others had not: that the only way she could be managed was when she was unconscious. He hoisted her to his hip and as he started running, he chortled, "You little heathen!"

"Shh! Get back," said one of the soldiers, and the other two fell back until the shadows covered them.

"What is it? I can't make it out."

"It's a man carrying a girl."

The third man swore. "Well, we can't just stand here." As they moved out of the shadows, one of them shouted, "You there. Halt or we'll fire."

George grabbed his burden tighter and bolted like a hare. Fifty more yards and he'd reach the horses.

He could hear the soldiers giving chase but they hadn't fired on him. He barreled into the brush, barely feeling the pain as the girl clawed and bit his arm. She seemed to have recovered fully.

"Buck! Damn you, Buck, where are you?" The horses jerked at their tethers as George plowed toward them, snarling, "Damned miserable idiot, serves him right to get left behind!"

"Heah!" Buck grunted as he crashed through the bushes. "I comin', Gawge, don't be mad."

"Soldiers, Buck. Make a run for . . . " The rest of his words were eaten up by the volley of a rifle. The girl was like a wildcat in his arms, and he slapped her across the face. The blow stunned her but she kept fighting. If he hadn't dropped his knife he could have done away with her on the spot.

The cry came again. "Give up and come out. You got ten seconds."

Buck's horse was resisting the mount, and the more Buck beat him, the more the animal snorted and pawed. There were tramping boots now, muttered words, and finally a loud ping as a bullet glanced off something close by.

Tossing the girl to the ground, George ran forward and pressed himself against a pine at the edge of the thicket. He barely had time to pull his pistol out before one of the soldiers reached the spot. The man raised his own pistol and aimed into the brush.

"All right, last chance—"

George's arm streaked out, slammed down, then raised again, the pistol coming up point-blank in the soldier's startled face. George fired and felt the spray of warm blood and flesh over his hand.

The two oncoming soldiers peeled apart and faded into the surrounding thicket. George could hear them. Round and round he spun, firing wildly until his pistol clicked empty. Throwing it aside, he started for the rifle on his horse, and from nowhere two bodies rose out of the darkness and dragged him down.

His face hit the dirt. There was an arm across the back of his neck that threatened to snap it, but he struggled until he could see Buck's silhouette outlined against the pale ground of the clearing. He was mounted but going nowhere, for as the horse thrashed under its excess burden, its hind quarters seemed to buckle. Buck's fist pounded between its ears, on the neck and sides of its face.

Suddenly the animal burst to life and ran forward into the moon-washed clearing, Buck slopping from one side to the other. George's eyes rolled up, his chin still crunched in the dirt as he spit through his teeth. "Stay on, Bucky boy. Stay on!"

But as he watched, the horse broke into a demon dance—lunging, kicking, shrieking. He could see Buck's massive shoulders rounded as he clung to the saddle horn, the reins long since wrenched from his hands. Poor clumsy bastard, thought George, and he tried to shout again but nothing would pass his twisted windpipe but a grunt.

When the horse reared up and began pawing the air, Buck lasted only a few seconds before crashing to the ground. Then as George watched in horror, the horse twisted on its hind legs so that its hooves were above the grotesque form. The horse dropped his feet. Buck screamed. The animal reared again, and came down. Again and came down.

At dawn the next morning George Greelee was tried by Colonel Appleby and sentenced to be executed by firing squad.

The early hour did not diminish the number of spectators, as was hoped, and even some of the officers' wives had defied their husbands to attend the first execution in Nacogdoches in a number of years.

Phillip seethed with helpless fury at Colonel Appleby's demand that the girl witness the execution, for though she held herself erect, her whole body quivered as she stared at the bound and blindfolded figure of George Greelee. The colonel had insinuated heavily that not only was the Indian captive responsible for this execution but was also to blame for the slaying of a brave soldier trying to protect her, and indirectly the cause of the tragic trampling of the other man by his own horse.

Up to now, George Greelee had made no sound. But when he heard six carbines fan the air to slap shoulders and the deadly *click-click* that followed, his plaintive moan broke over the hush. *"Pleeeease! I don't want to die!"*

Just as his voice waned, a loud wail rose from the murdered soldier's young wife, and she fainted. Phillip cursed under his breath, "Orders be damned," and hooking an arm around Silver's waist, he half shoved her through the spectators.

Before they'd gone a dozen steps, the rifles exploded in a sound no soldier ever forgets. The girl's body spasmed, she stumbled one step, and kept going.

No sooner had he deposited the girl in Walker's room than there was a racket at the front door, which Phillip had once again bolted behind him.

Colonel Appleby rammed a meaty fist at the portal as soon as Phillip lifted the bolt and marched to take up a stance behind Walker's desk.

"Aide-de-camp, this tragedy is a direct result of your irresponsibility," he began without preamble. "The major left the girl locked up and that is where she is going to stay. I am moving my things here to headquarters, and you will clear yourself out immediately. The girl will be put in The Stocks. You may do it yourself, or I will have it done for you."

Phillip's indrawn breath was audible and his dark eyes smoldered. A tense moment passed before he saluted with the same excess he had given Major Grayson the night before. "Yes sir, colonel sir!" He wheeled for Walker's room, but the ringing footsteps he left behind were voice enough.

In the days ahead, Phillip became a warden, a tailor, a nurse, a cook—everything but a soldier. No one was to go near the girl except him, thus his hours were consumed by his tasks, many of which were diametrically opposed to the colonel's rigid rules.

He saw that Silver had a means to stay clean by hauling buckets of water in the dead of night. He transported fresh dresses from Millie stuffed in his saddlebags, carried fresh fruit and whatever additional delicacies he could secret away inside his pockets, under his hat, or in the leg of his boot. But as a week turned to two, the girl grew more despondent. She lost all appetite and began to pace like a caged animal.

Night and day she paced, and if ever she slept Phillip could not catch her at it. She no longer offered him a sympathetic smile for his efforts or seemed aware of anything save the walls that hemmed her in. Her pattern moved from right front corner to back left, from right rear to left front, then back to the single barred window on the back where she would stare out for only a moment before taking up her path of X's.

After three days she appeared to be in some sort of trance. She would no longer change to fresh clothing, and it became increasingly hard for Phillip to force himself through the ordeal of obtaining it only to see it lie unused and trampled by her relentless feet on the earthen floor. Phillip began to realize that all the tender care in the world wouldn't take the haunted look from her eyes nor put back the pounds she had lost. Only one man could do that, and he was miles away.

Chapter 11

As the power of the Texas Indians declined, so did the number of soldiers stationed at the frontier forts. Walker's present task was to reassure the anxious settlements that withdrawing their remaining troop protection was essential for their future safety—a task he considered half military propaganda since no one could be sure the legions of Palo Duro would not swoop down to inflict a mortal wound in the intervening time. But it was impossible to make final plans for the expedition in September until the number of troops could be determined, the men marshaled in one group, and their ranks brought to some kind of order.

Fort Fisher at Waco was the last stop in his diplomatic tour. Living on the Brazos River, roughly the western edge of civilization, those residents were free from all but occasional Indian troubles, and were more receptive to his encouragement; yet by the close of the last day's meetings, Walker was exhausted from tension and frantic to get back to Nacogdoches. If he had not been under direct orders from President Grant not to travel alone and unprotected, he would have ridden straight through the night: Leaving the girl to face the fort alone was bad enough, but deserting her on the very heels of all that happened was driving him insane with worry. Unless Phillip had the wisdom and courage to disobey his orders, she would have been confined in The Stocks now for almost three weeks. No matter what she had done, she didn't deserve this.

Walker's men were sorely disappointed to find their last few hours in the saloon preempted by an order to be ready to move out in half an hour, even though another night's accommodations for the four of them had already been purchased. Without further explanation, their superior informed them that they would camp along the way if they did not reach the next settlement by midnight.

They left Waco around sunset, but only a few miles out of town the carriage threw a wheel. Walker sent both guards back to town to buy a new wheel while he and the driver, Lieutenant Franklin, set up camp.

Franklin was a nervous sort by nature and not one Walker would have chosen to accompany him had he not been too preoccupied that night to notice his attendants. Franklin jumped at every sigh of wind. Chafing at the delay and irritated at the lieutenant, Walker put on some coffee and sat down before the fire, determined not to be affected by his companion's case of nerves.

He stared at the darkening eastern sky and spoke casually.

"Texas is a big place. I guess I've seen just about all of it the last few years. The cypress swamps, the northern plains, the western desert, the Guadalupe Mountains—"

Franklin jumped up, snapped his rifle out and pulled the trigger back in one movement.

Walker scanned the surrounding darkness, and then gave a purposely bored sigh. "I really don't think there's reason to be nervous, Lieutenant Franklin."

"Nervous?" shrilled Franklin. "I'm not nervous, sir!"

"We're too far south and east, you know."

Franklin stayed crouched. He whispered as though others were listening. "That don't matter. I heard before we left town that Horse Back did some raiding just north of Fort Worth last week. Didn't kill the family but he burned the house and stole the livestock."

Walker leaned back on his elbows and crossed his ankles. "Fort Worth is three hundred and fifty miles from the canyon in Amarillo. That's a long way, even for Horse Back. Anyway, to most people an Indian's an Indian. The raiders were probably stragglers—renegade Kiowas or Apaches. But I'm sure it couldn't have been Horse Back."

Franklin eased the trigger into place and sat down, laying the weapon across his lap. "People don't have much trouble recognizing Horse Back," he contended stubbornly. "I've seen him myself, six months ago when we were scouting the Red River. He's as tall as you are—every bit of six feet four inches. Got a scar on his right cheek, too, but that's not what makes people recognize him. It's something else . . . something about seeing an old man looking like a strapping young warrior—you know, like he's . . . indestructible or something. Do you know how many times he's been reported killed? I heard a tale one time—"

"Here, have some coffee," interrupted Walker. He tried to change the subject. "Where are you going after the campaign in September?"

Franklin relaxed a little and took the cup. "Thanks. I don't plan to sleep much tonight, anyway. Well, I'll go home, see the family. I come from a little town—" Franklin leaped to his feet again, flinging the cup away to bring his rifle up. "There's something out there, Major, I know it!"

This time Walker had been so startled by Franklin's movement that he had bolted upright. His patience at an end, he stood up and ordered sharply, "Soldier, get hold of yourself."

Franklin's fingers tapped up and down on the rifle stock. "I'm in control, sir. But I know—"

Franklin's sentence broke off. Walker looked at him, first surprised then bemused at the comical expression frozen on the lieutenant's face: His eyes were round, the whites showing; his lips were still shaped over an unspoken word. Walker was about to offer a gentle jibe when the lieutenant's stiffened body began to tilt slowly, like a tree severed at its base. Then as his angle increased so did his rate of fall, until Franklin crashed face first at Walker's feet, an arrow protruding from the center of his back.

It seemed that the war cries broke out the minute Franklin struck the dirt, then they were all over Walker: naked bodies painted with black stripes, a great eyeball, a snake coiled to strike. He was thrown on his belly, his right cheek crunched against pebbled earth as a knee pressed into the back of his neck. Fingernails raked up his forehead, twisted into the hair above, and in the firelight he saw the glint of a blade, watched in stunned horror as it moved closer. Then the touch of cold steel against his hairline—

Suddenly there were more cries from the darkness, and the fingers loosened, the blade flicked out of sight, and finally the knee in his neck was gone.

A dazed moment crawled by when he understood nothing but that one more second had ticked past and he was not dead. He could see legs and arms swinging in silhouette against the fire as bodies scrambled away from him; he heard guttural voices scattering into the darkness, and, once, a scream that was silenced abruptly. And then for a moment it was very quiet and he heard only the crackle of the fire. He lay still and rested.

Gradually it came to him that his men must have returned just in the nick of time. There was blood in his mouth, gravel on his face, and a hideous pain in his neck. And where were his men? Was there anybody there at all?

With a groan, he got his hands under his chest. But before he could push himself up, two feet took up a stance on the ground just in front of him. And now he understood that it was not his meager command of soldiers who had saved him. For a befuddled moment he could only blink at the new set of moccasins in the dust.

Pain wracked his body but after a prolonged effort, he was standing on his feet. He tottered from side to side several times, but doggedly refused to fall.

At last his vision began to clear and his gaze moved up over a hard flat belly, a muscle-knotted chest, and finally a pair of dark eyes level with his own.

The Indian's time-ravaged face was inscrutable, its deep etching somehow at odds with his straight carriage and wide, unbent shoulders. And there was the scar on the right cheek—just where he knew it would be.

Holding the dark gaze, Walker spoke only one word—

the one that kept rolling around in his head like thunder.

"Why?"

The man wore no elaborate headdress, only a special scalp lock that designated his rank, and a loin cloth.

Walker said it again, louder, more demanding. *"Why?"*

Chief Horse Back's eyes narrowed and after a long moment, his piercing scrutiny gave way to a look of contempt.

"I do not know, *tivo*. Ask your God."

Their gazes stayed locked, each probing and measuring the other. Then a brave in the background muttered something in Comanche. With a final stare, Horse Back turned away, spluttered a quick command, and they were gone, glistening backs melting into darkness.

Walker never knew how long he stood there, only that shortly after he sat down he heard someone else approaching and knew that it was his own men.

The guards pulled up and dismounted, and behind them was a wagon driven by the smithy who brought the new wheel.

"My God!" cried one of the men, running toward Walker, who was trying to stand up again. Then looking aside, the man whispered, "Franklin."

"He hasn't moved," Walker said. "He's dead." Then his thoughts began to stick together, to settle eagerly into the habit of command.

"If you're up to it after fixing the wagon, I'd like to take the body back to Waco to be prepared for burial," he said shakily. "I'll send someone later and we'll ship it to his family. The smithy will need an escort anyway. Then we're pulling out again. Tonight."

After the wheel was mounted, the arrow was removed from Franklin and his body loaded in the smithy's wagon.

"Was it Comanches, sir?" asked Walker's man, holding open the carriage door for him.

The smithy spoke up. "That was no Comanche arrow. It was Tonkawa."

Walker looked at each of them. "Comanches don't range this far south."

"Well, I guess it's a good thing we came back and scared them off. I just wish we'd been in time to save poor Franklin."

Walker said nothing but clasped his forearm over his bruised rib cage and climbed inside the carriage.

As they turned back west toward Fort Fisher, the carriage swayed hypnotically as Walker stared out the window. Was Horse Back still out there somewhere, watching them? The carriage rocked gently but Walker's body tensed; his left fist folded under his chin as he peered into the inky blackness. What was Horse Back doing so far south? What moved the chief to save a white man — and of all white men, the one sworn to kill him? Would Walker Grayson report the incident to those old Indian fighters Miles and Mackenzie — and would it make any difference, come September?

A voice inside his head answered: I do not know, *tivo*. Ask your God.

Tension at the fort in Nacogdoches was running high under Colonel Appleby's control. He lacked Walker's easy grace of command and tried to inspire obedience with fear. His voice bore a natural gruffness; his soul contained not one iota of patience, and because he was continually goaded to ever higher planes of lordship by his ambitious spouse, his own wire-thin nerves readily transferred to others. Thus Silver Dawn was not the only one who prayed for Walker's return.

On Monday of the third week of Walker's absence, Phillip left his duties and rode into town to send a secret telegram to Waco: *Major Grayson, emergency situation, please return posthaste, Phillip Martin*. A few hours later a reply arrived in the main office. It was received by a furious Colonel Appleby.

Phillip was summoned.

"Aide-de-Camp Martin, may I inquire why you were sending a wire to Major Grayson without my knowledge?"

"You may inquire, sir, but I cannot divulge that information. It's of a personal nature."

The colonel bristled visibly. "As you well know, Major General Grayson is a busy man at this historic moment. I am responsible for the order of this fort at the present, so from now on I advise you not to go behind my back about any matters whatsoever. Is that clear, young man?"

Phillip eyed the telegram in Appleby's hand. "Is . . . that for me?"

Appleby wadded the paper and tossed it in the trash with a flourish. "It says Major Grayson has already left Waco," he snapped. "Now, I believe you have guard duties over a certain savage?"

But Phillip left with a wide grin. Enjoy, old boy. Your hours on the throne are numbered.

Every minute he was not trying to persuade the girl to eat or bathe, Phillip watched the road for Walker's carriage. Silver's condition had deteriorated. Her face was gaunt, her eyes hollow, her supple flesh wasting to stringy muscles and sharp bones. With no sunshine, her skin had faded somewhat, though it was still very dark.

Milly had thought it best not to give her any more of the new dresses for fear she would find some method of slashing them. That day she had managed to slip away from her disapproving husband and coax Silver into a bath and change of clothing. Giving the girl the same high-necked gray muslin she had lent her before, Milly hurried back to her place to repair and clean the other one. Later in the day she was able to get the girl to sit on the cot while she brushed the matted tangles from her hair.

When Milly surveyed her work at last, she sighed. There was great improvement in appearance, she supposed. But she sensed the girl's life force fading like flower under the sun, a much more alarming situation than that everlasting pacing, which occurred now only at early morning and late evening.

"This is worse," she told Phillip. "Restlessness means a strong desire to move, to be free. But this apathy. I . . . I think she wants to die."

Phillip gestured helplessly. "I've told her Walker's coming any day now. In fact, I can tell her for sure that he's already on his way. But if that doesn't help, I just don't know what else to do."

Milly raised her eyes. "She won't believe you. I don't think she would believe anything any of us told her."

After Milly had gone, Phillip stepped inside the cell. Silver was sitting on the cot, and he went to squat in front of her, showing her the bread and cheese he had brought.

"Do you think you could eat some of this?"

She nodded listlessly. He spread a napkin on her lap, sliced some cheese over the bread and handed it to her. Her hand trembled as she took it, and he saw her grimace as though the sight of food made her ill. But she took a slow bite and chewed.

"Don't hate him, Silver. I know it seems like he's been insensitive, but the opposite is true. It's just that his job is causing him a lot of pressure just now. *Suava-ti?*"

Silver looked at him. "One cannot hate one's own flesh, and we are one."

Phillip's jaw dropped and after a moment he tried to cover his shock by standing up.

"Look, I know you don't understand why he seems to have deserted you. But I have reason to believe he'll be back very, very soon. He'll straighten things out for sure. He . . . he cares very much what happens to you."

Her eyes rolled up solemnly. "Me know where Walker go."

"You do?"

Silver blinked several times, then turned to look at the wall. "It Walker's right to take many wives."

Phillip looked at her with pity yet her suspicions would come true soon enough.

He said jokingly, "Er . . . just how many wives are we talking about here?"

She faced him, surprised at his ignorance. "As many as he wants. He is a man."

As misfortune would have it, Walker stopped at the main office first, and Phillip missed his arrival because he was with Silver.

Being queen, Mrs. Appleby had established herself along with her husband in the right wing officers' quarters, and being next in command, Mrs. and Colonel Bigby had moved their things into the middle rooms. Both matrons were about to embark for town to do a little shopping when the door was opened for Major General Grayson. Glancing at each other with grim satisfaction, the two ladies resumed their seats beside the desk, while Colonel Appleby came to his feet and saluted.

"Major General, sir! Good to have you back," said Appleby with feeling.

Puzzled at the unusually warm reception, Walker grasped Appleby's extended hand. Then he pulled off his gloves and tossed them on the desk.

"I suppose everything has gone smoothly."

A condescending gleam came to the colonel's eyes. "No, Major Grayson," he said, pausing to watch the effect of his words. "I regret to say that there has been a terrible, *terrible* tragedy."

Walker paled. "Where is the girl? *Where is she?*" He leaned across the desk, hand darting toward the colonel's shirt front before he caught himself. When he had resumed a regid stance, he spoke with heavy meaning. "I trust the *white* woman I left in your care has not come to harm."

Colonel Appleby allowed himself a smug smile. "No, Major, the girl has not come to harm." His smile faded. "But a far greater trouble has befallen us. She has caused the death of two soldiers in your absence." He waited while Walker's face changed again, then suggested, "Perhaps you should sit down to hear the details."

Phillip was just locking the cell door when he heard voices behind him. Looking up, he saw a storm coming toward him. Walker was leading the pack, Colonel Appleby trotted behind him gesturing and shouting, and the matrons brought up the tail, waddling to keep up. Walker's expression appeared to be one of rage, and Phillip glared at the trio he knew must have already laid a web of lies.

Walker stopped sharply in front of him. "Open the door."

Phillip fumbled with the lock while Appleby continued his rant. "Ingratitude! It's an insufferable trait, especially in the heathen. You'd think she'd be grateful you took her out of sin and depravity, but no. She sneers. Defies respectable women!"

"That's why God Almighty has taken their land from them and given it to us!" Mrs. Appleby burst out, unable to hold back any longer. "Sodom and Gomorrah were destroyed for their heathen practices, and that girl is heathen no matter the color of her skin. She has chosen by her deeds to be one! My husband did the only thing he could."

"Try the other key," said Walker.

Phillip's trembling fingers wrestled up the next one and poked it at the hole, though he thought the first one was right.

"Please, Major Grayson," cried Mrs. Bigby. "Won't you answer us? Surely you don't mean to release her after everything she's done."

Phillip glanced up and for the first time saw the tight lines around Walker's mouth, the aura of barely restrained fury. Phillip looked away to hide a victorious grin; his hand relaxed, found the right key, and tripped the lock.

Walker threw back the door and rushed inside. Silver was huddled in the corner on the floor. Smothering an expletive, he hurried forward to lift her in his arms. The others fell back as he swept past them out the door and headed for the main building.

"He's going toward your office!" shrilled Mrs. Appleby, falling in behind them. Colonel Appleby said nothing as he turned to follow.

Walker outstripped them so far he had to wait for Phillip to catch up, then unlocked the main entrance. Inside, he paused only long enough to order, "Bolt the door."

As Walker disappeared through the exit that led to his quarters, Phillip strolled leisurely to the desk and sat down to assess the competency of his former administrator. If he read the major's mood right, such information would be very useful in the near future.

Silver lay trembling as the fearful bed gathered around her, but she dared not protest for she knew her dreadful deeds would have been told to her husband. Walker left her once and returned shortly to stand over her, his leathery brown face as lined as a map.

"I've got some matters I must attend right now, but I want it understood that you are not to move from that bed. Phillip is in the front office. All you have to do is call." His tone was the same one he would have used to a group of disorderly soldiers. When her eyes clouded with fear, he felt sick at his stomach. He preferred to crush her to his breast, to pet and hold her, stroke her cheek and tell her . . . But, he remembered bitterly, it had been clearly demonstrated he could not trust himself to stop there. He said more gently, "There's nothing for you to be afraid of. I'm here now and I won't leave you again."

After looking deeply into her eyes, he turned and left.

For the next few days, Silver lay in the big bed, which did not swallow her up after all. She could not understand why she was not being punished. Instead, a tray was fitted over her lap. On it was a plate heaped with steaming potatoes, thick slices of buttered bread, hot chicken browned over an open spit. The next morning, it was fried ham and eggs, grits floating in a pool of butter, a big crusty sweet roll drizzled with honey. Silver ate happily: Walker had come back—more sun-browned, more golden-haired, more handsome. Everyone at the fort would know now that she was not a slave. She was wife of the Big Chief.

Walker came at least twice a day, though he seemed uncomfortable and did not stay too long. Other times it was Milly or Phillip, but no one else. Silver could almost believe that only the four of them lived there.

Sometimes Milly read to her, and Silver listened avidly. There was an odd familiarity in some of the stories: the ugly baby duck that turned to a beautiful white bird; the silly short stories whose rhythm she seemed to know by heart, like the one about the cow that jumped over the moon. Unable to account for the way they comforted her, she decided that her people's stories and those of white eyes must not be so very different.

Horse Back had often bragged about his daughter's sharp mind, and once she had made it up, Silver began to master the perplexing use of pronouns. But other lessons were harder. Quohadie Teichas expected their women to work hard, but white men didn't feel that way. She watched in silent wonder as Walker moved about the room, tucking the cover about her feet though they were not cold, plumping her pillow until it bent her neck. Wisely, she waited until he had gone to put things back as they were, though it was hard to keep a smile when her neck was breaking and her feet sweating.

But she was learning. One word of complaint—one move to fix things herself—brought a menacing frown to her husband's face. If she failed to clean her plate, if she tried to get out of bed, if she reached for the hairbrush Milly had left her, he growled, "I'll do that!" In Silver's lifetime there had always been war, never enough food. No Quohadie Teichas had time to dote on a wife. Relationships between the sexes were simple and concrete. When the men were not making war or getting food, they smoked and sat in council. At night they bedded their women. Women worked from dawn to dusk, for all other duties were theirs. At night they lay with their husbands.

White eyes had so many rules that she would never learn them all!

She had been taught that a wife should be obedient. Yet when she tried to imitate Walker's slaves by saying "yes sir," he was not pleased at all. He had leaped from the side of the bed. "My name is Walker," he told her stiffly.

He said that she must get well and strong, yet if he found her out of the bed, he grabbed her up and put her back. She gloried in his touch and pressed close to him; but he only put her down more quickly and would not come near her again for a long while. She worried about that. Walker had not gone to marry the second wife as she thought or he would have brought the woman back with him. But she was out there somewhere, waiting for him.

Shortly after installing Silver in his room on the day of his return, Walker had gathered everything belonging to the Applebys and Bigbys and dumped them unceremoniously on the porch in front of an amused crowd. Afterward he sent a full report to Washington with a recommendation that both officers be passed over for promotion the coming January. In spite of his fury at Appleby's mishandling of the situation, he found the task unpleasant, for both men were too old to be offered many more upward moves before retirement.

Three days had passed, yet if there was quiet at the fort, it was the kind that heralds a storm. Initial fear had subsided into seething unrest. Walker knew the vengeful rumors being spread by the ousted colonels would undermine his authority as he continued to protect the girl. One story had it that the tall, leggy soldier who had been executed was Silver's rejected lover. Others said the soldier, and the half-wit brother who was trambled to death by his own horse, had seen the girl somewhere else, lusted for her, and followed her to Nacogdoches.

This morning Walker had ordered an inspection—a good reminder that the army forged ever ahead with its task of defending U.S. citizens. When he went back to the office, he did not look in on Silver but finished up the last of the late reports.

The front door was left open now, for the main office

was strictly avoided by all, and Phillip strode inside with another sheaf of papers in his hand. "Don't close up shop yet, here's another report. It's marked urgent."

Walker took the papers. "It's a report on the battle at Adobe Walls.* Have you read it?"

"Yes. It was a disaster for the Indians. According to one of the buffalo hunters, there were about a hundred warriors lead by Horse Back. They had enough muscle, too — Sata Tejas, Tabbe Nanica, White Horse, White Antelope, Yellow Bear, He Bear, and that young hothead Quannah Parker. I guess they meant to stop the slaughter of buffalo for good."

Walker scanned quickly through the document — written by a Tom Addington — noting times, places, numbers. "Twenty-five whites held off a hundred Comanches. That's a switch."

"Well, it seems someone woke early, went to the well, and caught sight of an Indian. He gave the alarm and the gates were closed. Two white men were caught outside, killed and scalped. With the whites bottled up inside the stockade with an arsenal of six-shooters and rifles . . . I guess bows and spears just weren't enough. And the Indians had no cover at all. Addington says the Comanches tried to knock the gate down by backing their horses into it."

Walker began to read. *In all my ranger days I never saw Indians fight like that. They were like demons. White Antelope and He Bear fell dead inside while being lifted over the top of the stockade. Horse Back had three horses shot from under him, but he kept coming again . . . I think he got away unharmed. Quannah Parker was badly wounded, perhaps he is dead. It was the bravest, most foolhardy fighting I've ever seen. I could not participate in cutting off the heads of seventeen such brave men and sticking them on top of the pickets . . . we heard the Comanche Death Song all night —* Walker stood up, threw the papers down, and went to the window.

* Adobe Walls was a trading post where buffalo hunters could sell hides.

179

'Are you okay?"

There was a pause before Walker answered. "I'm all right. I saw Horse Back."

"You *what?* When!"

Walker did not turn. "The night we left Waco. We were attacked by Tonkawas. One of the guards was killed—Franklin—did you know him?"

"Heard of him. But what kept them from murdering the lot of you?"

"Not what. Who."

"Are you saying . . . you mean Horse Back saved your skin against Tonkawas? The Tonkawas ride scout for us, they—"

"Are traitors to their brothers," finished Walker, turning to meet Phillip's gaze briefly, "and nothing is too low for a traitor." He went back to his desk and sat down.

"Have you told anybody about this?"

"I've sent a letter to Mackenzie, though I don't expect him to believe it."

"I do. I've heard about Horse Back doing a lot of strange things. There's a story that says he saved General Sherman's neck one night, too. Warned him about an ambush by Kiowas."

Walker was looking up at him intently. "How would you like to go home?"

Phillip was surprised. "For how long?"

"From now till September, when the campaign at Palo Duro starts."

Phillip began to grin. "Oh, I think I could stand it. Why?"

"I'm taking a leave. Going back to Louisiana to look for the girl's parents."

"So," said Phillip slowly, "that means you'll be taking her with you."

"Well? She can't stay here," Walker snapped. Then the idea of leaving the fort suddenly lifted his spirits. His eyes sparkled. "Perhaps you would rather I sent her with you."

Phillip glared. "I'm not afraid to be responsible for her if that's what you're insinuating. The fact is we get along

180

fine. *Real* fine."

Walker was still amused. "I see. Is that why she gave you the slip the first minute your back was turned?"

"Well, at least I didn't desert her like . . . Look, let's drop this. When are you leaving?"

"Tomorrow." Walker's eyes narrowed. "So. You two got to know each other real well in my absence. Did you . . . talk a lot?"

"I talked, she . . . Why don't we just drop it."

"It seems you've taken a real liking to the girl." Walker's brows lowered a notch. "In fact, now that I think about it, you took her side from the start, disagreed with everything I tried to do for her."

Phillip held his gaze. "So what? Why should that concern you? After all, you only want to find her real parents. Remember?"

A muscle ticked along Walker's jaw. "That's right. The girl's got a right to know her own folks."

For a long moment their eyes clashed. Then Phillip's dark ones lit mischievously. "By the way, what do you hear from Camelia lately?"

Walker sat forward. "Will you get out of here?"

"Okay," Phillip said, grinning when his back was turned.

At the door he looked back at Walker with exaggerated sincerity. "Since you could use a few pointers, you might try plain old kindness. She responds real well to that. And why don't you try to think of her as Silver. It's much more personal than The Girl."

Walker lunged from his chair with a heavy book in his hand, and Phillip rushed outside, dodging behind the wall to wait only a moment before sticking his head back inside.

"While you're at it, why don't you pick her some flowers? She responds to that, too." He ducked out of sight, hooting loudly.

Since his return, Walker had ordered Phillip to stay in the main office building with Silver while he slept in one of the barracks to try to ease tension; however, now that he would be leaving the gossipmongers, he had decided to move his things into the room which had been meant for Silver, adjacent to his own, which she now used. He was not convinced everything Phillip said was in jest, and it was surely no worse for tongues to be wagging over his aide's personal involvement with the captive than his own.

Walker took Milly to town with him to finish out Silver's wardrobe. They picked out a suede riding skirt, a cream-colored, high-neck blouse, some unmentionables that Milly did not show him, and lastly, a pair of high-topped moccasins—boots really, but soft and flexible. Perhaps if the vixen would not wear "white man's shoes," he would be able to coax her into these. They picked out a low-topped pair for her to wear under her dresses.

Pleased with his purchases, Walker knocked on the door to his room about dusk, and when a small voice beckoned him inside, he spread the whole pile of clothes across the foot of the bed, announcing, "We're going to take a trip. It's time for you to get up and try your strength."

Silver's eyes widened. "Where we going?"

"To my home, in Louisiana. Here, I'll help you stand."

He threw back the covers and stared. She wore a thin, thigh-length gown, obviously one of Milly's, and it was plastered against her breasts, her dark nipples peering at him like two eyes, her navel making a third. Walker found it difficult to breathe, impossible to remove his eyes.

Silver saw his half-lidded look. "I cannot stand. My legs shake."

Walker replied slowly, "I'll help you." But he did not move. Silver pulled a long leg over the side of the bed, pushed up on one arm, and sat waiting for assistance.

Walker came to himself. "Oh. Here, I'll just . . . " She did not need to be told and looped the right one snugly over the top of his shoulder. He trembled as he lifted her to a standing position, and it was not her weight that affected him. "Can you stand alone?" he asked hoarsely.

182

"I will try . . . "

He let her go but she tottered dangerously. With a frightened gasp, he stepped forward and grabbed her to him. "Careful! You'll fall and—" She had turned somehow until she was in his arms, two soft tantalizingly spheres pressing into his chest, her arms hooked tightly over his neck. He could hear his shallow rasping as he stared at the soft pucker of her mouth.

"T-that's good, now. Just hold still a moment," he panted.

"Umm, yes . . . very good." Her mouth came closer, swollen and moist, lips parted.

Walker put her away from him. "I-I think you can manage alone now."

She did, though she stood somewhat stiffly, her previously soft mouth now clamped and unyielding. "Yes, I can do," she said through her teeth.

"Silver, we need to talk. Sit down."

She looked at him. "You say to stand."

"I know, but sit down."

She eased onto the edge of the bed. Walker stepped back. His palms were sweating. Wiping them on his thighs, he pulled a chair from the wall and sat down facing her. The lamplight shimmered on her hair, darkened the bow of her mouth, made her eyes like crystals. He took a deep breath.

"I checked the families of Indian captives and there are three dates of capture that match your age. One of the families was from Louisiana, the other two I cannot locate."

Her face was closed.

He got up and began to pace, keeping his eyes trained on the floor. "It won't be a hard trip. We'll travel by stagecoach and stay at respectable hotels along the way." He stopped to peer at her but couldn't get past the gray flint in her eyes.

"Your Camelia at this Louse-ana?"

Walker looked at her at moment. "How . . . did you know about Camelia?"

"I know."

He fixed his boots to the floor, willing himself not to be affected by those limpid gray eyes. She had to understand, once and for all.

"No, she lives many miles from there, in Georgia. But we will be married in October. White eyes count the faces of the moons in months. That's about three times for the moon to be full."

Silver died quietly inside. After a moment, she held up her bare feet and looked at her toes, wiggling them.

"Feet of squaw like rock, from walking, walking. White eyes woman have good hard feet?"

Walker looked at the small, shapely toes, the delicate arch.

"No, I don't think they do," he answered distantly. His eyes came up to meet hers briefly, then he cleared his throat and finished in a different tone. "Which is what I want to talk to you about."

"My feet?"

"Yes," he said, looking down again. "No. No, I'm not talking about your . . . " He swallowed. "I'm going to marry Camelia. Look at me, Silver, and listen to what I'm saying. There can be no more lovemaking between us. Lovemaking is a word for what we did on the way to the fort." He couldn't bring himself to mention the incident after the ball in the same light. "I told you it wouldn't happen again and I broke that promise. But I'm making it again." He gazed hard into her eyes. "Do you understand what I'm saying?"

She lifted her legs slowly onto the bed, tucked them under the cover, and lay back looking at him.

"Yes, Walker."

Walker turned toward the window. "So, we'll pack up tomorrow and leave this hellhole the day after that. You'll be safe there with my family, and perhaps we'll find some of your white people."

"Yes, Walker."

The quiet answer was somehow like a knife in his back. He turned and left without glancing at the bed.

Part 2

This is the forest primeval. The murmuring pines and
    the hemlocks,
Bearded with moss, and in garments green, indistinct
    in the twilight,
  Stand like druids of eld, with voices sad and pro-
    phetic,
Stand like harpers hoar, with beards that rest on their
    busoms . . .

            Longfellow—

Chapter 12

Everyone at the fort must surely know by now that Silver Dawn was no longer a slave but the First Wife of Walker Grayson. Together as man and wife they were making a journey to meet his family, which would now be hers. Even the old hags who hated her must know this.

Yet long before dawn, when the sky was still black, they climbed in the carriage Phillip had waiting to drive them to the stage depot. Walker looked anxiously around as he helped her inside as though he wanted to hurry before anyone saw them. Her face like a stone mask, Silver allowed herself to be assisted into the dark coach. Walker then announced that he would ride up front with Phillip—to give him some last minute instructions, he said. Then the door shut her in darkness and the carriage lurched away while Silver squirmed to find a comfortable position in her new dress.

She would play his games for now, though she felt she was in a stranger's body wearing this high-necked pink dress with long sleeves, fitted waist, a skirt that draped in the front then drew up over a thing called a "bustle" which rode, like a small tumbleweed, on her backside—yes, all this she would endure for her husband. She could not make demands yet. Only after she was with child could she begin to assert her rights. Then she would show him that he could not hide her away—like the result of some momentary madness. He had married a Quohadie Teichas, and he would be wise to get used to the idea very soon.

They said good-bye to Phillip when the stage arrived. Walker once again assisted Silver inside the coach and her

187

hand tingled when he held it. But the contact only lasted the briefest moment before he had seated himself on the opposite bench.

"Better try to get some rest," he advised, crossing his legs then his arms, and pulling his hat down over his eyes.

Rest? On top of her head sat a large headdress with a pink plume and ribbons that tied under her chin. Curly cloth scratched at her neck. She could scarcely breathe in the tight wrapping Milly had laced about her. How could one rest if a tumbleweed sat upon one's back?

"Quohadie Teichas do not wear baskets on their backs," she said sharply.

He tipped the brim of his hat up. "Pardon?"

She jabbed the bustle with her right elbow. "Quohadie Teichas carry basket with hands or on head. When it rides on back, one cannot sit."

There was a flash of white teeth from the shadows.

"The bustle was Milly's idea. But I quite agree that it's a ridiculous thing to wear. You may leave it off tomorrow." He pulled his hat back down.

Silver clamped her teeth together and glared at his dim shape for a long time, but he seemed to sleep. Eventually she grew weary and leaned back, crushing the bustle and not caring. She dozed, and when she woke again there were rays of sun slanting through the windows.

She sat up and looked about until she found the reticule Milly had purchased for her. It was to carry her things, but it contained nothing, for she owned nothing. She tossed it aside and stared at her husband, feeling somewhat mollified that at least he was the most handsome man she'd ever seen. He wore a gray three-piece suit, matching hat, fine leather boots of a charcoal color. Above the vest, his white shirt was almost as frilly as her dress, with rows of tiny pleats that set off the charcoal string tie at his neck. He was slouched low in the seat, and her eyes slid along his flat stomach, over the soft mound of his manhood, down the muscular arch of his thighs.

Suddenly her eyes grew fixed at what she saw. They were together on the ground, their limbs entwined, their bodies writhing to a primeval rhythm. His mouth was locked to hers—searing it, draining it, leaving it empty and yawning until he filled it again. She remembered all the exhilarating, terrifying sensations of his mouth nipping and sucking the ruddy peaks of her breasts, of the fire that spiraled through her loins, convulsing her body like a birth pain. His hands clamped her hips, pressed her belly against the rock-hard ridge that swelled with wanting her . . .

She sat back with a gasp, then coughed to disguise the sound. She was trembling with desire. It was all she could do not to rip away her clothes and straddle him just as he sat!

Walker pushed his hat back and sat up, and Silver almost jumped off the seat.

"What's the matter?" he demanded. "Your face looks funny. The ride isn't making you sick, is it?"

"I-I am hot in this dress. I do not like it."

"You'll get used to it." He looked out the window. "We'll be changing stage lines soon. By mid-afternoon we'll stop and get a room . . . I mean *two* rooms, of course."

Walker leaned back and let his gaze roam over her. She looked stunning. Her hair was done up on top of her head, and the new bonnet sat at a perky angle. For a moment the vast gulf between them did not exist.

Neither did Camelia.

He shifted on the seat. "I think we'll go out this evening, find a good place to eat—if you'll promise to wear that dress. Without the bustle, of course."

Silver looked at her lap. "You like this dress?"

She got no answer at first but felt his eyes fastened on her face. Her ears grew warm.

"I like it very much. It makes your skin dark, lightens the silver in your hair."

Silver looked at him sideways. "Camelia's skin is white. You like Camelia's skin?"

Walker yanked his hat back down. "Why don't you try to get some more rest?"

With a hand beneath her elbow, Walker guided her

189

through the lobby of the best hotel in town. It made Silver nervous that the passing men turned backward so they could keep looking at her, and Walker must have noticed too; when they reached the lobby desk, he was wearing his fiercest face.

The clerk swept a trained eye over them.

"Sir, may I suggest suite twelve. It's our very finest, one we usually reserve for newlyweds, but for you and the missus we could—"

"We need *two* rooms," said Walker flatly.

The clerk blushed. "Forgive me, sir. The young lady is your sister?"

"Yes." Walker laid two bills on the desk, snatched up their baggage quickly, and led them up a stairway.

The room was beautiful. The sheer white panels on the windows were flanked by green chintz drapes and allowed the late sun to wash thorough. In one corner sat a white wicker chaise with cushions of the same green print. The canopied four-poster was done in matching fabric. A plush ivory rug was thrown over waxed pine floors.

"There should be a bathing chamber through that door to the left which connects our rooms," said Walker. "Just let me know when you want to bathe and I'll call for your water." Taking his own bag from the hallway, he went to the connecting door and opened it. Inside the chamber was a large white tub that stood on four feet shaped like a mountain lion's paws. Silver was impressed.

"I will bathe when the water is brought," she said.

Only a faint amber glow lit the windows when the maid finished filling the tub and deftly loosened the long row of tiny buttons on the back of Silver's dress. When the girl was gone, Silver laid the items from her suitcase on the bed. She wanted to keep hating the white eyes clothes, but she couldn't despise anything as lovely as the soft fragile garments Milly had packed. Milly said white eyes women put this luxury *beneath* their clothes where it could not be seen. Which seemed a terrible waste. Quohadie Teichas women would have even traded horses for such finery—

and they would not have worn it where no one could admire it.

Smiling, Silver realized that if these things were hers to keep, then she was a very rich squaw.

After stripping gleefully to her bare skin, she put on a misty white garment that hung to the floor but was almost invisible. She admired her figure through its gauzy layers before stepping into the bathing chamber.

The tub was filled with steamy water and frothy bubbles. She eased into it, sighing deliciously. Leaning her head on the rim, she glanced at the closed door to her left and wondered what Walker was doing behind it.

"Walker?" she called softly. Then again: "Walker?"

The door opened a crack but she couldn't see him. "What is it?" he called sharply.

"I like this tub."

There was a moment of silence, then one mumbled word: "Good."

"I do not have . . . what you call it . . . 'soap.' "

"It should be there somewhere."

"It is on table, but I cannot reach it."

The door opened far enough to admit a hand, which groped on the washstand until it closed around the soap. She waited as the door opened slowly wider.

Walker stood very still, and Silver's body caught fire at the way he was looking at her. They said nothing for a moment, then he moved a step closer.

"Here's the soap." He leaned forward, his eyes fixed on the dewy cleavage peeping above the water. Silver reached for the bar, deliberately raising her arm until she felt a nipple rise above the water's surface. Never moving her eyes from his face, she slid slowly back down. Her voice was soft and husky. "Thank you."

Walker ran the tip of his tongue over his lips. "You're welcome," he said hoarsely. As he stepped back to pull the door together, his eyes stayed glued to her chest until the moment the door closed.

Grinning, Silver finished her bath with plenty of splashing sounds to remind her husband of what he so foolishly denied himself.

She dressed again carefully. Her hair was somewhat damp in the back, and she hoped it would not all fall down because she would not know how to get it back up. Leaving off both the corset and the bustle, she put the garter belt around her waist and pulled on the hose. Next, she opened the case of trinkets that she and Milly hadn't the time to put on, but she did not know for sure how the silver loops fit onto her ears and she could not get the matching neckpiece over her head. Walker would know how.

She stepped into the dress and pulled it up over her bare breasts. Once her arms were in the sleeves, though, she found it impossible to reach the buttons in the back. Since white eyes were rich, all the women must have helpers to dress.

"Walker?"

She heard him come through the bathing chamber. "Pleased to come help," she called.

"Are you dressed?"

"Yes."

He came inside, his eyes going over her again.

"This dress cannot do, please."

He hesitated before he came to her and turned her around.

Walker stared at her bare back, his gaze moving slowly down to where skin peeped through the lacy garter belt slung low on her hips.

"White eyes women wear . . . other things. Under their clothes," he pointed out crossly. "I thought Milly got everything you needed."

"That is so, but you said I did not have to wear it."

Unable to deny that, Walker started at the neck, hooking the pink satin loops over the tiny pearl buttons, but after a very long minute, he stopped. "This is ridiculous. There must be a hundred of these damn things!"

"You bought it," she said softly.

Walker scowled at the back of her head. "Your English has improved. You sound like a white eyes woman with a

——— FREE ———
B O O K C E R T I F I C A T E

ZEBRA HOME SUBSCRIPTION SERVICE, INC.

YES! Please start my subscription to Zebra Historical Romances and send me my free Zebra Novel along with my first month's Romances. I understand that I may preview these four new Zebra Historical Romances Free for 10 days. If I'm not satisfied with them I may return the four books within 10 days and owe nothing. Otherwise I will pay just $3.50 each; a total of $14.00 (a $15.80 value—I save $1.80). Then each month I will receive the 4 newest titles as soon as they come off the press for the same 10 day Free preview and low price. I may return any shipment and I may cancel this arrangement at any time. There is no minimum number of books to buy and there are no shipping, handling or postage charges. Regardless of what I do, the **FREE** book is mine to keep.

Name _____

  (Please Print)

Address _____ Apt. # _____

City _____ State _____ Zip _____

Telephone ( ) _____

Signature _____

  (if under 18, parent or guardian must sign)

Terms and offer subject to change without notice.

6-89

ACCEPT YOUR FREE GIFT
AND EXPERIENCE MORE OF
THE PASSION AND ADVENTURE
YOU LIKE IN A
HISTORICAL ROMANCE

Zebra Romances are the finest novels of their kind and are written with the adult woman in mind. All of our books are written by authors who really know how to weave tales of romantic adventure in the historical settings you love.

Because our readers tell us these books sell out very fast in the stores, Zebra has made arrangements for you to receive at home the four newest titles published each month. You'll never miss a title and home delivery is so convenient. With your first shipment we'll even send you a FREE Zebra Historical Romance as our gift just for trying our home subscription service. No obligation.

BIG SAVINGS
AND **FREE** HOME DELIVERY

Each month, the Zebra Home Subscription Service will send you the four newest titles as soon as they are published. (We ship these books to our subscribers even before we send them to the stores.) You may preview them *Free* for 10 days. If you like them as much as we think you will, you'll pay just $3.50 each and save $1.80 each month off the cover price. *AND you'll also get FREE HOME DELIVERY.* There is never a charge for shipping, handling or postage and there is no minimum you must buy. If you decide not to keep any shipment, simply return it within 10 days, no questions asked, and owe nothing.

sharp tongue. We call them *nags*."

"Heap no good *horses?*" she spluttered.

He gave the dress a yank. "Close enough. Now relax your shoulders. The dress won't come together."

Twenty, twenty-one, twenty-two . . . He stopped again at the small of her back.

"Listen, don't wear this bloody dress again, do you hear me? How did you get out of it in the first place?" he demanded suspiciously.

"The girl who brought the water helped."

He bent again, squinting at the pea-sized buttons. "Well, just call her next time. This is . . . too hard."

With a huge sigh, he stood back. "There, it's done. But next time we call the maid." He turned her around. "Are you hungry?"

Her eyes lifted to his as she held out the jewelry case. "I want to wear these."

Walker's shoulders slumped. "Can't *you* put them on?" She shook her head.

Since she was facing him, he looped the silver beads around the back of her neck and began to fumble with the clasp in front. His knuckles brushed her breasts.

Suddenly he snatched the necklace away and tossed it on the bed. "Just leave it off. Finish up and call me when you're through!"

He marched out and shut the door loudly.

Silver slipped her pride and joy, the soft white suede moccasins, on her feet, then donned her hat and tied the ribbon, standing back to look at herself in the mirror.

Then slowly she turned toward the bed where the delicate white lace things lay scattered. It was sure enough terrible to have such riches and not use them.

She walked over and picked up the one Milly had called a "brassiere." It was a new invention to support the breasts, Milly said, so that one did not have to wear a corset. According to Milly, not many white eyes had them, and she should be happy that Walker was a generous man.

Silver fingered the intricate lace, remembering the way

193

it had looked on her, with her breasts showing through the lace.

Just as Milly had instructed, she put it around her waist with the snap in front until she had fastened the hook. Then, twisting it around, she pulled it up over her dress, put her arms through, and went to the mirror.

The pink satin peeping through the white lace was not the same as bare breasts, yet it was certainly pretty. Much better than hiding the garment away altogether.

She was lost in admiring herself when Walker queried through the door. "Aren't you ready yet?"

"Yes. Pleased to come in." She stood back and faced the door as he opened it.

At first his mouth only flew open and he did not say anything. Then his eyes got very wide, his eyebrows climbing to a point over his nose, and his head went back. Roll after roll of laughter exploded into the room.

Silver drew up stiffly and waited for him to stop sounding like a prairie dog.

"Please," he choked, holding his sides, "please don't be angry. I . . . I—" While he had a second fit, Silver looked at him with eyes of ice.

He came to her and pulled her rigid body against his hip, planting a brotherly kiss on her brow. "A thousand apologies, sweetheart. You have every right to be angry, and I will never, *never* laugh at you again." Silver could not keep from melting against him but her eyes were indignant and wounded as they rolled up at him. "Please don't be hurt," he said gently, "but you can't possibly wear that on the outside of your dress."

Silver pulled away from him. She could still hear laughter in his voice.

"What is use to have it and hide it?" she demanded, tilting her head to look down her nose at him—her favorite angle. "White eyes have many stupid ways," she said, glaring. "Someday I will tell you *all* of them."

Walker could not trust himself to speak. Turning her about, he unsnapped the lace brassiere and slipped it from her shoulders. Then he looped her arm through his and escorted her to the door.

194

In spite of his promise, he could never quite bring himself to complete sobriety.

Thoroughly relaxed for the first time in what seemed like months, Walker pulled a long cheroot from his coat and lit it.

Silver could not take her eyes from the confusing assortment of silverware.

"Thank you," said Walker as the waiter set two enormous steaks before each of them. When they were alone again, he smiled. "I promised you good meat, remember?"

Silver did not smile. "You also promise me horse."

Walker looked at her for a long time before he spoke. "Some promises are hard to keep."

Silver dropped her eyes to her food so he wouldn't see their gleam of triumph. She knew he was speaking of another promise.

She began to slice her steak and found the utensils hard to manage. Walker watched her but offered no assistance.

At the first bite, her mouth began to water uncontrollably. She could hardly manage not to gobble.

Afterward came a rich desert, more wine, and coffee. Her stomach pushed at the tight dress but she could not stop the ingrained urge to consume everything while it was available. If her people had only a small part of white eyes food they would never go hungry!

Finally she could not get another bite down, and pushed her plate back. An older gentleman at the next table caught her eye, and smiled warmly.

Silver fastened her eyes on Walker. "That man is looking at me."

Walker did not turn. "Things are different now. There's no harm in it. He's just admiring your beauty."

"I do not like the way he looks at me. I want to go now."

Walker sighed. "We can never escape, can we?" He called the waiter for the bill.

At the staircase, he handed Silver the key. "Let yourself

195

in if you will. I need to walk down the street and get tickets for the stage tomorrow. Can you work the key?" She nodded, and he left her.

After finishing at the stage depot, Walker was halted halfway up the street as two men were being thrown bodily out the front door of the local brothel by a stout, brightly painted madam.

"If I see the likes o' you in here agin, you'll git more than a kick in the ass," she shouted. The two men scrambled away into the shadows. When the madam spied Walker, her face changed. She sidled forward to lean against the door.

"Bless yore balls, stranger," she cackled, propping her hand on her hip and giving him a leer. "You're 'bout the best-looking hunk o' man I ever seed. How 'bout a free drink? I may not be much to look at anymore but I got some that is."

Walker tipped his hat and grinned. "I'm sure you do, madam. But I guess I'll have to pass tonight."

Her eyes twinkled. "If you're ever this way again . . ."

"I'll remember you." He gave her a visual raking that made her giggle.

Upstairs in the hotel, he was relieved to see that his ward was not standing helplessly in the hall unable to manage the lock. Tossing his hat on the bed, he had pulled off his coat and vest before he noticed that the connecting door to the bath was open. He stepped to it to close it, then stopped still. Silver's door was also open. She was standing before the bureau brushing her hair, wearing nothing but a transparent negligee that gave him a side view of full breasts, the taut curve of her buttocks, and a flat belly. He could not move. His pulse pounded with the fury of a buffalo stampede.

Unconsciously holding his breath, he grabbed the door and pulled it quietly shut.

At the bedside stand he took out the bottle of wine he had bought earlier and downed two quick glasses. On rethinking the matter, he drank two more before stripping to his underwear.

He was barely under the bedcovers when there was a tap

at the adjoining door. "Walker?" she called shyly.

"What!"

The door opened and Silver stepped slowly inside. She had not changed her clothing. The way she was looking at him made Walker snatch the sheet up to his chin.

She did not move, but just kept looking at him. Walker felt his eyelids twitching with the effort not to let his gaze roam lower.

"*Sil*ver," he barked finally.

"I will go now." She giggled at his expression as she slipped out the door.

Walker fell back and yanked the cover over his head, and waited for his pulse to slow.

Scarcely an hour later, he was thoroughly drunk and pacing a crooked pattern across his room. A thousand times he had gone to her door and fortunately found her sleeping.

But he knew he couldn't anyway. It was like an alcoholic taking the first drink, and then the next and the next. He was not that big a fool yet. The way *she* understood a relationship, it was a simple matter of horsetrading—her body for meat, blankets, and a pony!

After dressing again, he paused at the mirror to jam his hat on, grinning savagely at his reflection. He would find something stronger than wine and after that he would pay a call at the house down the street. By heaven, there were those who got paid to relieve a man in just such an emergency as this one!

The madam, who called herself Savannah, was delighted to see Walker.

"Guess I had you figured wrong, stranger. Come on in!"

Walker found his tongue too thick to speak, so he just grinned.

Savannah put an arm about his waist and pressed her overflowing bosom against him. "Listen. We got the best girls in the county. For just a wee bit more, you can have one in your own room. *All night.* The one I'm thinkin' about has customers at the hotel anyway—the clerk, for one. He's a real discreet gentleman."

"That's not a good idea," mumbled Walker. "Here will be fine."

Savannah frowned. "It's just a few more dollars. The problem is, we're just full up right now. You shoulda come earlier."

Walker pulled away from her. "Impossible. It's got to be here." Distress cleared his muddled mind somewhat, and he grew uncomfortable. "Look, let's just forget it. My mistake." He started to turn back out the door.

"Oh, not so fast, cupcakes," declared Savannah, pulling him around by the arm. She leaned close and spoke low. "I'll tell you what. The hotel next door helps us out a little at times like these. What about going there?"

Walker hesitated, the fire in his blood cooling with every passing second. "No, really. I . . . think I've made a mistake."

"Savannah, did you need me?" a sweet voice called out.

Walker turned and found a green-eyed wench with pale blond hair sidling toward him. She tucked her arm in his and looked up at him, running her tongue over luscious red lips. As she pressed herself to him, Walker's gaze devoured the tantalizing mounds that rose above her gown.

"Hello," he slurred, looking deep into her eyes.

"She'll take you next door, stranger," said Savannah. Then with a wink, she added, "This one specializes in *exotic* love," and she laughed raucously.

Walker allowed himself to be led out the front door and down the darkened sidewalk.

"My name is Elexia," purred his buxom companion. Reaching up, she trailed a fingertip down one hard cheek.

"Elexia . . . beautiful name," murmured Walker, his passion surging back full strength. "Perhaps a sample is in order?" Turning her, he pushed her gently against the planked wall, into the shadows. When Elexia felt the magnificent body against hers, she thought she would faint. It had been years—perhaps forever—since she'd had a customer like this one. A single night couldn't possibly be enough!

She opened her mouth, greedy but sensing she should hold back. He swept her against him, his arms crushing her without pain as he kissed her passionately. He was as ready as they got! she thought, gasping. "Hurry. Upstairs," she said, reaching down to stroke his manhood once before she pushed him back.

Walker's groan coincided with her caress so that Elexia didn't realize until he slumped heavily against her that he had been struck from behind. Then a man grabbed her to one side and Walker fell to the ground. With one hand over her mouth, the man held her tight and, though she fought hard, she could do nothing but watch as the second man heaved Walker over on his back and searched him.

"I got his wallet. Let's go."

The man holding her whispered fiercely, "I know you . . . where you stay. I'll come back and git you if you don't start running right now. And don't look back."

Then they were gone. Elexia ran to the door of the brothel as fast as she could. And she did not look back.

A short while later, Savannah ordered her two burly assistants to escort Walker to his own hotel. "Don't say nothin' to the clerk but that you found him on the street," she instructed worriedly. "It's the least I can do. Oh, by the way. Don't forgit to check his pockets in case the thieves missed a little."

When Walker had been stripped out of his clothes and deposited — still out cold — in his bed, the hotel clerk closed the door, muttering angrily. "Confounded fools that go messin' around this town at night."

"You think he'll be all right?" queried his assistant.

"He seems okay. He'll probably have a splitting headache in the morning, but it serves him right. If I didn't owe the madam a favor, I'd have told them to dump him back on the street."

It was just past midnight when Walker came to enough

199

to feel the cool hand on his brow. His eyes felt like hot burning balls and the inside of his mouth like cotton. His head seemed to explode with shards of light when he moved.

The hand on his forehead withdrew when he let out a grunt. Forcing his eyes open a little, he saw a woman standing beside his bed. Moonlight streamed from the opposite window, outlining the shape of her body through the transparent garment. He was still very drunk but he suddenly remembered the mission that had sent him into the streets. The ravishing creature before him was Elexia. Ready and willing Elexia . . .

His pulse quickened, and although his tongue was still sluggish, he managed to command in a sultry voice, "Come here." Lying on his back, he extended his hand, palm out.

Silver had come to investigate the noise and found Walker moaning in his bed. Now he had seen her . . . was telling her to come to him. Surely he must be very angry that she had come to his room, openly tempting him again to break his vow.

She made no move to obey.

"Come here," he said again. "I want to touch you."

His voice seemed to rumble through her, and Silver shivered as she crept forward one step, then two. His hand rose up until his fingertip could trace the tip of her breast. As the nipple hardened under his touch, Walker groaned, grabbing her wrist.

"It's been a long night, love. There's no time for games."

He pulled her to the side of the bed, wrapped one arm around her waist, and pulled her down toward him, opening her thin wrapper with his other hand. Making a noise deep in his throat, he nuzzled the full mounds that drooped to meet his face, taking first one then the other in his mouth. Silver braced her hand on his chest, panting and weak.

Walker drew her on top of him, rolling her over to the other side but holding her thigh over his hip. Obviously he had not gotten what he paid for—certainly not a girl who was expert enough to make him forget the one back at his hotel. In fact, he would have done well to have chosen a woman with a different build. This one had a body too much like the one he had to forget.

"Silver," he murmured as he pulled head to his. Drinking the sweetness of her mouth, he was unaware which name he used and was truly surprised when the girl reacted like a swooning virgin, her mouth trembling as she gasped for air. Her response stirred the smoldering heat inside him, but it was not what he bargained for at all. He wanted a brazen whore who took a moment's pleasure and went on her way — no strings.

"Come now, let's dispense with appetizers, my dear. I believe I have the right to make demands, do I not?" He took her hand in his and pressed it to his swollen shaft.

Silver let out a muffled cry and tried to draw her hand away. He always tempted her into submission like this but with the morning light he would be angry. She did not think she could bear that again.

Walker frowned. "Forgive me for saying so, but your talents are highly overrated." He forced her hand back, moving it against him. Silver tried to relax. There was no end to the surprises in *commar-pe*. But as she moved her hand as he had done, her curiosity and desire suddenly leaped along together. She moved her hand lower and felt the velvet sack that held the seed for many sons.

With a strangled groan, Walker pushed her hand away and pulled her thigh higher. She felt his hardness probing her and kissed him feverishly, fitting herself around him like a glove. He rolled on top of her and buried his face in her neck, his befuddled mind playing its tricks again. "I didn't want to love you but I've loved you forever . . ." His mouth came up to seek hers, ravishing it until her mind was splintering away into small fragments. "The smell of you, the feel of you . . . I can't think about anything else," he murmured thickly, running his tongue along her neck, under her ear, across her face.

Silver grasped his powerful buttocks and felt them flex as he plunged deeper, taking her higher . . . *higher* . . .

They seemed to drift in the spangled lights of heaven

for an eternity, and the flash of a second. When the flame was spent, he lay on top of her, his cheek on her chest while she twined her fingers through his curly damp hair. "How will I live without you?" he whispered.

Silver stroked his forehead and paid no attention to his ramblings. The firewater was strong on his breath.

"You will sleep now," she crooned softly. "I will never leave you, Walker Gray's Son. Till the sun does not climb the heavens I will not leave you."

Chapter 13

Though the comfort of her husband's arms was almost
impossible to leave, Silver dragged herself from the bed
around sunrise. A good squaw always rose first to have
the fires going.

She dressed in one of the new riding suits Walker had
purchased for her: a divided, dusky-blue suede skirt that
pleased her because it allowed freer movement. The
matching tall moccasin boots that laced up to her knee
were also a taste of home that she enjoyed. She put on
the little vest over the pale-blue, long-sleeved blouse, but
left off the high-crowned hat; she did not like head-
dresses.

She was still brushing her hair out over her shoulders,
admiring herself and thinking how pleasing it was to be
so very rich, when there was a terrible clatter in the next
room. She rushed to the door and stepped through the
bathing chamber.

Walker leaned at an angle, his hand propped on the
bureau and his eyes squinted together. He was naked
except for the sheet twisted about his waist. On the floor
lay the decanter of liquor he had knocked from the
bureau, and the amber liquid was pouring out in a pud-
dle.

Silver went to pick up the bottle, and Walker did not
move his head or open his eyes as he muttered, "I want a
drink. Get it, quickly."

Silver obeyed and he bolted the glass swiftly, taking a
deep breath afterward and keeping his hold on the bureau.

"You have bad dreams last night," she sympathized.

He cracked one eye at her. "How did you know that?"

"You make noise like one in pain."

Holding the sheet tighter, Walker shuffled carefully to the bed. Silver hurried beside him and wedged her shoulder under his arm, and when they reached the bed, Walker turned on one foot and fell backward into it.

"My *head!*"

"Too much firewater," noted Silver under her breath.

Walker crossed an arm over his face. "How convenient."

"I do not understand 'spy.' "

Walker jerked his arm up to squint malevolently. "Were you spying on me all night, for Godsake?"

"You say we ride long today," she reminded him, her mouth feeling strangely dry as her gaze roamed over the hard cords in his abdomen. The hair on his chest was gold in the sunlight; it grew into a point that then disappeared under the white sheet. As she stared at the sharp contrast of his dark-gold body against the bed, her blood seemed to get thick. She remembered the things he had said to her . . . had *done* to her. But as always, the next morning he was "sorry." Which meant to be sad about the way things had turned out.

She went to sit on the edge of the bed.

"I bring you water?"

"No," he grunted, not moving his arms. Silver's hand ached to touch him, to feel his hairy chest against her palm.

"I bring food?"

He made another noise, and by the sound of it Silver knew he did not want food.

"I'll be all right in a minute," he said finally, "when the room stops spinning."

"I get Medicine Man for you."

A shadowed memory darted through Walker's head, and slowly he moved his arm. "Last night. Did you by any chance . . ." He covered his face again. "Never mind. Just go back to your room and let me dress."

It was the same as always, thought Silver, her eyes turning hard. He wanted to make *commar-pe* but now he

204

was angry because he had done it. He wanted Camelia to be First Wife because he had promised her, and she was his own kind. But Camelia could not be First Wife because he had already taken one before her. So afterward, he always wanted to pretend that it hadn't happened at all.

She stood up quickly and looked down her nose.

"He who has black dreams is haunted by the Spirit Man," she explained coldly. Then her voice dropped to a soft chant, her eyes glittering from narrowed lids. "Spirit Man comes after those who speak with forked tongue."

Walker's voice was deep with amusement as he peeped from under his arm. "So he's coming after me, huh?"

Silver gave him a slow, measuring look. "This is for *you* to say, white eyes." She turned to make her exit with a straight back, ignoring the muffled chuckle behind her.

By the time Walker was fully dressed, the effects of the night were beginning to wear off. His wallet with a hundred dollars in it was missing—which was no less than he deserved for spending the night with a strumpet. And instead of a cure, his disease was worse this morning. He was consumed with erotic memories, visions not of Elexia but Silver, her slender body beneath his, pulling him into her like an eddy sucking a man down into the bowels of the earth.

He picked up his bags and went to the door, but paused to press his fingers to the small pain in his temple. When he did, he detected a subtle fragrance on his hand, the dry spicy smell of the woods in autumn. His pulse leaped, and something wild and vaguely savage stirred inside him.

Spicewood leaves. It had to be spicewood leaves. But, on his *hand?*

He decided he needed extra coffee before he went to Silver's room.

Three days later they disembarked from the stage in

205

the village of St. Martinville, Louisiana, and loaded into the hired buggy which would take them to their final destination.

Although it was late afternoon and the sky was ablaze with color, it was dusk on the dirt road that wound through dark copses of moss-laden oaks. Here the daylight was detected only as an amber blush that wrapped about their secluded world of deep shade.

Silver smelled the damp, musky breath of the swamps and felt the stirring inside her again, as though she were acting out a familiar dream. She had known an old chief who claimed to have lived once before as an eagle. Perhaps that was true of herself also. Or perhaps she was only remembering the pictures from Milly's storybooks that were also oddly familiar. For this was truly the Enchanted Forest, dark and mysterious; the trees were like bearded old gnomes; giants twisted and gnarled with age who stood, hands clasped with their fellows, and waited for the night, when they would dance to the tune of fairy flutes.

The driver turned the carriage, and now they seemed to look down a tunnel made by more ancient oaks whose limbs interlocked overhead. At the end, the tunnel framed the face of a house that was nothing like the gentle whitewashed "plantations" they had passed along the way. This one was like the castles in Milly's books, its walls barely visible for the thick ivy that grew on it like animal's fur. It was the great monster of the Enchanted Forest, its dark eyes watching, threatening. A tower on the left side thrust upward as though it struggled toward the light but was being dragged down by the encroaching vines. As they drew closer, she said in a small voice, "It has no 'veranda.' "

Walker turned to her and smiled, and she knew he was pleased with her observation. Then his eyes moved to the house again and his smile faded.

"The townhouse is two hundred years old and patterned after a castle in Scotland. There's a porch but it's recessed behind that black grillwork called wrought iron. We have a plantation house a few miles out of town

206

which I much prefer. That's where I grew up. But when this old relic came up for sale, my father was looking for a place in town and we bought it. Not long afterward, however, my mother became ill and died, so I've never had any affection for it."

"The river we crossed, it is not the same one in the Land of the Teichas?"

Walker scowled. "That's Tex-as," he pointed out, "and we are far from that river now. Very, very far from Llano Estacado." His face relaxed a little. "Anyway, that was a bayou, not a river. Most of the names here are French. That was the Bayou Teche, pronounced By-you Tesh. The house is known as Gray Shadows."

Walker leaped to the ground as soon as the carriage stopped, but when he reached to help Silver down, she shrank back, staring at the house. He followed her gaze and murmured, "Believe me, I don't blame you a bit."

As Walker was handing bills to the man up front, there was a shrill cry from the porch, and Silver looked as a young blond woman came running down the stone steps calling his name.

Walker had scarcely turned before the girl flew straight into his arms and began kissing him fervently, saying, "Walker, Walker!"

He seemed too stunned to move. His voice was astonished and not entirely pleased as he drew back to stare at the woman and gasped, *Camelia!*

Then others were streaming from the mouth of the great house—another young woman who had dark hair, a handsome older gentleman, and an older woman with very black hair. Behind them came more people. One was a tall thin man dressed in black and white, whose skin was black, making the whites of his eyes look very strange.

Silver had never seen a man with black skin. She slid silently out of the carriage and stood behind Walker.

"Oh, Walker, it seems like *years* since we've . . . " The blond woman's voice faded as she looked past Walker's shoulder. Her blue eyes were growing big and round but before she could speak, she was shoved aside by the

207

other young woman, who also hugged Walker.

Walker kissed the girl's cheek and seem to recover somewhat. "Amanda, I think you've grown an inch."

The dark-haired girl drew back a fist and hit his shoulder, first making a face at him then throwing herself at him again.

Silver had backed into the carriage behind her, and the driver leaned over to growl, "Miss! Step out of the way."

Silver obeyed without dragging her eyes from the blue ones that were fixed upon her, and the carriage pulled away. But the others had seen her now, and their faces seemed to freeze with shock.

Something had happened to all of them. No one said anything anymore, only stood as though they could not move. Finally, Walker reached around to pull her forward, and his fingers were like steel jaws on her arm.

There was a threatening current beneath his quiet words. "This is Silver Dawn."

As Samuel Grayson started to step forward with his hand out, Kathren moved in front of him and said icily, "I think you owe us an explanation for this, Walker Grayson."

Walker's eyes flashed as he looked at Kathren, and Silver was afraid of what he would say.

"Once upon a time this family was known for its hospitality. Has that also changed?" he inquired coldly.

Samuel moved more quickly this time and took Silver's hand in his. "I'm Walker's father, Silver. My name is Samuel." Though the man smiled, Silver could see he was very tense.

The black-skinned man came forward then and picked up their bags. "Mr. Walker, we's shore proud to have you back home," he said with feeling, as though the words had a double meaning.

Walker offered no further explanations as he took Silver's arm and marched them toward the mouth of the great house. The others followed in a stricken silence.

The arched door of heavy, carved wood was opened by a woman whose skin was also very dark but not like the black man's. Her eyes were frightened as she looked at

208

Silver, as though she already knew some disaster was afoot. She spoke English but Silver had trouble making out the words.

"Monsieur Walker, it ees goot to see yooh. Would zee young lady lack to go upstairs now?"

"Yes, Bertha, please," said Walker, giving Silver a brief, strained smile. He leaned closer. "You'll have time to rest before dinner. There's no need to change clothes."

Silver followed the dark, shriveled woman up the staircase, knowing now that the house had been built for the giant in *Jack and the Beanstalk*. All the walls were heavy dark wood with knife carvings. A great lamp of wood and brass hung in the foyer and even the lamps on the wall could not be lifted by ordinary men. A huge stone beast of unknown origin sat by the banister at the top of the stairs. It was somewhat like a mountain cat with eyes more ferocious and much fur around its neck. She did not think it was a white eyes god, but just in case she made a wide circle around it.

The dark-skinned one looked over her shoulder and smiled faintly. Her lips were thin, her teeth very white. "Zere be many rooms. I weel find yooh a goot one."

When they stopped before a door, the woman looked at her curiously. "Yooh are Monsieur Walker's goot frand?"

Silver worried over the words a moment, but she did not know "frand."

"I am Walker's wife," she said in her best English.

The woman's face looked as though she'd been struck. Gasping, her small clawlike hands at her throat and the whites of her eyes gleaming like an animal's from the shadows, she croaked: *"Zee Holy Saints preserve us!"*

When the woman could not seem to recover, Silver repeated firmly, "I am Walker's First Wife."

Slowly, the woman began backing on down the hall, her voice still weak with shock. "Come. Monsieur's room ees farther alonk."

The next door opened into another dark room of mahogany and blue velvet. Silver felt smothered.

"Walker's room?" she asked.

The woman hadn't followed her inside but stood stiffly by the doorway. Her eyes were still enlarged and she whispered when she spoke. "Monsieur's room ees zee next one, madam. Your bags weel come soon."

With that, she shut the door.

The vaulted ceiling of the dining hall was a work of ivory plaster covered by hand-painted murals forty feet above the dark gray marble floor. The mahogany-paneled walls reached a third that distance before joining the papered upper walls, also murals, and were decked at that juncture with brightly colored military flags pointing half-mast toward the center of the room. In between each flag was either a gold and leather-bound sword, a gleaming musket, or heavy brass shield bearing the coat-of-arms of the Graysons' predecessors. One wall consisted solely of an enormous stone fireplace with ornately carved mantelpiece and matching bookshelves. Above the massive twenty-foot table hung a monstrosity of black chains and spikes that sufficed for a chandelier.

Two hours later the dinner had been prepared and the table made ready—though some confusion still existed as to the seating arrangement. Since every single family member had vanished into the house's labyrinths shortly after the couple's arrival and could not be found for consultation, it was left to the French cook Jubal and his assistant Mrs. Peoples to wrangle over the rumor circulated by the upstairs maid, Bertha, who contended that the girl claimed to be Walker's wife! But, of course, she had surely misunderstood.

The Mistress Kathren had different ways from the first mistress. She insisted all guests at Gray Shadows be seated by name cards to "avoid embarrassing confusion." So Jubal wrote the names carefully on cards of expensive parchment and did the only safe thing: He placed Miss Camelia's name card to Walker's left, Miss Silver's to his right. Then he and Mrs. Peoples made a hasty departure for the kitchen to see what would come of their decision.

They knew a few moments later when they heard a

scream.

Stumbling through the door, they found Kathren's dark eyes murderous with rage.

"What in God's name have you *done?!*" she shrieked. Then without further ado, she snatched up Silver's card and marched to the other end of the table to plop it down, turning on them in a fury.

"What possessed you to take it upon yourself to move that girl into Camelia's place!"

"Madam, a thousand apolo-gees!" cried Jubal, twisting his apron in his hands. "I have misunderstood. Please do not be angry!"

Kathren jerked the edges of her brocade dinner jacket and fought for calm. "For this time only I will overlook it, but another mistake of this magnitude will cost you your job! Now get to the kitchen. The rest will be here any minute."

Silver followed directions to stand behind her chair until the rest of the family had arrived. Walker and Samuel came through the door laughing at some joke, but Silver sensed there was still tension between them. At some signal she missed, they began to take their seats. Silver sat down with them, but Walker remained standing.

He looked at her down the length of the table and said quietly, "Silver, this is my stepmother, Kathren." He pointed to each one. "My sister, Amanda . . . Camelia Rhinehart . . . and my father who, as I remember, had the good manners to introduce himself—"

His sentence was cut off by the sound of heated words outside the door, which stopped abruptly as two young men came inside and found all eyes upon them.

"You are late," snapped Kathren. "Please take your seats immediately."

Both men were tall and slender but one bore a remarkable likeness to Walker—the same eyes and hair, the same features in a younger and slimmer face. The other had black hair and dark eyes in a swarthy face. The latter smiled at Kathren apologetically as he took his seat.

"Forgive me, Aunt Kathren, I lost track of the time."

211

Walker held out a palm to the other man, who was still standing with an angry flush on his face. Walker finished as though he had not halted, smiling fondly. "And my brother, Seth." Then he looked at the dark man and said, "I don't believe we've met."

"This is Ferrell Cassadyne," said Kathren tersely, "my . . . great-nephew."

Conversation waited while the dinner bell was rung and Jubal brought in the appetizers. When he had gone, Samuel looked toward the end of the table.

"Silver, Walker tells me you've had quite a hard time of it lately. I hope you are able to locate some of your family."

Silver shot Walker an accusing look for telling them only what *he* thought. But she decided it wise not to employ her former refrain about her lineage. "Yes, me— I also hope . . . too." She blushed for the awkwardness of her speech.

Kathren jabbed at a sliver of cold turkey, making a scraping noise on her place. "Since you disappeared to the stables so quickly, Walker, we haven't had a chance to talk. Perhaps you can tell us more about your guest." Her lips were thin and tight as she spoke.

Walker looked at her levelly and finished chewing with infuriating slowness. Finally he wiped his mouth carefully.

"She was captured by Indians when she was very young. Her age matches that of a couple of families listed here in Louisiana."

"You're very kind to concern yourself with someone who means nothing to you," replied Kathren archly.

Silver stared at her untouched plate until someone intervened to break the terrible silence.

"My brother is a very kind man," said Amanda, glancing at Walker. "I'm sure Silver has found that out."

Next came bowls of black soup, which made Silver nauseous just to behold. She glanced at Camelia and saw that she also had not eaten a bite, and her lower lip was trembling. Silver looked away in alarm. What other disaster could be in store for this night? Did his family always act so strangely with each other or was it because Walker had taken a First Wife? If so, they must hate her very much.

After soup came salad; after salad came an entrée of braised mutton, gravy, and rice. Silver thought the meat smelled worse than the rancid buffalo the army sold her people, and she did not eat the mutton.

Kathren laid her fork down and looked at Silver very deliberately. "Is your food unsatisfactory in some way?"

"The food's delicious," snapped Walker. "We ate not long before we arrived. Well, Seth . . ." He turned to his brother. "I hear you've taken the plantation entirely in hand. In fact, Dad says you're pushing for a new production record."

"Yes, and the stables are breaking even now, too." He paused to look at the man named Ferrell. "One recent acquirement is a house of at least twenty good saddle horses —"

Ferrell interrupted smoothly. "I'm afraid Seth is referring to the fact that I took Rising Sun out for a run this afternoon." He smiled sheepishly and charmingly around the table. "I apologized to Seth, of course, but I guess I'm just used to having a thoroughbred under me."

"I don't object to the horse having a workout," Seth retorted. "What I resent is seeing whip marks on a six thousand dollar animal!"

"Here here, boys," said Samuel, glancing uneasily from one to the other. "I'm sure Ferrel won't repeat his error." He changed the subject. "Walker, I talked to Senator Randall yesterday . . ."

At the meal's end, Silver was rescued from retiring to the parlor with the other women when Walker stood up and asked if she could be excused for the evening to get some rest.

Inside her room, Silver lay in the giant bed and looked at its tapestry, which depicted mounted hunters following dogs through a swampy forest. But she had no intention of falling asleep until she heard her husband come to his room.

213

When Kathren excused herself and failed to return to the parlor shortly, the girls escaped for Amanda's room upstairs.

Camelia flung herself on the bed. "How could he do this to me! How could he—could he—*could he!*" she wailed, pounding her fist on the bed.

Amanda sat down beside her. "You know Walker's awfully softhearted, Camelia. He just feels sorry for the girl, that's all. So should we, by the way."

Camelia raised a tear-streaked face. "Her! Is that all you can think about? What about *me?* I've never been so totally humiliated in all my life! Oh, I don't know how he could have done this to me!" Her lament rose so loud that Amanda covered her ears. Only the sudden opening of the door startled the girl to silence.

Kathren stepped inside and closed the door behind her. Her face was pale, her red lips only a thin, quivering slash across her face. She spoke in a low voice, spacing her words like one controlling a fit of rage.

"I will not stand for it. I will not tolerate it. I've worked too hard to get where I—" She stopped as she looked at Amanda. "Do you know what he's done? Did he write and tell you?" Her voice rose. "Because if you had foreknowledge of this and didn't say anything, Amanda Grayson, I swear I will *never* forgive you!" She started toward the bed, her expression so contorted with fury that Amanda came to her feet at once.

"For petesakes calm down, Kitty. I don't have any idea what you're talking about!"

Changing course, Kathren went to the nearest chair and fell into it. She stared at the floor in dazed wonder. "Of all the possibilities, I never expected *this*. The scandal, the rumors—his whole career down the drain." She stomped her foot and her eyes came up flashing. "The time I spent working on that old prick—I tell you I won't *have* it!"

"There's no need for vulgar language, Kathren," Amanda reminded her sternly. "And who in the world are you talking about? Who did you 'work on'?"

214

"Lawrence Rhinehart. He's ready to take Walker to Washington, Amanda. We're not talking about a governship, we're talking about *Wash*ington, for the love of God!"

Both girls gasped in unison.

"How dare you talk about Camelia's father like that," Amanda hissed sharply, for Camelia's face was undergoing shocking transfigurations.

Kathren glanced briefly at the girl. Camelia was of no use now; she was nothing but another mouth to feed. Walker had ruined everything.

There was only so many avenues open for avenging an insult from the mistress of the house. Camelia screwed her face into a horrible mask of agony, allowing her eyes to well up with big tears, and then turned them on Kathren Grayson. "I . . . I can't believe you said that to me," she whimpered.

Kathren stared fixedly at the floor, her face so aghast it looked disfigured, her voice an airless whisper. "The girl is Walker's wife!"

The next morning Silver arose and packed away her clothes. It had been past midnight when she finally fell asleep, but she never heard Walker come to his room. His shock at finding Camelia in Louisiana seemed real, so she had decided perhaps he didn't lie when he said she was in a place called Georgia.

But now that Camelia *was* here, there would be much time for Walker to spend with her. Perhaps Camelia was what kept him awake so late last night, and perhaps they were downstairs, together right now.

The thought spurred Silver to dress with frantic haste. After wrestling herself into the dark-green riding skirt, the matching vest and blouse, she was in the process of pulling on her moccasin boots when there was a tap at the door.

"Madam, eet ees Preesy," came a lilting voice. "Ah come to help you."

Silver opened the door and found a dark-skinned girl

215

about her own age.

"But you haf already dressed." The girl seemed crushed by the fact. Then her eyes lit up as she looked Silver over. "You very *pret*-ty! Monsieur Walker very wise to marry you before dat Camile get him. She would mek a terrible wife, that *chew*."

Silver looked at Prissy with surprise and then with interest. She was a bewitching little creature with tangled black curls and black eyes.

"I do not know 'chew,' " said Silver.

Prissy reached back to pat her rear end meaningfully. "Dis ees *chew*." Silver was only beginning to grasp the new word when Prissy went to the windows and drew back the heavy blue-velvet drapes. "Eet ees a beautiful day. Maybe you weel go riding wit Monsieur Walker?"

The sore subject made Silver frown. "Me—that is, I, do not have horse," she said sullenly.

Prissy laughed. "But dare *all* you horses now." She talked as she whisked about the room, tidying everything in her path. "You come down to breakfast, den monsieur can show you dee horses. Dey are magneefee*sont!*" She kissed her fingertips.

When she grabbed the door and held it open, Silver hesitated to follow. "Camelia . . . she will eat now?"

Prissy gave a low chuckle. "Not at dis house. She bawl so loud las night dat everybody hear her. Everybody but Monsieur Walker. He went riding and come back very late, lak he bin running from Fee Folay. Ah wonder eef he knows she ees gone. Maybe she go ohm to Georgia, *oui?* Now you come along." She laughed to herself as she led the way downstairs.

Seth was alone at the table, and Silver almost mistook him for Walker. He stood up to greet them.

"Good morning, Silver. Prissy."

Though he only glanced once at the maid, it was a warm lingering one, Silver noted. Prissy's dark cheeks flushed a deeper shade as she curtsied and left them.

As Seth seated her, Silver glanced around the smaller eating room and liked it better than any she'd seen. The walls were white. There were hanging baskets of lush green plants around the bay window that matched the bright green floral curtains. Beyond the window was the patio, with low walls that spilled over with blooming flowers.

"I guess it's just the two of us," said Seth, sitting again. "Miss Camelia left last night for a hotel in St. Martinville, and Walker was furious, of course, that she left without a word." He heaped Silver's plate with fried ham and biscuits as he talked, smiling easily. "But we won't worry about that now, will we?"

Silver returned his smile shyly. "Walker have big angry words. He have heap many damns."

Seth laughed heartily, and Silver liked the way he threw his head back and his eyes sparkled and his deep voice rumbled up through his chest. He was different from Walker, who, if he laughed at all, laughed *at* her.

"I didn't think by the way you were looking at him last night that you had found any flaws whatever," Seth remarked, still smiling with mirth. Then he added quickly, "You're blushing. I'm sorry if I embarrassed you but it amuses me that you've seen through those layers of military training. Walker's got a temper like all the Grayson men, including myself."

He paused to pour milk into Silver's glass. "I usually go riding first thing every morning. Would you like to go with me?"

Silver was anxious to test Prissy's information. "I do not have horse," she said softly, watching his face.

Seth frowned over his coffee cup. "I'm surprised Walker didn't tell you about the horses."

Silver shook her head. "He say he give me horse but he has not."

Seth leaned back in the chair and smiled. Not only was his new sister-in-law beautiful, but apparently she was not all that interested in the Grayson wealth—unlike some he knew. He wondered why Walker didn't just announce the fact that he was married and forget Camelia.

"Then it's my pleasure to inform you that you own not one horse but an entire stable full of the finest thoroughbreds in the South. And with all due respect for Indian ponies, I have to say that until you've seen Grayson stock, you've never seen a real horse." He leaned forward. "Why don't we go on now, before Walker gets back? I'd like to see his expression when he finds out you've made yourself at home without him. He's got a jealous streak a mile wide." He laughed merrily, as if at some private joke.

Silver could not believe her eyes and watched with breathless excitement as Seth brought each of six horses out for her inspection. They were either black or deep red or something in between, but none were spotted. Their sleek bodies rippled with strength. Their shiny hides glistened like water in the sun. They lacked the short-bodied power of a good war-horse and seemed particularly hard to handle—and perhaps they would not make the best mounts from which to shoot arrows. But Silver could hardly wait to feel one of them beneath her.

"And this is Rising Sun," Seth announced proudly, leading a coal-black stallion from the stable hallway into the sunlight.

Silver's heart leaped inside her. What legs! Surely he could run like the wind.

"That one," she said firmly.

Seth laughed. "Oh, no, my dear—much as I'd like to oblige you since this is Walker's pride and joy. However, he's not only our prime breeding stallion, but we're getting him ready for the next race. Ferrel Casadyne took him out yesterday, but it was very foolish of him. He not up to the animal and that's why those cuts are on his back." Seth frowned at the wounds. "He's too high strung for a woman to handle anyway. He's got a very hard mouth." He grinned that mischievous grin again. "Although I'd really like to accommodate you . . ." Then he shook his head as he reviewed her slenderness. "No, I can't risk it. The saddle horses are just as beautiful. Wait until you see—"

"That one," said Silver, as she crawled through the fence.

"Watch out, Silver. Stay back!" The animal snorted and rolled its eyes, jerking at the tether.

Silver walked slowly toward the horse, speaking softly in Comanche, and the horse began to quiet down immediately.

Seth's face was blank with surprise. "Well, I'll be damned. He likes you."

When Silver took the bridle, the horse grew very still and stayed that way as she lifted halter rope over his head.

"Oh, no. You can't mean to—"

In one graceful leap the girl was astride. Seth's jaw hung slack for a moment. "I can't believe you did that."

"I am Quohadie Teichas," said Silver as though that explained everything. Then she reined the horse around, made a circle around the working pen one way, reversed and went the other way. "He have very good legs," she admitted.

Seth made no move toward his own horse. "That's the damnedest thing I've ever seen," he reiterated, his beautiful green eyes as big as saucers.

Silver pulled Rising Sun up in front of him, and Seth was even more amazed that she didn't seem to think she'd done anything out of the ordinary.

"We ride now?"

"But he—but you—" Seth pushed his hat down hard and stared up at her somewhat peevishly. "All right. But let's see how you do when the devil's got a clear path in front of him. Just remember that I warned you. He's got a hard mouth."

He mounted quickly, let out a loud *whoop,* and took off.

Chapter 14

"Is there anything you can't do on that horse?" Seth demanded as they pulled up at the stable again.

"Many things," said Silver, dropping to the ground. "He need much training."

Seth's mouth was open again. "Such as?"

"He would not allow me to shoot under his neck. He would not know how to run in battle." She laughed a little. "He seems to know only very fast. But I will work with him." She tied the reins to the fence.

Seth dismounted with a scowl. "Look at him. He's standing at the post like a damned plow horse." The stable hand had stopped working a mare to get Rising Sun; now he had stopped in his tracks. "Your eyeballs will fall out if you do that too long," Seth advised him. "Just let the girl stall him. It's obvious she can do it better than either of us."

Silver was beginning to understand white eyes men. "I do not think I can do it better than you or Walker," she demurred, and Seth glanced up quickly.

"Don't try that business with me," he said flatly. "I know the truth."

Silver followed Seth to the last stall, leading Rising Sun. Just as they stopped, there was a muffled sound from within the hay bin at their backs, and Seth wheeled around.

"Who's in there?" There was no answer and he threw the door open, bringing a startled snort from Rising Sun.

Silver gasped as she looked down. Protruding from the loose hay was a man's hairy, half-covered buttocks and underneath him was a female's naked lower anatomy, graphically defined by a dark triangle at the fork of her legs.

"You sorry son of a—" Seth grabbed Ferrell Cassadyne by the back of his rich silk blouse and hauled him backward. Rising Sun whinnied at the confusion and jerked his head at the rope in Silver's hand.

In spite of his half-clothed condition, Ferrell proved well able to defend himself, and the tumbling bodies banging against the wood enclosure sent Rising Sun into a panic. Silver talked quietly while she maneuvered the horse around and headed him for clear space again, but before they reached it, the scullery maid came scampering past, clasping her clothes abut her; she dashed ahead of Silver and the horse, and out the doors at the end of the hall.

Outside, Rising Sun started to calm down. That could not be said for Seth. When he came from the stable, his face was as contorted as his clothing was in disarray.

"I'm sorry, Silver." His cheeks were dark crimson. "I don't know what to say except—well, I've never been so disgraced in front of a woman in my life!" he said hotly, brushing the hay from his britches.

Silver began to laugh, holding her hand over her mouth.

Seth stiffened and looked at her. "What's so damned funny?"

"White eyes and *commar-pe*," she said with finality.

Walker was not surprised when he arrived at the stables to find his brother wearing an exasperated face. After all, he'd been with Silver Dawn.

He dismounted and tossed the reins to the stable hand. "I guess I should have warned you, Seth. She looks sweet, but don't let that fool you."

Seth frowned. "If that's the best greeting you can manage, I'm not surprised you think so."

Walker ignored him and looked at Silver. "Well, I see you've already had a tour of the stables. I was planning

221

to do that myself." His tone was still disgruntled.

"Which you could have done *if* you'd been here," Seth interjected. "As it turns out, we've done a little more than tour. Silver rode Rising Sun to the crossroads and back." He had stopped frowning and now the single dimple in his left cheek deepened. "In record time."

Walker stared. "I hope this is one of your tasteless jokes."

Seth crossed his arms and grinned. "Nope."

Walker's brows drew together as he looked at Silver again. "That was stupid—I guess you know that. It's a wonder the bloody beast didn't kill you."

"He ate out of her hand like a kitten," Seth put in happily.

Walker's head turned slowly toward his brother. "I don't believe you."

Seth lifted his shoulders. "Certainly can't blame you for that."

Walker moved only his eyes so that they peered at his ward between slitted lids. "You're starting to remind me why I left the ball and chain on you," he said with meaning.

Seth thought he was joking. "Oh, I hoped we could use her to help train the champions. She doesn't use a saddle so we could save a lot on equipment."

As his meaning dawned, Walker dropped his gaze. There was a dark oily stain lining the girl's new riding skirt. "You did. You rode that animal bareback." His voice rose. "I can't leave you alone for a blessed minute, can I?"

"Me have horse now," said Silver haughtily. "Heap *good* horse."

Walker gritted his teeth. "Do you have any idea how much I paid for that riding skirt? Don't you know anything about leather? It's ruined—worthless! You might as well burn it!

"What is one skirt? You are very rich white eyes," Silver accused.

"Rich but frugal," Seth murmured.

"If heap many buffalo did not rot on the land," Silver

continued, clenching her fists, "I would make new skirt like it—only sure enough better!" Her eyes were flashing like sunlight on new steel.

"Get back to the house and change immediately," bellowed Walker, flinging his finger in that direction.

Silver lifted her nose and spoke like one who has waited a long time for justice to be done.

"Me have heap many horses now." She threw back her shoulders. "Me have *best* horse. Me no ride mule who looks where the sun dies and where it peeps up at the same time—while his front legs go up *I-da-ho** and his hiny legs go where Dog Eaters see the Lake-With-No-End!** Me ride *my* horse now—Rising Sun!"

Walker's whole body had begun to shake before she finished, and Seth was choking to keep from exploding with laughter.

"Rising Sun is my *per*sonal property!" Walker roared. "Now go back to the house and get out of the filthy skirt before lunch!"

"Rising Sun is mine!"

Tears rolled down Seth's face, and as he stepped between them, he wondered if he'd misjudged his brother's leanings; he was about to take a right hook to his jaw, but he still couldn't stop laughing.

He took each of them by the arm and pushed, though it was somewhat like trying to maneuver two tin soldiers along the ground.

They were almost to the house before he recovered enough to clap Walker's shoulder and choke out, "It's g . . . good—" He guffawed and lost the rest. "It's good to have—" He laughed a full count of ten and Walker's face turned black. "It's good to have you back ho . . . ho . . . home." And he collapsed on the ground with laughter.

* Comanche for 'I am truly terribly cold.'
** The Gulf of Mexico.

223

"There's no need for these theatrics, *auntie*," said Ferrell, stressing the title as he downed a glass of port.

"No need —" Kathren's voice disintegrated into spluttering incoherence. After a moment she crossed the study to the door, closed and locked it. Then she came back to Ferrell and snatched the drink from his hand, slamming it down on the long high table that stood behind the sofa.

"How *dare* you," she hissed. "Every time I look up you're standing there with your hand out! How long do you expect to live off the fat of this good land if you keep throwing stumbling blocks in my path? That episode with the scullery maid. It makes me sick! If you think Samuel Grayson will overlook anything you do because you're a relative of mine, you're dead wrong."

Ferrell gave her a menacing glare as he picked up his glass again, drained it with measured slowness, then poured another. "What I think, dear *aunt,* is that I've been humiliated enough by this charade of yours. Why should I beg for what is rightfully mine?"

"That kind of thinking is dangerous," Kathren said uneasily. "You don't know Samuel like I do. He's a generous man but he's a stickler for integrity, and especially sensitive about the honor of the Grayson name."

Ferrell walked around and took a seat on the sofa, propping his boots on the glass-topped coffee table. "Not as sensitive as you, I'll wager."

Kathren had come to stand in front of him. "And just where would either of us be if I weren't! I'm warning you, Ferrell, if you plan to ride the gravy train, you'd best hearken to the rules or you'll end just like you started: with nothing but the shirt on your back!"

"Speaking of the gravy train," said Ferrell lazily, "I'm out of cash." When Kathren's face flushed with anger, he went on before she could say anything. "It's difficult to keep up with your little games without a great deal of money. This was your idea, remember?"

"You seem to think I'm some kind of bottomless pit! I told you, Samuel is generous but he's not wasteful. He wants to know how the household accounts are spent and goes over the books frequently. He gives me pointers on how to save, then he—" Her lip curled as she finished: "Spends any extra cash on Christmas gifts for the employees."

Ferrell chuckled. "I can see how that wounds you. Nevertheless, I'm out of money. There's a hunt tomorrow. I'll need something for the wagers."

Kathren gasped. "You expect me to finance your gambling?"

"Appearances, auntie. All the local swains bet. And besides the hunt, there's a race in two weeks."

Kathren spat with low rage. "I don't have to give you a damned thing."

"But wouldn't you like to do something about that luscious little savage Walker has brought home? You know, when word gets out that Walker's wife lived for years as an Indian captive, the gossip will ruin any chance he might have of a political career. So if you're planning on polishing the family name with the eldest son's glory, I suggest you get to work"

"I could if I didn't have to worry about you!"

"But why not let me help?" Ferrell suggested calmly, then grinned at the swiftness with which Kathren's anger turned to interest.

"In what way?"

"I have a few ideas. As you say, the Graysons have a low tolerance for dishonor. Now if the girl was say . . . found in my bed?"

Kathren's lips parted and she moistened them with her tongue. "Yes. Yes, the marriage could be annulled—quietly, before anyone even finds out they're married."

Grinning, Ferrell stood up. "I think five hundred should do me for now."

Kathren barely heard him and went on to herself. "I should get Camelia back here. She needs to fight for Walker—make him want her. He wanted her once, he can be made to again." She looked up at Ferrell. "Come to my office late tonight. I'll have the cash."

Ferrell gave her a peck on the cheek. "That's a good girl. Now no more talk about my leaving."

Kathren stared at his back as he went to the door. "For now, Ferrell. But watch your step."

Ferrell turned at the door and held her gaze. "You, too, auntie. This old house holds many secrets, but some are shrewd enough to discover them."

Kathren flew to the door but Ferrell kept walking down the hall, even when she snarled in a loud whisper, "What do you mean? Ferrell, what do you mean by that? Ferrell! Come back, Ferrell!"

Silver had grown fond of Walker's handsome, silver-haired father but during the next few days she saw little of either man because both of them were usually locked away in private, pouring over ledgers. Although Amanda seemed to be thawing without Camelia around and Silver continued to court her with smiles, it was Seth who stayed by her side, showing her about the estate and explaining everything with pride.

The townhouse grounds were limited to five acres along the Bayou Teche that were like an enormous tropical garden. They were maintained by tall, many-paned greenhouses and ten gardeners. A maze of paths wound through azaleas and camelias, oleander and dogwood and crepe myrtles, giant ferns, and banana trees, sego palms and fan palms. At every conceivable juncture there were fountains, statues, urns, and benches tucked away in this world within a world.

The lower floors of Gray Shadows claimed water through an apparatus Seth called a spigot. Rain was collected in a tower as high as the roof, and each floor below could make use of gravity to get water through this spigot. Silver was amazed that white eyes had time for so much building and planning new ideas. But then, if her people did not have to always fight for their land, maybe they would have thought of these things, too.

She loved the carriage house. It smelled of leather and horses and was full of black shiny carriages with gold or silver trim. And she liked the yeasty smell of the wine cellars, although going down into them made her feel like she was trapped in the earth's belly.

Yet with all Seth's entertaining, she needed her husband — who was too busy to notice her at all. She dared not slip into his room to tempt him, for he seemed to want to pretend she was a guest of the family, some distant acquaintance to whom he owed polite manners and nothing else. She didn't think he even realized she slept in the room next to his.

And, she was right. Late one afternoon she was in the tub and the door of the bathing chamber burst open.

For a moment, words seemed to elude him. Then he snarled accusingly, "What are you doing here?"

Silver peeped above a mountain of bubbles. "I am bathing."

He looked as if she had hurled some insult at him. When a pause of considerable duration uncovered no new or more effective words, he rumbled again. "What are you doing in *this* room?"

Her slim straight brows pulled together. "The maid brought me here." But there was a dab of bubbles on the end of her nose and, looking cross-eyed at it, she blew it away.

Her apparent unconcern blanched Walker's face. "You have no business in a room adjoining mine. My God, this house is in enough turmoil as it is!" he bellowed.

"You will send me away like Camelia?" Silver asked fearfully.

"I did not send —" He stopped to get a grip on himself. "As you've probably realized," he went on with ill-concealed irritation, "there's nothing I can do about it now without adding more fuel to the fire. But stay in your own room, do you understand me?" He pointed imperiously at the door behind her.

Silver looked at him quietly for a moment before she said, "I have understood for a long time now."

Walker only half heard as his gaze slipped down the creamy dark skin of her neck and chest. And when he checked himself and looked up, he met a pair of smoldering silver eyes whose source of heat was not anger. "Stay out of my room," he said, and slammed the door.

227

That evening at dinner Walker announced that he, Samuel, and Seth would be going to the plantation for a few days. Silver lowered her eyes to her plate and then lifted them to Amanda, aware that except for Prissy, she would be left alone in the enemy camp.

Amanda's conscience smarted at the girl's grieved expression. She couldn't keep ignoring her sister-in-law much longer. If only Camelia would quit sending those heart-wrenching notes begging for information — asking if anything had "gone wrong with the marriage"! With a little effort, Amanda managed to smile at Silver for the first time.

Silver was allowed to roam at will during the men's absence. She spent time with the gardeners, the cook and kitchen servants, and Prissy, when the maid had free time. And Silver discovered another strange white eyes custom. Prissy said that though she and Seth sensed some chemistry between them, they could never be married or love each other because he was rich and she was poor. They could not breed and be happy like the animals because they had to follow rules which they had made. But why?

As the days dragged by, Silver grew restless. These white eyes did not work, and what else was there but work? Those who did work were poor, but if one did not work, that one was rich. Very confusing.

It was late one stormy evening. Dinner with Kathren, Amanda, and Ferrell was a depressing affair because Walker's stepmother had not acknowledged by word or glance that Silver existed, and Amanda did not look up from her plate at all. Silver didn't know if she liked the man called Ferrell. He was very handsome, slim and swarthy with dark eyes and hair; he looked at her often, and his eyes were kind and warm. She smiled back at him shyly.

The sun was just setting and the night promised to be long. After her bath, Silver dressed again. There were a few books in her room but they had very big words and she tired of the struggle. When the great old house had settled into silence she took a candle and stepped outside her room. She still thought of the house as a silent beast, pretending to sleep but always watching. At night she could hear it breathe.

But something had gnawed at her all evening, a feeling of constriction, a longing for the wide-open spaces — and she could not bear her room.

From the balastrade outside her door, she could look down to the ground floor and see the round marble fountain in the center of the ballroom. Three stories above her head was an ornate dome which opened, Seth said, to circulate cool air throughout the mansion in summer.

Heading opposite from the main staircase, she followed the balcony around the next corner, found the stairs that led up, and climbed every flight until she reached the top floor. Looking down made her dizzy. There was nothing above her now but the circulator dome.

The upper level of the west wing appeared unused, so she took a candle from the wall before she turned onto that landing. Why white eyes must have so many rooms she could not understand. She wished she knew what was in them all.

There was nothing of interest. Here the landing was completely walled and there was no looking over the balcony to the ballroom below. Every door she tried was either locked or contained only a shallow square room barely big enough to stand in, which the maid Bertha called "closets." She had one in her own room.

Suddenly she stopped beside one door and held the candle higher to look at it. It was a smaller door, which she had found always opened to closets. But this one — She chewed on her lip and then tried the knob.

Behind the door was a steep narrow staircase, and as she studied it, the skin on the back of her neck began to crawl.

Horse Back claimed that his daughter's power to predict certain events was the result of her being born on the sun god's birthday, an explanation that went unchallenged although it was pure concoction from Horse

Back's fertile imagination; he was an accomplished story-teller who needed no more inspiration than the sight of an arrow to spin a two-hour tale at the campfire, deftly interweaving real-life experiences with fantasy.

Silver had never questioned anything Horse Back told her, nor did she this explanation for her ability. The spells when the gods spoke to her were widely spaced and frequently wrong as to detail. But her predictions of outcome were deadly accurate. When Silver doomed a strategic maneuver, the warriors quickly abandoned it.

She feared "the gift," dreaded to the point of feeling physically ill when the small pulses started in the back of her brain, yet she could not escape its grip until she knew the end of the matter.

The feeling was strong now as she climbed the narrow stairs, but she could not will her feet to stop even when her hand began to tremble, making threatening shadows flicker upon the walls.

Finally the steps stopped in front of a narrow wooden door, stained very dark like the rest of the house, and Silver knew she was higher than even the circulator dome. She also knew from the pulses inside her head that this door was always kept locked.

When she tried the knob, though, it was not.

Inside the door was another staircase. Her candle was burning low and she wanted desperately to go back to her room. But her feet kept moving, and now she was on a short landing. There was a small round window at the end and one door to the left. She went to it and stood, and after a moment tried the door.

It swung open silently, and Silver was rooted to the spot with a sense of horror. The dank air smelled of death, a peculiar sweet-sour odor she knew from experience to be the reek of rotting human flesh.

Suddenly a musty draft moved over her, snuffing the candle out. The walls of her throat stuck together and she could not breathe. She knew there was someone in the room even before she heard the sound of footsteps scuttling like dry leaves in a wind.

Her eyes adjusted to the darkness, and from the solitary window across the room enough light permeated to illuminate the white-shrouded shapes of covered furniture—and then a form, hunched and furtive, near the long mirror on the left wall.

"Go away!" rasped a voice. The form crouched and Silver could vaguely make out its claw-shaped hands pressing frantically along the edge of mirror.

Suddenly the mirror opened like a door and the figure vanished. Before Silver could take a step, the mirror closed again.

Her heart hammered as she tried to hurry back down the unlit passages, smothering a scream when she realized there were spiderwebs all over her face and hair and arms.

When she emerged on the top landing, she spared no time to recover but ran to the stairwell and down until she came to the second level.

She ran again until she reached her door, then stopped and stared aghast at it. She knew someone was in her room, and she could not force herself to touch the doorknob.

The door opened suddenly.

"Madam! Ah heard you running—" Prissy stopped when she saw Silver's face. "Come inside quickly." She grabbed Silver's arm.

Prissy led her to the bed and sat down beside her. "What has happened?" she asked urgently, seeming to know that a variety of horrors aboded in the great house.

"Someone," gasped Silver, "someone in that room. Someone evil!"

"What room, madam?"

"High—up very high," choked Silver, unable to catch her breath again.

Prissy put her arms about her. "Eet was dat old woman, Sheba. She ees mean, yes. Ah tink someone put a gris-gris on her when she come from de womb."

"She should not be here." Silver looked fearfully at the door. "Walker should send her away!"

Prissy sat on the bed, her mouth pursed indignantly.

"Dat ees so, but she come wid Mistress Kathren from Georgia. When dey come, everytin go wrong at dis house. De first mistress get sick and die, den Lady Kathren take over everyting."

Silver took a jerky breath as her heartbeat began to slow. "You do not like Mistress Kath-ren?"

"She ees bossy. She smile lak a fool at de men but when dey are not here, she ees vicious. Someday dey weel find out dis mistress ees not a good woman."

Silver's dreams were haunted by formless shapes, whispering shadows that cackled from the corners of her room. When morning came she was more exhausted than when she'd fallen into her bed.

Downstairs, she found Ferrell alone in the breakfast room. He came to his feet and offered her a chair. "Sorry, but everyone seems to be up and about but me. I'll ring Jubal."

When her food was brought, Silver could only stare at it.

Ferrell leaned forward and when Silver looked up, he stared deeply into her eyes. "You don't seem well this morning. Is there . . . anything I can do to help?"

He spoke so tenderly that Silver felt a lump in her throat. "I want Walker come home."

Ferrell sat back. "I see." He studied her a minute then said cheerfully, "Well, he may have deserted you but I'm available. And since you're already wearing your habit, why don't we go for a ride?"

Silver brightened. "My horse is Rising Sun. He have very good legs."

Ferrell laughed. "Indeed. Let's go."

When their horses were ready, Ferrell suggested, "There's not much room for riding here. Too many trees. I'll take you down the bayou road." With that he wheeled his horse and took off.

They thundered down the long avenue of oaks, out the wrought-iron gates, and turned toward St. Martinville. Silver beat him easily to the crossroads, but unlike the

Grayson men, Ferrell seemed to take his defeat with good humor.

They proceeded slowly as the road followed the jade waters of the bayou that snaked beneath mossy bowers of oak and cypress. Every bush was laden with scented flowers, and the blossoms filled the air with sweetness. Silver smiled. "This land grow many trees."

Ferrell pulled up his horse. "Do you think Rising Sun will tolerate being tied? Good. Let's let them rest here."

The bank beside the water was covered in spongy grasses and ferns. Silver looked at the water as they sat down.

"Do you know when Walker will come home?"

The first frown puckered Ferrell's handsome brow. "No, I don't," he replied shortly.

Silver looked at his profile, the hawkish nose with thin, flared nostrils, a rather harsh mouth.

"You like Amanda," she said abruptly. "She like you also?"

Ferrell gave her a guarded look. "You're very observant. How did you know?"

"I see when you look at her. Does she like you?"

Ferrell's experience with women was long and varied yet it came to him that he was totally unprepared for the quest upon which he had set himself. This one was a contradiction, shrewd but guileless, trusting but not a fool. He plotted his course carefully.

"I like Amanda very much but she is a snob." "I do not know 'snob.' "

Ferrell relaxed. "Well, it's someone who thinks they're much better than others. Amanda thinks her money makes her better, so she won't lower herself to show interest in me—though, of course, she's very much attracted."

Silver looked away at the water, for his eyes seemed to probe her mind. "You are not a rich white eyes?"

Ferrell cursed inwardly, for he had blundered into another corner.

"Oh, I have plenty of money," he said, holding out his hand. "This ring is worth more than that creaking old

233

house and everything in it. My . . . my father left it to me."

"What was his name?"

Damn her! he thought savagely. Thanks to his good mother, he was a bastard sired by God-knew-what drunken wharf trash. His thoughts darted frantically until he came upon a suitable answer.

"His name was David, after David in the Bible."

"What is a by-bul?"

For a moment, Ferrell's frustration waxed so great that he thought about throwing her on her back and being done with the matter. But after looking away for a moment, he turned back and smiled. "You have the most beautiful gray eyes," he said softly. "So pale and shimmering, like silver . . . like your name."

He had moved so close that Silver could feel his breath on her cheek. The way his eyes moved over her face made her aware of a sudden desire to be held against a hard-muscled body, to be touched and kissed. Before Walker she had not known this need, only infrequent and undefined yearnings, sometimes a desire to touch one of the young braves to see what his body felt like. But never this hunger that came at night and chased sleep away, that grew more intense the longer her husband persisted in his stupid vow.

The thought of Walker brought her up sharply. She got to her feet and brushed off her skirt, forcing a smile. "Take me to see more of this Louse-ana."

Ferrell spoke without enthusiasm. "Sure."

They had ridden only a little further when Silver came upon an idea to terminate the excursion. She was no longer comfortable with this man.

Turning the big stallion suddenly, she gave an exuberant laugh. "I beat you to stables!" And leaning forward, she had only to give the black stallion a squeeze with her thighs and the horse lunged forward so fast she lost her breath.

Silver was exhilarated and relaxed when she finished

234

the race—winning, of course.

Ferrell dismounted quickly and was beside her before she could leap to the ground. With a warm "well done!" he put his hands about her waist and lifted her down.

Jones had come to hold the stallion from force of habit, and it was fortunate. When Ferrell stepped close to lift Silver down, the horse reared into the air, snorting and behaving with his customary orneriness.

Ferrell snatched Silver out of danger and pulled her against him, swearing, "That bloody bastard!"

While Jones tried to calm the horse, Ferrell was so preoccupied with glaring at the animal he didn't seem aware that his arm was clasped tightly across Silver's back, nor was she at first. But after a moment, she realized that his hand had become mysteriously trapped under her armpit so that his fingers pressed softly but firmly into her right breast. She even imagined that they moved ever so subtly in a caress.

She tried to ease away from him but his grasp tightened.

She almost gasped with relief when he finally released her.

But then he turned her to him, his hands on her shoulders. "Are you all right?" he asked solicitously.

Silver noticed with alarm that Jones was leading Rising Sun to his stall and was now out of earshot unless she deemed it necessary to scream. "Here, let's take a look," Ferrell was saying like a kindly father.

His hands moved gently over her neck, down her arms, felt her ribs. Silver stood like one frozen, and tottered stiffly when he turned her around and began running his hands up and down her back. Suddenly he bent and took her thigh within his hands, squeezing the length of her leg—as though a Quohadie Teichas could be injured by so little!

She was getting very angry.

Ferrell stood back and looked at her, his eyes knowing and warm. "Well, thank God you have no broken bones. But you may be very sore. I keep a special ointment in my room." His voice thickened. "It would be wonderful

235

massaged into your back and legs, your . . . upper body."

Silver stepped away from him and jerked her riding jacket back into place, her voice just short of a sneer. "On my back you would see many stripes from the whip. On my ankles you would see how I wear chains of slavery for many moons. I will not need your 'ointment.' "

She saw his dark eyes flare but he smiled when he spoke.

"You are a remarkable woman, Silver. I'm most proud of our friendship. Why don't you go on to the house and tell Jubal to make some fresh coffee?"

Silver's gaze remained hostile as she watched him lead his horse into the stable.

After standing for a moment to collect himself, she turned toward the house, walking so slowly that she was not out of hearing distance when a dog began barking frantically from inside the stable. By the time the snarls rose to frightened shrieks, she was running toward the double doors of the stable.

She ran down the hall, turned and ran down the next one, and at last found Ferrell Cassadyne, riding whip in the air. On the ground cowered a formidable-looking dog with close-cropped ears and bobbed tail. Its face was laid open to the bone and there were bloody stripes across its shoulders. It shrank into the corner, alternately snarling and yelping with pain.

Silver's right hand whipped like lightning to the little leather sheath under her hair while the left one shot out to catch Ferrell's wrist, halting his downswing.

In his blind rage, Ferrell only snatched absently to free his hand but when he couldn't he turned. Then he gasped—first in surprise that the iron grip belonged to a woman, then in horror at the knife raised over the back of his neck.

Ferrell did not move another muscle as he stared into flashing crystal eyes.

"That dog live here. He is mine. Do not touch him again or you will find your scalp hanging on the door of

236

your room." The threat was delivered tonelessly, coldly, and Ferrell felt the prickle of death running along his skin. She meant it.

He relaxed his arm. "You don't understand." He felt disgusted to hear the wheedling note in his voice, but he went on. "These are guard dogs. They're kept chained because they're killers. This one got loose." Then with sudden inspiration: "The dog attacked Rising Sun."

The girl had released his wrist, lowered her knife, and stepped back; she did not seem afraid he would overcome her in a burst of anger.

"Rising Sun can care for himself. This dog is mine." She looked down at the animal, who was not moving now. "If he lives, he will no longer wear chains. Where are others?"

As fright passed, Ferrell's anger surged up to choke him, and if it wouldn't destroy everything he had worked for, he'd have turned the little beggar's own knife on her. As it was, he could barely reply for the murderous rage inside him.

"I don't know what you're talking about," he said frostily.

"You say there are other dogs. Where are they?"

Ferrell's eyes gleamed suddenly. If he could do nothing else, he would give the twit enough rope to hang herself.

"They're kept in pens behind the carriage house."

His anger abated enough that he could breathe more normally as he watched the young woman stride briskly out of sight, carrying herself with a morbid sense of purpose that reminded him of an executioner going to his duty.

He started for the house—and the unlocked marble-topped liquor cabinet. It was his only recourse, for in that single, blind flash of bloodlust, he could well have undone everything.

He would sit quietly and drink. And think. Then he would be calm and able to enjoy the scene when the chips started to fly.

Chapter 15

The livery boy made a noise in his throat when he looked up and found a dark, slim figure silhouetted in the door of the carriage house. Although he saw a female shape, there was something so menacing in its stance that a chill ran through him.

Snatching off his hat, he croaked, "Ma'am?"

"Where are the dogs?" said the shadow.

"De dogs, ma'am?"

"The guard dogs who live in chains."

It did not seem wise to question the young woman's authority. "Outside, ma'am. Around de corner," he whispered.

When they reached the pens, the brood of black, sharp-faced dogs leaped at the bars, snarling.

"Dey are vicious, ma'am. Don't go near dem," he warned. But the young woman began speaking softly in a strange tongue, and the dogs quieted.

"Unlock the cages."

"Ma'am, we only let dem loose at night and pen dem by offering food de next morning. Ah m-must not. No one could move about for fear—eet would be very dangerous."

The strange-colored eyes came around slowly until they rested upon him. "It will be very dangerous if you do *not*."

The boy's hand shook as he unlocked each cage. He did not, however, open the doors but scrambled into a nearby tree to watch.

Silver opened one cage at a time, praising each stiff-legged black devil that emerged. The animals gathered about her timidly, their slick bodies wagging all over as she touched them lightly on the head and continued talking to them, and when she moved, the pack swam about her like frisky pups. As soon as they were out of sight, the boy jumped to the ground and tore out for the back door of the mansion.

Ignoring Jubal's irate squawk, he rushed through the kitchen, down the hall, and burst into the sunroom adjacent to the back patio where the mistress worked on her books in the mornings.

She looked angry at the interruption but he blurted out between gasps. "De young woman! She—she came. She . . . she ees a *witch!*"

Kathren frowned. "What are you talking about?"

"De woman ees a witch! She let de guard dogs loose and put a gris-gris on dem. Dey followed her like pups. Ah saw wid my own eyes. She ees a witch!" he shrilled.

Silver did not flinch as Kathren's pacing brought her dangerously close to an impact, nor did her face change when the woman wheeled abruptly and stuck her face so close that her nose almost touched her own.

"This is the last straw," Kathren stormed in her face. "What makes you think you can come here flaunting your despicable marriage and daring anyone to say anything about it? What? Tell me? Do you presume that you are now the mistress of the house—that you can march about ordering *my* servants around? That you can turn up your nose at my food, spit on my hospitality and—" She drew back a little at the soft glitter in the gray eyes, and finished with an imperious flourish of her finger. "You will *not* flounce to the stables and ride any horse you choose, and you will not go anywhere *else* on this property and take it upon yourself to make changes without my permission. And if you do it again, I will personally see that you are thrown off this property and Walker can go to hell if he doesn't like it. Do I make myself plain?"

Silver tried hard to remember this screeching woman

was her mother-in-law, but her jaws flexed angrily and she lapsed into her former misuse of pronouns.

"Me have dogs and horses now, and me say they not wear chains."

Amanda intervened quickly, for she thought for a moment that Kathren would leap on the girl and claw her eyes out.

"Kathren," she threatened, "I think we should let Walker handle this. You had better remember to whom you are speaking."

Kathren got a grip on herself before she did something she would regret. But her hands knotted at her sides as she gritted softly, "All right, we'll let it rest until the men come back. But don't you ever, *ever*, take it upon yourself to alter so much as a crooked picture in this house again."

That night Silver lay in bed and worried until she was ill that Walker would be angry when he returned. But she also worried about the animals whose lives were in danger, and even about the old woman who haunted the upper rooms. Was this Sheba kept in chains by Mistress Kathren? Did Ferrell chase the old one through the dark hallways and beat her like he did the dogs? She remembered the smell of the room, the way the old one disappeared into the wall. She must tell Walker of these things when he returned—if only she could manage to capture him alone.

And there was only one opportunity to do that. She would risk his anger and go to his room after the others slept. He had said he did not like the great house either so perhaps he would want to take them away when she told him about the evil there.

The men returned from the plantation the next morning, laughing and in high spirits.

Having slipped out to the front porch alone to wait for them, Silver was sitting in the swing, hidden by the ivy-covered lattices, when the men dismounted and Jones came to take the horses around back. Kathren did not

240

notice her when she walked out to the front steps and waved gaily.

"Samuel, darling! I've missed you." She ran down the steps and into her husband's arms. They were all laughing and talking when they came upon the porch.

Samuel and Kathren were the last to go inside and just before they did, Kathren spotted her in the swing. Her only acknowledgment was an icy glare.

Silver waited, then wandered slowly through the hall toward the breakfast room, where she could hear Kathren's lively chatter.

The men were seated and Kathren was ordering Jubal this way and that as he scurried to set out yet more food.

Suddenly Walker looked up and saw her standing in the door.

His eyes seemed to catch fire when he looked at her, and for a moment Silver was so mesmerized by the dancing, gray-green orbs that she forgot her purpose. It was as though no anger had ever passed between them—just the fiery sparks that erupted when their bodies touched.

Then Kathren, following his gaze, chirped, "Oh, Silver, do come in, dear. Have a seat right there beside Walker."

Stunned, Silver obeyed, stumbling a little because she was unable to drag her eyes from Walker's as she went around the table.

His voice was almost timid as he turned to look at her. "Hi. How's it been going?"

Silver blushed and lowered her eyes, but Kathren pretended the question was a general one.

"Well, there's been a rather nasty misunderstanding, I'm afraid, but there's no need to bother you men with it. You've got enough to tend to without worrying over our domestic tranquility."

Walker was instantly alert. "Misunderstanding?"

Kathren had risen impatiently to take the platter from Jubal and began heaping the plates with steaming grits and ham.

"Well, it seems that Silver didn't understand about the guard dogs." Kathren allowed her lips to thin a little but took visible pains to force a smile. "But I'm sure she had

241

no idea of the tragic results when—"

Walker's fork clattered to the table at the word "tragic," and he looked around at Silver.

"What happened?"

Kathren sounded alarmed. "Oh, you mustn't be angry with her, Walker. As I said, it was just a small misunderstanding."

"What . . . happened?" he repeated distinctly.

Kathren shot Silver a defeated and apologetic smile, and went on.

"She turned the guard dogs loose. They attacked poor Randy, the livery hand, and almost killed him. But she couldn't have known, Walker. You mustn't be angry with her."

Amanda's eyes had grown progressively wider during Kathren's manipulation. She knew there had been no attack on the livery boy—she'd seen him this very morning and he repeated his tale of how the girl "spoke dat heathen tongue and de dogs obeyed!" He seemed quite awed and not the least bit near death.

She used a tone that commanded her brother's immediate attention.

"Walker." He looked at her. "Everything is fine. Trust me."

But Walker glanced at each of the women, then stood up stiffly. "Silver, could I see you in private, please?" And without waiting for a reply, he grabbed her by the wrist and led her from the room.

He didn't speak until they had gone out across the back patio to the railing that overlooked the bayou. Then he whipped her around to face him.

"Did you turn the dogs loose?" he demanded hotly.

Silver's lip trembled. "M-me do. Me see that man hit dog and dogs live in cages and me open doors so they go free."

The muscles in his jaws twitched, his eyes shimmered, and for a moment Silver thought he would strike her.

"If you cannot be trusted," he said carefully, seeming to drag each word from his throat, "I will have no qualms whatever about locking you up. There are plenty of rooms where you can spend your time without being a menace to the entire household."

"The Great Spirit no make dogs to live in cages!"

"They're in cages for a reason—and you're not going to get around me with tears, so don't start!"

"Me Quohadie Teichas. Me no have tears—me no roll eyes like Cah-meel-ya." She demonstrated. "And stick out the lips." She demonstrated again. "And me no speak with two tongues. Me go home where laws are same for whole village, not like white eyes who—"

She broke off and dodged when he flung out his arm to point toward the house.

"You will not disrupt this household like you did the fort!" he thundered. "Now march back straight back in there and apologize this instant!"

"No!"

Walker gasped, his face quivering in a series of apoplectic distortions.

"No?"

Silver spat, but made sure she missed. "No!"

Now he spoke softly, his jaws clamped until water would not have passed through his teeth.

"You will do what I tell you to do this minute or so help me God I'll tan your backside until you won't walk for a month of Sundays!"

Silver's chin jutted and her hand crept toward the back of her neck. "Me not your slave. Me—"

He grabbed her arm and snatched her forward so that her head snapped back. He followed a gravel walkway through the deep shade of tropical growth, and Silver had to run after him to keep from pulling her arm from its socket. Tears blinded her, making her stumble repeatedly, but in spite of her clawing she could not get free.

Safely away from the house, Walker went directly to a stone bench, hauled her around and across his knee, and immediately the hair at the back of her neck parted. He saw the necklace was not a necklace, and the knife inside the little leather sheath was not homemade. He jerked the knife away and tossed it on the ground, and when she fought him, he leaned his body over her shoulders to

243

hold her down. Then he started whacking.

Silver screamed in rage and humiliation. Only once had Horse Back spanked her (she had defied him to go on a hunt with the warriors), but she had never forgotten it.

"Kiowa-che tivo sata! Nei may-way-kah ein, moo-be-er!" she shrieked, then decided a translation was in order: "Scoundrel white man dog! I will kill you, you snake!"

But Walker didn't stop until he had completed ten licks, at the end of which he stood up and set her on her feet.

"That's only a little sample of what's to come if you don't have the grace to appreciate the hospitality of this house and behave as a guest. Otherwise, you will reside here as a prisoner until I find the unfortunate man who sired you. Till that time comes you will mind your own damned business and stay out of affairs that don't concern you!"

He wheeled and started up the path. Silver stood transfixed with rage.

Then she was running. She gained his backside so swiftly that Walker barely had time to turn before she sprang through the air at him.

Silver was as shocked as he to find herself straddling him from the front instead. His arms flew around her back to keep her from falling, and hers grabbed at his shoulders as she toppled backward.

Suddenly his eyes locked to hers, and for a split second they were as still as two statues, nothing moving but the hot flashes of light between their eyes. Then his arm slid up the back of her neck and he grabbed her face to his.

The first fierceness of his attack waned to a hungry, languorous, insatiable kiss, and Silver felt the quivering response of her body. She clung to him like a leech, knocked his hat off as she curled her fingers in his hair, hooked her legs around him until he would have had to pry her off. His tongue darted inside her mouth, and she could not get enough of it.

Then he walked, pressing her to him with a hand on her buttocks, her hips moving sensually at the touch of his belly between her thighs. Around the corner he moved to a patch of grass near a fountain and laid her down.

"You'll learn." His voice trembled. "You'll learn one way or the other."

She shivered as he moved over her, his face dark and his arms like columns of stone on either side of her.

"Me not walk in white eyes shoes," she murmured thickly.

He spread her unresisting hands against the ground and lowered himself. "Then I will teach you the hard way." His eyelids drooped as he looked at her mouth.

"Then teach me white eyes ways . . . your hard way . . ." She lifted her head and nibbled at his mouth, and with a groan his head swooped down. His mouth left trails of fire on her face and neck, and when the footsteps approached she registered the noise like bird chatter in the trees.

"Well, I'll be damned. And here I was rushing to the rescue."

Walker gasped and rolled off of her, and they lay panting, their eyes still glazed, as Seth continued to chuckle merrily.

Prissy could not coax Silver into lunch with the family nor entice her to eat the cake she brought to her room later. According to Silver, Walker had been so angry when Seth found them together that he had stalked off without a word—not even helping his own wife to her feet. And in turn, Seth muttered all the way back to the house that his brother was not only a fool but inconsiderate, bull-headed, and stupid. Silver seemed afraid that Seth had gone directly to Walker after depositing her in her room, which would make matters worse.

Although Prissy had fretted for several hours to produce the new hairdo, it didn't lift Silver's spirits. In fact, though she claimed to like the new fullness and the wispy

245

tendrils pulled around her face, Prissy got the firm impression Silver would never submit to the ordeal of curling her hair again.

Prissy felt the prick of resentment as she helped Silver into a pale, silver-blue muslin with a high neck, long sleeves, and wide white lace collar. Things hadn't been easy for the girl, but at least she was able to dress beautifully and sit down to a meal with the family as Walker's wife.

"You look beauteeful," said Prissy wistfully. "Walker cannot stay angry for long."

Silver raised one brow. "You do not know Walker."

"Come now," said Prissy, suddenly impatient. "You look lak a princess, you are married to a prince, and you still aren't happy. What eef—" Prissy was looking at her thoughtfully and Silver waited for her to go on. "Dere ees really no need to be sad," Prissy went on soberly. "Tink eef you wanted someone you could never have."

To Silver's astonishment, Prissy turned away quickly and left the bedroom.

As Prissy started toward the stairs, she heard footsteps coming up them. She glanced over the railing, afraid it was the mistress coming to check on Silver's delay.

For a moment Prissy stood frozen by the sight of Seth Grayson stepping lightly up the staircase. They always carefully avoided any moments alone, and she should hurry back to Silver's room before it was too late. But she couldn't take her eyes from him. Such a man! The tight, butterscotch riding breeches clung to his long muscular thighs; the tall boots made his legs even longer; and the flowing white blouse was opened negligently at the neck, revealing a deep bronze chest furred with gold hair.

She came to herself and turned quickly, meaning to scamper back to Silver's room.

"Prissy, wait!" Seth ran the last few steps until he was on the landing, and stood so close that Prissy's head seemed to fill with the musky cologne he wore.

"Yes, Master Grayson," she said weakly, looking up at him.

"I . . . I forget," he murmured, his gold-lashed eyes searching her face.

Prissy dropped her gaze. "Maybe you weel remember later." She started to step around him.

"Wait. I mean . . . oh, yes. I was coming to see if Silver would come down for dinner—though I wouldn't blame her if she refused."

"Yes, she ees coming," nodded Prissy, but further words deserted her.

"It's frustrating to watch the way they're bungling this marriage," he went on, "especially when it's obvious they care so much for each other. Don't you agree?" She felt his eyes probing her face like soft fingertips, though she could not force her head up.

"Yes sir," she whispered.

"I think they're fools," he said, his voice lower.

"Yes sir."

"Prissy." His tone brought her face up and her eyes were held to his as she knew they would be. He moved toward her slowly, towering above her so that she had to bend her neck. "Prissy," he murmured again, then his head darted down.

One taste, not touching her anywhere else—that was all he meant to take. Then his arms were around her and he couldn't stop kissing her.

Prissy felt the wall against her back, felt the strength at last of the tall, hard body she had watched shamelessly whenever circumstance permitted.

"We cannot!"

"I know," he murmured against her mouth. "They can and won't, we can't but would. It isn't fair, Prissy!"

Prissy thought her heart would burst with its pounding. "You must stop," she croaked, not opening her eyes as his lips slid across her cheek. "Please!" she gasped.

He stood back, breathing hard. "For now. But I have to see you again. I'm *going* to see you again."

Prissy ducked her head and moved around him, heading for the stairs. "Maybe, Monsieur Grayson."

"Prissy!"

She stopped, holding to the banister for support.

"Look at me."

She turned and raised her eyes, and she thought her face would melt from the heat of his gaze.

"Soon," he said. "It has to be soon. One fool in this family is enough."

Prissy could only nod mutely and pray her knees did not give out before she reached the bottom.

Silver was glad she wouldn't have to go to the dining room alone.

"You look ravishing as usual," smiled Seth, looping her arm through his. "Don't you feel the slightest bit of pity for my brother? He'll have to suffer through the whole meal watching you and knowing he can't have you for at least two hours." When Silver blushed, he grinned wickedly. "I'm sorry, I shouldn't have said that." When she smiled her forgiveness, he quipped, "Because he deserves every minute of it."

They talked and laughed as they strolled through the foyer toward the dining hall, then fell silent when they heard Kathren's lively chatter punctuated with trills of laughter.

"Well," observed Seth dryly, "the clouds seemed to have lifted.

Two wide double doors gave entrance to the dining hall. As Seth and Silver stepped within their frame, both of them stopped abruptly. Seated next to Kathren was Camelia, and next to Camelia was Walker. His mouth was half opened as though he had been speaking. When he saw Seth and Silver, it opened further. Silver looked at the floor, unable to stop the flush of outrage climbing up her cheeks.

Kathren's gaiety deserted her as she spoke to the late arrivals. "As you can see, we're waiting dinner on you."

Seth only smiled into Silver's eyes as he took her to her chair on the other side of Walker, then seated himself next to her.

Kathren rang a bell, and as Jubal began to set tossed green salads in front of each of them, Silver struggled to hide her anguish and humiliation. And for a moment, it seemed she wasn't the only one to feel awkward. Not a soul spoke; only the muted jangle of silverware, the rustle of clothing as bodies sought an increasingly elusive position of comfort, and the little contented clucking noise that Jubal made as he laid before them his special croutons seasoned with garlic and red pepper.

Finally Kathren glanced around the table and smiled. "I'm sure you're all as delighted as I am that Camelia has finished her business in St. Martinville and returned to us. My goodness, it's been as though we'd lost a member of the family in her absence!"

No one joined her nerve-grating little laugh. But Silver noticed that Camelia didn't seem to feel awkward at all. She scarcely took her eyes off Walker's face, which at the moment was partially hidden behind his wineglass as he leveled a predatory look at Seth, who, in turn, was smiling secretively as he took his first bite.

Samuel was not smiling. It seemed that no sooner had his life become worth living again than the family was coming apart at the seams. And for the first time he began to see that his new wife was a woman like other women; one who couldn't resist dabbling in the romantic affairs of those about her. Camelia would never have come back to Gray Shadows without ample encouragement.

Silver picked at her salad with polite interest but had no intention of eating leaves like a buffalo even if her stomach had not already been in turmoil. Her hand shook so badly when she tried to lift her fork that she quickly laid it down. She could feel Walker's gaze on her and twisted her neck up to one side until she could see his face.

Gray-green orbs bored her through. Silver looked back to her plate, feeling strangely guilty. Had she only imagined a flicker of pain beneath his eyes?

"Camelia," said Kathren, "you must tell me the name of that fragrance you're wearing. It's absolutely bewitching."

Camelia's laugh was too shrill. "But you guessed it,

Kitty. It's called Bewitching."

"And so it is," murmured Walker, sipping his wine and probing Camelia with a warm look over his glass.

The blonde blushed prettily. "I bought it yesterday at Zack's. And he has the most divine little hat in the window. Why don't you go shopping with me tomorrow, Kitty?" She popped a forkful of dewy leaves into her mouth and chewed daintily.

Silver was not surprised that Camelia liked buffalo food.

"I'd love to," tinkled Kathren, then sweetly to her husband: "Can you manage without me, dear?"

"I'll try." Kathren sensed an ironic tone beneath his bland smile so she fluttered her lashes at him in a perplexed way.

Camelia laid her hand lightly over Walker's. "Remember when we spent the whole day at the French Market in New Orleans? I must have bought a hundred dollars' worth of clothes that day!"

"Of course," said Walker, looking into her eyes. "Do you still have that cute little green bonnet, the plaid one?"

"You remembered!" Her eyes misted with joy. "Of course I have it. You told me how much you liked it."

Samuel cleared his throat, eyed his wife at the other end of the table, and said crossly, "You'd better see what's keeping Jubal. I'm starving."

Kathren rang the bell again but chattered on as Jubal hurried in with heapings of shrimp gumbo and side dishes of boudin—thick sausages stuffed with rice and seasonings.

As Jubal lifted two untouched salad plates from the table, Walker handed him his wine goblet. "A refill, please." Jubal darted a glance at the mistress, who was scowling.

"Oui, monsieur, *un moment.*"

In a subtle movement not lost on Walker, Seth leaned closer to Silver. "Why don't I show you the local racetrack while they tend to their shopping? Rising Sun will be competing there in less than a week—if you haven't made a house pet of him by then," he grinned.

"The horse should know nothing but the inside of his stall and the track in the meantime," said Walker tersely. "You can't expect him to rise to the competition after he's been coddled to death by a female."

Seth arched a brow. "Oh? And have you witnessed this 'coddling,' my dearest brother? Undoubtedly not or you would have seen Rising Sun turn in record times. Come out and watch her work him in the morning."

Walker's glass struck a blunt chord against the mahogany table. "Perhaps both of you need reminding that the horse belongs to me."

Smothering an outright laugh, Seth fixed his plate with a grave stare of pity and regret, as though his brother's childish remark embarrassed him terribly.

Silver had no such compunction. "Rising Sun is mine also," she announced, her eyes flashing around the table.

Seth nodded thoughtfully at his gumbo. "Yes, that was my understanding of the law . . ."

Walker leaned around Silver to look at his brother's profile. "Then undoubtedly you've been listening to Silver's version of 'horse trading'—a matter of heathen tradition which does not extend to the state of Louisiana. She's confused." He bolted down the rest of his wine.

Suddenly aware that all eyes had turned in his direction, Walker felt compelled to explain further this matter of a trade—which could be grossly misconstrued. So he set his glass down.

"She has a lingering obsession to own a horse of her own and I promised her one." He bent a jaundiced eye upon his ward. "She has mistakenly assumed I meant *my* horse."

So interesting was the table conversation that Ferrell Cassadyne had forgotten his appetite for rich, south Louisiana cuisine and lounged in his chair, arms crossed, one finger propped against his cheek, listening avidly.

"Far be it from me to interfere in a family matter," he said, "but Silver and I went riding together the other day and I must say I've never seen anyone handle a horse with such ease, especially one with a reputation for making short work of a long list of stable hands."

Though his voice was so soft as to barely be heard, a round of startled gazes swung upon him, the most piercing of which belonged to the eldest son. But Ferrell looked Walker in the eye and said quietly, "I agree with Seth. You should come out in the morning and watch her work with him."

Samuel's recent goal had been to turn the management of his estates over to his sons completely so that he could enjoy his golden years with Kathren. There were times, however, when his offspring evidenced swift and unaccountable regressions into spoiled brats; and it also came to his notice that Kathren not only lacked the skill to control them but often seemed to encourage them in such lapses. She was actually grinning at all this folderol.

Smugly pleased that his voice still had the power to silence a disorderly room, Samuel said clearly, "I think this conversation has gone far enough. Every animal on this property is fed and maintained with money from my pocket, if not directly then by money from varied foundations that I established for each of you when you were in diapers." He looked around at each of them. "It is my opinion that if Silver handles the animal as well as claimed, then the family can only benefit. And we do — in case you've forgotten — work as a family unit, do we not?"

Pleased with the silence and lowered gazes, Samuel went on. "I would like to see Silver and Rising Sun together myself. In fact I *invite* you all to the stables in the morning." He met his wife's scowl with a beguiling smile. "Kathren, see that you're finished with your office duties by eight o'clock sharp. A good queen keeps in touch with the very smallest matters in her kingdom."

At seven forty-five the next morning, Amanda stood frowning at her reflection as she brushed out her hair in front of the mirror.

"I know you ride well, Camelia. But take my word for it. This is not the time for a demonstration."

252

"I haven't done badly so far," Camelia replied. "You saw the way Walker acted last night—just like I knew he would. That's why I came back. Kathren said if I'd—"

Amanda caught the other girl's eyes in the mirror. "So. You and Kathren have a plan, do you?"

"I intend to seduce him," said Camelia flatly. "He doesn't care a fig about his wife and I just can't imagine how she forced him to marry her. But she did. She must have."

"Oh?" said Amanda. "Then you could have a very serious problem on your hand, couldn't you?"

Camelia's smile faded to a look of horror. "You don't think . . . oh, my God! I never thought of that. Oh, Amanda! Your father would simply die if Walker has sired a heathen brat!"

Amanda glanced at the clock and rose to get her riding jacket. "Apparently you and Kathren haven't covered every possibility after all."

"You're being mean, Amanda. And I can't believe the way you're acting; not sticking by a friend who's been treated so despicably by your own brother! Besides, I see you've put on your riding habit, too."

Amanda stood before the mirror to give the brown velvet skirt a final pat. "Yes," she said mildly, "but only in case I feel the sudden need to make myself scarce."

Camelia wheeled for the door. "I'm not waiting on you a minute longer. You're just trying to impress Ferrell—pretending all the time that you can't stand him. Well, he's as handsome as any and according to Kathren a very wealthy man. Besides, you'd better latch onto whatever's available. You're not getting any younger, you know."

Amanda's gasp came too late to be heard as Camelia closed the door loudly. Ferrell indeed! Amanda fumed. For two cents she'd rid the house of every one of its guests in the time it took to swat a fly! Not a single minute had she had alone with Walker—there was no time for anything between the inane struggles of the women around him. Ferrell Cassadyne! She was only thankful he'd been too interested in the savage girl to pursue *her* lately. He disgusted her, made her flesh crawl.

Ferrell indeed!

Her brown curls jiggled and her color ran high as she flounced down the stairs and swung around the post at the bottom step.

"Oooh!" The squeak was torn from her as she collided with Ferrell's chest and his arms clamped around her.

"What's the hurry?" he chuckled. "Afraid you'll miss the show?"

She jerked away from him. "There wouldn't be any *show* if it weren't for your goading. I just hope the girl doesn't kill herself trying to show off for all of us."

"Rest assured there's no danger of that," he grinned.

Amanda drew herself up. "It's almost eight," she reminded him coldly.

His face was hurt. "Amanda, I've never been anything but kind to you, yet you act as though you despise me. I even thought of asking Samuel for a few pointers . . ." He spoke with boyish innocence. "I wanted very much for us to be friends. I think you know that."

"Please," said Amanda tightly, "don't bother Daddy with any more family problems." Her face hardened with the effort to say the words. "You are a guest in this house. Please forgive me if I've been rude."

Ferrell smiled. "Forgiven." He held out his arm gallantly and Amanda saw no course but to take it.

Chapter 16

Dressed in mustard-colored riding breeches with similar white blouses and tall boots, the two men lounging against the fence could have passed for twins. The tallest and heaviest, however, wore a fierce scowl whereas the younger was serene and perfectly content to let the silence between them lie untouched.

Camelia swung her hips as she approached, almost gasping with delight at the sight of the men. How many families could boast not one but two such specimens? If it weren't for his cold lack of interest, she would have happily pursued Seth in Walker's absence; but loyalty ran so deep in the Graysons that her shy and subtle overtures had been immediately rebuffed.

"And where is everyone else?" she chirped.

Walker gazed toward the paddock where Jones was trying to manage Rising Sun and said nothing, so Seth answered, "They'll be along in a moment. In fact, there comes Silver now."

Camelia's heart nearly burst with hatred as she watched the sleek, tanned savage walking beside Samuel, smiling at something he said. She turned to Walker.

"I'd love to try my hand at Rising Sun, too." She added teasingly, "I've always wanted to give him a run but dared not ask permission."

Walker turned around and leaned away from the fence.

"Absolutely and unequivocally *no*." With that he turned for the solitary open field that lay beyond the paddock and the one mile oval practice track within its circling, white board fence.

Camelia pouted to Seth. "He knows perfectly well I can sit a horse better than any woman in this state — I have a wall full of trophies to prove it!"

"We're well aware of your reputation," said Seth easily, "and because you know horses, you should certainly realize that placing for confirmation or even in a stee-plechase isn't the same. Besides, Rising Sun is a one-man horse." He grinned. "Excuse me. A one-woman horse."

Kathren had found some last minute chore to detain her, but Ferrell and Amanda arrived at the track shortly. Amanda took the first opportunity to rid herself of Ferrell by perching on the top rail of the fence like a young boy.

Rising Sun was in high spirits and Walker's heart climbed in his throat as Silver and Jones parried with the horse. Although Walker had managed to hide the fact successfully, he was curious to see if the girl's ability matched her reputation. He was also feeling no small pride that she had so impressed Jones and Seth, momentarily forgetting that he'd had no part in her equestrian training whatsoever.

Silver glued herself to the horse and when Jones fired the pistol, the animal sprang forward. He hugged the inside corners and extended himself down the straights; nevertheless, Silver sensed a tension in him, an excited and almost frenzied constrainment. She knew nothing of a good clock time but she did know he was not running as well as he could.

They finished the lap with Rising Sun barely breathing hard. Jones looked at his watch. "Not nearly as good as yesterday," he said with obvious disappointment.

"But a beautiful sight anyway." Seth smiled at Silver. "You look like you were born on that animal."

She acknowledged the compliment with a brief smile but immediately frowned again as she walked the horse in a slow circle. "I want to go again."

Jones looked at the men for approval. Silver saw Seth and Samuel nod enthusiastically but Walker just kept looking at her, his eyes deep and inscrutable.

She guided Rising Sun back into the chute and Jones called "Ready up . . ." and fired. The stallion burst from the enclosure and they were off again.

After another lap, Silver stopped the horse in front of them again, and Camelia said in a bored voice, "That's very good, Silver."

But Silver was totally absorbed in her mount. Her cheeks were bright, her hair windblown, and Walker could have cared less about the lap time.

"Again," she said, looking at the men.

Camelia shifted her weight, hoping her restlessness would rub off on the others.

Noting her ploy, Amanda called out enthusiastically, "Give him another run, Silver. It's exciting just to watch you!"

Silver turned the horse back toward the chute a third time, then pulled him up before she reached it. The others watched with new interest as she slipped lithely to the ground and began working with the saddle strap. Instant concern flashed from one face to the other that perhaps she had found some undetected injury.

Jones was under no such misconception and hurried to her. "No, ma'am, don't do that. It's okay for a country stroll but—"

The saddle was small and light—and now on the ground. Jones looked at the men helplessly.

Deep lines scored Walker's brow but when Seth and Samuel looked at him askance, he nodded. "I think she knows what she's doing."

Camelia's soul fluttered to despair at the pride in Walker's voice, but she could think of nothing to say as Silver mounted and positioned the horse in the chute again.

Amanda climbed down from the fence. "Walker, I hope you're right. I've never seen anyone take a race lap riding bareback." Walker swallowed tightly, wondering if his swelled pride might cost him too much.

Suddenly, a choking fear leaped into his chest as he imagined her taking a spill. "Stop her. Stop her, dammit!"

It was too late. The pistol cracked the air and Jones pulled the chute lever simultaneously.

Adrenaline shot through Silver's veins as they cleared the steel gate, for she felt the animal's power break loose with the fury of the black storm cloud that ravaged the plains. She could feel each ripple of movement as though it came from her own body, the bunching contraction of backstrap muscles, the accordion effect of unwinding vertebrae, then an explosion of power, like an arrow catapulted from the bow. His mane stung her face as she hovered low, clamping her legs about the rib cage and feeling the vibration of air as his mighty lungs blasted and sucked, blasted and sucked. Her captivity, her torture, even her abduction from her homeland was almost worth this one moment.

Both rider and horse were properly winded when they stopped in front of the cheering group, which had expanded to include several stable hands and Rising Sun's personal jockey.

Jones was dancing in circles looking at his watch as though he'd found a gold piece.

"The angels in heaven must be shoutin'," he sang jubilantly. "That beats his time for the national championship last year!"

As Silver climbed down and Jones grabbed the reins, Rising Sun was doing his own dance of excitement. Seth swung over the rails on one hand and ran to hoist Silver in his arms, swinging her around. "You did it!" he chortled, and gave her a smack right on the mouth.

Walker spun on his heel, but Camelia seized him by the arm, pained to see the jealousy flaring in his eyes. "Wait, Walker, you promised I could ride him."

Walker stopped abruptly, clenching his teeth as he stared at her incredulously. "What *is* this obsession with my horse?"

"Oh, please, Walker. I don't want to run him — just make a small circle — oh, pretty please!"

"Ride him then," he snarled, "but hurry up. I've got better things to do than watch these childish performances."

Camelia scrambled quickly through the fence, undaunted by the fact that everyone was too busy laughing and talking to notice her. They would, soon enough.

She snatched the reins from Jones. "Walker said I could ride him — just a small circle," she said tartly when Jones's jaw dropped.

"Have you ridden bareback, miss?" asked Jones worriedly.

"Of course, you fool. I took first place in the state for showmanship this year." Before Jones could say anything else, Camelia leaped up toward the long black back.

To have a strange figure come at him so suddenly was like touching spark to a keg of dynamite, and Rising Sun shied to dodge the noisy young woman's assault. Jones grabbed tight to the reins but the stallion's nerves were keyed high from the run, and he suddenly knew a fierce desire for freedom. As he rose on his legs, his right front hoof came up Jones's chin, knocking him backward. Jones lost his grip on the reins, and Camelia, seeing an opportunity for glory, grabbed them.

"Whoa now, boy, ease up," she cooed, and Rising Sun gave himself over to sheer panic. With a shriek that was half rage and half fear, he rose up once more, hooves in the air.

As the deadly blow fell, Silver slammed against Camelia in a single leap and knocked her clear, but it was only by the hair's breadth of a second that she dodged aside in time to save herself. She snatched up the reins before the horse could bolt and urged him well away from the others before she began to calm him.

Camelia was bawling loudly, and when Seth only stood there looking down at her, Walker was compelled to cross the fence and go to her aid.

He bent to lift her and she screamed.

"My arm! My God, I think that savage has broken my arm!"

"Nonsense," gritted Walker under his breath. "Calm down. You're hysterical."

"Hysterical with pain—*ooooooh!*"

Checking the tremor on his lips, Seth offered soberly, "Why don't you help her to the house, Walker? That does look like it's going to be a nasty bruise."

Walker's whole face was clenched as he glared at his brother. He found no alternative to assisting Camelia, insomuch as he would have had to peel her off of him to escape.

Suddenly Camelia screamed again and, turning loose of her captive, crumpled to the ground. *"My ankle!"*

Walker's lips thinned until they almost disappeared as he lifted Camelia into his arms. When he looked over his shoulder, Silver was watching him with calm disgust from the back of Rising Sun, who was also watching with an odd, humanlike expression of curiosity.

Walker thought he heard a snicker in his brother's voice.

"You go ahead with Camelia, Bubba. I'll help Silver stall the horse."

Camelia almost wept with a sense of loss when Walker's arms withdrew as he deposited her in her bed. She moaned pitiably, and Kathren left them to go downstairs and order up compresses for the ankle.

"You'll need to stay off of it for at least twenty-four hours," Walker advised her. "I recently had the same problem. It may be a while before you're up and about. If it's a sprain."

The pain in Camelia's ankle underwent a remarkable recovery. She pushed up on her elbows. "Oh, I'm sure it'll be okay in a few minutes." She had no intention of being laid up while Silver was prowling free.

"Oh, Walker, don't go!" she cried when he turned for the door. Her eyes implored him. "We haven't had a chance to be alone for a moment, even though I know you're . . . occupied with others now."

Walker's mouth twitched. "But I'm sure it's not proper to call on a lady in her bedroom."

Camelia's heart leaped at the words. "You mean if I

weren't in my bedroom, you wouldn't see anything wrong with us being . . . well, together?"

Walker looked at her curiously. "I should hope not. Why would I?"

Camelia stalled by squealing and grabbing her ankle, and Walker sat on the edge of the bed and took her foot in his lap, rubbing the ankle.

"Oh, that feels so *gooood!*" she whimpered softly, then her eyes filled with tears and she raised them to his. "It could have been so good with us, Walker. Why did you have to ruin everything?" she blurted.

He looked at her again. "I hope you're not referring to my bringing Silver here. She was a slave when I found her and had been for almost two years. I couldn't let an animal continue that kind of suffering, let alone a young woman."

My God, so you married her? thought Camelia. But she carefully forced the outrage from her face. He was so defensive that she would have to try another approach.

"Well, I do feel very sorry for her. I'm too tender-hearted for my own good, I guess. But what about us? Surely you don't expect me to just accept all this humiliation with my head down?"

Walker frowned. "Silver has nothing to do with our relationship and is no reflection on my respect for you in any way."

Camelia was so confused she dared not stumble on any further. She sat up in the bed, very close to him, her big blue eyes limpid.

"Then hold me," she said quietly. "For just a minute. Please."

She slipped into his arms, her cheek against his chest.

Walker put his hand on her back, surprised to feel vaguely uncomfortable with her emotional display. Probably—he thought wryly—because he'd become so accustomed to independence in a woman.

"You're shivering," he said.

"I'm cold . . . so cold." Her breast pressed against him, and she smelled sweet—not wild or erotic, just

261

sweet.

"I think we need to spend more time together," he said. "I mean, before we do anything else. We don't really know each other, Camelia. Or at least not well enough to make any sort of commitment."

Camelia's eyes were round with disbelief and hope. What else could he be saying except that he had come to his senses at last? That his only option now was a quiet divorce so they could go on with their wedding plans!

Her heart tripped with joy, and as she sat away from him, she prayed she was not pushing too hard.

"I think you're right that we must be very sure about everything. But I don't think we'll make much progress until . . . you do something about Silver."

"I'm going to the county seat tomorrow and do a little checking. I hope to find some of her family soon."

"And?"

Walker shrugged. "That's all. That's all I've ever wanted to do was help her."

Kathren returned with a cold compress and Camelia could hardly wait for Walker to leave. He looked on for a moment, then said he would check on her later.

As soon as he was gone, Camelia hissed, "Shut the door quickly!"

Kathren returned to sit on the bed. "What is it?" she whispered.

"You've got to find out what's going on. Walker's talking about *us*. About a relationship!"

Kathren's lips curled. Times like these she lamented the folly of thinking she could palm off this shallow-minded twit on a man like Walker. Unfortunately, she had no better plan at the present time.

"You're mistaken, Camelia. I know the Grayson men too well. Walker wouldn't continue to see you while he's married to another woman."

"But there's something we don't understand. He says he only wanted to help the girl. He must have *had* to marry her for some reason."

Kathren's shock was genuine. "Oh my Lord. You don't suppose she's . . ."

"I don't know, but you've got to find out." She finished in a wail. "I can't go on like this any longer!"

Kathren was just about to enter the library when the fates miraculously turned in her favor. She heard Walker's voice boom out, "My *what?*"

Seth repeated angrily, "Your wife. I said I treat my horse better than you treat your wife, dammit! And I'm getting sick and tired of—"

Walker took a step, his eyes darkening to deep sea-green. "Wait just a minute. Let me get this straight. Are you talking about Silver?"

Seth replied stiffly, "Who else?"

Walker eased back until he felt the chair against his legs, and fell into it to stare vacantly toward the windows. After a moment, his powers of speech returned in the form of a barely audible whisper. "I'm not married."

"You're *what?*"

Walker blinked up at him, then came to his feet with a shout that rattled the windows. "I said I'm not married, by heaven! Now where did you get this absurd—no, let me guess," he corrected with a savage sneer. "Would it have come from the proud wife herself?"

"And why not?" Seth bristled. "Sure she told us, and it's a good thing, since you neglected to fulfill that duty yourself. What I don't understand is why you're trying to hide it, like you're ashamed of her or something."

As Seth's voice waxed toward the same angry pitch as his own, Walker raised a hand to silence him and went to the door.

Kathren darted around the next corner just as Walker's head poked out to check the hallway, but after the door closed she didn't resume her eavesdropping; she had everything she needed already.

Walker locked the door and came back to collapse weakly into the overstuffed sofa again.

Seth looked at the pallor around his mouth. "You're not joking."

"Joking? Do I look like I'm laughing?"

Seth shook his head. "Something crazy is going on here."

"You're damned right it is." Walker shoved his glass out for a refill. "And I'm fed up—do you hear me?— *fed up*. I can't believe she'd tell a bald-face lie like this just to get her hands on my horse!"

Seth couldn't keep from laughing as he sloshed more brandy into Walker's glass. "I know he's a prize, but really. Don't you think she might have another motive for telling this story? I hardly think a young woman who looks like Silver would go to such lengths for a horse." He chuckled at the thought.

Walker replied dolefully. "Then you don't understand the savage mind. She's Comanche. She would sell her—" He stumbled over the word *body* and changed it. "She would sell her own soul to get her hands on a horse. It's a matter of vanity, a literal feather in her cap to own the very finest. And anyway, that's not all of it. She's obsessed with escaping to Horse Back."

"Isn't that the old chief you're trying to smoke out of the canyon?"

Walker's hand shook as he downed his drink. "The same. He raised her from a child."

"If she wants to go back to him so bad, then maybe you should think about—"

"Drop it."

Seth knew how far he could push. He changed course by giving his brother a wide grin.

"I can't figure out how you got yourself into this mess. One woman thinks you're married to her, the other thinks you're engaged to her." He wagged his head with mock sorrow. "Damned position for a man to be in. What are you going to do about it?"

Walker stared thoughtfully. "I have a motto," he said after a moment. "When you don't know what to do, don't do anything."

Seth lifted a brow. "You wouldn't be planning on paying the two lovelies back, would you? Or maybe you're just thinking how a man might enjoy such a predicament."

"Me?" asked Walker, spreading his hands.

Seth was still grinning as he sprawled in a chair and propped his boots up.

"I'll admit not many men could resist having two women fight over him. The question is, which one do you want? Or do you even know?"

Walker gazed beyond the windows to the flowers swarming over the patio planters, and his mischievous smile turned bleak.

"It's not always a question of what we want, is it?"

Seth took a long, thoughtful sip of his brandy. "No, it's not," he said quietly.

Silver walked forlornly down the path from the back patio, past the fountain where she and Walker had almost . . .

She looked at the ground in front of her. Almost was not good enough anymore. She had given up everything—all her past and everything she knew—to come with him peaceably, to be a good wife. Her heart did not hurt so badly for her home anymore, and she would not even keep trying to escape to the plains if only she and Walker did not live in the great house and if only he would worry as much about the wife he already had as he did the one he was going to take very soon.

She heard footsteps and looked up.

"Hello," said Ferrell, striding boldly forward to take a seat beside her on the bench. She did not look at him as he went on cheerfully. "You were magnificent this morning. It's too bad you've tied yourself to a man who appreciates you so little."

Silver was stung. "It is not for you to say how my husband treats me."

Ferrell scooted closer. "I only say that because I care what happens to you. I may be the only one here who does."

Silver stood up, anger flushing her face. "I do not hear these things!"

Ferrell's patience came to an abrupt end and he

265

sprang to his feet, grabbing her arm. "You're alone among the wolves, my sweet. You'd know that if you'd seen your husband in Camelia's room—oh yes, he was. I saw them there together. Saw him rubbing her ankle, her leg."

Silver tried to wrench her arm free but could not. "Do not touch me, *tivo sata*. You do not remember that I almost cut your throat." And she tried to jerk free again.

Ferrell snorted bitterly, bringing his face close to hers.

"A mistake you will not repeat if you know what's good for you. You've got enough enemies in this household—some you don't even guess."

"Me not prisoner, me—I am Walker's First Wife. I will tell him you beat the dogs," she threatened.

He released her suddenly. "Walker's got other worries. Besides, what's he going to do, send me home?"

"He will do something. He will not let you beat the dogs!"

Ferrell laughed in earnest. "Life is more complex, I'm afraid. A struggle between the brave and the cowardly, the strong and the weak . . . a challenging game which never tires me, especially when I always win." His dark eyes moved down over her slowly, and she felt naked.

"You are evil," she whispered, backing away.

Ferrell looked at her lips with longing, moistened his own with the tip of his tongue. "But evil always triumphs . . ." For a moment he seemed to lean toward her, then changed his mind and moved back. "Watch your step around here, sweetheart," he advised cockily. "Walker is a busy man, and this is a very large house. Tragic things have happened here, terrible accidents. Some even say Gray Shadows is haunted."

"Me tell Walker," she repeated airlessly, and Ferrell laughed, stopped himself short, then threw back his head and kept laughing as he walked off.

After an hour's haranguing, Walker gave in.

"All right, let her ride him then. But if anything

266

happens to her, I'll hold you both personally responsible."

Samuel and Seth grinned confidently. With first place points in the upcoming race on Saturday, Rising Sun would take the national championship for the second year.

Silver had lost interest in roaming the grounds after her encounter with Ferrell and stayed in her room. Toward evening, she undressed, bathed, and put on the short garment Milly had called a "chemise," for the room was very warm even with the windows opened.

She was trying to think of some excuse not to go down for the evening meal when she heard Walker moving about in the next room. She went to his door and tapped on it.

"Come in."

He was just sprawling into the chaise and lighting a long black cigar.

"Good evening," he said softly, his eyes going over her warmly.

A thrill licked through her veins at the way he was looking at her, but there were more pressing matters on her mind.

"I do not like Ferrell," she announced, careful to use the correct pronoun.

Walker smiled lazily. "That makes two of us."

"I want you to send him away."

Walker felt a familiar hardening in his groin as he looked at the dark, twin circles peeping through her chemise. He shifted uncomfortably, reminding himself not to become a pawn of his own devices. The little minx had blatantly installed herself as mistress in his home and he doubted his family would ever overcome the shock of it; not to mention the fact that once again she managed to portray him as a user of women, a callous bastard who engaged himself, then blithely married another woman and installed the wife under his betrothed's very nose.

He patted the chaise. "Come sit down, dear, you look a little tired."

267

Silver walked forward but did not sit down. "Will you send him away?"

Walker made a face of impatience. "I said to come sit down."

Silver obeyed, and as soon as she did, he put a fingertip under her chin. "You look . . . lovely." His voice was low and husky.

"Ferrell is evil. This house is evil," Silver went on hurriedly, angry that he was distracting her with his touch.

Walker trailed his finger under her chin, down her neck, slowly down her chest to the crevice between her breasts. Silver pulled back, anger and quick passion warring inside her.

"Ferrell likes me. He wants to touch me."

Walker's eyes came up swiftly. "And did he?"

"No. But he wants to."

"I can't say I blame him," said Walker easily, the knot of anger in his chest relaxing. "Anyway, I can't send him away. He's a relative of my stepmother. And certainly not because he likes what he sees. He'd be a fool not to," he added with a lascivious grin.

Silver stood up quickly. "You will not send him away?"

Walker grabbed her wrist and pulled until she fell upon him. Holding her against him with one arm, he crushed out the cigar with the other.

"Let's don't talk about Ferrell anymore. There are more important things for a husband and wife to do." Holding her head back with his fingers in the back of her hair, he ran the tip of his tongue lightly around her lips.

Silver fought off the sudden languor that made her feel floaty. Her life was in danger but now he had decided to forget his stupid vow because his man-lust was too impatient to wait for Camelia.

"Husband protect his wife," she insisted, pushing at his chest.

"And wives obey their husbands," he murmured. "You have no choice in the matter at all. Think of it as return

268

payment for your new . . . property." His mouth reached up toward hers again, but Silver dodged her head, then scrambled from his clutches and stood glaring down at him.

"If you will not send Ferrell away, I will not lie with you."

Walker's eyes flared. "Now we're getting to the heart of the matter, aren't we? Well, white eyes don't operate that way, sweetheart. You say you're my wife, so you'll act like one. You won't go climb on my horse without my permission or take over anything else that belongs to me." He stood up and moved toward her. "My hat's off to you. You've gone from a captive in chains to mistress of a mansion in a few short weeks." He scowled fiercely. "And can you believe it? I thought all you wanted was my horse!"

Silver's voice trembled. "Me try to get away when you mate with me—to stop you. Me Quohadie Teichas, me no want to marry *tivo sata!*"

Walker narrowed his eyes. "Tell me one thing—for my own peace of mind, since the event seems to have slipped my mind—just when did this wedding ceremony take place? Was I drunk? Unconscious?"

Silver clenched her teeth. "If you do not remember, why you come to lie with me now? Why you not go find Cam-eel-ya instead? She drops her wet tongue like a dog when she even look at you. She is only angry because she cannot be First Wife. But she cannot ever be, not even if you sell me. And if you do, me run away to Horse Back!"

Walker looked at her incredulously.

"I can't believe it. You're so steeped in pagan custom that you're perfectly willing for me to marry Camelia, when you think I'm already married to you!"

Her head jerked to a lofty angle and her lip curled when she spoke.

"I do not care if you marry ten wives. I hope you sell me very soon. Then I will leave this evil house!"

Walker stared, his eyes snapping furiously. Then he pivoted with military crispness and went to the door to

269

hold it open.

"Dress yourself," he said coldly. "And be at the dinner table in ten minutes."

Chapter 17

Only when starvation threatened did Quohadie Teichas resort to eating their few paltry hens, yet Silver had torn the crop from too many of them to be interested in the chicken and rice Jubal served with pride that night. Also, she had learned which dishes were apt to be endowed with heavy doses of red pepper, and after having choked almost to death on such, she warily shifted the rice from spot to spot on her plate and bided her time for desert, which was always good.

Although Kathren looked disapprovingly at the constantly changing arrangement on Silver's plate, she made no comment. Silver was relieved; she was still so angry at Walker that she could not cope with anything else.

She kept her head down and barely listened to Samuel's discourse on Walker's brilliant future in politics, a discussion to which Walker himself rarely contributed anything.

It was only when Kathren insisted he speak at some upcoming function that Walker interrupted.

"I'm afraid you're being a little premature, Kathren," he said with polite firmness.

"Nonsense, Walker. As the saying goes, if you don't toot you're own horn, nobody'll do it for you. And anyway, you shouldn't think of the Ladies Auxiliary as a political commitment. They're all just so proud of their hometown hero, you know that." She smiled winningly.

Walker looked her in the eye. "I'll be happy to address them on a nonpolitical subject. That is all."

Kathren swallowed her defeat with aplomb; she would work on the matter later and really had no intention of

271

pressing him further because he'd been so guarded with her since his return.

But after conceding happily, "They'll be drooling over you so they'll hardly notice your theme anyway, love," she went on speaking as the thoughts came to her. "Oh, I just had a marvelous idea! Why don't you tell them about the upcoming campaign, how President Grant himself gave you the enormous responsibility of bringing those bloodthirsty Comanches in tow? In fact, you could show Silver to them. You know, that's quite a feather in your cap—returning a captive to her native homeland."

Kathren was appalled the moment she heard herself. But as the frown grew on Walker's brow, and before the storm cloud on Samuel's face could burst, she recovered like a cat landing on its feet.

Her eyes brimmed as she looked across the table, speaking in a choked whisper.

"Silver, you'll never know how glad I am that Walker did rescue you. I had a daughter once, she'd be about your age if she hadn't been kidnapped—" Her voice broke and she grabbed clumsily at the table napkin to wipe her eyes.

Ferrell suddenly strangled on a sip of tea and began coughing, but surrounding that splutter was a thick, stunned silence.

Samuel's light blue eyes were wide with grief. "My dear Kitty! Why have you never told me about this daughter?"

Kathren blew her nose loudly. "There was no need to burden you," she sniffed bravely. "Besides, I found out some time later that she . . . she died in an Indian camp."

Walker glanced shrewdly around the table but made no mention of the fact that the state of Georgia had rested well beyond the bounds of Indian troubles for almost forty years.

It was Amanda who came swiftly to her feet. No woman who had suffered her own daughter in Indian captivity could possibly have treated Silver as Kathren had done, before Amanda's very eyes.

"May I be excused?" Amanda asked curtly. "I have a terrible headache."

Samuel glanced worriedly about his family circle as

Amanda's footsteps echoed a rapid staccato on the marble tiles. Then he saw the crushed hurt on Kathren's face and his eyes reached the length of the table to caress her.

"My dear, I'm sure Walker can manage to entertain the women next week. And since you so love to host such things, why don't you have the meeting here? Maybe Jubal could serve some of those *pralines au petit lait,* like before. What do you think, kitten?"

Kathren gave him a tremulous but subtly promising smile. Their gazes were still locked when Silver stood up suddenly. She was never one to let pride stand in the way of adopting an enemy's maneuver if it seemed particularly successful.

"May I be excused?" she parroted, "I have a terrible headache."

As Kathren's head swung around, her ruby lips looking almost black in her white face, Seth clapped a hand over an offending snicker, and Samuel opened his own mouth but no words came to him before the young woman had turned and headed for the door.

Kathren's face trembled with outrage as she looked at Walker.

Walker gave her a lopsided grin and shrugged. "She learns real fast."

Silver's veneer of civilization was showing ominous cracks by the next morning, but there was no one up and about to notice. She dressed and went to the kitchen.

The stove was a large brick rectangle in the center of the kitchen, lined with a firebox of the finest steel, and with five circular heating grills on top, which allowed for the preparation of numerous dishes at once. Four brick ovens built into the walls completed the chef's paradise—if one could take the heat when all were in operation at the same time.

Jubal danced happily from his stew pot to the perpetually heated skillet, dabbed it with fresh butter and flipped a pastry into it; then he poured his guest a large mug of coffee, so delighted for a mouth to feed that he was once again able to overlook his disapproval of the young mistress spending so much time with the servants. The child could not be charged for her ignorance, being raised a heathen and all. Besides, it was no small treat to see Mistress Kathren outmaneuvered.

Jubal hummed merrily to himself. Gray Shadows had not known such excitement since the old days, when young Master Walker hid a baby 'gator in the flour bin.

Sensing this was a day she needed to feel very strong, Silver screwed up her face and drained the blackwater politely, but when Jubal announced that Master Grayson would be gone for the day in search for her family, it rose to the back of her throat. She almost choked on one bite of the sticky sweet roll, and did not take another.

"Where is Prissy?"

"Prissy weel not be in today at all, madam. Thees ees her day at home."

"Where is her home?"

Jubal was stirring the blubbering stew pot with a wooden spoon. He waved his free hand disdainfully.

"Down the road at the Acadian veelage."

"I would turn which way?"

Jubal stopped stirring, his small black eyes squinting suspiciously. Despite the fact that he found her company fresh and honest, her uncommon beauty a delight, and her unconventional ideas amusing, it was not his intention to become caught in the cross-fire between the two mistresses. Better to miss her company than his paycheck.

"Madam," he said gravely, "you cannot go to the veelage. You are zee wife of Monsieur Grah-sone."

Silver raised one brow. "Then I can go where I choose."

Jubal folded his hands over his apron and smiled down at her pityingly.

"But madam, you do not understand thees things. Prissy is *Cajun. L'Acadien*. She ees of the working class."

The girl's blunt tone belied the innocence of her wide gray eyes.

"You work."

Jubal drew up stiffly, his nostrils flaring. *"Mais, la difference!* I am Creole. *Mon pere* was cousin of Napoleon the second, Duke of Reichstadt, himself a son of the first Napoleon and Marie Louise. *Ma mere's* ancestors followed

274

La Salle's mission into zee Mississippi Valley only a few years later." He thumped his chest. "I am Creole!"

"Prissy is a good woman," said Silver heatedly.

Jubal flung his hands out. "I did not say she ees otherwise!"

Suddenly he remembered to whom he was speaking, and the little Frenchman struggled to control himself, closing his eyes briefly while his lips moved in supplication. Finally he was able to explain.

"Acadians are French who were exiled from Nova Scotia. They come many, many years later, a poor and wretched people who float up the bayous from the Gulf." He gestured with the long spoon like a maestro's baton. "Raft after raft of squawking chee-kins and flapping underwear! They stop and build their veelages and cling together like orphans. They fish zee bayous and scratch zee dirt for food. They are too poor to have education so their French ees polluted with what we say, 'backwoods Engleesh.'" He frowned with obvious regret. "Although some are now making professions of every kind. But," he said and waved the spoon threateningly, "a mistress of Gray Shadows does not go to their veelage. Eet ees not done! Mistress Kathren would fly into very little pieces. She would . . . Madam? Madam, where are you going?"

Silver had stood up. Now she grabbed the pastry from her plate and popped it into her mouth whole, and Jubal sucked in a quick breath: There was a menacing gleam in the child's eye as she chewed with slow relish, afterward pausing to lick each of her fingers. Then, still looking at him with those feral eyes, she ran the tip of her tongue around her lips like a lioness polishing off a carcass.

"I must go see these savages for myself," she said, and left.

Silver heard the music long before she saw the humble log houses scattered along either side of the smaller stream that forked from Bayou Teche. A wooden footbridge arched over the narrow waterway of sluggish backwater, and from there a path twisted through the village. There was a little white stucco chapel with a red-tile roof sandwiched between log cabins, a barn that served as the livery. Silver's spirits lifted as she followed the path. She could hear music—strange music quite unlike the mournful sounds Kathren made on the violin. This was a sound that made her feet step quickly along and her heart swell with a song.

Women bending over steaming wash pots smiled shyly and waved as she passed. Lovely dark-skinned children seemed to be everywhere, the smaller ones playing in the dirt, older ones leading a team of mules or herding a flock of chickens. Everyone was busy and smiling, and the air reverberated with the sounds of accordion, guitar, and fiddle.

Beneath the shade of a sprawling oak, a group of women were gathered at a loom similar to those in Silver's own village, but more elaborate. Fascinated at the bright pattern rolling onto the catch beam, she stopped to observe.

"Mistress!" came a cry of delight, "Mistress Silver Dawn!"

Prissy gathered up her long cotton skirt and ran to Silver, embracing her affectionately before she heard one of the older women clear her throat in a stern reminder. Prissy drew back, embarrassed at forgetting herself but still bubbling with enthusiasm. "Ah caint believe you come to see me lak dis!"

"Walker is gone. Jubal did not want me to come, but I do not care," Silver grinned.

Prissy grabbed her by the hand and pulled her toward the women at the loom. "Dis ees my mistress, de younger Lady Grayson Ah have tole you about," she announced proudly.

The women bobbed their heads and smiled merrily, though they were obviously worried at her presence. They were plain women, some broad or plump, others thin and wiry with white aprons over dark skirts, and three-cornered scarfs over their hair. Silver smiled courteously; the middle-aged squaws were always the backbone of a village.

"I can make cloth, too," she said, looking eagerly at the loom.

"Ah have dis chance to get away and you want to make cloth," said Prissy, waving mischievously to the women and propelling her captive along the path.

"Poppa, he shoe de horses. We go see heem, ho-kay?"

They crossed another footbridge flanked by low-hanging oak and cypress that reached overhead. Silver was so enchanted that she clung to the wooden rail until Prissy had to pull her arm again.

Children ran to them as they passed, touching Silver's riding skirt or grabbing her hand. Most had dark features with intelligent but mischievous black eyes, yet a few had the coloring that Silver associated with true white eyes.

A dark-eyed urchin no more than six pulled at her skirt, and when Silver looked down, he flashed her a smile. "Come wid me. Ah show you a crawfish dat long." And he measured a span of two feet with his hands.

"Ah'm gon sweetchy you tail, you little gaga," said Prissy. "Get yourself back dare in de yard." She scooped him up, gave him a playful swat, and set him down with a prod in the right direction. "Deese cherins lie lak dere daddys," she grinned at Silver. "A big tale's de only ting a Cajun lak better dan fay dodo."

"Fay-dodo?"

"Yah, you know . . ." She spread her arms over her head and kicked her feet this way and that. "Een Engleesh you say 'party.' "

When Silver looked at her blankly, Prissy put one hand behind her back, patted the other over her lips, and hopped from foot to foot, singing, *"HOO woo-woo-woo, HOO-woo-woo-woo."*

Silver laughed. "I do not dance like *that!*"

"But now you know *fay dodo.* Let's go see my poppa."

They stopped in the doorway of the barn, and Prissy's voice rang out over the clang of the anvil.

"Daddy! Put you hammer down. Ah haf a fran to see me."

Jean-Pierre Fontenot was a small man, but muscles stood out like knuckles under the dark leathery skin of his arms. His white work apron was smeared in grime and axle grease, and he wiped his hands on it as he came toward them.

"Dis ees Mistress Silver," Prissy announced. "She leev wid de Indians all her life and now she ees mistress of Gray

277

Shadows lak Miz Kathren. Silver, dis ees my poppa."

A tall gaunt man remained at the anvil, propped on a head-high walking stick of smooth, twisted white wood. The tip of his white beard was long enough to tuck in his belt, and there were tufts poking from under his pointed hat. He wore a green twill shirt that belled out past his hips and matching britches stuffed in tall wading boots. Though he didn't impose himself, Silver saw him watching them with interest.

Jean-Pierre winked at his daughter. "Eef you bruzzers see dis angel, dey weel be more worthless dan dey are now," he advised Prissy. Then he winked at Silver. "Dey only do tree tings good: make dodo, make gogo, or get chookay."

Prissy pursed her lips. "Ah tole you all Cajuns lie, Silver. My bruzzers all work de juga cane for de Graysons." She lowered her voice. "Dey only sleep, make love, and drink on de weekends."

Silver was both amused and confused. Surely these happy people were not the "poor wretches" Jubal had spoken of.

"I have four brothers, also," she said. "They are Quohadie Teichas, Antelope Eaters, and mighty warriors of the plains. But I have not seen them for a long time."

Jean-Pierre sobered. "Dat ees bery sad." He took Prissy in the crook of his arm. "A man has no reason to leev without hees family. But come. Talk to old Loup while Ah work. Somebody must earn bread for this brood. Dey wake up like chicks — wid dere moufs open."

Silver sensed an aura of mystery about Loup. Although he had followed their conversation eagerly, he had not spoken, and now, when Prissy said simply, "Dis ees Loup," he only looked at her with the faintest hint of a smile. The whites of eyes were large and yellowed but the irises had the clarity and depth of green moss under a pool of water.

"Loup ees our local legend. Writers of history and picture takers from everywhere come to see heem," said Prissy.

"I am Silver Dawn." She smiled hesitantly. "My father is the great war chief of all Quohadie Teichas."

Loup fixed the girl with an unblinking stare and dropped his voice. "My daddy he was half buffalo. The other half was 'gator."

When no hint of laughter or disbelief came to the girl's face, Loup cocked his head, his eyes bright and intense. "Where do you come from, heh?"

"The plains of Llano Estacado. And you?" Silver spoke with grave respect. Perhaps this one was a Spirit Talker.

Loup relaxed, his eyes twinkling now that the conversation had swung back on course.

"When Ah was six or five, my mama tote me to de side of de road een a toesack and lef me for de garbage wagon." He gave a wicked little cackle and watched Silver's face avidly. "But Ah don stay in de sack, see. Ah go hide een a barn and Ah hides good. When de shootin' she start, nobody see li'l Loup under de hay. Ah crawled everywhere through de city streets but only after dark, 'cause French soldiers dey hang on de cathedral at Notre Dame, and dey shoot what move, uh-huh."

Prissy grinned. "You are wasting all you good tale dis time, Loup. Silver doan know any white man history, only Indian."

Undaunted, Loup leaned upon the twisted stick while the tail of his beard lapped upward with a breeze.

"*Ma mere* was half Washita Indian, half congo."

"Congo means water moccasin," interrupted Prissy. "You know that snake?"

Silver's eyes widened. "I sure enough know that one."

Loup nodded slowly, deeply satisfied. "Den you know the blood of Loup Pedeaux, why de writers come far and wide to talk wif Loup."

"Yes," said Silver with awe. Then palm out, she passed her hand before her face in a vertical line. "I knew a Spirit Talker, an old chief. He was an eagle once."

Loup's face flexed with surprise and the air of superiority was replaced by a look of stupification.

Prissy burst out laughing. "You have found you match dis time, Loup Pedeaux!"

She was still laughing when they came to the footbridge again but stopped suddenly, her eyes fixing straight ahead. Silver followed her gaze and her heart tripped at the sight of the long graceful stride, the wide shoulders and proud head of thick blond hair. But it was Seth and not Walker.

Seth's preoccupied frown melted. "Hello," he said. His voice changed subtly and he looked only at Prissy when he spoke.

Prissy's mouth opened but there were no words, just a small noise.

Silver was glad to see him, but when Seth looked at her, he frowned again.

"I was ordered to bring you back, Silver. I'm sorry, but this time Daddy sided with Kathren. He looked a little tired so I didn't press the issue."

Tongue-tied, Prissy stared at the ground, and Seth's face mellowed again as he looked at her. "But anyway, now that I'm here why don't you show me around, Prissy?"

Later they sat on the steps of Prissy's house eating bread and cheese and drinking goat milk cooled in the well. Prissy sat between them and could speak almost coherently now.

Silver was touched and intrigued as she watched the darted looks, the way Seth and Prissy spoke of mundane things while an undercurrent of excitement heated every word with hidden meanings. She was sad that she and Walker had had no such time of courtship.

Though Silver was content enough to be an inanimate object, time was slipping past, and she could envision Kathren Grayson waiting on another set of steps, shrieking like a mouse struck by the hawk when she spotted them returning late. If Jubal were right, she would be even angrier if she knew they had been associating with "wretched people," and the ensuing family strife would somehow be Silver's fault once again.

Reluctantly Seth heeded her entreaties to leave, and Prissy walked with them to the edge of the green, sun-drenched meadow where their horses were tethered. The grass was starred with red, violet, and white wildflowers and, pretending a great interest in them, Silver walked a little beyond so that Seth and Prissy could be alone.

Prissy felt dwarfed as she stood close to the big roan horse and his owner, for the top of her head barely reached Seth's shoulder. He held to a strap on the saddle, and Prissy felt trapped as he towered over her.

He lifted her chin tenderly to look into her eyes.

"I am coming back here, maybe tonight. Will you meet me?"

Prissy swallowed, the sight of his sun-bronzed skin and burnished hair making her heart flutter. "Ah'm afraid, and you know why," she said hoarsely. "And dat means dat you do not think much of me, because a tryst ees all you can offer."

She tried to look away but he lifted her face.

"I keep thinking . . . what if that's all we can ever have? I don't think I'm strong enough to turn it down. Are you?"

The force of his gaze drew her to him until their faces were close. He moved to kiss her but stopped. "Are you that strong?"

Prissy swayed toward him, her lips parting and her eyes limpid with desire. But Seth pressed his hand lightly against her throat, holding her back.

"No, my black-eyed gypsy," he whispered. "One kiss is not enough. Tonight. Watch for me tonight."

Prissy could not break the spell to even nod, and watched numbly as he left her standing and went to the other side of the horse to mount.

"It's time to face the music, sis," he called to Silver, and when she started walking toward them, Seth looked down at Prissy again. "Tonight."

Prissy was still stiff and staring up when the horse's movements forced her to jump out of the way. Seth laughed and touched the brim of his hat. "Good-bye, *ma chere*. But only for now."

Prissy watched as he rode away with Silver and could not summon so much as a small wave when he grinned over his shoulder and blew her a kiss.

She was still standing in the same position after the riders had disappeared into the woods.

The foreboding silence at the dinner table marked the passing of the storm; however, just because it was punctuated by the incongruous merriment of jingling silverware did not mean another one wasn't brewing on the horizon. For when Silver and Seth had returned that morning,

Kathren was not waiting on the front steps but Samuel was, his face looking swollen and red with anger. He had found Kathren crying in her room, saying that she had utterly failed to earn the respect of his children. She had become frantic with worry and sent Ferrell to look for them. His report that he saw Seth and Prissy Fontenot standing in a meadow, entwined passionately, was the last straw for Kathren. She felt she had utterly failed to uphold the honor for which the Grayson family was known.

Samuel's fit of outrage waxed so hot in relating the incident that Silver had dashed around him and fled to her room, mortified that Kathren had finally turned Samuel against her. But even from her room upstairs she could hear the angry shouts between Seth and Samuel.

Later, Samuel came up to her room and apologized, explaining that he must "protect" Kathren against feeling like an outsider. Apparently, however, he was still angry when Walker returned from his search of the captive records. More hot words had passed between Samuel Grayson and his firstborn son. Though Samuel privately admired Silver's courage, her wit and intelligence, and even — truth be told — her very difference, the strain was telling on the family.

Kathren had, however, recovered from her upset sufficiently to attend the evening meal, and now her voice seemed to shatter the silence.

"Silver, I've been meaning to tell you that I've planned a small tea for the Ladies Auxiliary next week. I would be grateful if you'd help me plan the menu. Walker has agreed to give the program."

"Kitty, I would be glad to help you, you know that," said Amanda, glancing apologetically at Silver. "I'm sure you know that Silver hasn't had experience with this sort of thing.

When Walker just kept eating, Amanda glared at him and said to Silver, "Maybe you'd like to add your own part to the program. I'm sure you could enlighten us from a different point of view, for instance you could enumerate the injustices done to your people."

"Or maybe," said Kathren easily, "you could tell them

about your wedding." Her laugh was a harsh tinkle. "You know how we women are about such things, and I must admit I feel cheated in not getting to witness my stepson's ceremony. By the way, what was your wedding date?"

Walker was torn between an angry protest at Kathren's deliberate baiting, and wanting to hear himself about this mysterious event. To date he had not concluded there was any basis for the girl's claim, which meant that she had brazenly lied. The motive that compelled the lie was what interested him — assuming it was more complicated than her lust for a horse. He stared without expression at his plate but his pulse pounded with stress.

Silver smiled, pleased to have her status openly acknowledged. "I was bitten by a congo and afterward Walker took care of me and—"

"That's a Cajun term," corrected Kathren tersely. "The snake is called a water moccasin."

Ashamed to have blundered into a sore subject, Silver apologized, then went on. "We were married three moons after that, when Walker was taking me to the camp at Nacdoches."

Walker's brow furrowed as he juggled the memories into chronological order.

Kathren clasped her hands together. "How romantic. But don't stop there, tell us everything!" And her eyes were wide and innocent. "What did you wear for the ceremony?"

"If we had been in my village, I would have worn a white doeskin while the women sang the Comanche Lovesong for the dance that comes before. But for the wedding ceremony itself, Quohadie Teichas do not wear any clothes at all." Her lips curved shyly. "Do white eyes wear many clothes when they breed together?"

Apparently brain signals could get crossed under extreme stress. Walker's esophagus closed when it should have opened and his windpipe opened when it should have closed, and he inhaled a large cloud of fiery spray from his wineglass. Had it not been for the spontaneous and combined efforts of the bride on his right and his fiancée on his left, he knew he would not have lived to remember and later enjoy the spectacle of stunned faces at the table.

283

But when the interruption served only to postpone a new outbreak of war, he deliberately continued his splutter, intermittently gasping loudly, until the family had come half out of their chairs to rush to his aid. It seemed prudent to hold his throat and gasp a minute more, and so he did, until by squinting carefully, he could see the anger and outrage turning to fear.

Then he staggered to his feet with remarkable swiftness and pulled Silver up from her chair. "Please, dear," he choked, "help me to my room, I need to lie down."

"I'll help, too," said Seth quickly, and it was only when the three of them were out of the room and in the safety of the foyer that both brothers exploded into shrieks of laughter, and Silver could not decide which one needed her supporting shoulder more.

The national racing circuit was new but growing rapidly. Although the first Kentucky Derby had been held only the previous year, the aristocracy craved the accoutrements that separated them from the working class, so many of whom were destroyed by the war. Thoroughbred racing had quickly become the "gentlemen's game."

However, the officials at Evangeline Downs were in a tumult over the Grayson's entry. The horse was one of some fame and they had enthusiastically heralded his race with flyers and clippings and, quite frankly, there would be much unrest if the horse was not allowed to compete. Though the rule book, still under revision, made no reference to the sex of the rider, they were certain that it was highly improper for a woman — and a novice at that — to compete; such a precedent would open the doors for more confusion as women everywhere, some of them excellent trainers, decided they, too, wished to race. Furthermore, the young woman in question demanded she be allowed to ride bareback, a dangerous proposition and one that likewise was not covered in the rule book. In the heated discussion behind the closed doors of the official box, no one voiced the regret that overlaid their outward objections, namely that they could have doubled the ticket sales had they known the unusual nature of Grayson's entry.

Efforts to prevail upon Samuel Grayson to enter his regular jockey failed and so with admirable resiliency, the officials began to plug the new entry as "daring" and "provocative," a tactic they hoped would stem the flow of criticism should objections arise from the other participants.

Walker was unable to disengage himself from Camelia long enough to express his pride to Silver; he could only stare up at her in the dazzling silver-blue habit and long charcoal boots, and subdue the desire to yank her from the horse and kiss her soundly. Then the crowd pressed about them, bearing Silver and the horse along with it. Silver twisted her neck and was still looking back at him when they disappeared from sight.

The time while the horses were in the chutes was restricted to mere seconds, so that even with her training, Silver was not prepared when the gate opened.

Rising Sun came off the starting line dead last and by the time they reached the first curve, attention had already shifted to the lead horse, and Rising Sun was all but forgotten.

When Grayson's entry began to pull up the outside lane, however, the mood of the spectators made a fickle shift, and the American love for the underdog gained momentum. There were shouts of encouragement and soon Kathren looked behind her, aghast to see a gang of dandified, obviously wealthy young men screaming "Rising Sun, Rising Sun," and stomping their feet to the rhythm. The crowd took up the cry, though it seemed impossible the animal could make up the lost ground.

Ignoring Jones's advice to pace the horse until the last stretch, Silver leaned low until she could no longer see for the flying mane in her face. There was no time to waste on white eyes advice; she made a sound low in her throat, and the power surged beneath her like the blast from a cannon.

Walker had disengaged himself from Camelia to lean far over the rail, screaming until his voice cracked. And Samuel, in spite of his wife's valid concerns should Silver Dawn really win—there would be tremendous publicity—was so excited he feared his heart would burst from its frenzied strokes. Finally the entire crowd was chanting and stomping their feet: *"Ris-ing-Sun! Ris-ing-Sun!"*

When the horse made the last turn and started thundering down the final stretch with the closest contender six lengths behind, the sound of the crowd grew so deafening that each member of the family was forced to watch, alone with his own thoughts, as the bulging chest broke the finish ribbon; no conversation was possible.

By the time the Graysons reached her, Silver was wearing a wreath of roses and carrying a gold banner bearing the title National Champion. Walker clawed his way through the throng of newspaper reporters and admirers, and when Silver saw the pride on his face, tears spilled down her cheeks.

A voice boomed above the noise, and the jubilant din abated only long enough to hear the announcement.

"And to the first female winner of a thoroughbred race in these great United States of America, the National Championship goes to Miss Silver Grayson and Rising Sun of Grayson Estates Incorporated, St. Martinville, Louisiana!"

Walker could only get close enough to grab Silver's ankle, and when she looked down and saw him, her face flushed with a smile. "I did it good and well?"

Walker's grip was loosened as the horse was propelled through the pressing throng, and only then did he find his voice.

"That's my girl!" he shouted, grinning and waving. Silver twisted her neck until she thought it would break, but his face was quickly swallowed up by the crowd.

Too exhausted to do more than take a light meal in her room, Silver crawled into bed that night and went instantly to sleep. But sometime later she woke to a noise from Walker's room. Hoping he might pay a call, she pulled on a robe and splashed her face with water. Her hands stopped in midair when she heard the whispering wavelets of a woman's voice.

Slipping through the bathing chamber, she went to the door and listened. But there were no more sounds, not even the normal clomp of his boots or creak of the bed as he settled down for the night. Resisting a shameless urge to knock on his door, she went back to bed. While he courted his second wife so boldly, the First Wife must not interfere. He must come to her now, for she had done all she could.

Walker returned to his room the second time. He had managed to coax Camelia back to her own quarters — he hoped for the night.

He went inside silently and undressed in the dark. After a stiff drink, he fell across the bed, waiting for the numbness to come. Not one instant had he been alone with Silver since the race; Camelia had clung to him like a spider monkey and the more pathetically desperate she became, the more his conscience smote him.

He fell asleep, and she came through the mists toward his bedroll. A creature of wild beauty, a symmetry of perfectly formed limbs, walking with the grace and fierce price of a lioness. And he knew from that moment that she was his, meant from the foundation of the earth to be his.

He did not know when he awoke and climbed from the bed. It was impossible to distinguish reality from dream; to stop what he was doing no matter the consequences.

Silver blinked through the deep fog of sleep and saw the form standing over her bed but she wasn't afraid. He stood there for a moment, and she could see that he was naked. She pulled back the satin coverlet and raised her arms to him, and he moved over her like a shadow. The sweet dregs of sleep blended her senses into a honeyed languor. Moving in the grace of a dance, they rolled, she over him, he over her, kissing and touching, their bodies seeking leisurely, taking the unhurried pleasure of couples tuned and primed to each other for a lifetime.

Walker raised above her for a moment, and she could see the hard planes of his face in the moonlight. "I think I love you," he said quietly.

"Is your foolish vow at its end?"

"All fools pay for their stupidity. I've paid for mine long enough, I think."

"Will we have many sons?" She leaned up to kiss the end of his nose.

"Ten."

"And daughters?" she kissed him again.

"Fifteen."

"And I will always be First Wife?"

"White eyes take one wife, one mate for life. You are the only wife, for always."

When she raised to kiss him, the shaft of love thrust deep and she froze, her mouth opened against his in a small moan. Then she wrapped her arms about his neck and they lay motionless for a time before the love dance began. And even then there was no thundering race to its climax but a soft swelling, a seed springing to life, bursting its dormant husk to explode in gentle showers of warmth and light.

He slept afterward as he always did, but Silver was too filled with euphoria to think of sleep. After a little while, she went out on the balcony and stood naked in the moonlight, her heart full and content.

She began to sing:

Nei mu-su-ite ah mah-cou-ah,
Nei mu-su-ite ah mah-cou-ah,
A-ya-a-ya Ie-yah-ya, ya,
Nei mu-su-ite ah mah-cou-ah . . .

"That's beautiful, what is it?" said Walker behind her.

She turned and moved softly into his arms. "It is old Comanche song. I do not know white eyes song or I would sing it for you."

He kissed her with tender nips, holding her face between his hands. "I prefer Quohadie Teichas." Releasing her, he stepped back into the shadows of the door and looked at the moonglow of her form as though trying to commit it to memory. "I can't seem to get enough of you."

"You will keep trying?"

He paused. "Yes, as long as I live. I knew it today, when I saw you ride."

Silver smiled. "So you like woman who is good with horse."

288

Her banter didn't alter his intense expression. "I like a brave woman. One who has the courage to overcome any obstacle. Your battles make mine look puny."

"You are wearing your *bree-chez*. Are you leaving me now?"

"Only for now. But tomorrow things are going to start to change around here, and that's a promise."

She dropped her head, afraid that what she was about to say would also change things. "Sometime white eyes do not keep their promises."

He stared for a long time without speaking, then turned silently into the shadows. She heard the door closing a moment later.

Chapter 18

Walker was sleeping like a dead man two hours later when the plumb, soft woman's flesh moved against him. Murmuring huskily, he turned to wrap himself around satin thighs, to hunch sensually against the smooth, slightly mounded belly. His hands groped for the silken stands of hair and he touched a springy pad of curls. But he was still so possessed by the previous experience that he didn't notice. Already he was hard, and pushed at the fork of her legs, rotating his hips.

"You can't do this," he mumbled into her hair. "I told you. Tomorrow."

Small round breasts slithered up and down his chest. "Oh, Walker, I knew you'd feel like this!"

Walker jerked fully awake. "Camelia! My God, what are you doing here?"

Her hands grabbed at him like a child after candy, unskilled, bruising his manhood when she tried clumsily to grasp him, and her hand spasmed with fear when she actually did.

Walker scrambled on his knees until he reached the lamp, but his fingers trembled so badly he couldn't strike the match. Again the clutching hands came at each side of his naked waist, then slipped under his arms and up to twirl in the hair on his chest.

"Camelia, stop it! You've gone mad." Still he could not light the wick, for now she had grasped his manhood again, pinching the foreskin until he felt he was being nipped to death by a small terrier. Throwing the matches

290

aside, he got his feet on the floor and lunged to the safety of an upright position. Whirling about, he could barely make out the nude figure against the moon-glowing sheets. "You've got to get out of here," he rasped. *"Now."*

The tears in Camelia's throat were real. "How can you say that to me after bedding that Indian whore! I can't help it if I'm still pure and don't know what to do." She buried her face in the pillow and began to weep loudly.

Walker crawled across the bed on his knees but sat back on his heels, well out of reach.

"You must hush this instant! You're shaming yourself and me, Camelia. In the name of all the saints, take what pride you've got left and go!"

She raised a tear-stained face. "Go? Where would I go that my shame wouldn't follow me? You've disgraced me before everyone! I can never lift my head again. You've done this to me and you say I have shamed *you!*"

Walker touched her shoulder. "Camelia, I'm sorry. I never meant for any of this to happen. I took Silver from slavery and brought her here to find her family. I never meant to . . ."

Camelia stared through the shadows. "To fall in love with her?"

"I didn't say that."

Camelia covered the hand on her shoulder. "But what about me? Now that you've ruined my life, what about *me?*"

Walker's chest tightened at her pitiful tone. "I don't know," he said hoarsely. "I just don't know. How can I promise you faithfulness when I can't keep . . . Camelia, go to your room now. We'll talk about this in the morning. I think you need to go back to Georgia as soon as possible."

She lunged and threw her arms about his neck. "Not until you've taken me like you've taken that savage!" She tried to kiss him but Walker twisted his head, attempting to disentangle her arms; finally gaining the floor again, he backed away from her toward the balcony. But slowly she approached, swaying her hips as she glided across the

291

room.

Camelia threw off the mien of crushed idealism and her voice took a waspish turn.

"I'm not going anywhere. You promised to marry me and you're going to do it, Walker Grayson. Anyway, you're not married to that little savage. She made the whole thing up."

Walker had backed out onto the balcony. "I never said I was married to her."

But forward she came, pale skin glowing in the moonlight. When she had hemmed him against the balcony railing, she snaked her body up his, the points of her high round little breasts following the movement of her hands up his chest until her weight hung from the noose of her arms around his neck.

Again Walker attempted retreat, but his naked buttocks colliding against the cold metal railing made him clutch to the nearest object in reflex, and Camelia, taking the circling arms for an embrace, wiggled herself tightly against him and reached for his mouth hungrily. She kissed him with such a ravaging force that for a moment Walker saw no way to escape without hurting her.

"Stop it!" he said harshly, and used considerable effort in prying her loose.

But it was too late to alter the course of events to come, for the young woman watching from the next-door balcony had already moved silently back into her own room.

The mansion was wrapped in predawn darkness when the dirge began. It started like the cry of a wolf, low on the musical scale, but rising as swiftly as a gust of wind to a sonorous outpouring of grief.

Kathren bolted upright in the bed, terror closing her throat until she could only clutch at Samuel's shoulder for the first few seconds before she found her voice.

"My God. What was that?"

As Samuel raised on one elbow to squint at his wife, it began again.

"Merciful saints," he breathed, then noticed the whites of Kathren's eyes shining in the shadows. "I'll get the gun," he said gravely, and fumbled to light the lamp beside the bed.

The servants were wakened one by one and, listening to the agonized wail, many of them deemed it wise to remain in their beds. Camelia had slipped into Amanda's room after she was rejected from Walker's, weeping and talking incoherently, and Amanda had hardly dozed off when she heard the sound. She slung her feet over the side of the bed and began pulling on her slippers and robe. However, Camelia's eyes were glazed with fear; she pulled the cover over her head and refused to budge.

After dismissing Camelia with as much grace as possible, Walker had, for the second time, succumbed to a deathlike slumber. He missed the opening prelude, and by the time Seth came to rouse him, Samuel had had time to pinpoint the location of the noise if not the exact source.

So when Seth guided Walker onto the front porch, they saw the whole family standing huddled on the front walk, their nightclothes turning them to little ghost figures under the last but brightest rays of moonlight. A few of the servants were clustered around—Jubal in his night-shirt with the pointed tip of his nightcap hanging over one eye, and the butler and the upstairs maid clutching each other in a posture of horror.

The sound rose again, waving on the still air, and the hair on Walker's neck prickled like the feet of a thousand insects.

He rushed down the steps toward the moon-washed figures, who were pointing and gesturing, excitement making their movement jerky so that they looked like marionettes in comical blue-tinted nightclothes.

Randy the livery boy threw himself against Kathren's backside, his fingers digging unabashedly into the flat buttocks beneath her gown as he took up his refrain in a howl which rivaled the one that had brought them from their beds: "She ees a weetch! We are doomed, Mistress Kathren, de Fee Foolay come to get us all!"

Kathren wrenched herself from the boy's grasp and barked, "Jubal! Do something with this squalling calf before I take a whip to him."

While Jubal scurried to obey, latching onto the lad with one arm across the boy's throat, Walker followed the collective gaze of the group to the widow's walk four stories up and positioned directly over the porch; it was flanked by two towers whose dark spires thrust against the brightening eastern sky. On the widow's walk, a figure dressed in a white shroud was pacing back and forth.

"Go back in the house, all of you," said Walker, and his tone of command made the group subside into anxious twitters.

"How did she get up there?" whispered Seth. "The only entrance to the west tower is through the west wing. Those passages have been sealed off for years, and she couldn't have come through the east tower; the stairs collapsed last spring and we tore them out. It's a straight drop five flights to the basement."

Walker spoke to Samuel. "Dad, please take everybody back inside. All I need is Seth."

"What's wrong with the girl?" Samuel stared with consternation at the pale figure. "What's she saying?"

Walker gazed unblinkingly at the widow's walk, for when he heard it now, in its fullest form, he recognized the dirge he had heard echo across the plains after a thousand battles. His body raised in chill bumps, vibrating with the dying echoes so that he could not move a muscle until the last mournful note had faded.

"It's the Comanche Death Song. Please, Dad. Take the others inside."

When the family had disappeared into the house, Walker pulled Seth into the shadow of the giant alley oaks and stood rubbing his hands briskly over his bare chest and arms.

"Let's give her some time to settle down. I wouldn't want her to get so upset that she . . ." He didn't finish but a vivid memory of her leaping from the hotel balcony flashed through his mind.

"I . . . I really didn't realize she was so different," whispered Seth.

Walker glanced at him briefly. "I could write a book on the subject."

They thought a minute.

"Well," said Seth finally, "the only way I can see to get up is just to scale the front wall, maybe through those grapevines. But they're old and probably rotten."

"Where is she?" said Walker suddenly, stepping to the edge of the shadows. "I don't see her, do you?"

Seth squinted, but the full moon had dropped low over the mansion in one last blaze of brilliance as daylight approached, and it blinded him.

"No . . . I don't think—"

"There!" said Walker, pointing to a flash of luminous white that disappeared before Seth could spot it, seeming to vanish into the walls of the towers. "Come on," he urged, "let's move around to the back of the house. At least the moon will be at our backs and we can see better."

They stopped at the corner of the carriage house and the mansion squatted before them like an ancient gray beast, its massive lines already turning vague in the twilight.

An eternity passed and they saw nothing. Seth muttered, "Dammit, I don't see how she could have gotten down short of sprouting wings." He looked at Walker. "She couldn't have gotten down, could she?"

Walker squinted but couldn't detect so much as a flicker of movement. "I've learned not to discount any possibility where she's concerned," he replied bitterly. "Let's go look around."

They poked at bushes and trampled ruthlessly through Kathren's flowerbeds, yet uncovered nothing except a few startled birds on the roost. Walker was fighting a sense of panic. Almost an hour had passed.

The others were waiting in the tomblike silence of the parlor, and when Walker and Seth pushed the door open abruptly, there was a female squawk of surprise.

Kathren recovered before the younger women and began firing questions at Walker.

"Did you find her? Is she armed? Is there any danger of—"

Walker looked quietly at his father. "I want you to get Harriot."

Kathren let out a gasp. "Then the girl *is* dangerous. See here, Walker Grayson, you have no right to withhold information that could save our lives—and I know you are not telling us everything you know about this girl. Why would a man go after his own wife with a bloodhound unless she was a danger to all of us?" Her voice rose. "I demand to know what you intend to—"

"Kathren, for the love of heaven hush your squawking." Samuel spoke harshly and ignored her startled look as he went on. "Randy, you go get Harriot and bring her to the back door. Muzzle her just in case—though I don't think she would harm the girl if she's working without other dogs. Now I want the rest of you to go somewhere—preferably upstairs to your rooms—and stay out of the way until we get to the bottom of this." He looked at Walker. "I can't understand what's come over the girl. In fact, there's a lot I don't understand," he added meaningfully.

After the women and servants trudged off in search of rest, Samuel looked at his younger son.

"Seth, I'd like to speak to your brother alone."

"Yes sir," Seth replied instantly. But he paused at the door to glance once more at Walker before closing it.

Samuel went to the mantel and got his pipe, and Walker took a seat on the sofa, waiting patiently because he knew each step of the little ritual by heart; three taps against the stones to clear out the old ash, a sniff at the fresh tobacco pouch and afterward a pinch between his fingers. Then he would study the pipe like the most intriguing puzzle while he made little strokes with the gold-plated tamper Melissa Grayson had given him twenty-five years ago.

The match flamed and Samuel cupped his hand over it

to touch it to the tobacco, making little sucking noises on the pipestem until the smoke puffed from the corners of his mouth.

He looked out the window at the tree shapes turning milky blue against the gold sunrise.

"I like Silver," he said thoughtfully. "I really feel a genuine affection for her though I've only known her a short time."

Walker watched his back and said nothing.

"Is she stable?"

Walker was surprised and annoyed. "She's perfectly sane."

"But could she be dangerous?"

Walker leaned his face into his hands. "I honestly don't know," he said after a moment.

Samuel came to sit on the couch and touched his shoulder. "Son, I don't question your feelings for this girl. They are apparent every time you look at her."

Walker started to protest but found no way to do it without making himself a fool. After Silver's description of the Indian wedding ceremony at the dinner table, he had remembered something he had once known but forgotten: To an Indian, the act of coitus *was* the wedding ceremony. Was he—of all people—to claim ignorance of Indian customs, when, in fact, he had sent many a soldier home because such ignorance endangered lives or the delicate balance in some treaty negotiation?

As to caring for the little savage . . .

"I know you love her, as I love Kathren," Samuel went on softly, kneading the thick shoulder under his hand. "It's our duty to protect and cherish both of them, and I'm trying to stand behind you on this, son. But—"

The sound of the door opening interrupted him. Kathren stood clinging to it for a moment before she could speak.

"Come quickly," she gasped. "The carriage house."

The sun was up in full strength, setting every bead of

moisture to dancing light. In the distance a rooster greeted the morning; crows hawked in the trees by the carriage house, and the musty breath of the swamp had been washed from the air by the morning freshness. It seemed a day like any other day, and Walker couldn't shake the feeling that he would wake up any moment to find Silver smiling from the doorway of his room. Or gazing into his eyes in that half shy, half seductive way she had.

Seth was waiting for them on the back patio.

"There were no lamps on at the time, but Randy thought he saw somebody lurking inside," he explained. "It's black as Egypt in there with no light, but he figured it might have been Silver because a few minutes later he found that the guard dogs were loose."

"Well, that does it," said Kathren. "You'll just have to call off the search, Samuel. I will not have you risking your life for that girl."

She made *that girl* sound like a foul word, and Samuel looked at her curiously.

"That girl, Kathren, is your daughter-in-law," he reminded her quietly.

"And we're wasting time," said Walker. "Seth, you go in the front of the carriage house and I'll circle around back. Dad, why don't you and Kathren just wait for us . . . inside the house."

"Don't you dare try to shut me out," said Kathren hotly. "This is my house and my family as well. I have a right to know what's going on."

The French doors to the patio rattled, and when Walker turned, he saw Ferrell, Amanda, and Camelia in their bathrobes; he jerked his head at Seth and they hurried off, leaving the older Graysons to explain.

After circling the carriage house twice, both inside and out, they had found nothing. At the kennel pens in back, one dog had been recovered and locked up, but the other three were missing.

Seth thought aloud, "Having lived on the plains all her life, I don't suppose she can paddle a boat."

Walker considered the matter for only a heartbeat before he barked, "Quick—I'll check the boat landing and you cover the garden paths." And he took off running.

The overhanging veils of moss blocked his view until Walker had scrambled halfway down the steep path that dropped to the bayou; when he could see the boat landing, he stopped dead.

She was sitting cross-legged on the weathered gray planks that extended over the water, her brown legs peeping between the tatter streamers of the cream muslin frock he'd purchased for her in Nacogdoches. The top part covered only her left shoulder, for the right one had been slashed away. The missing guard dogs were curled in black heaps about her, but as Walker stood staring, one of them raised his nose to sniff the air.

The movement alerted Silver, and she looked up.

Her body snaked upward and in the bat of an eye she was on her feet. Walker opened his mouth but before he could say a word, she had brandished a foot-long butcher knife.

There were shouts coming not far away and Walker ran down the rest of the steps, hoping to abort the scene before the witnesses could arrive.

He was halted just short of the pier, however, when the dogs rose with a chorus of snarls and stood stiff legged, their fangs bared and dripping.

"Silver, don't do this," he said breathlessly. "Don't make a spectacle of us in front of the family and servants. We can talk. Whatever is wrong, I can fix it."

Her snarl rose over those of the dogs.

"Ka-nei-mah nah-ich-ka ein! I do not hear you, you two-tongued snake!"

Her head was dropped from her shoulders, her eyes were paled to lustrous crystal, and a vivid memory flashed through Walker's mind of the day she was first brought to him in chains. Every ounce of ground gained appeared to have been lost.

Their eyes locked in a test of wills and Walker didn't allow himself to even blink until he saw her hatred faltering by the little quiver of her eyelashes.

"I don't understand," he said simply. "Is this your idea of a marriage? Of trust? You speak of our children in one breath and threaten my life in the next."

Her eyes flared hotter and as Walker's foot eased down on the edge of the pier, she gestured with the knife; he finished the movement by bringing his left foot up slowly to meet the other one, mentally noting that he was past the danger of tripping on the little step-up.

Then he heard his faithful followers scrambling down the embankment behind him, their voices hushed but excited, and Walker grimaced with fury.

"Silver, look at me," he coaxed again softly, for her eyes were fixed beyond him.

But a shriek interrupted before he could go on.

"Oh, my God! Look at her arms — I'm . . . I'm going to faint!" The voice was Kathren's.

Walker saw what had provoked the scream. The girl had taken the knife to her arms and legs, and made thin, shallow slashes. It must have been what she was doing when he found her, for bright red blood was just beginning to drip from the wounds.

"It's part of their mourning ritual," Walker said over his shoulder. "They are light cuts — nothing dangerous. Now please. Go back to the house."

The family and servants retreated further up the embankment but not so far that they could not see.

"I know something has happened to upset you," Walker began, "but all we have to do is . . . My God." His voice was thick with disgust. "What is that in your hair?"

A satisfied gleam came to the lustrous gray eyes.

"Ashes and grease," she intoned, and Walker recognized a cadence, a warning rhythm like the wind first rippling the water before it whips it to the frenzy of a gale. And when she spoke again, he was not surprised to hear a full-blown chant.

"Ashes and grease," — she swayed — "signs of mourning, songs of death," — she swayed — "river of buffalo turned to blood, The People cry for the lost land . . ." She closed her eyes and lifted her face: *"Habbe we-ich-ket . . . Habbe we—"*

"Silver, stop it!" He took a quick step along the pier and Silver snapped her head up, the trance broken and her senses tuned to everything about her.

"Do not take another step, white-man dog, or I will rip open your belly and let the wolves drink your blood!"

There was a strangled noise behind him and Walker hoped one or more of the women had fainted into blissful oblivion. In the meantime Randy had joined the group. Samuel motioned the boy toward the dogs and when Randy called out, one of them trotted past Walker, disdainfully ignoring him, and submitted to Randy's leash; however, his efforts failed to coax the others into following suit.

Only the knowledge that she could move like a striking adder checked Walker's urge to rush her. In addition, only one backward step stood between her and the water, and he entertained serious doubts that he could outswim her.

He tried once more, his words tumbling over each other like a man pleading for his life. "Talk to me. Tell me what I've done to hurt you. I know I'm not perfect, but we're a family, Silver. Families work together—"

"I am not your family!" She curled her lip so that her small pearly teeth glistened against the dark setting of her skin. "I am Quohadie Teichas, daughter of Horse Back. Your soldiers take my homeland and carry me far from my real family. You give me white eyes clothes and teach me white eyes ways." She paused to spit in a gesture of contempt, and the fire in her eyes burned hotter. "So I wear your clothes though they hurt my skin and I speak your tongue until I do not know my own—I give you my body to bear many sons and for all this, you are still *tivo sata* to me—the white man dog whose promises are like bitter waters, for they ease a man's throat but sour his belly until he dies!"

Walker's chest ached with all the things he couldn't say. At last his throat opened to release one word, and he poured everything into it.

"Silver."

For a moment she wavered, and Walker imagined flesh-colored lines streaking down the smut on her cheeks. But a voice rang out behind him, clear and not at all faint.

"Then go back to your precious Horse Back, you little heathen!" screamed Camelia. "Nobody wants you here. You've done nothing but bring this family grief since the day we laid eyes on you!" She subsided into a fit of bawling, but there was no other sound.

Silver stared at Camelia briefly, then at Walker; and when she stooped to brush aside the tattered skirt and replace the knife in a belt strapped to her thigh, Walker's knees seemed to melt from under him and he smiled his relief, raising his hand as he moved toward her again.

She stopped him with a look that chilled his blood, and made the cramp in his chest grow tighter. "And so I go," she said softly and, wheeling around, she sprang into a perfect dive.

Walker's eye shuttered like a lens, freezing her for a flash of time while her body was suspended and arched like a sailfish over the still, emerald water. Then her feet followed the path of her steepled hands so perfectly that she broke the surface with no more splash than if an arrow had pierced it.

The house creaked and shuddered as though it sensed the impending storm. The thunder rumbled closer and occasionally a flicker of lightning lit the tall windows of the library.

Walker had managed to light a weak fire with a few scraps of kindling that had escaped spring cleaning, and stood by it now, hardly conscious of his shivering or the green silt from the bayou drying in his clothes, making them stiff as sun-dried canvas.

Seth had taken time to change but his hair was still damp, and he ran his hands through the unruly curls as he stood in the doorway looking at Walker.

The slump of his brother's shoulders did little to quell his own uneasiness, and he paused to pour a drink before joining him at the fireplace.

"Looks like it's going to rain again. The mud hasn't dried from the cane fields since the last one," he remarked. When Walker looked at him, Seth's spirits took another plunge. "You're thoroughly drunk," he noted.

Walker gazed at the fire while he emptied his glass, and Seth teased, "We've weathered worse storms than this — and I'm not referring to the one outside."

Walker said nothing as he turned from the fire and went to slouch into the overstuffed sofa, twirling the empty glass slowly in his hand. Seth followed to sit beside him, continuing in a light tone. "Tomorrow will never know the difference. Daddy will cool down, you'll sweet talk Silver, and two years from now this will be family legend. We'll tell it bigger each time and laugh ourselves to death." Walker glanced at him, and Seth blurted, "Okay, maybe it'll take ten years. But heaven's gate, man. You lock her away like a wild animal then wonder why she acts like one! By God, I don't blame her," he said, frowning indignantly. "I'd have slit your throat a long time ago."

"You don't know what you're talking about," mumbled Walker thickly, finding a grim satisfaction in his slurred words. "This is not going to blow over."

"How long are you going to keep her locked up?" Seth demanded, ignoring his prophecy.

"That depends on her."

"So you think she'll just lay down arms and come crawling to you if you punish her long enough? Well, I think you're a fool. What you're doing is driving her away."

"I'm not driving her anywhere. She's the one who's so damned determined to run off."

"She loves you."

"She hates me, she hates you — she hates anything with white skin, and I honestly believe she'll hate her own kin if I ever find them!" Walker blurted passionately.

"Then why haven't you done right by her?" Seth insisted. "If you know she can't make it in the white man's world, why in the name of your own honor haven't you let

303

her go back to the Indians?"

Walker considered the orange firelight for a long time, and when he turned, Seth gave a start at the red swelling around his eyes. "I can't," he said miserably. "I love her."

Seth searched a moment then said softly, "You've got a funny way of showing it. I'd have sworn you were planning to slaughter the only people she—"

In a flash there was a hand on Seth's collar that made the fabric squeak in protest.

When Walker realized what he was doing, he stared with disbelief into Seth's face, then snatched his hand away violently.

"Consider this, all-wise one," he hissed savagely. "If I take up for my so-called *wife,* I'm accused of betraying the family honor. If I protect my family from my wife, I'm accused of disloyalty and brutality. And if that were not enough, my own brother sinks the knife deeper!"

A sheepish look passed over Seth's face, then his anger flared back. "What I said is true. You're not the only one who's suffering from a culture gap around here, so don't expect my pity!" He looked at Walker intensely. "Listen. I'm sorry, okay? It's just that you're messing things up so bad I can't stand it—not when I know that . . ."

He looked at the fireplace a moment and then went on. "The family may not like it one hell of a lot, but look what you and Silver have already accomplished. First Silver springs the news practically on the eve of your wedding to Camelia—"

"I never married her," Walker contested. "I slept with her and that's the same thing to a Comanche."

"Whatever. Anyway, now she lives here as a legitimate family member and I haven't seen the roof cave in. Nobody has collapsed—and all that really remains is to get rid of Camelia, smooth the family's feathers, and go on your merry way with everything you ever wanted—*if* you had the wits to see it."

Walker waved his hand. "You talk riddles."

"I talk good sense; you're just too drunk to follow me. Go find this white family of Silver's, let her meet them—

you underestimate the call of true blood. But before you do anything, go upstairs and talk to your wife. Make love to her. But most of all, stop holding her prisoner. You're just confirming the family's accusations that she's nothing but a heathen who will slit our throats at the first opportunity."

"She might. She's already killed four men."

Seth blinked. "I'll pretend that was the babbling of a drunken fool."

"Then you'd be the fool." Walker heaved himself from the sofa and walked to the fireplace again, shivering though his clothes were almost dry. "Neither of us are weaklings and it took the both of us to overcome her and drag her from the water."

"So? She's very strong. Would you rather she drowned?"

Walker ignored the quip. "When she was a slave, she was brutalized and in return she killed herself an Apache or two, and later two soldiers that tried to rape her."

"She was defending herself. I admire that."

Walker turned around. "I've never known anyone so proud and fierce. But it doesn't change anything. She can only be pushed so far, and then God help the idiot who pushed her."

"Who did?" Seth asked softly.

"Who did what?" Walker snapped impatiently.

"Who pushed her? Why don't you make her to tell you what caused the return of the savage? If she were my wife—"

"And did she tell *you*, my brother?" Walker scoffed. "Or didn't I see you almost break your neck on the stairs in your hasty retreat?"

Seth flushed. "It was too soon, that's all." He covered the slash in his shirt with one hand.

Walker set his glass on the mantel and started toward the door.

"Where are you going?"

Walker's liquor-dulled eyes flashed suddenly clear.

"I'm going to bed before I have to sleep wherever I fall.

305

And I suggest you get some rest, too. You see, I've decided to take your advice. I'm leaving tomorrow and I won't come back until I've found some of her family." He smiled grimly. "In the meantime, we'll see how you fare at being warden. But don't underestimate your adversary. She's strong as a wounded bear, wild as a mustang, and cunning as a lynx." He touched his brow in a mocking salute. "I hope you enjoy your job." And he staggered out the door.

Seth tossed down the rest of his drink and sank low on the sofa, staring at the flames until there was nothing left but embers.

Chapter 19

Kathren threw a finger to her lips until the halting footsteps faded down the hall. Then she tiptoed to her bedroom door and listened.

"That was close," she whispered irritably. "I thought Walker had already gone to bed."

Her knees shook as she started to return to the red satin chaise where Ferrell was sprawled, a nightcap of Samuel's best French champagne in his hand. A limb banged on the window as the wind picked up, and with a shudder, Kathren changed direction for the nightstand by her bed, taking a small gold flask from the drawer.

"It's a night to remember," murmured Ferrell, eyeing the flask.

Kathren tossed him a glare, pulling the vanity stool closer and taking a seat. As she took a bracing nip from the bottle, Ferrell laughed unkindly.

"Usually nothing gets to you. What's the matter? Does it make you squeamish that your husband is sleeping next door and that he might wake to find your so-called nephew in your room?"

"He won't wake, I've seen to—" Kathren broke off and glared. "What 'gets' to me is when you exhibit stupidity. Surely you can be more original than an *accident*. So Camelia gets thrown from a horse, what would you do then? Are you so vain as to think you can arrange the demise of all three heirs—how would you space these accidents, one a month? One every six months? At that it would take almost two years to get what you want."

307

She took another swig of liquor, snapping her head back and making her glossy black curls dance; then she smiled at him with a tinge of regret.

"As to your suggestion, it's so preposterous that I know you are joking. No man is so enamored of a woman that he will include the bastard son of the second wife in his will. Not even I —"

"Don't waste a good performance." There was a small tick in Ferrell's left jaw. "I've seen the will."

Kathren went white. "You conniving little . . ." She stopped and stared a moment, then smiled slowly. "I've bred no fool," she said huskily. "You might be ruthless, intelligent and ambitious, but certainly no fool. I'm very proud of that."

Ferrell toasted her insolently. "Thank you. But you, my mother, are a liar. You weren't going to tell me about your success, were you?"

Kathren dropped her gaze. "I was afraid you'd move too fast. You do that sometimes. For instance, this notion of helping me by getting rid of Camelia is nonsense. It's true that she's become nothing but a nuisance — she couldn't seduce a drunk sailor, much less a Grayson," she sneered. "But I'll think of something on my own." She scowled suddenly. "What made you snoop out the will? That was very risky. You could have been caught."

"I've noticed the lines of dissipation in your husband's face and I know he doesn't abuse his liquor. And he's so tired lately . . . and perhaps distraught by nightfall — when you crawl into his bed?"

Kathren was surprised. "I never realized you resented my physical relationship with Samuel." She studied him intently. "Why are you looking at me like that?"

His dark gaze probed a second more, then dropped to the glass in his hand, and Kathren saw that the knuckles beneath the sparse black hairs were whitened. She stared thoughtfully at his fingers — long, tapered fingers that at the age of ten could span enough ivory to render a perfect performance of Chopin's *Fantasie Impromptu* on the Steinway in the parlor of her employer—then Melissa Winebrenner. Kathren's breath caught at the memory. What a waste of talent and looks and intelligence! she thought.

But he was only the son of a servant, a bastard at that, and Melissa's praise and encouragement had turned out to be a pious indulgence to tickle her own ego, for when a twist of fate disclosed the sordid fact of Ferrell's conception, Melissa's parents promptly dismissed their daughter's private maid and the bastard son, and Melissa would not look her in the eye but folded her hands on her lap and bowed to their wishes without a word of protest. At that moment Kathren had fully realized the vast gulf that separated her from everything she wanted. With unswerving single-mindedness, she began to funnel every thought and all her energies into bridging that gulf.

Kathren's face mellowed with an almost forgotten maternal tenderness. "I've done everything for you," she said softly.

Ferrell threw back his head and hooted cruelly, transforming her smile to an ugly grimace of horror.

"Your 'everything' is what binds our hands now, my dear mother," he said acidly. "After all, there's only so much room in the attic."

Kathren's blood congealed in her veins and her heart seemed to stop. Her path to the decanter on the bureau weaved drunkenly for her head was spinning like a planet out of orbit.

She poured another drink and watched the dark profile of her son. She noticed that his drink hand was perfectly steady, whereas her own hands trembled so fiercely that she could hardly still the tinkle of the glass against the bureau.

"Ferrell, you must listen to me. Anything I have done, I have done for you. And it's taken me years—years of humiliation and defeat. But it's all within our grasp if only you do not do something foolish."

Her anger kindled as she thought of decades crumbling to ruin — all because of the one for whom she had toiled. She moved until she stood in front of him, drawing upon her favorite weapons of aggression and intimidation.

Suddenly she hissed, "How dare you threaten me, you sniveling upstart!" She threw her shoulders back and continued coldly. "Rest assured that any tidbits you have gleaned are only pieces of an elaborate tapestry — one of my own design and making while you were nothing but a bad-tempered, vain little brat in short pants, swaggering about the Winebrenner estate like you owned it! It's no wonder I was dismissed. Had you not been such an odious little creature, I might have managed Melissa and kept my employment there. Instead I was forced to the streets again — selling myself to feed you!"

Ferrell's eyes had not left her face, and they were still laced with the light of triumph. "I think you 'managed' Melissa Winebrenner Grayson quite well. In fact, I applaud you. A self-educated apothecary . . . my God, what an accomplishment."

The brandy sloshed onto Kathren's icy fingers. "I beg of you," she whispered. "In the name of the bond between us, do nothing to jeopardize what's in the palm of our hands!"

"In *your* greedy little palm, Mother. You have it all, everything you ever wanted — and I don't believe for one minute you plan to risk it on my account." He grinned suddenly. "And I don't expect you to, of course. I certainly wouldn't do it for you."

Kathren's expression was that of a mother who beholds a monster coming from her womb, and Ferrell's teeth flashed whiter and brighter. "In fact, I'd be downright disappointed if you showed such stupidity, the way I was when I found out you keep the very one who could condemn you under your very skirts. Very

310

stupid, Mother. You should have done away with her before we left Georgia."

Kathren gasped the word. "Sheba!"

"Of course now I'm glad that you didn't." Ferrell examined his manicured nails. "Otherwise I'd still be in the dark, where you prefer to keep all your . . . *mistakes*. And Sheba did prove to be rather loyal. It took my best charm to persuade her. However, I still think she has outlived her usefulness."

Kathren exploded. "How dare you tell me what to do when if it weren't for you I'd—" Kathren threw her hand over her mouth, tears filled her eyes, and in an instant she was sobbing quietly.

The hardness in Ferrell's face showed small chinks then larger cracks, and he hated himself more than he did her as he went to put an arm around the heaving shoulders; his words sprang not from compassion or warmth but from a grim sense of duty, and a childhood habit he'd never quite overcome.

"It's all right, Mother. I know how hard you've worked. Everything will turn out for us, you wait and see."

He knew it would, too. This time he would see to it.

Walker had not slept any by three A.M., and once more he crawled from his bed of torture, threw a robe over his shoulders, and crept down the hall to the room where he'd locked his wife away.

Never was there any sound from within and this time was no exception. Furtively he rapped on the door.

"Silver?"

Nothing. He rapped again, then groped for the key in the pocket of his robe as a sudden vision of her lying dead on the floor flashed through his mind.

He realized his foolishness when he cracked the door and saw her sitting cross-legged in the window seat, her form silhouetted, for the storm had veered to miss

311

them completely and the moon was out.

His remorse fled. "What has kept you awake, milady?" he inquired sarcastically. "Are your talents failing you and it takes all night to make a simple knife?" Then he inhaled sharply as he saw the flourish of a blade wink in the moonlight. He took a step, and his feet crunched on the pieces of a broken mirror.

He stood still and looked at her shrewdly. "I've often wondered," he said softly, "how a Comanche warrior would handle such an unruly squaw?" And he saw the shard of glass waver slightly, for he had known the answer before he asked. "Good," he taunted. "It's comforting to know I'm doing the right thing."

He locked the door behind him and before dawn made good his vow. After leaving a waspish reminder of duties on his brother's door, he saddled his horse and rode away in the darkness.

Seth was humming softly as he climbed the stairs with a breakfast tray. Although he clutched a key in his hand, he knocked politely before he opened the lock.

Silver was sitting where Walker had left her, in the window seat.

Seth cleared his throat to cover a gasp of shock. Sunlight poured into the room and what he saw was a stranger with a smut-blackened face and greasy streamers of hair hanging in her face. She sat slumped, holding a blade of slivered mirror in her hand, and for a moment the fear crossed his mind that the girl was truly unbalanced.

But her next words dispelled that worry. "Take away your white eyes food, I will not eat it," she said huskily.

Seth looked indignant, and teased, "You most assuredly will, young lady. I cooked it myself, just for you."

Her hand moved and the blade flashed, momentarily blinding him. "Then leave it, *tivo sata*. I do not wish

312

to see your pale face," she warned savagely.

Seth set the tray on the bureau and turned back toward her.

"I'll respect your need to do this, just as I'll respect Walker's conviction about locking you up. But I don't believe for one instant that you would harm anyone in this house."

Then he turned and shut the door behind him, and Silver heard the latch click as he locked it.

After a minute, she left the window seat for the first time, went to the bed without touching the tray, and found the peace of sleep more quickly than she would have imagined possible.

Downstairs, Seth set himself to a second but equally disturbing problem, and launched an attack at Jubal first, for the cook was so tuned to gossip that he could frequently predict incidents in advance—though the phenomenon was due to the size of his ears rather than neurological endowments.

When Seth burst through the kitchen door, Jubal's plump effeminate hands were awaiting the pastry he'd spun into the air; but the noise brought his head around and the dough struck his stiffened fingers, spread over his knuckles, and dropped in pieces to the floor. After that, Seth could elicit nothing from the angry Frenchman but dark mutterings, and he was in a fine rage himself as he stormed into the breakfast room to confront Kathren.

"It has come to my attention that Prissy Fontenot has not been back to work since the other day when I went to her village," he announced stiffly. "Where is she?"

Samuel set his coffee cup down. "Don't use that tone to your stepmother. Prissy has been . . . dismissed."

Seth's eyes darkened to jade. "Why?"

"Kathren thought it best," said Samuel, dropping his

313

gaze. He rubbed his fingers against his left temple where the now familiar pain had started.

"I want her reinstated," said Seth flatly.

"You should have thought of that before, dear," purred Kathren, spreading her bread with butter.

"What is that supposed to mean?"

Kathren looked at him with pity. "Darling, I know you are a grown man with certain . . . well, needs. But you'll have to learn to be more discreet and not flaunt your affairs."

For a moment Seth stared, unable to believe either the insult or his father's impassive reaction. "If you were a man, I'd do something about that poisoned tongue of yours," he advised coldly.

Samuel touched the center of his chest. "Please," he murmured, and his lips felt numb. His forearm was crushed against the table's edge as he sagged forward, and he could neither move the limb or straighten up.

Seth stared in dazed horror; Samuel's lips were blue, his face frozen in a horrible contortion.

"My Lord!" Kathren screamed, coming from her chair. "Look what you've done! Quick—get Doc Adams!"

She had yelled the second time before Seth could break his feet loose from the floor, but afterward he couldn't stop running until he reached the stable stall, threw open the gate, and grabbed Rising Sun's hemp halter.

Though the horse dodged and rolled his eyes, he seemed to sense his truculence would not be tolerated and submitted while Seth threw the heavy work saddle over his back. He was rewarded shortly thereafter by the touch of boot heels in his sides, a loose rein, and the soaring joy of freedom as he launched himself over the paddock fence and thundered down the bayou road.

"Your heart sounds fine. Perhaps it was a constriction of the muscles around it," said Dr. Adams. "Have you eaten anything unusual today?"

Samuel shook his head, feeling as ill as he looked. "I've just been having a few aches and pains lately—an old man's bones settling." He laughed unconvincingly. "It's nothing but a little indigestion. You know how women get so excited over these things."

The doctor frowned. "I didn't mean to imply that you're perfectly healthy." He spoke to Kathren. "I don't envy you your task, but see that he comes by my office next week for a few tests."

"Oh, I'll come," agreed Samuel quickly. "If I ever have another spell like this, I'll be on your doorstep before you can snap your fingers. You can bet your boots on that."

Dr. Adams gave him a sour look. "If the Good Lord can't get your attention with a willow switch, He uses a razor strop. If that don't work, it's a timber and in extreme cases of bullheadedness, a corner post right between the eyes. My advice is not to wait that long—which is what you'll be doing if you a wait for another attack."

Samuel waved him away. "You're a pessimistic old grump. That's why I have this ravishing nurse to take care of me." He patted the bed and took Kathren's hand when she sat down beside him. He grinned up wickedly at the doctor. "She knows just what to do."

Doc Adams turned to his bag and opened it briskly. "At last Friday night's poker game you took everything but the shirt on my back. I certainly don't intend for you to miss this week's game."

He straightened with a needle in his hand. "Complete rest is what I order, and I'll give you something to aid you," he said, tucking the corners of his mouth in a small malicious grin.

Samuel eyed the instrument. "That's not medicine—it's revenge and you know it," he glared.

315

"But it works so fast," murmured the doctor. "Much faster than pretty nurses."

"Leave it to a Frenchman to invent such torture," muttered Samuel, rolling to his side.

Samuel was asleep in no time. Kathren could not find Seth and half feared that he had slipped away to the Acadian village. But his rebellion had become only a minor irritation in view of what she now suspected. Even when she passed the room where Silver was locked away, she cast no more than a brief contemptuous glance toward it before marching on for the west wing.

The hunched figure whirled furtively as the door opened.

Kathren held the candle up, narrowing her eyes. "All right, let me have it," she demanded. "What are you hiding behind your back?"

"Mistress, my mistress," quavered a thin voice, "the moon in her eyes, the stars in her hair—"

Kathren blew out the candle and now she could see the glow surrounding the twisted figure like a halo. She crossed the room in three strides.

"Give it to me!"

The gnarled hands fumbled in agitation and lost their grip on the burning candle. Sheba screamed as it toppled, for the hot wax scalded the dark shrunken skin on her hands. Kathren reached out and jerked her forward just in time to avoid disaster when the frazzled rug shot up a little smoking flame.

Kathren stomped until she was certain both the candle and the rug were extinguished, then she whirled about with a backswing that would have dropped a grown man.

Both candles were snuffed now and the room was smothered in gloom or else Sheba might have had time to duck; she was strangely agile and often missed punishment with a cat-quick movement. But Kathren's knuckles landed with a crack of bone and squish of flesh, and Sheba cowered to the floor, flinging her arms up to protect her head while she blubbered and squealed with fright.

"That's only a sample, as you well know!" hissed Kathren. "How many times have I warned you about this. Not only are you going to roast yourself alive, but the rest of us as well. Now get up!"

Sheba's bawling hushed immediately. For one thing remained clear in her cobwebbed brain: Continued disobedience was not the path to mercy.

"I 'ave sinned, O Lord, I 'ave sinned grievously in Thy sight—"

"Shut up and listen to me." Kathren grabbed the reeking wool coat and lifted the woman by the shoulder of it, her flesh seeming to crawl with lice at the first touch. No matter what discipline she meted out, the creature continued to bundle herself in the moth-eaten coat she'd found a week ago in a forgotten chamber.

With new rage at having to touch her, Kathren took hold of the scrawny throat and held tight while she ripped the garment away, feeling faint as the odor of excrement assailed her.

"Give it!" Sheba shrieked, braving anything to clutch at the prize.

Kathren snatched it from her grasp and threw it toward a sheet-draped chair like one tossing a viper from his bed. Then, gagging but determined, she marched to it, bundled it in the furniture cover, and flung it toward the entrance door. "I should have burned it before now," she said, turning and striding back purposefully across the room again.

Sheba shivered in terror, crouching into the corner made by the bureau and wall, next to the single window which was the sole source of light.

"Dark!" wailed Sheba. "Dark!"

Kathren struck her another stunning blow, and the grizzled head wobbled on its thin neck as though it would topple to the floor. But Sheba quieted again, and even began to grin pervertedly, her toothless gums gaping and her eyes glazed with a strange pleasure. "My baby luv me," she crooned, reaching out to stroke at Kathren's forearm.

Kathren quickly stepped back to avoid the scaly, clawlike appendage.

"Yes, of course I do. That's why I can't let you have the fire sticks. You know that. Your hand is not steady."

"I know, I know," Sheba echoed thinly.

"Now," said Kathren, in complete control again. "I must know if someone has been here besides me. You must think very carefully, for when you do, you are very smart indeed. So do not answer hastily."

The crone crawled upon the cedar chest below the window and sat down. She was small before, but age and arthritis had shrunk her even more until she was not much larger than a dwarf. The once taut skin, stained olive with Mandingo blood, that had made her the highest paid courtesan in New Orleans, now hung in dark leathery bags from her frame. Her raven hair had turned white as bleached bones and stood from her head like a cap of thistledown, thinner but still kinked by her African genes.

Her silhouette swayed as she pondered the question, and Kathren did not press her.

At last Sheba stopped short and sat very still. Then she began like a storyteller, her reedy voice pitched high.

"She come. The one with the Spirit, the one whose hair has caught the moonbeams."

Kathren's jaw sagged with shock. "When! When did she . . ." That question was useless, for Sheba had no conception of time. Kathren passed a hand over her eyes before going on. "Did she see you? Did you talk

318

to her?"

There was no answer. Already the memory had left, and Sheba rocked again, humming softly.

"Now listen up," said Kathren sharply. "The girl doesn't matter, but was there a man? He would have been tall and dark, and he would not have left without trying to talk to you."

Sheba's gums opened in a beatific smile. "Our boy," she whispered, clasping her hands joyfully. "Our boy— yours and mine, he said. A fine boy."

Kathren's heart skipped a beat. She swallowed the dryness in her throat and went on. "Did you show him the secret door?"

"No key!" Sheba shrilled, rocking faster. And when it seemed she would go off on another tangent, Kathren pulled a candle from her pocket and lit it.

"No key!" Sheba cried again, leaping down from the chest to follow her mistress.

Going to the long, age-blotched mirror, Kathren pressed the edge until it opened, then she groped along the dark wall for the lantern hung well out of Sheba's reach. When the lantern was going, she extinguished the candle and put it in her pocket.

A little ways along the tunnel, Kathren stopped at a door and spoke coldly over her shoulder. "You are not allowed inside, you know."

She unlocked the door, stepped inside, and closed it bluntly when Sheba tried to peer around her.

Although the west wing had been unused for many years prior to Samuel Grayson's purchase and none of the family had guessed the existence of the room beyond the mirror, Kathren was grateful she'd left nothing to chance and, kneeling, she lifted the loose floorboard. The room was airless as a tomb and by the time she had retrieved the small wooden box, sweat plastered her dress and ran into her eyes.

The box was intact, and she almost put it back without checking, feeling certain that no one—not even her crafty son—could have discovered its hiding place even if Sheba had divulged the presence of the room and the doorlock had been picked.

There was a glass *clink* as she moved to put the box back, and again she drew it out, placing it on her lap. Her hand trembled as she tripped the padlock, for she had unconsciously memorized the exact tone of the bottles rolling against each other—a tone that did not ring with the same depth now.

An observer would have thought Kathren unmoved by her discovery, for she quickly snapped the box lid shut, replaced the padlock, the box, and finally the loose floorboard over it.

The lantern light did not waver as she stepped into the passageway and locked the door behind her, and she did not speak until she had secured the lantern on its high hook and Sheba had followed her into the outer room beyond the mirror.

Then she turned and started for the old woman, who had begun to bounce around her in the manner of an ape. Kathren advanced like a leopard stalking its prey until Sheba was cringed against the wall.

"You have sinned grievously against God and now He will turn from you," Kathren hissed. Her eyes glittered and she used a hypnotic tone. "He will no longer hear your pleas, and when the Dark One comes for you, nothing will save you!"

A low wail began in Sheba's throat and Kathren silenced it with a light, almost playful cuff. "The Dark One will not correct you in love, as I do. He wants your *soul*. He wants to see you roasting by a hook in the back of your neck—sshhh! Hush now." Her voice became a croon as she controlled her revulsion enough to stroke the lice-infested white hair.

"If the evil one hears you, he will know your deed and come for you. He may even appear in the body of another, like the man who calls himself 'our boy.' He came to tempt you before, you see, and you let him do

320

it."

"No key! Sheba could not let him in your secret room!"

"Ah, yes, but he is very smart and you shouldn't have let him into *this* room. But not only did you do that, you showed him the mirror and told him about my secret room, didn't you?"

Sheba clutched her head and moaned.

"Did you . . . tell him what was in the chest?"

"Nooooo! Sheba no tell! Fee Foolay come get me!"

Kathren glanced at the cedar chest below the window but went on rapidly. "Time has run out. The whole household will be searching for me, so I'll have to trust you. But do not ever leave your door unlocked again. The Dark One has been here, in this very room with you. He is so shrewd that he has even unlocked my secret box without a key. That proves he is the Dark One—he knows magic.

"Now. I must go quickly, but think about what I've said. And when I come back, I will tell you what to do—a special spell to keep you from the Evil One. But you must follow my instructions carefully."

Samuel's color was returning by noon and he was able to eat a little. Ordinarily, Amanda's clinging and whining and fussing over her father would have irritated Kathren unbearably but now she found it gave her time to eat and think in silence. Though she was aware of Ferrell's intense regard across the table, she ignored him unless it was to give him a bright, pleased smile. However, as soon as lunch was over, she followed him as he headed for the stables and began her attack with a matter-of-fact tone.

"Samuel mentioned this morning that having extra guests has been a strain on the family. I told him you'd be happy to take a room in town for a while." To soften the blow, she hooked her arm through his and made as though she would walk him to the stable.

Ferrell stopped short, jerking away from her. "You put a halt to that notion, I hope."

Kathren batted her eyes. "But what could I do? I dare not defy him."

"Don't make me laugh. Use your witchcraft on him—it worked well enough to get the will changed."

"A mistake which I'm regretting more by the minute!" Kathren returned hotly, dropping her girlish mien to stick a long bejeweled finger under his nose. "Now you listen and listen well. My plan is proceeding perfectly—or it was until you arrived. Certain drugs in combination can have fatal results, which leads me to believe that perhaps your dabbling in my medicine chest was something more than a prank to needle me. Maybe it was only a test run and you are planning on having your inheritance early."

"That's crazy. I only wanted him to sleep a little later this morning so I could talk to you. I didn't realize his loving wife was adding something to his nightcaps."

"I want those vials returned immediately or I'll let Samuel have his way and you will be *out*. Do you understand me?"

Ferrell lifted a brow at her outburst. "You really are upset. Don't you trust your own son?"

"Like a snake," said Kathren flatly.

Ferrell was beginning to grin. "So if I return your witch's potion, then I may assume there will be a bed here for me tonight."

"I want them *now*."

Grabbing her shoulder, he pressed a quick kiss on her cheek, but his grip was tense and painful. "That's my mom," he winked, and turned back toward the house.

Samuel insisted Kathren continue with plans for her meeting of the Ladies Auxiliary Club in spite of his morning illness, for he felt much better by late afternoon.

Moving behind Kathren's vanity stool, he laid his hands gently against her neck and brushed her crown of ebony curls with his lips. "You're beautiful," he said huskily.

She smiled knowingly at him in the mirror. "I see you're perfectly recovered. However," she said through pouted ruby lips, "I'm thinking of loading you with black coffee all evening just so your mood will hold until the meeting is over."

Samuel frowned and turned away. "I don't know what's got into me lately, I can't seem to hold my eyes open past eight o'clock." He paused by the bed to slip out of his bathrobe, and Kathren's eyes lit as she admired the still muscular back and broad shoulders. In addition to everything else he had given her, Samuel was both lusty and tender in bed; she'd never once considered stepping outside of marriage to satisfy her admittedly insatiable sexual appetite.

Then her smile slipped and a cold dread uncoiled inside her when she thought of how close Ferrell had come to taking all that away from her. Though she had the vials safely in her possession again, it was possible he might get his hands on some more. He was a resourceful devil—no one knew that better than she.

She stood up, taking the diamond necklace with her as she moved in front of Samuel. She pressed her back close to his naked chest. "Help me, dear. You know I can never clasp these things with my long nails."

Samuel closed the hook, then bent to trail his lips along the ivory skin of her neck, murmuring thickly, "Do remember about that coffee tonight, my sweet. I plan to be wide awake when those old biddies leave."

Turning within his arms, Kathren drew his head down and kissed him hungrily. His arms circled her and crushed her to him until passion gripped her so fiercely she knew she must stop now. She pulled back

323

breathlessly and looked into his eyes.

"I won't forget. And don't *you* forget: You are the light of my life. I would die if anything ever happened to you." And she meant it more than she ever had.

Pecking him playfully on the nose, she turned back for a final look in the mirror. She would cut back on the doses after tonight—no, it would be safer to leave them off all together until Ferrell tired of his games and moved on to bigger and better things. Which she prayed would be soon.

She paused at the door with a parting taunt. "I think you should start on the coffee now," she said gravely, but Samuel was wearing a preoccupied look as he fished a note from his coat and read it.

"Damn. I swear I can't remember anything anymore. There were two things I wrote down and then forgot where I put the reminder."

"What is it, dear?"

He wadded the paper up and tossed it aside. "The first thing was Sheba—now just hold up before you get angry. I'm not talking about having her put away. God knows I gave up on that a long time ago. And she doesn't bother anything—we hardly know she's around. But I saw her in the kitchen the other evening and she smells abominably. You'll either have to clean her up or keep her away from the kitchen. I couldn't choke down a bite of food afterward. Besides, Jubal is terrified of her."

"I'm sorry," said Kathren meekly. "I know she's awful but I feel—"

Samuel held up his hand. "I know how long she's been with you and I admire your devotion. Just please get her cleaned up." He grimaced again.

"And what else?"

"Oh, yes. A letter came to the warehouse office more than a week ago, but I could never think to ask you about it. It was inquiry from some distant relative about a Miss Susan . . . Susan Prichard, that's it.

Seems she was working here as a maid some time ago—in fact, it was about the time that Melissa died. I was so distraught then that I scarcely knew my own name, so I certainly don't remember this maid. I thought you might, since she would have been working directly under you."

The reference to her days of servitude would have brought a sharp retort from Kathren had she the wits to notice. But she stood stiff and unblinking as the blood drained from her face, leaving her mouth a grotesque, crimson-black slash. "I don't remember anyone by that name," she whispered.

"What's the matter, dear? You look ghastly." Samuel started toward her but Kathren came to herself with a shrill laugh.

"Me? I'm fit as a fiddle and you know it. But I've got a million things to do, so ta ta, love. And don't forget our rendezvous!" She blew him a kiss, darted out the door, and shut it.

Outside, she leaned against the massive oak portal for fully five minutes until the sickening whirl inside her head ceased. Then she hurried for the stairs that led to the top level, pausing only long enough to remove her keys from the nook behind a faded ancestral portrait. She must work quickly; her guests would be arriving in less than an hour.

Chapter 20

When Kathren opened the door, Sheba gave a frightened squeal and dashed for the corner.

"Shut up!" warned Kathren impatiently, setting the lamp down and heading straight for the cedar chest under the window.

Suddenly the crone leaped and placed herself between her mistress and the chest.

"Mine, mine!"

Kathren struck the shrunkened face with a doubled fist, not once but twice; the head wobbled drunkenly but Sheba staggered back toward the chest and draped herself over it, whimpering, "Mine, mine!"

Sheba wore nothing now but a thin cotton shift that rent when Kathren grabbed it to haul her out of the way. After taking another blow or two, Sheba retreated, blubbering and moaning, to cower in the corner.

There was a padlock on the chest and Kathren's frantic haste kept her from finding the right key immediately. In the meantime, Sheba had stopped crying and now crept closer, a sly look of glee on her shrunken face. "We take her out, yes?" she asked, rocking on her bare, crippled feet.

Kathren looked aside with cruel smile. "Yes, and then down the bayou she goes. And if you open your mouth with one complaint, I'm going to tie you to this and send you down with it."

Sheba cringed against the wall but only a second later she was drawn toward the chest, peering closer as Kathren raised the lid.

"The gardeners," she quavered. "You said the gardeners would dig her up!"

"It's amazing how much you remember when you want to," snapped Kathren, beads of nausea popping from every pore as the reek of putrification rose from the sepulcher. She made a gagging sound. "No wonder this air is tainted. I don't see how you bear it!"

Twisting her head away, Kathren lifted the bundled linen, extending it full length from her, and instantly her arms ached with the weight of it. She had never imagined that mere bones could be so heavy, and surely nothing else remained after so long.

"The mirror, quickly!" she gasped at Sheba. "And bring the taper with you for light. There are two extras in my pocket."

"They will find her," Sheba threatened once more, eyeing the bundle with pathetic longing as she pressed gnarled fingers along the edge of the mirror. "And I'll be alone now," she sniffled.

Kathren brushed past her into the small tunnel. "You will be worse than that if you don't shut up. The 'gators would much prefer fresh meat."

When Sheba froze with terror, Kathren gave a snort of wild laughter. "That's better. You should remember what can happen to those who meddle in other people's secrets." Then she sobered quickly and ordered, "Hold the light up and don't fall behind. Time is running out."

Providence was with her and Kathren found Camelia alone in her room, dressing for the meeting.

"Oh, you're still here," she said, looking surprised. Camelia turned from preening. "Still here?"

Kathren dropped her gaze and murmured, "I'm sorry, I shouldn't have said anything." She turned to go.

"Said anything about what?" demanded Camelia. "Is it about Walker?"

Kathren waved her handkerchief, then pressed it to her mouth and mumbled. "My meeting . . . I must go."

Camelia came toward her. "It is about Walker. You must tell me!"

"It's not my place. Really, I—"

"Kathren, please! How can you torture me so?"

"Oh, all right. I suppose it would be better coming from someone who cares for you. My dear . . ." Her eyes brimmed. "Walker is going to ask you to leave. He loves Silver, he told me so."

"I don't believe you," Camelia gasped.

"Do lower your voice, my darling," Kathren pleaded. "Already the servants are snickering. You'll bring more shame to your family if you carry on so. All of society will be talking about you, pitying you—why, no man will look twice at a female spurned."

Camelia grabbed the sides of her head and whispered, "Oh, Lord, what can I do?"

Kathren thought a minute. "I know, and it's so simple I don't know why I didn't think of it before. Just leave before he returns. He won't have the chance to disgrace you with rejection, and no one need ever know the details but you and me."

Camelia swayed on her feet and Kathren thought for a terrible moment that the girl would faint. But she whispered weakly, "Get Amanda for me. I cannot do this alone!"

On her way to the stairs Kathren was smiling, though her face sobered long enough to peer anxiously into her stepdaughter's room.

She widened her eyes dramatically. "Amanda, you must go to Camelia at once. Something awful has happened and she needs you."

Then she smiled again as she tripped lightly down the stairs.

328

In no time it seemed the carriage was taking the girls down the long oak alley now lit with lamps for the soon arriving guests, and less than half an hour later the meeting had begun.

Upstairs, Samuel Grayson was sprawled across his bed sleeping, the empty pot of laudanum-laced coffee beside him on the nightstand, while downstairs Kathren stood before seventeen members of the Ladies Auxiliary Club who were gathered in the parlor.

"Walker could not come tonight," she announced, glancing again at the mantel clock to tabulate each passing minute. At the moans of disappointment, she went on. "However, in his stead I have prepared something for you myself. It is in keeping with the club's high goal of promoting human understanding by studying both our past and present problems. What I have is a true life drama, a sequence of events that began in the distant past and has stretched forward in time to touch me personally. It's the tragic story of a young white woman who was captured and subsequently reared by the Indians. Most of you have heard the rumors, but now I give you the truth."

Kathren paused for effect, pretending to look at her hastily scribbled notes, which consisted of only half a dozen lines but fully covered the intent of her speech. Then she raised her eyes slowly, sadly. "It rivals the story of Evangeline, for it is a tale of love and hate, of honor and betrayal . . ."

Sheba hobbled down the hall of the second floor, hefting the weight of the mistress's sacred key ring and remembering the feel of her new robe, a deep wine-colored velvet that trailed far out behind her and was given by the mistress herself, to keep forever. She had wanted to wear it on this mission but the mistress had turned mean and hateful, saying that the garment might trip her feet.

She did not falter in deciding the right door, for she knew every room by heart, even the twin master bedrooms that belonged to the mistress and master.

The door creaked open and the sight of the silent darkness made her shrink back. But she moved forward finally and peered inside.

"Angel Girl, come stand in the light. I, Sheba, give you your freedom!"

There was a slow movement in the gloom and Sheba trembled. In spite of her mistress's reassurances that the Angel of Light would bless her for her deed, she had learned to be wary of the spirit world.

"Come forth," she hissed again, and a pale form materialized from the shadows. Sheba motioned with her knotted fingers. "Come! I show you the secret path to freedom." She screwed up her face, trying to remember the words, then grinned toothlessly. "Freedom to go to your people!"

None of the lamps along the hallway had been lit; only the glow from the ones around the marble fountain permeated upward, faintly illuminating the layers of balconies and dying again before it reached the center dome above. But Silver could see enough to be revolted and frightened by the old one, even if the smell of death did not reek from her until Silver felt light-headed with nausea. She was torn with indecision, for plainly the old woman had set her free, and seemed to know all about her.

"You are a Spirit Talker?" she asked fearfully.

"Spirit, yes!" rasped Sheba, nodding her cap of white wool. "I set you free and the Spirit blesses me!"

Silver dodged away as Sheba's wrinkled claw made a motioning gesture, but when the crone turned and started toward the stairs, she followed.

The lower floors were silent and dimly lit, and Silver's racing heartbeat slackened. Though the Spirit Talker was leading her boldly through the main living area, there was no one about, as though everything had

330

been planned for her escape. A superstitious confidence began to beat in her breast. The gods had heard her pleas and forgiven her for disgracing her people with the white eyes; now they returned her to her homeland, and a chant of praise rose in her throat so that she had to swallow it back.

Nevertheless, she fell further back as the increasing light revealed the figure rocking before her. She had seen many Spirit Talkers in the full glory of their profession, every inch of naked skin painted, with only the tip of a buffalo horn covering the head of their manhood, layers of claws circling their necks, the sharp talons of an eagle hanging from their ears; and when only ten years of age she had accidentally stumbled upon a religious rite performed by a young brave whereby a rope was passed through his breast and he was suspended and whirled from a medicine pole in an effort to insure his entrance into the Happy Hunting Ground, deep in the heart of the earth.

Though such gruesome practices were apparently necessary, Silver could not believe that even the most heinous of deities would accept a creature such as this as a mediator. Yet she had already tasted freedom in her dreams, and she could not stop her feet from following.

As they passed the kitchen, Sheba turned inside. Only a small lamp burned on the wall, but Silver looked immediately at the large chopping block where Jubal prepared his meats. Then she looked at the Spirit Talker, who nodded and gestured for her to hurry.

Silver picked up a fine carving knife, tested its blade with the tip of her finger, and her chest constricted so that she could barely breathe. The savage revenge she owed the white man seemed from another lifetime, and she couldn't bear to think of using the instrument on any of the great house. For the hateful Kathren was Walker's mother, Camelia was weak and stupid and no brave took delight in such a paltry prize; Amanda was

Walker's sister, and then there were Seth and Samuel and Jubal and Prissy—even Ferrell had laughed with her once.

Her hand shook violently. "I can*not*."

"You must or your path will be broken!" urged Sheba, motioning frantically.

Silver gripped the knife and closed her eyes. There was no other way. Walker had spoken of the Law of One Wife and taken Camelia almost in the next breath. If she stayed she would have to bear them lying together night after night, year after year, and even the pain of thinking about it made her want to kill them both.

She jerked her head at Sheba, and then followed after her.

The old one stopped again, this time in front of two massive double doors.

Silver was puzzled. "This is no secret path."

The crone waved a finger at the door and bobbed her head emphatically. "You must go. The path to freedom!"

At the same moment Silver stood looking apprehensively at the parlor doors, Kathren stood on the other side, front and center of her guests on a small raised platform, keeping track of the number of footsteps from bedroom to parlor by allowing one per second, sixty per minute—and if nothing had gone wrong she could begin now.

Silver squeezed the brass latch quietly, pulled the door open, and stared in shock. In the next second she would have bolted at the sight of Kathren in a dazzling green taffeta gown and looking directly at her. But the words she heard mesmerized her:

"The sad end of the story will come, fellow members, when Walker—who has fought so bravely to rescue Silver Dawn—rides away to the northern canyon to destroy her father, the mighty Horse Back!"

A hissing snarl of rage exploded into the silence, and for a moment, the women guests only froze in their seats, not realizing the sound came from behind them. Kathren felt a triumphant exhilaration speeding through her veins. Her timing could not have been more perfect: Sheba had followed instructions to remain beside the girl, and together the pair struck a tableau that turned even her own knees to water.

Her eyes flew wide and she gave in to the urge to gasp, alerting the others to the source of the blood-curdling hiss.

Then bejeweled coiffures swung as though controlled by a single cord, and they saw.

The little figure of Sheba caught the eye first. A grisly caricature in ghost-white cloth, out of which twisted the arthritic limbs hung about with blackish, wrinkled bags of hide as rough as an alligator's. Above the shrunken face flamed the cap of brilliant white hair, and the dark sockets below it were but deep hollows that could have been only the sockets of a skull, for her eyes had died and shriveled in the perpetual gloom of the upper rooms.

Now a maniacal smile spread her thickened lips so that a string of saliva drooled from her pink gums like a silver thread. She clapped her clawed hands in glee and rocked on her crippled feet, and finally she could express herself in no other way but to extol in a high thin wail: *"Golden Angel of Light, riding the moon when she comes, to bless me, to bless me, sweet Angel of Light!"*

As for the ladies of the auxiliary, one glimpse of the smaller figure had frozen them in a paralysis of blind, superstitious terror. But it was the sight of the savage that undid them. Sinewy, honey-gold thighs gleamed from the tattered streamers of her dress, the equally naked arms were tensed with the graceful power of a ballerina so that there could be no doubt of the

333

strength behind them. The once beautiful cream muslin bared a glistening shoulder and alas! — the voluptuous curve of one large, firm breast.

And to those who got as far as the face came images of old, conjured by a hundred whispered nightmares: The Savage. The hair greased until it hung in strings, the face blackened in the name of war, so that the pale eyes shimmered all the more brightly with bloodlust.

But the catalyst was the long narrow blade of the carving knife glinting in silver splashes of light. Even Kathren could not have predicted the results.

Fumbling with a little-used leather thong of keys, Walker checked a curse at having found himself and his guest locked out. They had ridden for hours, were exhausted and hungry — and if that were not enough, the front drive was lined with the carriages of guests, his family having apparently discounted the fact that he might return any day — or night. Perhaps, he thought viciously, they hoped he would not.

He laughed uncomfortably. "This is the last key. It's got to be the one."

With a squeak of protest the key turned, the massive door creaked on its hinges, and they looked into the deserted and dimly lit foyer of thick red carpet and dark mahogany walls.

Walker shrugged. "I guess the servants have gone to bed. I didn't realize it was so late."

Jamie Daniels took a gold watch from the pocket of his crisp navy uniform — one of the few keepsakes he'd kept in memory of his long dead family. "It's only quarter of eight."

Suddenly there was a scream, and Jamie had heard nothing like it since the day he lay in the bushes and watched the naked red body pounce upon the corpse of his father. His blood chilled with dread, and he instinctively crouched.

334

"My God," whispered Walker reverently, "what was that?" He took only one step before another sound broke from deep within the interior of the house, and he could only liken it to the shrill screams of a dying animal. No, animal*s*. Many, *many* of them . . .

There was only one door to the parlor and it was blocked by the crone and the savage. So the sea of women surged backward in the opposite direction, a tidal wave of crinoline, brocade, and muslin that dethroned Kathren. Only by reaching the safety of an armchair and climbing upon it did she escape the stampede of dainty, sharp-heeled boots or she knew she would have been trampled to death.

The room could not contain them: Women shrieked and pressed themselves against the windows until Kathren feared the panes would burst into showers of splintering glass. She warned them in her best soprano but no one heard her.

Heavy, marble-topped lamp tables were skidded along like the refuse on a swollen flood, and lamps and china and bric-a-brac went crashing to the floor. One woman succeeded in climbing the walnut bookcase, and only the fact that it was anchored by mortar to the adjacent wall saved her; when one foot slipped, she clung by her hands from the uppermost shelves, her feet dangling, while she emitted one continuous, ear-shattering scream that was swallowed up by the greater volume below her.

For a petrified moment, Sheba and Silver had stood rooted by an equal if not greater fear as the spectacle mushroomed like the smoke of an explosion feeding on itself for new energy. Then Sheba gave up a shriek and tore out for the stairs to the upper rooms. Silver whirled in search of a way out of the house.

She was confused and passed the doors to several quicker outlets without knowing it, circling toward the rear of the house. When she stumbled into the cavernous dining hall with its vaulted ceiling reverberating with the commotion from the parlor, she was gripping the knife in a frenzy of fear.

The two men rushed through the foyer and when they also passed the dining hall, the echoes tricked them: They turned at once and, together, swung open the two massive doors.

"Silver!" It was a cry of despair as well as shock; she was as Walker had left her—filthy, wild-eyed, and brandishing a knife. He believed that if he could have reached her, he would have throttled her.

Silver gestured with the knife and rattled a heathen warning. Walker did not pause to look at the young man beside him—he could not bear to see the ruin of several days' work etched in Jamie Daniels's horrified face. Instead he motioned. "Cut her off that way!"

While his companion bolted around one side of the twenty-foot dining table, Walker took the other route. She might go back the way she came but she couldn't get past them to the foyer.

He shouted as he went. "Silver, put that knife down and come here, dammit! I'm warning you, I'm going to—"

He didn't finish because in one leap she had landed on the table as effortlessly as a bird lighting on a twig. However, he continued his pell-mell skidding, watching with twisted neck and wide-flung eyes as Silver leaped along the table in the opposite direction, finally landing on the floor with a soft thud.

Through the doors she went, and after losing several valuable seconds changing their momentum, the two men followed in hot pursuit.

Seth was puffing and red-faced.

"I can't go another step!" he said, pulling Prissy against him and laughing as he spoke.

"Ah doan doubt that. You have not stopped since de

band began at sunset," she chuckled, her cheeks flushed and her dark eyes sparkling.

The music started again and after a few rollicking bars by the accordion, a small spritely old Cajun began to sing in French. Seth pulled Prissy from the circle of lanterns into the shadows. "If I'd known you spent all your nights like this, I'd have paid you a call long ago. The only thing that bothers me is, how do you have any energy left to work?"

"Our motto is: *Laissez les bons temps rouler*—let de good times roll! We just doan roll em till de work ees done," she grinned.

Sweeping her up tighter, Seth kissed her on the mouth affectionately, then his face sobered. "I can't bear to think of going home tonight. I can't bear to think of leaving you. Ever."

She tried to pull away. "Old Jean-Pierre weel box your ears eef he see us. With us dere ees no 'kept women,' an no making gogo for fun. You bed a woman, you marry her."

"I know," whispered Seth, nudging her nose with his. "That's what I keep thinking about. Having you every night, dancing with you, kissing you . . . making love to you." His head swept down and Prissy turned her face quickly.

"Please doan talk about tings dat cannot be."

Seth pulled her along with an arm around her waist, and they started down the path toward the bayou, the moon lighting their way.

"You dance and sing like a professional, you know how to work hard, you're intelligent—good grief, Camelia would faint dead out if she had to add two and two, and I saw you run a grocery ticket in your head this afternoon. I tried to beat you, but not only did you finish first, I got the wrong answer. You could do anything you set your mind to, including running a plantation.

"We are not talking about de same ting an' you

337

know it," she said sadly.

"But look at Walker and Silver—"

"Dey haf many problems."

"Which they'll work out because they love each other." He heard a sniffle and stopped, swinging her around to face him. "You're not crying are you?" he asked in alarm.

Prissy brushed her cheeks and dried her fingers in the folds of her skirt. "Ah am not."

"Good," he said softly, and started walking again.

"Grandfather ees at de *fay-dodo*. Come an' let me show you hees house. Eet ees better than a plantation."

Their view of the house was framed with jagged curtains of moss, in black relief against the moonlit bayou. Within the ruffled frame of moss, the slope of the porch roof and railing were also in silhouette. The bayou ran so close to the porch that a man could pole fish without leaving his rocking chair.

And there were several rocking chairs available. Seth and Prissy took one each and sat in silence, listening to the swish of sluggish current, the lugubrious screech of a giant crane as he lifted himself from a cypress stump and flapped around the bend. The crickets and frogs sang.

"Lord," Seth sighed contentedly, "what would a man want with a plantation when he had this."

"Ah love eet here," agreed Prissy. "When Ah sit here, eet seems dere ees nothing else een all de world to do."

Seth turned his head on the chair back. "You're good for me."

She was looking at him but her face was in shadow. She didn't speak for a long time and when she did, he could tell her voice was choked. "You must be very sure of dat."

"Before what?" There was no answer, and Seth stood up slowly. The rocker creaked back and forth, and the sound was hypnotic, and peaceful. He lifted her to her feet and stood so close their noses would have touched if Prissy were not so short. "Tell me again what happens when a couple makes this gogo, as you say," he said huskily.

Prissy's ears grew warm at his tone. "Dey weel be married before de cock crow eef dey are caught."

"Shotgun wedding, huh." He stooped quickly and took her in his arms, rubbing his nose lightly against hers before he kissed her deeply. "I never did go in for big weddings."

Prissy's heart hammered as he laid her on the cotton mattress of the little bunk by the window, and when he moved over her and the moon drenched his face, she drew a quick breath.

"Maybe you are de biggest fool Ah haf ever known," she said, and drew him down on top of her.

He kissed her eyelids, her nose, her chin, then moved to her neck. As a fire spread through her body, Prissy gasped and moved wantonly against him. "Dere ees not much time, an Ah doan even know how long it takes to become a wife."

He undressed her slowly, his eyes sparkling with silver-blue diamonds as he looked at her. Then his head dipped, his lips trailed over her bare breast. Prissy grew rigid with anticipation as his mouth hovered over the taut and straining nipple, and when he pressed to her, she came to life again—the languid drowsy movements of before but now with desperate longing.

No man had ever treated her like Seth, as something tender and precious. There were not many young men her age; there were far more girls; the few that lived in the village Prissy had known since childhood and they were like brothers. But this was a man—the strongest, the most handsome, the most passionate, and she knew with a kind of sixth sense that he would die for her. He was that kind of man. The thought added joy to the new and wild sensations flooding her body.

She unbuttoned his shirt quickly then her hand slowed as she reached to place her palm on the lightly furred chest. She could hear him breathing as though he had run a long way.

She whispered breathlessly. "Remember, my beautiful golden man. We Cajuns play for keeps."

Seth stared at her mouth as he lowered his head. "So do we Graysons."

They kissed hungrily, the kiss growing deeper until kisses were not enough. Prissy barely knew he stood up quickly and undressed. And though she would have liked to admire his hard length at leisure, her body seemed to move of its own will—she need not even think.

At first she grunted a little at the pain, but the small burning was swept away by a budding pleasure, a tingling heady euphoria that gripped her whole body. He moved, and she sighed; he moved again, and she sighed again, and the sound aroused Seth until he was drunk with desire.

When they floated back to reality, they were sweaty and their bodies were stuck together, but neither of them moved.

"You haven't asked me one question," said Seth, his eyes closed against her cheek.

"And what ees dat?" Prissy murmured.

"You haven't asked me if I love you. That's what all women ask at this time, isn't it?"

"Ah am not 'all women.' " She pressed his head into the crook of her shoulder. "Eef you plan to marry me, den you'd better learn dat, for sure."

Seth drew back to look at her. "Cajuns are damned funny people," he chuckled, only half joking. "Here you had me thinking I would be tarred and feathered for taking your virginity without honorable intentions, yet you don't question my feelings for you."

Prissy's black eyes twinkled. "Why Ah ask you eef you love me when Ah doan love you?" Before his look of shock could turn to anger, she went on. "Ah lak you, but Ah doan love you. As Grandpa say, love dat come quick, she go quick. When we haf lain many nights together and you haf cooled the fever of my brow, and Ah have soaked your tired feet, fed you and watched over you; when you haf pulled your son from my womb—then we weel talk of love. For now, eet ees enough to drink your beauty, and know that you are mine."

He pressed his cheek to hers and held her so tightly that Prissy thought he would crush her bones. "I can't leave you. I can't leave these happy people and go back to that house. Not tonight."

"You weel go. You must."

He raised his head again, and his face was hard. A little wave of fear washed through Prissy at the look in his eyes. "Watch me," he said. "You just watch me."

"Then nothing I can say will persuade you," Walker said again. They were standing in the morbid quiet of the foyer and young Lieutenant Daniels's cheeks were flushed as he pulled on his gauntlets.

"I appreciate your efforts, Major General, I really do. But I'm afraid my sister is . . ." He paused and could not go on.

"You've seen her at her worst," Walker pointed out. "I've spent a lot of time with her, Lieutenant. And while I don't claim to understand everything she does, I know part of the blame is mine. I knew something had upset her—but it makes my blood boil that instead of talking to me about it, she defies me to help her. I . . . I locked her up in her room. Then I compounded the insult by leaving her to fend for herself—I keep forgetting how well she does that," he finished thoughtfully, half to himself.

But the lieutenant would not look at him. "You needn't make excuses for her, sir. She'd have ripped either of us to the bone if she'd had a chance."

"But she doesn't know who you are yet," Walker

insisted. "You're just another uniform."

Jamie opened the door and stepped onto the front porch. It was just after midnight, and in the lamps from the porch he could see a young man waiting in the driveway with his horse.

"I meant what I said, Major Grayson." Jamming his hat on, Daniels looked at Walker. "I mean it more than ever now. There is more for me to revenge than I realized. I want to be part of the September campaign. If you petition my commander, I'm sure he'll release me from shoving a pen for that long. I'm a soldier, not a secretary." He frowned.

Walker kept looking at Jamie; in spite of his dark hair, the likeness to Silver was unmistakable in the pale, black-lashed gray eyes.

"You will be in contact?" prodded the lieutenant. "About the campaign?"

Walker sighed. "I'll think about it. That's all I can promise you now."

"That's all I can ask." Lieutenant Daniels squared his shoulders and held out his hand. "It's been an honor to know you, sir. Your name is mentioned in the highest circles, so I'm all the more humbled that you took time to try to help my . . . my sister."

Walker shook his hand firmly. "I regret that things have not turned out differently."

The flutter of the long dark lashes was almost imperceptible. "You cannot regret it more than I, sir."

"Good evening, Lieutenant Daniels."

"Perhaps we'll meet again, in September."

Walker managed a nod, the lines in his face like the scarred walls of the Llano Estacado.

Chapter 21

It was around four in the morning. Her knuckles were bleeding from smashing out the small panes around the window seat and then the splintered wooden frames which held them. After inching down the trunk of the tree below the balcony window, there seemed to be no skin left on her thighs, only raw bloodied flesh. There was a time when she would have scoffed at such minor abrasions but white eyes ways had softened her; the pain was like the fiery sting of many ants, a distraction she could ill afford.

The stars had faded and the eastern sky was streaked with gold by the time Silver dropped to the ground, and now it would be a race against time to get what she needed and be on her way before the household awoke.

Finding the french doors on the patio unlocked, Silver stepped inside. Even the great house itself seemed to sleep for once; there were no sighs, creaks, or moans. She crept through the dark silence, feeling her way through the den to the kitchen door.

There was no lamp burning at all in the kitchen, yet she found a knife from the chopping block and tied it to her thigh with the strips she'd torn from the bedsheet. When she finished, her fingers were stuck together with the blood from her legs and arms. Groping until she found a damp dishcloth, she wiped them, then began to stuff a half dozen cold biscuits she found into her knapsack, also made from bed linens.

Her self-imposed fast was two days old — she had not

eaten since the first time Walker locked her away — and now her mouth watered until she drooled like the Evil One upstairs. Letting her nose guide her, she finally found a ten-pound slab of smoked pork and wished she could devour every scrap of it. Instead, she tore off chunks and stuffed as many as she could into her mouth as she hurried on to find the front foyer, which was the shortest route to the open fields that lay beyond the oak alley.

She started a little when she saw that a lamp in the foyer was still burning low. Though its light was feeble, she felt exposed, and pulses of adrenaline quickened her blood as she stole across the plush red carpet toward the arching front doorway.

When her bare foot struck something solid but strangely soft, fear almost choked her. She stumbled but the movement was like that of a fleeing deer and her flight ended at the heavy door. She leaned against it weakly until she could get her breath again.

The moment gave her pause for thought. In the end it was not curiosity over the object in her path that made her turn but the lure of the wide curving staircase she had passed. Her chest ached with unshed tears. Just one peek at his sleeping form was enough — a kind of farewell, however brief. A moment she could treasure because there would be no harsh words or bitter accusations.

Every instinct warned against such foolishness but the temptation was too strong. She could not put an eternity between them without a last farewell, for there had been joy mixed with the pain. So much that if it weren't for warning The People of her husband's attack, perhaps she could have eventually adjusted to Camelia as Second Wife. Sharing a man with other wives was hardly a new concept to her.

But now the pain of parting grew intense, and her head turned slowly in the direction of the staircase.

At first she saw only the horizontal lines that marked

the steps. Then her eyes dropped to the mysterious, elongated shape on the floor below them.

A nameless dread filled her as she moved toward it. Then she knelt and touched a human head, the hair springy against her palm.

Her fingers moved over the features like a blind man reading Braille. The skin was waxy and cold but the identity unmistakable. A wracking sob tore up from her throat.

She never knew if it was the creak of a floorboard or a clairvoyant prompting that made her look up, but as soon as she did, the tall shadowed form on the staircase moved too, and a face materialized from darkness; he came lunging down the stairs two at a time.

She whirled and sprang to the door but its massive weight resisted her until she thought she could feel a rasping breath on the back of her neck. The touch of cold fingertips on her elbow was the final shock, and she wrenched the door open and shot through it like a bullet.

Across the porch, down the steps—her feet flew as never before, their rhythm pounding out the dead man's name. The open fields no longer beckoned. Instead, she rounded the end of the mansion and headed straight for the swampy lands along the Bayou Teche where she might be able to lose her pursuer.

Kathren's hysterical grief was not feigned. Each time the sedative wore off and her eyes fluttered open, the sight of Ferrell's dark face leaning over her sent her eyes rolling up again.

Walker had been the one who discovered the body, who questioned the servants over the whereabouts of Seth and Amanda, and who sent word for Dr. Adams. The long years of discipline and the habit of command held his emotions in check, yet it seemed hours before anyone came. In the meantime he sat near the sofa where he'd laid his father.

He was still sitting there when Dr. Adams arrived. After a cursory examination, the white-haired gentleman touched Walker's arm gently. "He's gone, my boy. Gone." The words seemed directed at himself as well.

The sheriff and his deputy were ushered into the library, and Walker replied to the questions in a low monotone, his eyes never leaving his father's face. Only when Lucas Rains, the undertaker, arrived did Walker rise abruptly and take the law officers out onto the front porch.

"It looks like he took a blow on the back of the head," said Sheriff Hancock.

"I know." Walker stared down the alley of century-old oaks that were Samuel's pride and joy.

"Where were you when it happened?"

"Asleep."

"Who found the body?"

"I did."

The sheriff started to lay his hand on the younger man's shoulder, but something in the gray-green eyes stopped him. "You know how folks around here felt about him. I won't stop till I catch my man."

"Neither will I," replied Walker matter-of-factly.

A high wail of agony sounded from inside, and Walker knew Amanda had come home at last. He left the two men on the porch.

Sheriff Hancock and his deputy mounted but as they turned their horses, someone called behind him. "Sheriff, wait up. I have some information I think you'll be interested in." And a man stepped from the bushes next to the corner of the house and started toward them.

Walker saw to it that the body was prepared and buried that very afternoon in spite of strenuous resistance from Kathren and Amanda. Seth agreed they wanted no part of a lengthy and public service, and the

346

women were in no shape to prolong the argument.

The file of family and servants, dressed in black, trudged up from the cemetery in the garden and across the front lawn of Gray Shadows. On the front porch, Walker handed Kathren's arm to a maid and, when the others had gone inside, turned to Seth.

"I've got to find Silver."

"Do you think you can?"

"I've got to. I can't think straight until I know she's safe."

"You know what this means. It was one of us. Somebody living in this very house."

A shudder ran through Walker's body. "I just can't think about it yet, but I'm taking the bloodhound right now and I'll probably be gone all night."

"I'll go with you."

"No, I'm going alone."

"Then I won't be here when you get back."

"What are you talking about?"

"I need to see about . . . my own woman."

Walker stared. "Is there something you want to tell me?"

"I'm married to Prissy."

Walker felt as though the wind had been knocked from him. It was a moment before he moved at all, but suddenly he pulled Seth to him, embraced him roughly, then shoved him away again. "If I'd had your courage in the first place, Silver would be here with me, where she belongs."

Seth attempted a lopsided grin. "I'd say it was more of a hard head than a weak heart. But you'll find her. Something tells me she's not as determined to flee as she pretends."

Walker found it difficult to speak at all. "I'd like to believe that. I just can't." He turned and started down the steps then stopped mid-stride when he spotted two riders coming up the drive. The man in front was Sheriff Hancock.

347

The sheriff dismounted slowly and looked from one brother to the other, his grieved blue eyes finally resting on the older Grayson.

"I'm afraid I have a warrant for your arrest, Walker. I have an eyewitness and the testimony of several servants who heard your quarrel with your father just before he died." He held Walker's astonished gaze. "I'm sorry, son. This is the hardest thing I've done in my whole career. I hope you understand. I don't have any other choice."

The trails switched and turned back upon themselves until by the time the sun was setting, Silver realized she was facing north again, the direction of the mansion. It had taken her all day to make one huge, futile circle.

She had meant to follow the bayou upstream, which would take her in a northwesterly direction, but the banks were so choked with vines and creepers that she had veered away from the stream. Her flesh crawled when she thought of the snakes that must slither through the murky waters, for the pain of a snakebite almost rivaled the bite of George Greelee's whip.

As the sun began to set, she searched in vain for a tree to climb, but the great oaks reached skyward to escape the tangled undergrowth, and there were no limbs low enough to reach.

Her legs and arms were caked with thick black mud that chilled her to the bone when damp mists started rising from the swamps; she stopped frequently to remove it with the knife edge, gritting her teeth as the blade scraped over skin that was already raw and bleeding.

At last the twilight faded to full darkness, and she slammed into trees, stumbled through briars, and sobbed as sharp sticks lacerated her feet. The biscuits she'd stolen were too little too late, and she wept more bitterly to remember how many trays of food she had scorned. Now she was so weak she could manage but a few steps before stumbling, and finally each stumble became a fall into the oozing black mud. The forest came alive with grunts and tweaks and muted rustlings, the call of strange birds, occasionally a splash as some nameless reptile took to the water. But she had no way of knowing if the water led to the bayou or it was just another inland pond like others she had passed.

She had fought the swamp all day, and gained nothing. Nestling in a clump of shaggy, damp grass, she tried for the first time to rest.

When she awoke the moon was high, but it didn't penetrate the ceiling of tangled creepers and mossy limbs enough to allow travel.

She sat up and listened intently to a distant sound, possibly the one that had wakened her. It sounded like a dog but none she'd ever heard before.

As the noise approached, she decided that perhaps the gods had intervened; a dog at night would be hunting and maybe she could coax him into sharing his prey. Or take it from him.

The racket grew louder, seeming to rush upon her swiftly, and she jumped to her feet.

Peering over the tall grass, she saw the flash of a lantern and ducked down again. There was a man with the dog!

She whispered in Comanche as the animal with baggy skin came snuffling up to her, and she commanded him to go away, *"Ein nea-dro, sata!"* she hissed but a cold wet muzzle nudged her face even as she shoved, and the dog whined happily.

She could hear unhurried footsteps breaking twigs, and the rustle and swish of branches rebounding. She took the knife from her thigh and in spite of the dog's interference, managed a crouching position.

Then there was a sound to her left and she turned, straining to see through the blackness.

Now it was to her right, and she whirled again. Only

when a pair of arms closed around her did she realize she'd become the victim of one of the oldest Comanche tricks. The second noise was a ploy to distract her.

She was so stunned she didn't resist as the arms turned her about. And then it was too late to do anything. Something struck the side of her head and she went limp.

Amanda's eyes had become oriental slits in her swollen lids, but the flood of tears had not begun to dry.

"You must send for S-Seth," she told Kathren.

"Dear, I told you I've tried once already." Kathren's tender tone turned to a sneer. "He's so involved with that little twit, Prissy, that he doesn't have time for us. Just forget about him. We'll get Walker out of jail ourselves. Why, Maxwell Clinton never lost a case, they say. He could get the devil himself cleared of charges."

Amanda stopped crying to frown. "How dare you imply that Walker isn't innocent!"

"I didn't mean—oh, I'm so upset I don't know what I'm saying anymore!" Kathren garbled through her handkerchief, her voice rising to a wail again. "How am I supposed to handle all this at once? We're left with nothing, Amanda. All our men are gone. *Gone!*" Her heart-wrenching sob put the young woman's to shame.

Amanda tried to comfort her but Kathren threw off her hands. "Everyone's deserted us. Only you and I remain in this house of death!"

The sight of her stepmother's grief was overwhelming, and Amanda decided she had never fully realized the extent of Kathren's devotion to Samuel.

"I'll go myself," Amanda announced, wiping her puffy eyes with a handkerchief. "Seth has got to come home and that's that. He'll know what to do about getting Walker out." She rose from the rumpled bed and headed for the closet.

"What are you doing?" Kathren demanded, her words suddenly clear and forceful.

Amanda yanked her riding skirt from a hanger and tossed it on the bed. "I'm going to the Acadian village to get Seth. I didn't believe it at first but all the servants think he's there. Even *you* believe there's something between him and Prissy."

"But you can't leave me. I couldn't bear it without you, Amanda." Kathren broke down again, twisting her hands and weeping first with hard little chuckling sounds and then the great noisy inhalation of one suffocating.

"Okay, okay," soothed Amanda. "We can wait until tomorrow, I suppose. And then I'm going, Kathren. Seth's place is here with us, doing what he can to help Walker. Besides," she finished thoughtfully, a chill running down her spine, "someone pushed Daddy down those stairs. Suppose it was someone living here with us . . ." She did not finish, for the only one in the house she didn't trust was Kathren's nephew.

"I know who did it," said Kathren savagely. "It was Silver. She knew she was going to be sent away and she pushed him. *Oooooh!*" She snatched the younger woman to her breast so tightly Amanda thought she would choke. "What would I do without you," she sobbed.

After whimpering on Amanda's neck for a moment, she raised her face, tears streaming, and spoke like a wounded child.

"Let's get our nighttime toddies and go to bed, can we? And could I . . . could I sleep with you, just for tonight?"

Amanda swallowed, her eyes brimming as she patted Kathren's shoulder. "Of course you can. Now wash your face and go fix our toddies. I'll get your face cream and your nightgown and bring them here to my room."

"You're a saint," Kathren quivered, blinking bravely.

351

Then she rose and left for the kitchen.

It was well after midnight when Ferrell returned to the mansion. Amanda was sleeping soundly. Kathren had built a small fire in the library where she sat snuggled in a velvet lap robe enjoying a glass of brandy.

Ferrell opened the door then pushed it wider. "It's like an oven in here. This is August, for heavensake," he said irritably.

"I'm chilled," replied Kathren, pointing to the stool at her feet. "Sit down and fill me in."

Ferrell had taken time to change from his muddy clothes into Samuel's wine-colored smoking jacket. Kathren smiled wistfully at the shapely, black-haired legs that stuck from under the knee-length hem. "You look so boyish and innocent in that, it's enough to blind a mother's heart."

"You could never raise an innocent, Mother." Ferrell pulled the robe about him carelessly.

"You were successful?"

"I took her to the cottage in the swamp."

Kathren stared. "*Alive?*"

Ferrell folded his arms on his knees. "You are no longer the master of this game. When I'm finished with her I'll let you know. As far as anybody else knows, she's headed for the Texas plains right now."

Kathren gave him a cold appraisal then hissed vehemently. "Do you think that I would dare interfere with your petty revenge after what you've done? You've taken the man I loved when there was no reason—"

"Balderdash. I cut myself in early, that's all. If I'd trusted you, I'd still be the unwelcomed nephew."

"Silver can clear Walker," Kathren insisted. "You said she saw you. You must do away with her before Seth returns. Amanda is going to find him herself in the morning."

352

Ferrell chuckled. "Oh, *ma mere*. If I'd known life with you could be so stimulating, I'd have tracked you down long before now." He was still looking at her with amusement. "I checked on Amanda before I came down. I'd say she'll hardly know her name in the morning, let alone that she must find her brother."

Kathren rolled her eyes. "Thank God you didn't find me sooner or we'd be in the poor house right now." She leaned forward and touched his arm. "Seth will come anyway, very soon. Your petty little revenge is not something we can afford right now. You must do it soon."

"In my own good time, Mother." He grinned lazily. "But first I will show her the wrath of a man scorned."

Gooseflesh tickled the back of Kathren's neck, and not for the first time she wondered if he would stop at anything to get what he wanted. Anything at all.

Silver winced as she opened her eyes and found sunlight streaming into the bare stone cottage. She had hung by ropes around her wrists, her back against the cold stones, for over three hours, and she wished now that she had never drifted off to sleep. Her hands were numb from the ropes, but now as she put her weight on her feet, they, too, had gone to sleep and began to throb.

Suddenly she caught the sound of footsteps outside. He was coming again. Quickly she wiggled her feet hard to get the circulation going.

The loose boards of the rotting door rattled, and Ferrell stooped into the room.

"Ah, my sweet. So you're awake. Shall I light a fire?" he asked cheerfully. "The swamp air is rather chilly."

There was but one piece of furniture, a stout wooden table set in the center of the room, and in the middle of it her knife was stabbed, its blade shimmering in the morning sun. Ferrell unwrapped the cloth he had brought and put it over the table; then he began to spread the table with a slab of cheese, a chunk of bread, and two apples.

"You've become so thin since you arrived at Gray Shadows. I prefer a little flesh on a woman." He jerked the knife from the table and looked at her, turning and walking toward her slowly.

He brought the knife tip up under her chin. "First we eat. After you are refreshed a little, we'll finish that business we started in the garden. You do remember that day, don't you?"

The narrowed silver eyes glittered with the venom of a cobra. Ferrell whispered, his breath touching her face. "I'm impressed. It's truly inspiring to see such courage." He bent closer, his lips parting to take her.

The knife tip kept Silver from moving her head, but her aim was perfect, and she stared wide-eyed a second later at the spittle hanging from the end of Ferrell's nose.

His face contracted with murderous rage, and Silver closed her eyes and prepared to die, already feeling the slice of steel as the knife separated the soft flesh beneath her chin.

When she heard a great bellow and realized the knife tip was no longer at her throat, she opened her eyes and saw that Ferrell had stepped back and was rubbing his face against his sleeve like a cat with peanut butter on its nose. Finally he looked at her, and his voice shook.

"If you knew how close you just came."

Silver snarled contemptuously. "I know, *tivo sata*. I know how low is the man who finds helpless women to torture because he is too much white belly to challenge a man."

Ferrell laughed. "My good lady, you are hardly helpless." He came toward her again. "Which is what I find so attractive about you."

354

"I am Walker's wife. He will kill you."

"If he ever gets out of jail. But in the meantime—"

"What is this jail?" Silver demanded.

"Jail means a prison. A cage that he cannot get out of." He smiled with relish at her stricken face. "Yes, my dear, he's been taken by the white man's law for killing his father. He'll probably hang."

Her heart seemed to stop and for a moment Silver thought she had died, for how could one live when his heart had stopped? Then the rage came—waves of it that suffocated her.

She dropped her head so her enemy couldn't see her expression.

"Now, that's better. There's something very attractive about a woman's grief. It makes her vulnerable, you see. That's what most men like—a soft yielding woman . . ." He reached out to place the knife tip between her breasts, against her skin. Then he slowly pulled it down the middle of her belly, and the ragged remains of the dress split and fell away.

Silver shrank from the lust in his dark eyes as they roamed freely over her, touching her breasts, her navel, and settling at last on the area that interested him most.

Ferrell touched his groin briefly to rearrange something there, and then looked at her again with a lewd grin. "Shall we eat first?"

He cut the rope from the metal hook in the stone walls and pulled her to the table by the end of it, her hands still bound. "Eat," he commanded softly.

"I cannot. My hands are tied."

Ferrell sliced some cheese, stabbed it with the knife, and brought it to her lips. Silver took it, and their eyes locked as she chewed slowly.

He continued to feed her a piece at a time until Silver jerked her head away. "If you do not stop, *tivo* there will be more than spittle on your face."

After dragging his gaze over her slowly, Ferrell said,

"So. Now it is time." He stabbed the knife into the table with a small splintering crack, then reached out and molded her breast with his hand, cupping it and watching her face.

Silver neither moved nor showed any emotion.

He trailed his hand lower, and still she did not move.

"Perhaps I've misjudged you," he said, licking his lips. "Perhaps there is truth to those tales about the lustful nature of savages."

She looked at him, and after a moment ran the tip of her tongue over her lips as he had done. "Perhaps," she said, and her voice was like velvet.

She could hear him breathing raggedly as he moved to take her against him. The touch of her breasts on his chest seemed to work some magic on his body so that he writhed and tried to pull her closer. With her wrists crossed there was no place for her arms but between their bodies, and Ferrell reached behind him impatiently and jerked the knife from the tabletop.

After cutting the rope on her wrists, he threw the knife out the window, and Silver forced her eyes not to follow it.

Then he pulled her into his arms again, and the fact that she remained unresponsive and stiff seemed to delight him. "You're not as cold as you would have me believe or you would have tried to break away before now. The demolition of the parlor was not accomplished by a timid, fearful woman," he husked, grabbing the mounds of her buttocks in each hand to caress them.

Silver moved her hand slowly, as if she wanted to resist the impulse but couldn't, and laid her palms lightly on his shirt front. "Walker is hairy," she said softly. "Comanche have no body hair." She stared curiously at his chest, moving her hands a little.

Ferrell stepped back to strip off his shirt, and Silver let her gaze roam over his naked chest. "You have much hair," she murmured, and she looked down so

356

that her eyes lingered on his belt buckle.

Ferrell seemed to run completely out of oxygen, and a madness seized him. It had been a long time since sweet Anna in Georgia, and since coming to Louisiana, all his time had been consumed with his plans; night after night, thinking of the lovelies, Camelia and Amanda, sleeping so near but scorning even the most subtle overtures.

He hastily unbuckled the belt and pushed the tight riding britches below his hips, forgetting that his gaping mouth quite marred his dark good looks.

"You have good body," said Silver, looking at his throbbing manhood as though she could not take her eyes away. She raised her hand tentatively — a maiden enthralled with the forbidden fruit — but held it midair.

There was a noise in Ferrell's throat as he grabbed her hand and pressed it to him.

Possessed of extraordinary powers of concentration, Silver lent all of them to remembering every detail of her love lessons, and her fingers worked their magic. Ferrell was gasping, groaning, moaning, begging her to stop — not to stop. She looked at his face, saw his eyes were dazed like a blind man's, and she knew the time was now. Gathering his velvet sack into one hand — wishing it were his evil soul — she crushed with all her strength.

Ferrell doubled over and finally fell completely to the floor, writhing like an animal in the throes of death. Silver dashed quickly outside and just as she dropped to her knees to search for the knife, he stopped screaming. Her hands ruffled the grass like a woman after her last sewing needle.

Just as her hand brushed the cold steel, she heard a noise and looked to see him standing in the window.

He started to crawl through it and Silver got to her feet and stumbled into the brush. But she knew he would overtake her; his body was hard and lean whereas hers was starved and weak. She could not run

357

at all without stumbling.

He thundered and crashed through the brush like a wounded buffalo, and finally she could not go on, so she stopped and turned.

His eyes flared with a strange light, and he even smiled as he came toward her.

"I will kill you," she warned breathlessly.

He said nothing, only stared at her with a look of mindless hatred.

Silver did not retreat one step, so now he was very close.

He lunged.

She jumped back, flexing the knife. "I will kill you," she said again.

"First you have to be stronger than I am. And we both know that is not—" He lunged again, catching her off guard. His hand closed over the wrist of her right hand and twisted, bearing down, down—until she was on her knees before him and her paralyzed fingers began loosening on the knife.

A sadistic smile curled his lips, and his chest seemed to expand as he looked down at her, bearing her ever closer to the ground as she gave in to the crushing pain.

The knife fell from her grasp at last and his teeth flashed wicked white. "Now we will finish—"

Silver watched his face as it twisted with perplexed horror. Then his body stiffened like a frog speared through back, but she didn't move until she felt his blood spreading warm and sticky over her left hand— the one that had whipped up to catch the knife as it fell from her right hand.

When she jerked, the blade came from his belly with a sucking sound, and Ferrell was still staring with wonder as he dropped to his knees!

"Your evil is come upon you, *tivo sata*," she sobbed, and backed away from him.

He was looking up at her now, his eyes wide and

staring sightlessly. Only when he tilted forward was there a look of comprehension in them. Then his face struck the ground with a heavy thud, and Silver ran.

"Do you understand?" queried Kathren. "If you do, nod your head. Good girl. Now at the count of three you will open your eyes. One. Two. And three." She smiled warmly. "Aren't you feeling better now?"

Amanda looked at her blankly. "Yes . . ." Amanda's eyes clouded. "My tongue . . . my head." She flushed with embarrassment. She formed the words in her mind, but they wouldn't come out right. She tried to push up on her elbows.

"Isth it mor-nan?" she slurred, and her cheeks reddened again.

"Of course, darling. We just had our coffee. We were talking just a minute ago. Remember?"

Amanda frowned and rubbed her temples. "My th . . . thongue." Quick tears came to her eyes when she heard herself, and Kathren stroked her brow.

"It's that silly medicine Dr. Adams gave you. I was the same way. It'll wear off. I think I'll go fix you some orange juice. That should perk you up."

When Kathren was gone, Amanda sank back and closed her eyes, jumbled pieces of a nightmare floating in her head. She remembered clearly that her father was dead, her brother in jail for his murder, but she didn't care. No, she did care—she *must* care. Yet when she thought of the facts, no storm of emotion came. And in the next moment, she wondered where she was.

She opened her eyes and looked at the nightstand, eyeing the porcelain roses embossed on the lamp's base. Her mother had made her a mask for the Mardi Gras, a mask of roses like these. She remembered putting on the mask, and Melissa laughing at her with delight.

Her lips trembled, for now she saw something different. She was walking down the long alley of oaks toward the house and there was a tall dark-haired woman standing on the porch. *Your mother is dead, Amanda,* said the woman. *Your mother is dead . . . I'm sorry, so sorry.*

Her eyes rolled tiredly toward the window, and what she saw made her face twist up slowly. She tried to scream but no sound would come from her throat. She could only watch in mute horror as the naked woman began to smash out the glass; it spewed like glittering shards of light, a sparkling fountain of water drifting in slow motion, swirling weightlessly and soundlessly through the air.

When the woman crawled into the room, Amanda could feel her lips working silently but her body would not move. Fear choked her as the woman came toward her, her body smeared with black mud from the swamp—and blood. Much blood.

But she finally realized that the woman was part of her nightmare, so she didn't try to speak anymore, even when the apparition padded softly across the room and leaned over her bed.

"Amanda, you must come with me. You must help me save Walker!"

Amanda stared.

Silver turned and hurried to the closet, ripping out the first thing she came to. She slipped Amanda's riding skirt over the blood and dirt, pulled on a blouse, boots with no socks, and rushed back to the bed. Amanda had not moved nor changed her expression.

"You must come," Silver pleaded, taking her by the wrists. "Ferrell killed our father Samuel and now he himself is . . ." She paused, for there was no need to go on. The black spirits were powerful; they cast spells and sometimes their victims never recovered.

"I cannot leave you to them, Walker's sister. And there is not more time. I am sad for this but you must leave the great house. You must come with me now, and if you fight me I will have to strike you."

She pulled Amanda from the bed roughly, hoping the pain might jar her to her senses. But Amanda flopped on the floor like a beached seal, her catatonic state breaking only enough to strike new terror in her heart as she looked up at her tormentor.

In spite of Amanda's uncoordinated resistance, Silver grabbed a bare foot in each hand and headed stubbornly for the window.

They were halfway there before Silver gave up. The girl's body was weighted with numbed muscles, and her own strength was failing quickly; it would be certain death for both of them to try to escape down the balcony.

Her face flushed when she looked at Amanda, for the girl's thin gown slipped up to her waist, and her pale legs spread to leave her secret parts exposed.

Silver recalled in anguish how the men had lifted her skirts—when they dared get close enough; or spied on her when she bathed, laughing wickedly and pointing at her. And the final desecration, when they tried to mount her.

"My sister, I hope you do not hate me for this. Please believe that I save your life."

Outside in the dim hall, Silver turned toward Amanda and hoisted her feet to each side of her hips. The hall echoed with her panting as Silver threw all her weight into her labor, cringing with pain herself when she thought of Amanda's delicate skin burned by the friction of the carpet.

"Just a little ways to go," she said, and Amanda's dark eyes never left her face.

As the balcony turned left to the stairwell, Silver found the closet where she'd seen the maid put linens.

She pulled Amanda's gown back in place and tried to arrange the pillows around her comfortably. After ripping off strips of sheeting, she used one for a gag and the other to tie Amanda's cold, stiff hands. At last she stood back. Amanda's face was a pale oval in the darkness.

"I will come back for you when it is safe." She touched Amanda's cheek with the back of her fingers. "I am Quohadie Teichas, daughter of Horse Back. I do not break my word."

Amanda watched as the door closed, and suddenly she was in the belly of the earth, suffocating with the darkness and the horror, until at last she sank back and knew nothing.

Chapter 22

"Mistress, we so very much appreciate your gesture, but I myself have nowhere to go," argued Jubal. "I have leeved in Gray Shadows for many years."

Kathren's frown grew angry. "I've tried to be tactful and kind but now I'll spell it out for you. This family has just suffered a great tragedy and we need time to ourselves. Surely you can understand that. Besides, there is only Amanda and myself here, so there will be no work to do." She sniffed indignantly. "I'd think you'd all be thrilled to have the time off. You could . . . well, you could visit relatives."

"I have no relatives here," complained Jubal's assistant, Mrs. Peoples.

"Then stay with friends," snapped Kathren. "Go shopping, catch up on business—oh, do I have to make a list? You are dismissed for the entire week and if you cannot find something to do with a paid vacation, then I cannot help you. Now go, the lot of you!"

Locking the kitchen door behind them, Kathren went back to her search. Earlier, when she had returned with her stepdaughter's orange juice "toddie," she had found the shattered window, and Amanda gone. Kathren realized at once that the girl had stumbled in her drugged stupor and fallen against the window.

However, she explained to the servants that a bird had flown against the glass and ordered them to clean up the mess, after which she set about getting rid of the entire staff until she could locate the witless missing girl. If they discovered Amanda in her present

363

state, there would be an uproar, for no doubt the stupid chit had sustained noticeable injuries by now.

Two hours had passed when Kathren closed the last door. Counting all four levels, there were in excess of a hundred rooms; she had covered them all.

"The idiot," she snarled, pushing sweaty hair from her forehead. The girl had obviously wandered outside, and with no servants to help search, it was unlikely Amanda would be found until the drugs wore off. "Damn that son of mine," she muttered, "playing house with the little savage down in the cottage while I'm fighting for our lives!"

Then she had another thought. Ferrell had killed once to get what he wanted. When he finished with Walker's wife, he would have killed twice. What if Amanda stumbled in his path? Might he not think to rid them of another nuisance?

Kathren paled at the thought. Already they were walking a tightrope, when if he'd only left things in her hands . . .

Spluttering a string of oaths, she pulled on a pair of tall rubber boots under her skirt and started down the path for the cottage.

The oaks were turning black against the sunset as Sheriff Hancock tried one more time.

"Mrs. Grayson, I don't need to remind you that there have been two murders in this house. Now you say you've given all the servants time off. Please let me prevail upon you and Amanda to come into town for a few days. My men have been out all day looking for this 'savage' as you call her, and they're exhausted; I won't ask them to stay here for your protection. Do it for my peace of mind if nothing else. You could stay with Walker's aunt and uncle."

Kathren's face was ravaged and pale yet she held herself erect. "This is my home. What danger is there if the little heathen is gone, as you believe?"

"I believe what Walker has told me, Mrs. Grayson.

He said she would have headed straight for Texas. Besides, my men have combed this area clear to St. Martinville, and she's just not here."

"The girl was Walker's wife so naturally he thinks he knows her well," said Kathren snidely. "What about the things *I* told you—that Samuel and Walker were shouting, and the girl could easily have overheard them."

"Walker says she was locked away upstairs."

"She was sup*posed* to be locked away upstairs when she destroyed my parlor and scared the wits out of my guests," said Kathren tartly. "That a man is forced to lock his wife away at all should tell you something, sheriff. She escaped, she heard Samuel's demand for Walker to send her away, and she took her revenge by killing my—" Kathren caught herself in time. "My nephew."

Hancock sighed wearily. "I know you've got a good case. That's why we've not only posted lookouts along the roads but sent wires ahead to Texas. However, my point is this. Walker says—"

"Please do not say that to me again! What did you expect—that he would admit his own wife was capable of murder? Really, Sheriff Hancock. You expect me to take his word after he . . . well, he might have murdered his own father?"

"Walker made no such claim," the sheriff said quietly. "He told me outright that the girl had killed soldiers who tried to rape her." He looked at Kathren oddly, his eyes seeming to spear her. "I didn't realize until now you thought Walker Grayson had actually killed his father. I find that very disturbing, Mrs. Grayson, very disturbing. I've known both men for years."

Kathren was suddenly misty-eyed, her voice soft with regret. "I did not arrest him, Sheriff Hancock, you did."

The sheriff put his hat on. "It could have been one of the servants, perhaps one with a grudge," he said stubbornly. "In any event, this house is not safe for two women alone. What about Amanda; is she afraid? She could ride back into town with me right now—"

"I've told you, my stepdaughter is peacefully sleeping off this trauma. I will tell her about my nephew's death when she is able to bear it. If she wants to go to Belle and Guy's later, I'll see she gets there."

Kathren tensed all over, hanging breathlessly on the sheriff's next words. After finding Ferrell's body, she had waited hour after hour not knowing if the lawmen would discover the Indian wench and cart her off to jail, or perhaps discover Amanda instead, wandering dazed and drugged about the grounds, babbling heaven-knew-what incriminating statements. Her knees went weak with relief when he spoke.

"All right, I'll say no more. When your nephew's body is released for burial, I'll send word. Again, my deepest condolences. I didn't know Ferrell Cassadyne but I'm sure he was a fine man. I know Samuel was." Hancock shook his head. "Dirty business, murder. So hard on those that are left—" He looked at Kathren suddenly. "I'm sorry, I didn't mean to go on like that."

Kathren stood in the doorway, holding to it for support as the sheriff went down the steps to his horse. Stumbling upon her son's body that morning was a gruesome shock that almost sent her over the edge. But there had been no bond between her and the baby who had brought such trials upon them. Pregnant prostitutes were not in demand; her business was ruined for many months and there was no money. She lived off garbage cans and handouts in the streets of Atlanta and later, when she was able to attract customers again, she paid sitters for her newborn son.

Then she obtained employment as young Melissa Winebrenner's personal maid—a demanding but promising position. And Kathren had learned to make the best of every situation. Thrown into such prestigious social circles, Kathren was soon having an affair with one of the wealthiest businessmen in Atlanta.

But her son's obnoxious ways soon ruined that as well. He stole things he didn't need, tormented the Winebrenner livestock and household pets, destroyed personal property. Soon after Kathren's dismissal from

366

the Winebrenner estates, the man she was seeing broke off their relationship.

Later came the years of separation when Ferrell went to claim his fame, gambling away every penny he extracted then returning for more, holding her past over her head. Yet after years of living in filth and degradation, Kathren Morrison—alias Kathren Cassadyne alias Kathren Lovall—had followed her former mistress to St. Martinville, and in fourteen short months was mistress of the manor. She'd had it all at last—everything she wanted. But Ferrell couldn't wait: He wanted, and he took.

The sheriff untied his horse, holding the reins as he glanced at the massive walls and towers above him. The sun had rushed to a sudden death, taking with it the amber light that washed the turrets and spires till the old house looked like a fairy castle. Instead, there was only a stark and menacing silhouette against the faded mauve sky.

Sheriff Hancock shivered without realizing it. "You are a brave woman, Mrs. Grayson."

"So I've been told," said Kathren smoothly. "Good evening, sheriff."

Kathren's agitation grew as darkness seeped through the windows. The drugs should have worn off by now; which would mean that Amanda had found her way back from wherever she had wandered. Kathren prayed she had; an accident or even a suicide would be highly suspect just now. Although—she pursed her lips irritably—the thought of Amanda hanging to her skirts for the next few years was unbearable. There were no hopes for marriage in the offing.

But she could not get rid of Amanda now. Another time, perhaps in a few months when interest in the tragedies of Gray Shadows had lagged.

Kathren had paused at the foot of the staircase to light a wall lamp, when she grew still and rolled her eyes up to scan the tiers of balconies above her. After a moment she moved out near the marble fountain, standing directly below the high circulator dome as she searched again, listening intently.

The fountain gurgled and chuckled but there was no other sound. Yet she was more certain than ever that she had heard a soft thud.

As a precaution, she went to the stairwell in the foyer and propped two small wooden stools on the steps; finally she blew out all the lamps in that area. If someone tried to come down through the foyer she would at least be able to hear them.

Kathren's mind was turning quickly as she went back to the stairwell in the ballroom. Sheba was locked away in the upper rooms, for she took a perverted interest in all forms of death and in her excitement, her tongue might be loosened. However, in her long months in the upper rooms, she might have uncovered another route back into the main house. In which case Amanda, having returned, could have happened upon the old witch running loose and could now possess dangerous knowledge. Perhaps there would *have* to be an accident . . . or perhaps "a servant carrying a grudge."

Checking the pistol in her pocket, Kathren started slowly up the steps, her eyes pealed on the spiraling balconies above.

Then she heard it distinctly—a moan, perhaps a mumbled word. As she took the pistol from her skirt, the skin on the back of her neck prickled.

Silver groped and struggled with the confused Amanda inside the closet, not daring to use a light though she could tell her fingernails were leaving marks on Amanda's face as she pressed her hand across the girl's mouth. Surely her sister would hate her forever, but there was no help for it.

"You must believe I am trying to help you," she whispered. "I get you up, then you must try to walk. Ferrell killed your father. I saw him on the steps. You must help save Walker. Think of that only, my sister—

that we must help Walker."

Through the hours of isolation, of darkness and terror, the drugs had started to wear off a little, and Amanda's mind began to function again. There was a ring of truth in what she heard, yet her body was still stiff and uncoordinated. She could do little except lean upon her sister-in-law, and when she did try to speak, Silver pressed a hand over her mouth again.

Amanda lifted a leaden arm and placed her hand over the one that was on her mouth; she squeezed, trying to let Silver know that she understood what to do.

Silver loosened her grip slowly. "The spell is gone," she whispered. "Now we must try to get away. There is great evil here. We must go and find Walker. He will know what to do—" Both girls jerked at the voice.

"Step away from her, Amanda."

Silver gasped. A woman's form stood at the top of the stairs barely two yards from them, outlined by the weak light thrown up from below. But Silver didn't need light to know what the woman held in her hand—the ominous *click* was enough. Horse Back was champion of the tournaments with the rifle as well as the bow, though his daughter had never overcome a fear of the noisy firesticks. She went rigid at the sound.

Kathren raised her voice. "Step away from her, Amanda. She killed Ferrell this very morning, and Sheriff Hancock has been searching for her all day with men and dogs. She's a murderer!"

Amanda tensed, the whites of her eyes glowing in the gloom as she rolled them over her shoulder at Silver, who was holding her from behind.

Silver loosened her grip. "You must decide who speaks with forked tongue, my sister. I tell you that Ferrell was evil. He wanted to hurt me."

After a moment Amanda answered with a squeeze of her hand. Then she exaggerated her slur. "I . . . can't stand alone, Kathren. I'm sick."

Kathren stepped closer. "Give me your hand, Amanda. As for you, you little savage, if you make

369

one wrong move I'll pull this trigger. Amanda!" she repeated sharply. "Take my hand."

Amanda slid her foot forward then made to lean her weight on it. Only she never stopped leaning. Pretending to faint, she fell forward into Kathren.

Kathren's finger slipped and the trigger snapped. Silver shuddered at the sound but there was no time to waste. Amanda and Kathren tottered, clinging to each other on the precarious edge of the stairs. Silver lunged for Amanda and yanked her back to safety. Kathren flung out an arm for the banister post to keep from falling to certain death.

Raising the acrid-smelling pistol again, her voice shook with rage while the girls cowered where they had fallen.

"Get up both of you! You haven't fooled me, you little bitch!" she snarled at Amanda. "You fell deliberately. You've listened to that heathen's lies, so you can just go the way of the rest of them. Both of you, get up and move down the hall!"

Silver could see the flash of the pistol and her throat went dry. She reached for Amanda, then drew back as she felt the warm stickiness of blood on her hand.

Her eyes glimmered as she looked up at Kathren, speaking in that low guttural voice that had given more than one man reason to pause.

"You have hurt her, *tivo sata*. You will pay for this . . ." As she spoke she felt her thigh where the knife was strapped, so caked with dried blood and mud it had chafed her raw skin all day while she eluded both Kathren and the horrible white eyes who brought dogs to hunt her down.

Kathren chortled maliciously, "You make threats from your knees, savage. Now get up!" The gun waved menacingly.

Silver's legs trembled with weakness as she stood up. She had tried several times to raid food from the kitchen, but had been interrupted each time.

"Get up," Kathren repeated when Amanda wallowed like a horse in quicksand.

"I c-can't!"

Kathren pointed the gun at Silver. "Then drag her."

Silver's lip curled as she emitted a sound like a rabid wolf, and Kathren stepped back, the hair on her neck raising as she waved the weapon. "I said drag her!" she threatened again.

The silver eyes were so murderous that for a moment Kathren feared the savage would attack her, and that was a disaster she wished to avoid. It would take hours to clean up the evidence of blood on a wooden floor.

Her breath of relief was almost audible when the savage bent toward the wounded Amanda.

Kathren allowed their laborious trek to pause as she took something from behind a picture. Then on they went.

When they finally came to the door to the recessed staircase at the end of the west wing, Silver was certain she had reached the limits of her endurance. Her heart fluttered weakly and when she crumpled to the floor beside Amanda, she knew she couldn't get up. Yet all it took to inspire her was the blunt nose of the pistol in her face and Kathren's raised voice.

They proceeded up the narrow stairs with no light.

When they reached the door that was their destination, Kathren felt in a small nook and produced both candle and matches, then unlocked the room which Silver remembered so well.

There was a demented cackle from within, and Silver stiffened when the door opened and she caught a glimpse of Sheba's twisted figure and glowing cap of hair. Again the stench of death filled her nostrils and a sick feeling of dread sapped her muscles.

"Inside," ordered Kathren, setting the candle holder on a dusty bureau while Silver dragged Amanda into the room.

"I have brought you more, like I promised," Kathren told Sheba, and the crone began to hop about them, her dark leathery face split by the pink slash of her toothless gums.

"Two!" she chortled. "In the chest?"

"You will have the silver-haired one for certain." Kathren gave Silver a sadistic smile. "This one will not be missed. But I haven't decided yet about Amanda's fate. It will be blamed on this one, of course, and on top of everything else she's suspected of, I don't think anyone will be overly anxious to locate her—especially when they think she's headed for Texas."

When Sheba crept up close and tried to finger the pale hair, Silver let out her most savage snarl, and Sheba jumped back with a yelp of fright. But a moment later she was edging closer again, the little raisin eyes sparkling from the folds of her face. Silver's fingers itched to touch the knife on her thigh, but her fear of the gun held her back.

"Later," hissed Kathren impatiently. "Now listen carefully, Sheba. There is no one below. You must go to the pantry in the kitchen where you will find several short lengths of rope hanging on nails. Bring them to me along with a knife. And don't dawdle. Be back here in five minutes or I'll come after you."

Sheba pranced and cackled her way to the door, then with a last hungry survey of her new guests, she disappeared.

"Amanda is Walker's sister," said Silver. "She has been sick, she will not remember this. It is I who have caused you grief. Keep me and let her go."

"Keep your advice to yourself, you whoring savage. Do you think I need the likes of you telling me what to do—*you,* who killed my only son?"

"Your . . . *son?*" said Amanda.

"Yes, my son!"

Kathren paced, her body tense and the pistol gripped like a lifeline. "Ran him through with a knife, leaving him for his own mother to find!" She whirled on the girls, her face ugly with hatred.

"Kathren—oh, Kathren!" said Amanda quickly. "Lord, I didn't know about Ferrell. Why did you tell us he was your nephew?"

372

Kathren took two strides and slammed the back of her pistol hand across Amanda's face, knocking her against Silver.

"This one is also your family!" cried Silver, clutching Amanda's shuddering body against her. "Why do you torment her? She has done nothing to you!"

"She's nothing but a millstone about my neck. She's a hard-hearted bitch just like her mother," sneered Kathren.

"My mother loved you," began Amanda. "She gave you a job."

"Melissa patted her smarting little conscience is what she did. She *owed* me that job. She owed me for letting her parents kick us out into the streets to eat the garbage from the tables of snobs like herself. Besides that, she needed me. She needed someone to look down on so she could feel superior."

Silver's eyes were glued to the gun as Kathren paced a circle.

Kathren ranted on.

"She wrapped herself in her finery—*'Don't you just love this new gown?'*" Kathren mimicked. "*'Oh yes, mistress. Anything is beautiful on you.'*" Kathren stopped to shove the gun in Amanda's stricken face, and both girls shrank back with a gasp.

"But she paid. Oh how she paid! It took months for her to die, don't you remember, Amanda? And I her faithful nurse got to watch it all." Kathren threw back her head and laughed. "Oh, yes, every hour of agony I watched—do you really know how bad it was, sweet Amanda? Certainly not. You were too busy with your parties and beaux—so let me tell you."

She leaned down, the candle throwing skull shadows on her face. "There were headaches—blinding headaches. And nausea and chills, dysentery, loss of memory, hallucinations—I gave her all those months of agony, *Miss* Amanda Grayson. Still it was not enough pay for what she had done!"

Amanda trembled violently but she couldn't say a word.

The door creaked open and Sheba skittered inside, her eyes glazed as she hopped from foot to foot.

"Lights coming!" she garbled, flecks of foam gathering at the corners of her mouth. "Up the drive — Sheba see them!"

Kathren whirled around. "What are you talking about?"

"Somebody coming," shrilled the crone as the pistol waved in her direction. "The Spirit of Darkness comes!" And she fell to her crippled knees and clasped her clawed hands in supplication. "Lucifer, Star of the Morning, look upon us with —"

Kathren jerked her to her feet by her hair, and the crone let out a screech. "Shut up, you babbling idiot. Who's coming? Where?"

"Don't know, mistress!" moaned Sheba, her eyes for once bulging because of the searing pain in her scalp. "I see the light a-coming up the drive!"

"We must go quickly," said Kathren.

After pressing the edge of the mirror to open it, Kathren touched the pistol point to Silver's right temple. "No sound comes from the hidden chambers," she whispered. "One false move and this will splatter your brains to the very ceiling."

Sheba followed them inside and Kathren pressed something that made the mirror close behind them. The candle was burning low and Silver felt suffocated by the close walls. Amanda staggered repeatedly, her loss of blood making her weaker.

For a while Kathren allowed the girls to descend the stairs buttocks first because they were so weak; but their pace proved too slow, and Kathren used the sharp toe of her boot to spur them on.

Silver thought they would go down forever. The taper had burned out, making their tortuous journey more painful as they bumped and tottered along, fearing each step would be the last before they tumbled headlong into the bottomless blackness.

When they finally stopped, Kathren fumbled in the dark, and when the match struck, both girls jumped back with a squeal as a coal oil torch burst into flames, illuminating a large, oblong room.

The walls were the same gray stone as the house, the floor nothing but black spongy earth. Through a thicket of tall cane at the end of the room, a canal of murky water entered. There was a small tunnel through the cane, and Silver soon saw the reason for it: a tiny canoe lay beached on the slippery bank a few yards away.

"The bayou comes here," said Silver, awed.

"Not the bayou," snorted Kathren. "The swamp waters—black and full of these!" Taking a dirty newspaper from a nook in the wall, she tossed strips of something black and shiny into the water. Then with the paddle from the canoe, she began to splash the inky surface.

"Come, my pets! Come to Momma—" Kathren hushed to cock her head and listen.

"Go to the listening post, quickly!" she hissed at Sheba, and the crone hobbled to a six-inch hole in the stone wall, holding her ear there for a moment. Her squinted eyes widened until the whites showed.

"They come! On the stairs!"

"Damn! There's no time to tie them up." Kathren turned back to the girls, leveling the pistol at them as she spoke. "Move into the water."

Silver's heart melted when the gun's muzzle turned upon her and she had no intention of balking. Yet when she reached down for Amanda, she found the girl's body wound up like a steel coil.

"No!" shrieked Amanda, hugging the ground. Silver pulled her toward the water anyway, and Amanda's voice rose to scream of hysteria. "Noooo! *No!* Kill me please. Kill me, Silver, don't let her . . ."

The rest of her words were incoherent. Silver ignored her protests, using all her force until they were both in the edge of the water; the swamp was their only means of escape from the mad woman with the gun.

"I can swim good and well," she whispered, but Amanda's body convulsed; her fingernails clawed the muddy black bank even as Kathren stalked toward them making threatening motions with the gun.

Suddenly there was a soft swishing of water near the entrance. Amanda's head riveted toward the sound and her mouth flew open in a silent scream.

Silver looked. Toward them came two, three, four— her throat closed up and she couldn't breathe.

Slithering along in the water came scaly heads and slitted eyes that glowed gold. Silver trembled with religious terror. Even the most powerful Spirit Talker in her acquaintance could not conjure up such devils as these.

Mesmerized, Silver could only stare as the gold eyes slid silently along on the oily black surface, when suddenly the eyes disappeared.

Silver gasped. Instead of eyes, there was pink, corrugated flesh and on either side of it, jagged teeth. Then with a catlike hiss, the powerful jaws snapped together like a white eyes trap, and Silver trembled until her teeth chattered with superstitious fear.

Kathren seized the moment; she shoved the paddle into Silver's back, and when that one fell, all that was needed was to push Amanda off the ledge of the shallows.

The canal was deep. Just as she heard Amanda's scream, Silver felt the black water close over her head.

Kathren snatched Sheba by the hand and ran with the flaming torch toward the stairwell. There was no need to look back, for the fate of the other two women was sealed.

"I don't like it," said Seth, and he yelled again. *"Ah-maan-dah! Kathrennnn! Where are yooou . . ."* His voice echoed off the vaulted dome of the roof not far above their heads. They were on the fourth level, and thus far they had found neither family nor servants, had heard nothing but the dry voices of timbers sighing, and the reverberations of their own screams.

"Maybe they went into town to stay with Uncle Guy,"

Seth suggested, though his tone was unconvincing.

Walker looked at him. "And for that you hit Deputy Walley and broke me out of jail?"

"I don't know any more than you do what's going on here. But we both know that Kathren has lost her mind to send every living soul off this place after two cold-blooded murders. I know something's not right here and you do—Listen!"

After a pause, Walker motioned with his hand and they started down the dark hall.

Seth stopped, knelt down and picked up something. "That's funny," he said.

"What is it?"

"Matches," he said, standing up.

"Shh! Listen, I heard voices."

"What would they be doing out here on the west wing?" asked Seth.

Suddenly a door opened and ahead of them, down the hall, there was a blinding light. They both squinted, throwing up a hand to shield their faces.

Kathren could not believe her eyes. Shoving Sheba back the way they had come, she slammed the door after them. "Run!"

Walker and Seth were right behind them and burst through the second door in time to see the bright orange glow lining the mirror.

"What the hell's going on here—that was Kathren!"

They ran to the mirror but after several blows to it produced no results, Walker fitted his fingers around the edge.

They had brought no light and the room was lit only by the rising moon slanting through the single low window on the right-hand wall. As Walker fought back a choking panic, he heard Seth thrashing about in the darkened corner, and in a moment he felt a hand on his arm.

"Stand back. We'll break it," said Seth, and laid the brass lamp base to the glass.

Although the mirror shattered, one touch told them the door panel behind it was made of solid cypress.

Walker shoved past him and began tapping on the wall to the left of the cypress panel until he could locate the wall studs.

"What do you think?" panted Seth.

"I'm going to try to break the wall. If that lamp still has a wick and you have matches on you, you'd better get it lit."

Taking a run at the wall, Walker heaved into it with his right shoulder and burst through the wood veneer that supported the tattered and splotched wallpaper; the wall exploded with the sound of splintering wood just as the glow from Seth's lamp spread through the billowing dust.

Inside the small bare room was a door leading right, but it was locked.

"My turn." Seth handed the lamp to Walker, stepping backward a few paces to launch himself for the door; the last one brought a bark of surprise from him. One of the loose floorboards buckled and popped out of place, and the length of his shin scraped along raw wood as his foot fell through a hole.

Walker rushed to him with the light. "If you've broken your leg, I'm going to . . . What's that?"

Yanking his leg from the hole, Seth muttered a curse. "A loose floorboard—"

"No, look. There's something under the flooring . . ." He knelt and grabbed the stout wooden box, hefting it up through the opening.

"Leave it," said Seth. "Let's go after Kathren. Amanda could be in trouble somewhere. That's probably something one of the servants stashed away—now come on, let's go!"

Walker laid the box on the floor and stood up. "We'll come back and check it out. I don't like what's going on here. Why on earth is Kathren running from us?"

The door to the right collapsed with minimum effort. Along the hall they found two more doors which opened left into empty rooms, but farther along there was one to the right.

"We're headed down again, let's keep going," said Seth, but Walker paused at the door.

"Put out the lamp," he whispered.

"What?"

Walker only touched his arm. Seth doused the light and when their eyes adjusted, both of them saw the faint orange line along the bottom edge of the door.

"She's in here," Walker whispered again.

For a moment they listened for sounds.

"She saw us come after her and she's bound to have heard us walking down the hall," said Walker.

"I think we should just call her."

"Okay, try it."

"Kathren, are you all right?" Seth reached out and tried the door. "It's locked," he whispered, and now Walker tried.

"Kathren, stop this foolishness and open the door!"

There was no answer.

Seth was aiming his boot at the door when Walker's hand stayed him.

"Wait."

"What's the matter?"

"I don't know exactly; just don't stand behind that door. Move toward the wall."

Following his own directions, Walker stood well to the other side, stretching his boot around to give the portal a stout kick near the floor.

The two men plastered themselves against the wall when bullets splattered the door in triplicate.

After the echoes died, Walker whispered, "There's your answer. I just pray to God that nothing has happened to Amanda."

Chapter 23

There was another hard kick at the door, but this time Kathren was wise enough to save her last two bullets. Sheba was wrapped around her legs, blubbering incoherently, and her arm ached with the weight of holding the torch up.

It was over now but for one thing, and after that she could accept her fate. All that remained was to bring the last of the mighty Graysons to the dirt, and she had only two bullets to do it.

"Kathren! Put down that gun. This is your last chance."

Kathren reared back her head and replied in a hyena laugh.

"Your threats are useless, you stupid fools. Do you think I would let you take me now? Do you think I'd spend my last days rotting in some four-by-four cell?"

The door seemed to be blown apart, pieces of it splintering and flying across the room. Kathren ducked her head, for she could do no more with the crone hanging in a death-grip about her legs.

She waited until she saw the shape of a man in the blazing light and pulled the trigger. The figure reeled against the wall, and then the second one came, and she fired again. She chortled, grabbing Sheba's white fuzzy mop in her fingers and almost yanking it out by the roots as she hauled the crone away from her.

Then her laughter died as the haze from the gun cleared and she saw both brothers, wounded and staggering, yet still on their feet. Seth was hit in the leg and could only stumble forward but Walker's was a shoulder wound: He rushed her.

Without hesitation Kathren whirled to the window behind her and broke it with the blunt ball of wadding on the end of the torch. Her skirt ripped as Sheba tried to cling to her. Sheba was scraped off like butter from a knife as Kathren scrambled through the opening.

Between the two turrets, washed in the fiery light from the torch, the ledge was only four feet wide. There was nothing save a sheer drop from the other rooms, but here there was an old timber used by the builders. If she could cross it, she would have access to the widow's walk on the front of the house.

The crone made it through the window and was once again tangled in her skirts as Kathren staggered along the ledge, dragging the old woman's weight. Already she could hear the men clambering out the window back behind them.

As Kathren tottered out onto the end of the beam, Sheba chattered and whined and clutched at her; one push would rid her of the crone for good, but Kathren found she couldn't force her hand to the deed.

Suddenly the small twisted figure seemed snatched away from her by the wind, and when Kathren whirled around, she saw Sheba held like an infuriated child in Seth's hands, stamping her bare crippled feet and flailing her arms about. Walker was coming along the ledge, stepping carefully around Seth, but stopped before he reached her, and Kathren scooted her foot further out on the beam.

"Where is Amanda? Tell me where she is!" Walker growled, holding his bleeding shoulder.

"In the belly of the swamp 'gators!" Kathren laughed, and when Walker's face twisted in the orange torch light, she added, "And so is your precious savage! They're both dead—eaten by the swamp scavengers and at this very moment being digested—don't come any closer!" She thrust the torch in his face, laughing again when he jumped back.

"You're lying," Walker shouted. "Silver ran away."

Kathren turned away from him and tottered out onto the beam with both feet.

Walker screamed to stop her but Kathren wobbled along, the torch waving as she tried to balance.

Her dance became wilder; she toppled to the right, now to the left. "Kathren, wait there!" he shouted. "I'll come get—"

It was over so quickly. Her foot slipped, and for a moment she straddled the beam. But when she reached to grab the timber between her legs, the torch fell, spitting cloth cinders and afterward a spray of hissing sparks as it slid down the voluminous folds of her skirt. The soft cotton poofed into flames, and she screamed as she tried to beat out the flames licking up her face.

Only the fleeting image of her pitching sideways would be left to Walker, for in the blink of the eye she was gone, her scream strangely musical as she tumbled through the darkness in a blazing ball of fire.

The crone sprang from Seth's arms with superhuman power and before Walker could realize she was coming, Sheba was at the lip of the roof. With the light of the torch gone, he could see her crippled figure rocking back and forth in the moonlight. "My baby! My precious baby!" she groaned, holding the glowing white cap of her hair.

"Sheba, get back!" barked Walker.

She crouched and swung her head toward him, and when she spoke again, she sounded as sober and sane as a judge. "My daughter is gone," she said quietly, and twisting her body as nimbly as a sprite, she leaped spread-eagled over the side.

There was no scream, nothing at all until Walker heard a faint crunch, like a sack of dry twigs tossed lightly upon the ground.

When Kathren had left them and taken the torch with her, the hole of stagnant water became a black wet death. Though Silver could hear Amanda floundering and gasping, she could do nothing to help her. Treading water with one hand while she reached for the knife with the other sapped the small burst of energy that came with the knowledge of her impending death. Fleeting seconds of strength were all she had left.

Then there was a sudden blast of breath that filled her nostrils with the stench of rotting flesh, and once again the catlike hiss. Her right hand cut upward, parting the weight of the water with an excruciating lethargy, so that she knew the outcome already and let the momentum shove her back and under the tainted grave of brackish water.

She waited for the crush of those ridged teeth as she sank through the swirling midnight, thinking that she would not now save Walker's sister and redeem herself. To leave him was more terrible knowing that she was taking Amanda with her—the last act of her life, the last in a series of tragedies sparked the moment she began to ache for Walker Gray's Son, a white eyes chief.

Suddenly it came to her that the knife was not in her hand—and why it wasn't. In the next flash of time she remembered the hard shellac of scaled hide against the V between forefinger and thumb—the jar as the hilt slammed against the flexing underthroat of the great beast.

But it was too late. There was just a thimble of breath left in her lungs—and then there was none. Her arms gathered the water to her like a woman taking wash from the line, but she was too deep; the black water had no end, and the moment came when her mouth opened and the small crushed sacs of her lungs expanded in the final gasp that would fill them with tainted black water.

Walker and Seth stood peering over the rim of the roof. "There's no need to check.

"We should. Miracles do happen."

Walker waited until the flames began to die. "Go check if you want to, but I'm going to make sure that wasn't a trick to throw us off. Then, if there's no sign of Silver and Amanda up here, I'll get Harriot and search the swamps until I find them."

Seth swallowed. "How do you know Kathren was lying about what happened to them?"

Walker couldn't admit that he didn't, so he started back along the ledge toward the broken window.

The lamp was still sitting on the floor in the hallway, and once it was giving light, they left nothing to chance, checking and rechecking each room for hidden doors and chambers, knowing it would be easy enough to pass over an unconscious body stuffed in a secret place, like the little wooden chest. If a door failed to give, they broke it down and felt over every square inch of the room before continuing.

Farther along the hallway there were no more doors, only damp bare walls.

"Where does this lead?" asked Walker.

"I've never seen any of this."

"Let's go back. The other way is sure," said Walker. "We could have Harriot on the trail in a few minutes and we might need every second."

Even when the air rushed inside her, it was a moment before Silver could realize her face had burst the inky surface of the water. A few feet in front of her she could hear the churning and thrashing as the fatally wounded monster provided a meal for his brothers.

Her gasping finally stopped and she floated limply, stroking only occasionally, until first her feet and then her knees touched ground. The cave was still smothered in gloom but for the entrance, where moonlight was streaming through the cane. Silver crawled through the mud, feeling everywhere on the slimy bank until finally she touched a shoulder.

"Amanda," she croaked, shaking the girl.

Amanda came awake with a shriek and began batting the air wildly, her fingernails accidently scratching Silver's face as once Silver's had done to her.

"Oh, Silver — Silver, it's you!" cried Amanda, fumbling in the dark until she could crush the other girl to her. "I thought you were a goner, for sure."

"I do not know 'goner,' " choked Silver, for the arms about her neck were strangling her.

"Never mind, you're not, thank — oh my God," Amanda broke off and went rigid. *They're still here.*

"But perhaps they are not as hungry now," advised Silver, rolling her eyes toward the churning water. "We should be very quiet. They could change their minds if they hear us."

Together they crawled from the shallow water and huddled against the wall, eyes trained on the misty moonlight that filtered through the canes at the entrance.

The crunch of bones and ripping of flesh died to contented if somewhat hair-raising sighs, and finally there was the swish of water, the shadow of snout and head, and the weaving of the water as the long bodies slithered out through the cane.

When her hands were dry, Silver searched the wall until she found Kathren's stash of matches and candles, and brought a lighted taper to where Amanda was shivering wretchedly.

She looked down and said, "I eat or I die."

"Then you die. I wouldn't touch my little toe in that water if I sit here till I rot to a corpse."

Silver sat down beside her, looking at the water longingly.

"Rattlesnake is good for food. The evil-water-dogs are not so different." There was a gagging sound beside her, but she went on absently. "If the knife was still in the carcass and I could bring it to shore, it would be little trouble to build a fire and — "

A hand clutched her throat lightly. "You may have saved my life," said Amanda in a low voice, "but if you do not shut up, I will throttle you."

Silver abandoned her idea reluctantly.

"If we go up the stairs, Kathren will be waiting for us," she pointed out. "If we stay here, the beasts with yellow eyes will return to fill their stomachs again."

Amanda huddled against her shoulder, shivering. "I'm too weak to climb the stairs anyway."

Silver returned to her former theme. "That is why we must eat. A few strips of roasted meat . . ." Her voice trailed away, for the gray blush of dawn lit the cave now and she could see Amanda's face well enough. She shrugged. "Then we must escape through the water."

Amanda spoke slowly and distinctly. "You . . . are . . . crazy."

"There is no other way. Soon Kathren must return to see if the evil monsters ate us."

Amanda eyed the entrance. "The bank couldn't be more than a few feet from that door—providing the cane thicket doesn't go far." She paused thoughtfully. "The only cane on the banks near the house—that I can remember, at least—are just below the carriage house. I just can't remember how thick it is. I couldn't last long in the water," she warned, "even with you helping me—and Lord knows you can barely stand yourself."

"But are you strong enough to swim without eating first?" insisted Silver, and Amanda gave her a long, hard look.

"I'm as strong as I shall be—for I will not be eating before I leave this hole."

Walker and Seth sprawled on the sofa, exhausted, both wearing bloody bandages and layers of swamp mud.

"Sheriff Hancock will be after our hides. We'll probably be hearing from him anytime now," said Seth, tilting his second glass of straight bourbon. "Do you think he's going to believe us when we explain about the bodies on the lawn?" He bent suddenly to rub the bandage around his shin, and muttered, "Damn that

386

ornery old cuss! With hands like that, Adams should have been a wrestler."

"I think the good doctor doesn't like being dragged out of bed in the middle of the night," Walker replied, easing back against the sofa with a groan of pain. His body felt like he'd been dragged by a herd of wild mustangs. "You better be glad he patched us up after you let it slip that we were going straight back into the swamps."

"What I'm glad about is Kathren's sorry aim. A little higher and I might have lost my—"

"We shouldn't have stopped looking." Walker held his glass up and brooded at the amber contents. "It's getting light now. We shouldn't have stopped."

Seth swept his eyes over him. A stubble of golden beard covered his jaws; mud from his boots was making soft plopping sounds on the carpet, and blood from the shoulder sling was seeping through to stain the sofa back.

"You'd have collapsed if we'd gone much longer. You look like twice-chewed 'gator bait."

The choice of metaphors was a mistake. Walker came to his feet and sailed his glass around the room. It struck the hearth and shattered violently, for it was thick German crystal.

Walker limped to the window to look out. The gray blanket of dawn was bringing out the humped shapes of shrubs, the heavy braids of moss hanging like lace under the oaks.

"You are not my brother if you give up," Seth told him quietly.

"I should be mourning my father instead of—" He paused. "Dad never gave me anything but love."

"You're forgetting that he meant to throw you out of the house. No, that's wrong—you're not forgetting, you're forgiving. Maybe because you realize you can't lay generations of stupidity on a single person. Not Samuel, not yourself . . . and not Silver." Seth saw the wide shoulders hunch, and his heart pounded with stress. He had never seen his brother cry.

He went on quickly. "I think you've forgotten what kind of woman you married. If half the stories you tell are true, I don't think we need worry about Silver Dawn."

He grinned thoughtfully a moment. Then he got up, ambled to the fireplace, and clapped Walker on the shoulder roughly. "Yeah, I'd say—"

Walker doubled over, grabbing his shoulder, and Seth murmured, "Sorry, I forgot."

Walker frowned and held his shoulder. "I know what you're trying to do and it won't work. So forget it."

"You don't want it to work," Seth frowned back. "You just want to feel sorry for yourself."

Walker turned away and hobbled to the sofa again. "You won't make me mad either."

Seth dogged his trail and sat down beside him.

"I'm serious. What we better be worrying about is finding Amanda. Silver Dawn can take care of herself." He chuckled wryly. "Maybe you've forgotten, but she does it rather well."

Walker leaned forward and dropped his face into his hands, and Seth sat tense and uncomfortable for a moment.

Presently he said, "Don't worry. You'll get her back. Only I'm afraid that when you do, it'll be just like before."

Walker finally looked at him, and his eyes were glittering a little.

"And how's that?"

Seth waved his hand airily. "Oh, you'll try to dominate her and order her around the way you do everybody else." When Walker's eyes narrowed, he shrugged. "And she'll stick a knife under your nose and remind you that you are only a stupid white eyes." He grinned maliciously. "I will be watching with relish while she tames you."

Walker's jaw hardened. "We'll see about that. We'll just damn well see about that." He stood up unsteadily. "Come on. Let's go check the outbuildings again."

Sheriff Hancock spoke with obvious regret.

"I don't know what to make of all this unless Kathren simply went off the deep end over Samuel's death. Maybe she was taking some of those drugs—my word, there enough in that thing to do in all of St. Martinville." He stared at the wooden chest. "Well, Cassadyne is gone and there's no witness against you, but his statement is on record. I have to warn you that you're not cleared yet, Walker." He looked at the chest again. "Where do you think Kathren came by all that stuff?"

Walker was pacing impatiently, ready to begin the search again.

"When my mother was growing up, Kathren was her nurse. They had known each other for a—can't we go over this later?" he said shortly. "A few seconds could mean the difference between life and death."

"You're right." The sheriff stood. "My men have already spread out around the house and will work in an outward circle." He looked at the brothers gravely. "I hope Kathren's threat was only the ravings of a woman insane with grief. But if she was that far gone, I guess you realize she may very well have harmed the girls."

Walker shook his head. "I don't understand any of this. Kathren disliked Silver but she got along fine with Amanda."

The sheriff cleared his throat. "There's one other problem I have to mention. If . . ." He looked at the frowning brothers then went on reluctantly. "If we find your wife, I'll have to take her in—at least until we can investigate further."

"What are you talking about?" Walker demanded ominously.

"Kathren accused her of killing Ferrell Cassadyne. She said they were . . . er, together at a cottage in the woods. She said Silver was the last person to see him alive."

Walker's eyes were like ice. "If she killed Cassadyne,

389

she had good reason. I'm not a man of idle threats, Hancock. You find my wife, you better bring her to me before you take her anywhere. And no handcuffs."

Sheriff Hancock jammed his hat on. "I'll pretend you didn't say that. Threatening an officer of the law is—"

There was a sound at the door, and the three men turned.

Amanda was hanging against Silver, supported by an arm that trembled violently. The faces and forms were hardly recognizable, for only strips of flesh peeked from the covering of black mud and weeds and shreds of torn clothing. The gunshot wound in Amanda's shoulder was only a flesh wound, but its dark stain had mingled with the swamp silt to form crusty ridges on it as well as on both women's cheeks, and red splotches on what clothing remained to them.

For a moment they were all like actors who'd forgotten their lines. The sheriff's jaw was hanging, Seth and Walker stood frozen and staring, and the two girls tottered on wobbly legs within the doorway.

Then Amanda gave in to the rushing dizziness in her head and fainted. She fell to the floor because Silver could not hold her up; she could only cling to the door, gasping.

Seth ran forward and lifted Amanda.

"Sheriff, you're the only servant we've got right now. Upstairs, second door at the end of the next landing!"

They were left alone, and Silver couldn't drag her from her husband's face nor could she read anything in his expression but disbelief. Her throat began to clog disgustingly and she tried to remember that she was Quohadie Teichas.

Still he stared, not moving toward her, and she thought that saving Amanda had not been enough. If only her tongue would move, she would remind him that her job was done and she would leave as quickly as possible. But it would not move, and so she stared back.

He started toward her so slowly that she decided her

legs would give way before he crossed the room.

And then he stopped a good distance away, his eyes traveling up and down her, clouding by degrees, the skin around them pulling into deep lines like a man looking into the sun. Sweat popped from his pores like dew and ran down his creviced face until he had to wipe it with the sleeve of his shirt. His arm shook as though gripped with palsy, and she noticed that he was also covered in the glutinous swamp mud.

Walker searched for words but none came. His arms ached to hold her, but he had closed that avenue forever with his unthinking cruelty, more brutal in ways than her months of slavery. She stood before him like death—gaunt, stricken with tremors, her body smeared with blood. Yet she stood proudly. Defiantly. As well she should—he thought with anguish. Instead of following her dreams she had stayed with Amanda.

Even the sacrifice of his pride seemed a profane offering.

"If you cannot climb the stairs, I'll help you." He stared unblinkingly, hanging on her reply; then he realized it was presumptuous to think that she would allow him to touch her, even in the capacity of a servant. He was not worthy of even that, and he had started to drop his head when she said, "I cannot walk the stairs."

Walker looked at her, and the lustrous silver quality crept into her eyes until they glistened like wet marble.

"I . . . I could get Seth."

"Seth is with Amanda." After a moment Walker started toward her like a man dragging a great timber behind him.

He was surprised at how weightless she felt, or that his shoulder did not ache when she leaned against it. He was even more surprised when her arms lifted around his neck as he turned for the staircase.

Had the stairs always been so tall? The hall so long?

He stared ahead of him, not changing his expression as her arms tightened about his neck.

When they came to the door of his room, he paused

and stood there. Then he leaned one shoulder against the wall, and finally his head dropped so that their foreheads pressed together, very tightly, and for a long moment they did nothing but hold their heads together like bull rams, their eyes squeezed together at the same time.

Walker said nothing as he shoved away from the wall and opened the door to his room.

He laid her gently on the bed and stood back looking at her.

"I'll haul some hot water."

"To haul water is woman's work."

"It's a slave's work, and I am your slave." He knelt in front of her, and Silver felt a knot rise in her chest.

She wanted to believe what she saw in his face yet she had believed so many times. White eyes were masters of deceit, were they not?

She was surprised to hear herself say, "You are not my slave, you are my lord. My husband."

He ducked his head and she stared at the springy curls on top of his head before she reached out gingerly to touch them.

But he rose swiftly without giving her a glimpse of his face. "I will get the water," he croaked.

He seemed to relax as he worked. In fact, he grew so diligent that his efforts sheened his face with sweat, and she thought that she would have reaped more peace knowing he had eased his body with the water first.

She smiled, blinking rapidly. To consider the husband first and he her in the like manner—that was the way of *commar-pe*. And so she could trust a little. Only a little.

Walker's face was flushed with heat and exertion when he held his palm over the tub, as though it were a gift whose merit had not yet been determined.

"Well, I guess it's ready."

Silver looked at the circles of steam rising from the

392

tub, then raised her eyes to his, twinkling. "My legs shake."

A light leaped into Walker's eyes and he stared lingeringly a moment. "Then I'll guess I'll have to help you." His gold lashes fell to half-mast as he came toward her.

He carried her the scant distance to the tub and set her down beside it but stayed close, his head tucked over her bare shoulder so that his breath grazed her skin. "Do you need . . . any more assistance?"

She lifted her face and looked at him. "There are no white eyes slaves to undress me."

He turned her until she faced him squarely, leaving his hands on the joints of her shoulders. "Only your husband. Is this man's work?"

Her eyes glowed. "It has always been so."

He slipped the shreds of cloth over her shoulders, drawing his hands slowly down her arms and catching his breath when he saw a trail of chill bumps break out behind them. He rasped as though there were clogs of dirt in his throat.

"You must hurry with your bath."

"But I am not in the water."

His head jerked up and he stared into her face. "So you have found your method of revenge," he said gravely.

She tilted her head and looked down her nose, trying not to smile. "And do you not deserve it?"

His gaze roamed to her breasts again, and Silver could hear his breath sigh like a breeze in the treetops. "My punishment may be more than I can bear. Perhaps I could persuade you to postpone your toilette. I really see no need—"

A gurgle of laughter escaped her, and Walker frowned as she shook her head slowly.

"No, my husband, I truly must bathe first. What man would want a body such as this in his bed?" She dropped her dark lashes, making the pale gray irises like half moons below them.

He grabbed her nakedness against him. "I would."

His mouth swooped down like an eagle after prey.

"Please." Her lips murmured against his and when Walker felt her swaying surrender, he fought like a gladiator to subdue himself. A woman couldn't help these untimely and frustrating notions—yet he was determined that she would have her female way. It was certainly time she had her way about something.

His efforts at restraint left his face swollen as he allowed himself one more burning look at her body; then he lifted her and lowered her into the water, drenching his shirt to the elbow because he let go with great reluctance.

He bathed her slowly, leaning over the tub and watching her face as he stroked and caressed, and she purred and arched. Suddenly he stood up, arms dripping water onto the carpet.

"I'll use the cistern at the back of the house," he said hoarsely. "But be finished with this nonsense when I get back."

He left abruptly.

Though the bath had given her time to rest, the heat of desire left her body so heavy that Silver could barely hobble to the bed. She collapsed upon it and lay for a moment before sliding under the cover.

When Walker opened the door he was wearing a towel about his waist. Damp blond curls fell over his forehead and matted his chest. He was carrying a tray of food.

He sat down on the bed, giving a little shiver as he spoke.

"Cold water has temporarily taken the edge from my hunger but I warn you, eat quickly."

Yet he fed her slowly, watching her small pearly teeth take each bite. Finally the food was forgotten. Their eyes were locked, and there was no world beyond the charge of current flying between them, no future but the bloom of passion and joy.

He laid the tray aside and gave her water to rinse

her mouth. "My turn to feast." He took the glass from her hand, lowering his mouth to hers, plundering inside until she was gasping and pleading for rest—and then for more.

Suddenly he drew back and whipped the offending sheet aside. She was exquisitely formed, sleek and sinewy as a cat, her breasts round and firm as ripe melons, and . . .

He frowned, for they were curiously white, and below them he saw a triangle of more white skin framing a smaller triangle of crisp curls. He remembered the shape of the strange undergarment she had once worn, and his frown deepened.

"Will you always roast yourself under the sun, or will the day come when the Indian brown is satisfied to fade to white?"

She put a finger to his lips. "We will not speak of such things now." She looped her arms around his neck, raising herself and kissing him deeply until she felt the blade of muscles in his shoulders relax.

He resisted for a moment more, then crushed her to him, holding the embrace while he lifted his hips to move over her. He found no words of love more eloquent than the volcano roiling within his groin, and he plunged deep in one stroke.

Silver clasped her thighs around his lean flanks and for a paralyzed breath of time they held the pose, not moving. Then clamping her hips to him, he rolled them, and when she was on top, he lifted her backward with fingers laced in her hair until he could take the dark tip of each breast in his mouth.

With a bearlike growl he rolled them again, his body pinning her to the bed, driving violently, lifting her into the sweeping clouds above, where there were no bloody battlegrounds. And when she felt the final jerking convulsion of pleasure, she cried out his name, clinging to the instant of oneness until the last possible moment.

They sank to earth and he held her so close her bones seemed to crunch; he wept against her neck, and she caressed the back of his head like a mother comforting a child.

"You will never leave me again, white eyes, for I will follow you to the four winds. I will haunt your night dreams and give you visions by day."

Walker pressed his face into the soft flesh of her neck and could not speak.

During the night Walker slipped away several times to check on Amanda, but the sheriff had ridden out to get Dr. Adams, who after cleaning the wound and administering a mild sedative, proclaimed that plenty of food and rest would see the girl back to health in a couple of weeks. He also declared hotly that if any more Graysons got shot up, they should call somebody else.

Silver slept so deeply that each time Walker returned, he spent many moments bent over her, listening for a barely audible breath and almost collapsing with relief when it finally came.

It was close to dawn before he found the same state of repose for himself, yet when Silver opened her eyes, he was propped on one elbow, his face close as he watched her.

Her eyes touched his heavy brow, the thick gold eyelashes blurred by a ray of morning sun, the fine bronzed skin carved by the elements, and the firm curve of his mouth.

"I cannot get enough of looking at you."

He smiled, and his teeth were glossy white and even as the ivory keys of a piano. "Will wonders never cease? I was thinking the same thing myself. When two minds turn as one, I guess there's hope after all."

Silver's face clouded suddenly when she remembered. She made a move to get up. "Amanda! She was wounded and—"

Walker stopped her with a heavy thigh across her belly.

"It was only a flesh wound. The doctor has seen her

and she'll be fine, thanks to you."

Silver lay back against the pillow, timid because she could feel her cheeks grow red.

"It's the truth," Walker insisted, mistaking the cause of her high color. "Amanda told me herself. She owes you her life."

Silver dropped her gaze. Suddenly there were more memories, and they were not of Amanda. In fact, she could barely remember what the girl looked like. There was a kaleidoscope of erotic visions whirling about in her head—which must surely have come to pass seeing as how she was in her husband's bed and they were wearing no clothes. Apparently he deemed it such a natural state that he made no effort to disguise his arousal. There was something very hard against her thigh and her cheeks grew warmer as she tried to remember exactly how much of the last few hours she had dreamed and how much might be—could possibly be—real?

A chuckle rumbled in Walker's chest. "What's this? You're blushing like a shy desert flower, when I would have sworn a few hours ago that I married a wild—"

Silver silenced him with her finger once again.

"White eyes talk too much." She frowned and cut her eyes sideways. "Also, he like to make *commar-pe* at night but is very much soor-ee when the sun rises." Her glare became a real one as she thought about the matter.

Walker kissed her finger, drew it into his mouth, and held it lightly in his teeth as he spoke around it and watched her face. "Do I look sorry?"

Silver frowned more fiercely but it was hard to think of anger when his hard hairy body was touching hers, his skin so hot. Her heart beat fiercely.

"You look like a dog with a bone." She pulled her finger from his teeth, and her voice sounded breathless. "Or a mountain cat who is very truly hungry."

He moved quickly, touching her lips with his and letting them linger while their breath mingled like two wines; he ravished her with kisses that were feathery

397

and light, then hot and demanding, and finally she was tugging and straining to get at him, snaking herself around him like a boa crushing its prey.

"*Tivo sata,* you are like firewater in my blood. Give me your body or I die!"

Walker laughed, holding her legs around his waist.

"Such impatience, my dear. You have much to learn about love. It should be tasted slowly, not devoured in one bite."

"You have many moons to teach me that," she growled impatiently. "Mount me now, white eyes, and keep your much talking for later."

Chapter 24

The decision was mutually satisfying to both couples: Seth and Prissy would live at Gray Shadows. Walker and Silver would move to the plantation in the country.

Walker turned the pair of matching bays up the oak-lined drive of Bulah, but his attention was focused on his wife. Her pale hair, tangled with the butter yellow ribbons on her wide-brimmed straw hat, floated and swirled about her face as she tried to look everywhere and hold her hat in place at the same time.

"I like this house!" Silver exclaimed. "But where are the horses? I do not see any horses." Walker opened his mouth to answer but was cut off. "And where is the juga cane Prissy told me about? She said we had very much juga cane."

Walker laughed at her Cajun pronunciation and Silver jerked around to frown at him.

"You're spending too much time with your sister-in-law. "It's *sugar* cane," he explained with a grin. "And we do have it—nine hundred acres at Bulah alone. It's growing all around you." His arm swept the fields beyond the oaks.

Silver was disappointed. "It is only very tall prairie grass."

"But wait till you taste one of those ripe, juicy stalks." Walker licked his lips in a seductive gesture.

"I do not believe you are talking about juga cane, my husband." She smiled with promise as he urged the bays with a flip of the reins.

Silver leaned back to enjoy the view. "Now I know

we are very rich," she said dreamily, for at the end of the shadowed drive sat a white plantation house, eight massive columns rising up through the veranda roof so that it looked like one white eyes house on top of the other one. She sighed and snuggled against Walker. "And it has many windows. I will be very happy here."

A short week later Walker stood on the breezy veranda watching his brother's carriage move up the drive. He grinned when he spotted the flounces of crinoline fluttering from the step-through doors, and before the carriage had stopped rolling, Prissy scrambled down unassisted, the skirts of her new yellow muslin swirling like a cloud confection as she sprinted up the steps.

"Where ees Silver?" she demanded, her cheeks colored with excitement. "Ah have good news and Ah must tell her quickly."

Walker looked beyond Prissy and winked at Amanda, who led at a more decorous pace the entourage of servants disembarking from a second carriage. Her brown eyes sparkled and though her arm was still in a sling from the gunshot, her spirits were as high as Prissy's.

"She really does have wonderful news," Amanda assured him, pausing to kiss his cheek. "We must tell Silver at once. Where is she?"

Walker grinned ruefully. "I'm afraid she's busy with the payroll. Apparently the mental block suffered by Quohadie Teichas when it comes to learning white eyes ways does not apply to the system of U.S. currency. She mastered the entire method of exchange in an hour."

The party filed inside with the women chattering and Jubal squawking like a fish wife as he held his proud pot of gumbo clear of disaster. "Zee young ones, they turn my hair white already," he muttered, and Seth held the door as the cook swept imperiously past him.

The voices faded into the hallway and Seth went back to the edge of the steps to offer Walker a cigar. "So. Your poor Indian slave is now running a thousand-acre plantation," he said merrily, holding the match to Walker's cigar. "It didn't take her long to get the hang of it."

"You don't know the half of it," Walker said lazily, but the twinkle in his eyes belied his mournful tone. "She's planning to clear out the rest of the swamps next spring and plant more cane."

Seth's face clouded suddenly, and he pulled a piece of paper from the pocket of his fawn-colored waistcoat. "This came today. I believe it's the order you've been waiting for."

Walker took the telegram reluctantly, knowing already what it would contain. After a brief glance he tucked it into his coat and gazed across the green meadows of cane, puffing little curls of smoke around the cigar held in his teeth. "This is the first of September. I think we'll be ready to start harvesting in three weeks."

Seth propped his boot on the railing and followed Walker's gaze. "If the rest looks like this, we'll have a good crop. By the way, should you have some extra hands I think we're going to need them at Belle View and Oak Manor. The overseers there are already complaining that they'll be shorthanded. Of course, Mackenzie's march has begun by now, and I suppose you'll be leaving soon. Without you here to supervise the work, I'm sure Bulah will need all her extra hands." He stared at Walker intently.

Walker tossed the cigar over the railing and turned for the door. "Let's go eat, little brother."

Walker fell out laughing when Prissy made her announcement at the noon meal.

"My cycle ees one week late today." She beamed expectantly, waiting for a reaction.

Silver looked befuddled, Seth was choking on his wine, and when Amanda joined Walker's outburst, Prissy's dark brows slanted fiercely.

"Doan believe me eef you weesh," she said indignantly, "but you weel see. You weel not laugh when

401

dat creaky old house ees filled with forty or thirty sons!"

Silver understood at last and a misty smile lit her eyes. "I believe you," she said, glancing at Walker. But he was too busy recovering his composure to notice the look she gave him.

"I'm really sorry if I offended you, Prissy," he said when he could speak. "Believe me, I'm not laughing at your wonderful news, but the time and place you chose to deliver it."

Seth's flushed face showed no sign of amusement. "We'll have to discuss the fine points of social etiquette again," he murmured.

An hour later the three women were giggling and whispering like schoolgirls as they strolled across the back lawn, finally stopping at a bench beneath a spreading oak.

"And you haf not told heem?" Prissy exclaimed.

"It is too soon, I could be wrong," said Silver, holding a late-blooming oleander blossom to her nose, although she had already learned that the beautiful scarlet petals were not fragrant.

The men caught up and sprawled before them on the grass, alternately teasing and admiring the women on the bench, and the hours seemed to fly past in a teenage whirl of playful taunts and lively contentions, male pitted against female, until the sun began to drop and slant in misty-gold bars through the bastions of moss.

At the end of another week Silver was certain that her husband's seed grew within her, but she had not told him. Indeed, they spoke of little except trivia, and she watched helplessly as the thing that lay between them became a chasm neither knew how to cross. He didn't realize that she had learned of his plan to kill her father through Kathren, and in the feminine way women have of testing their men, she waited to see if he would be honest with her.

Although he was obviously brooding about the matter—for his appetite had lagged, his sleeping was disturbed, and he spent much time staring into the distances—he refused to broach the subject even when she gave him opportunity. She could not really hope that a warrior such as Walker Grayson would betray his own nation, yet she could not believe he would murder her father and brothers and sister, either.

Then one morning she found him at the sunny little office near the back veranda and stood watching him as he folded two letters and put them into separate envelopes. His face was so hard and tight it seemed it would crack if she spoke, and she suddenly knew the papers had something to do with his secret army plans.

Sensing her presence, he turned as though startled, and when she saw a fleeting look of guilt cross his face, her heart died inside of her.

He did not smile though his voice was soft. "How can you look so beautiful this early?"

"You see only what lies in your looking glass, for unless the sun of your faces touches mine, there is no light."

She was not smiling either, and Walker got the point. "I have to make a trip," he said, and he watched her face.

All he got was a familiar expressionless mask, so he said, "Aren't you going to ask me where?"

Silver lowered her gaze and fingered the little book of white eyes poetry she had been reading.

"When I look from my new kitchen window, I see the great twisted arms of oak and hear the mockingbird's voice." Walker had to strain to hear her. "And in a moment I am standing back and seeing another woman, at another kitchen window. She seems very tall and I have to look up because I am very close to the floor—a plain wood floor. The woman is singing as she cooks, and I know her voice."

Walker waited, his lungs suddenly empty and the back of his neck tight as a vise.

"This woman . . ." Silver paused then went on with difficulty. "This woman is not the wife of Horse Back. The words she sings are not Comanche—but Horse

403

Back is my father and he will always be!"

Walker came to his feet and crossed the floor. When he pulled her to him she turned her face away, but he forced her to look at him. "No Quohadie Tèichas lets a white eyes see his tears." He brushed her cheek with his thumb.

"But I am not Quohadie—"

Walker stopped her words with a kiss, and she didn't try to speak again as he held her close.

The horse blew foam from his lips and pranced at the rim of the canyon. Below, the valley floor was dotted with small campfires glowing orange in the night. Walker raised his eyes to the full moon and stared a moment before kicking his mount into a gallop. The animal was the sixth in a succession of horses he had bribed, borrowed, and ridden into the ground during his desperate race against time.

He had first come to know Col. Ronald S. Mackenzie several years back when Mackenzie was selected by the army to be Walker's henchman for the Indian campaigns in Texas. Though the colonel was a veteran Indian fighter of some reputation, Walker had lost respect for him after Mackenzie's foray against the plains Comanches two years earlier.

In that tragic comedy of errors, Mackenzie had marched after the elusive Horse Back, who was always on reservation lands when they went to look for him but forever being reported as a burning, looting renegade by the new Texas settlers. When Mackenzie had camped that night, Horse Back—having learned the army's plans from captured Tonkawa scouts—struck first. He had only two hundred warriors. Mackenzie had six hundred not counting Apache and Tonkawa scouts.

Horse Back entertained the army with a feint while He Bear captured their horses and mules, crippling the expedition. MacKenzie returned to Camp Cooper in defeat and humiliation.

Horse Back's band of warriors was not guilty of the Texas raids as charged; rather it was Lone Wolf's band of Kiowas. So after that confrontation, Horse Back smilingly rode an army mule out the head of the canyon and straight into the Agency for Indian Affairs to boast of the incident.

The old trader Emmor Harston recalled what Horse Back told him: "When I tell Agent Smith about my raid, I watch to see what he think. His face pretty soon get heap damn mad and he say, *'Go take dem horses and mules back to de white chief!'* But me no do. Me keep dat father mule, he heap good."

While the incident was humorous, it was also pathetic, for it demonstrated all too clearly what some would come to realize many decades later: That no matter how many times they were betrayed, the Indians had a childlike and naive perception of the white man's intentions, and they held it to the very bitter end. No matter how many treaties were broken, they would believe the next lie when it came. Horse Back little realized that what he considered a "good joke on white chief Mackenzie" was really another link in the chain of events that turned Mackenzie's mission from one of patriotism to one of revenge.

Another link came when Mackenzie sent a detachment from Fort Concho looking for Comanches they could fight, and the soldiers followed fresh tracks to a camp. The unit later returned with what captives they had not butchered, and Mackenzie's victory turned sour again: The village had been a "hospital camp" made up of wounded warriors, old men, women, and children. Wounded men were killed on their pallets, over a hundred women and children were left dead, another hundred and thirty women were raped during the battle by soldiers who later boasted of their feat.

The red-faced Mackenzie ordered that these "unusual prisoners" were to be treated well, yet because of lack of coordination between the agency and the army, the women were kept prisoners for months.

When Walker uncovered the facts afterward, he

stormed into Mackenzie's office and demanded his resignation. He did not get it—Mackenzie had too much backing in Washington. But from that time on the two men found working together an unbearable trial.

Suddenly, Walker's horse shied and then reared straight in the air. He grabbed for the saddle horn and gave a startled curse when he saw the shadowed form of a man standing directly in the path of the horse's falling hoofs. He forced the animal's head around to make him pitch sideways, but in doing so only narrowly missed going over the cliff's edge himself, horse and all.

Walker was engaged in a furious outburst of profanity as he dismounted, but there was no one to hear him except his frightened mount. The man was gone.

Yet as he made his way on foot down the rocky trail, he knew someone was following him—not by any sound but by the raised hairs on the back of his neck. In places the trail was so steep and narrow that he had to crawl, and each time he knew there was someone close enough to run a blade between his ribs. Finally he came to a rocky ledge and stood to look over the sides. The campfires were still burning, and he knew the slaughter would be a success if he could not find Horse Back in time. Even those in flight for the reservation had been shot down by the army.

Although he heard nothing, something made Walker turn. The figure now stood in front of him. With the sheer drop at Walker's heels, he knew escape was impossible. With no idea whether this was the right Indian, Walker started talking and didn't stop until he had finished a brief description of the army's mass movement, now plowing across the land two miles southeast of where they stood.

"You have come too late to honor your debt, white eyes," said the voice of the shadow, and Walker instantly recognized it.

He took an involuntary step forward but froze in his tracks when the warrior dropped to a crouch.

"It's not too late if you move now!" Walker argued

406

heatedly, frustrated that after all he'd undergone in getting here, the stubborn chief would refuse to at least make an attempt to flee.

The old Indian straightened slowly and looked over the ledge to the moon-swept canyon floor. His body tensed and for a long moment he said nothing. Then he turned back to Walker. "Go then, white eyes. Your debt is paid."

And he scrambled off the edge of the cliff like a mountain goat and disappeared.

Commander General Pierpont sat in his Washington office staring at the letter of resignation on his desk. The captain handed him a second letter and as Pierpont took it, he raised a bushy brow.

"This too?"

"Yes sir. It was brought by a rider straight to Colonel Mackenzie two weeks ago. He sent it on to us."

General Pierpont only briefly scanned the first letter from Mackenzie, for it was a glowing account of his victory at Palo Duro, which was already old news. Although Horse Back, Quannah Parker, and several more had escaped the massacre at the canyon, they were forced to turn themselves in after Mackenzie slaughtered over one thousand Comanche horses. Winter was coming on and with no horses, no weapons or supplies, the refugees had no choice.

The "real bad" chiefs and headmen such as Tabbe Nanica, Big Bow, and Horse Back received special treatment. They were spread-eagled to stakes in the ground and lashed with a plaited buffalo-hide whip.

For weeks Comanches straggled into the fort to escape the desolation behind them. They were greeted with clubs at the gate and many did not live to set foot inside.

The general turned his attention to the second letter, and his ears burned as he began to read. Although it was addressed to Colonel Mackenzie, there was no doubt that the stinging indictment of the army's Indian

407

policies included himself.

After tossing the letter down on his desk, General Pierpont pulled out a drawer and lifted an expensive rolled parchment, decorated and sealed with a handsome American bald eagle in gold leaf. He looked at the name on the commendation, then dropped it in the wastebasket beside his desk.

"Walker Grayson was one of the finest officers I ever knew," he said quietly, still staring at the leather-bound wastebasket as the captain closed the door behind him.

Henrietta, Texas
Spring, 1882

Two-year-old Martha was the last to succumb to sleep, and Silver was exhausted with nerves and the days of travel as she crawled into bed.

She gasped as Walker rolled on top of her with an animalistic growl and began kissing her neck, tickling her ribs until she was almost shrieking.

"If you wake up this brood of hoodlums you have sired, I am going home," she threatened, and then immediately burst into giggling as Walker tumbled her this way and that, tickling and caressing. In spite of their noise, not a child stirred. Even the oldest, Jamie, was for once beaten by the day's excitement, and kept up his steady breathing.

Through the years Silver had grown accustomed to her husband's sudden and rambunctious attacks of lovemaking, and now, though she would have preferred privacy, her body yearned for the release of tension. Before long they gave up wrestling and tickling for languorous sighs and lazy kisses, forgetting that they were surrounded by three dreaming children. Walker had been forced to become an expert at snatching sweet moments between the call of the plantations and the demands of his overactive offspring. Silver often mused that the only spot they had not tried was the kitchen table—and even that offered certain advantages since she liked to do most of her own cooking and

408

spent many hours in that room.

Although she dropped instantly into a deep post-coital sleep, she was awake and up long before dawn.

She had not been pacing the confines of the small hotel room for more than a minute before Walker sensed she had left their bed. He began wearily to drag into his clothes.

"Perhaps something terrible will happen," Silver worried aloud. "The agency says one thing and changes its mind with the wind."

"He'll come," Walker insisted, finishing the last button and pulling on his boots. "I've been checking and they've already made it as far as Boggy Station. Don't worry, they'll be here. That trader Emmor Harston is coming with them, and the army wouldn't let a civilian do that if there was any possibility of trouble. Besides, it's been seven years since the Indian wars. Let the memories go. You should be looking forward to seeing Horse Back again, not borrowing trouble."

He went to the mirror and gave his thick, unruly hair a lick with the brush; Silver kept up her pacing, chewing her lip.

"But we have come so far! The trip was so hard on the children—I do not want this to turn to a bad memory." She pivoted like a soldier and marched in the opposite direction, having unconsciously picked up the nervous habit from her husband. "If my brother comes, there could be trouble. He is a hothead."

Walker's voice was faintly impatient. "That was the old days, Silver. Quannah walks the white man's road now and from what I hear, he's doing a good job."

The baby awoke with a sudden yelp, like a puppy whose tail has been trapped under a boot. Silver began unbuttoning her blouse as she went to the bureau drawer on the floor, which doubled well for a baby's bed.

"I cannot believe he has changed," she said sadly. "He was very bitter I last saw him." Walker had taken her to the reservation shortly after the great battle at Llano Estacado to prove to her that Horse Back and

Quannah had not been killed. It was a fine reunion, and Walker could hardly hold back his own tears. Now, however, Silver had not seen her father in seven years.

"Horse Back was bitter, too, at first," he reminded her. "But both men have had to change. We all must change. That's the way life . . ."

He didn't finish as his eyes lit on the little girl nursing greedily at her mother's breast. He was always both awed and humbled by the sight, and crept toward them softly, aware of the somehow brutish crunch of his boots on the floor.

He traced the firm full contour of the suckled breast with his fingertip, then drew a circle on the downy cheek of his baby daughter. Bending, he kissed both spots tenderly, and when he raised his head, his eyes were burning with determination.

"Don't worry, my beauty. Nobody is going to ruin this day for you or he'll answer to me."

The Indian wagons had been sent to pick up Indian Agency freight from the railroad.

The excursion was entered into enthusiastically by Comanches hungry to escape the reservation, and the caravan of sixty some odd people bore all the trappings of an excited wagon train heading west, only the faces inside were not white but red.

The wagons overflowed with boxes, camp equipment, and bedding, poles and teepees, and food for the horses. There were no bridges, which required the squaws to get out and push each wagon up the rocky shoals at each creek crossing, but they labored without complaining. There would be many trinkets and beautiful cloth awaiting them at the small frontier town.

Neither the Comanches nor the white family who awaited them so eagerly realized that the story of Horse Back's visit to Henrietta would be told around the campfires of both races for many years to come.

Walker had ridden out in search for the little caravan, and Silver waited anxiously at the railroad depot, the baby on her hip and holding the four-year-old's hand. Her white brother's namesake, Jamie, who was almost eight, stood apart from the group with the dignity that befitted a male of his years.

Although Walker smiled when the chief waved in greeting, his eyes were tinged with sadness as he looked at the old warrior, who now wore white eyes britches and shoes, a leather vest over a well-worn shirt. The only vestige of his former glory was a simple scalp lock tagged with a feather which was obviously not eagle. Without weapons, there could be neither eagle feathers for adornment — nor hides for moccasins, so the Texas or *Teichas* Indians had grown to know the discomfort of corns and bunions.

"My father," said Walker, and the old chief grinned. "My son, father of my grandchildren."

"Your daughter is waiting at the depot with the children." Walker answered the searching question in the dark eyes.

"That is good," beamed Horse Back. "My people have chased the *cona-woka-poke* for three suns and still they have not seen this great wonder." He spoke of the train, the fire-wagon-horse.

Walker grinned. "Well, engine nine comes in around noon. You'll get your chance if we hurry."

When they arrived in town, Silver was still standing as Walker had left her, and his heart went out to her. Her back must be breaking under the load of chubby little Melissa Ann.

Yet Walker stayed back, pretending to adjust the strappings on his horse, as Horse Back stepped from the wagon with great dignity and headed for the young woman.

Silver handed the baby to Jamie — in spite of the boy's fierce look of disapproval — and tried to keep the tears from her eyes when she saw the mighty Horse Back in his white man's clothes.

She walked out to meet him and dropped on one knee before him.

"My father."

Horse Back's voice was choked. "Rise my daughter. The old customs are gone now. If a man stands still, the days run off and leave him." He made her stand so that he could kiss her forehead, and looked into her watery eyes. "I am well. I still have many wives and many sons and daughters. Quannah could not come. He is gone to see the Great White Father in Washington, but he sends his sister his love."

Silver raised her eyes, larger and more luminous than the first day Horse Back had lifted her into his arms.

"Prairie Flower is Quannah's Indian sister," said Silver, and she pressed her lips together to keep them from trembling. She had determined that the truth be spoken at last—if only this once. She went on. "The girl child of Cynthia Ann Parker is his half-blood sister. But I . . . I am his . . ." The word was a new one and she struggled with it. "I am his *adopted* sister."

Horse Back dropped his gaze for a moment, and when he could speak again, he said softly, "But more loved than any of my children."

Walker took the baby from Jamie and propped her on his hip. "They want to see the fire wagon," he told Silver, looking at his watch. "In fact, I hear the whistle now."

Horse Back went suddenly stiff. "That is very short time." Then he wheeled away toward the waiting wagons, still loaded to the hilt, for the occupants were too frightened of the approaching noise to disembark.

Horse Back began shouting in an unbroken string of Comanche.

Walker looked on nervously. "What's he saying?"

Silver was wearing a disturbed and puzzled frown. "He is telling them how to arrange the wagons."

The married couple watched in stunned silence as the wagons were lined up parallel to the tracks so all would have a clear view.

And the great steam engine belched and honked—the din growing like that of a cyclone sweeping upon them.

Like their owners, the Comanche horses had never seen a fire-wagon-pony either. Of one accord, they began to snort and rear wildly, jingling the harness strappings as they lunged to get free.

Some of the nimbler braves leaped from the wagons and ran to hide behind the depot, leaving the women and children in the wagons. Engine number nine clamored into the depot, its stack belching smoke like a dragon, its brakes shrilling piercingly, and the horses bolted in a frenzy of shrieking and bucking.

Nothing could stop the pandemonium at that point. Hay, pots, pans, teepees, poles, crates, and women and children were scattered across the nearby prairie. One of the horse teams headed across the tracks in front of the slow-moving train and kept going until it was halted by a wire fence, and one of the posts overturned the wagon. The Indians inside hit the ground running, and fled for the nearest hiding place.

Gesticulating with his arms and dancing in an angry circle, Horse Back shouted orders, but to no avail. When the noise started to die, he began to curse the amused engineer, half in Comanche and half in a hilarious mixture of both languages, punctuated freely by the "heaps of damns" he had learned from the white eyes.

Silver and Walker remained to enjoy their kin for longer than expected, for several days were needed to patch broken wagon beds, repair a warped coupling pole, and doctor three crippled horses. But it was agreed by all that Horse Back's visit to Henrietta would not be forgotten for many moons.

From that day on Walker noticed that his wife seemed to have reconciled her station halfway between two worlds. If Horse Back could walk the white eyes road, so could she. Though Jamie Daniels paid periodic calls to the Grayson plantation and seemed genuinely glad to see his sister, the two could not spend much time together before friction arose. Yet, Walker mused, their family had grown very large indeed. Since Seth seemed to be aiming for Prissy's goal of "forty or thirty" children (they had six at present), and Uncle Guy and Aunt Belle had moved into Gray Shadows with them to help out, the great house had ceased to creak and moan but rattled with children's voices and laughter.

Walker's thoughts broke off abruptly, his fork paused midway to his mouth as he caught the gleam in his wife's eyes.

His own narrowed, and he said slowly, "Not again." But he could see it was too late; the spell had already struck her.

"I must be free," she said gravely.

"But I'm hungry—I've got to go to the syrup mill this afternoon and later I must go over the ledgers—"

"Mrs. Peoples!" Silver called, jumping from her chair. "You will watch the children?" she asked, and her eyes were sparkling.

Mrs. Peoples glanced slyly at the master and saw that, as always, he was putty in the mistress's hands. "I surely will. You two run along," she purred.

Silver dragged Walker across to the stables, and though his responsibilities were already too vague to recall as he contemplated the afternoon, he pretended to be ornery.

"I don't know how you expect me to get any work done if I'm going to be dragged into the woods every few days and raped by my own wife," he grumbled.

Her answer was a high-pitched giggle, and he followed, muttering irately. He got his sorrel from the paddock while Silver led Rising Sun from the stable.

"And I guess you're going to make me ride bareback like a savage," he rumbled.

Silver mounted the tall aging stallion in one leap. "You do not have time for a squaw blanket if you keep up with me." And she kicked the horse into a gallop, which Walker could not hope to match on his own horse. Especially with no saddle.

She had beaten him to their spot so much that by the time Walker arrived, as breathless as his mount, Silver had stripped naked. She poised like a graceful swam, arching every muscle for maximum effect while Walker's eyes caught fire, and he half stumbled and half fell from his horse.

He came after her with no intention of playing out her ridiculous fantasies that they were two savages roaming alone and free on the Texas plains. Her body was as perfectly formed as ever, and a lusty arousal seized him so quickly and so thoroughly that his run slowed to a hunched stumble.

"Don't jump in that water! I am not going to get wet, I swear it—"

But it was too late. She arched out, hooked her body down into a perfect upside-down U, and pierced the still green waters of the bayou.

Walker stripped out of his clothes. "You'll pay," he gritted, hobbling clumsily as his boot hung in his britches, for in his lust he had forgotten to take them off first.

Silver cackled and pointed fiendishly, for his dignity was further maligned because his off-balance hopping set the most proud and intimidating of all male weapons to jostling comically.

When he succeeded in stripping completely, he walked out to the edge of the bank and looked down at her in the water, and Silver's laughter choked off in her throat at the sight of him.

Her eyes glowed like soft white crystals in her wet lashes.

"There was never a stronger or more handsome warrior than mine," she said soberly.

Walker gave her a wolfish grin to disguise a faint embarrassment at the adoration in her eyes.

"I can play the savage, too—as you have well learned," he taunted huskily. He lifted his arms for the dive and Silver watched in fascination as his muscles rippled and gathered strength till his body was ribbed with taut cords all the way from the broad shoulders to the lean flanks and bulging, muscular thighs. The cascading wave blinded her, and while she shook the water from her face, she felt his arms circle her waist under

415

the water. She wiggled, pretending to fight him, and suddenly his head broke the surface, his face dewed with beads of water.

"I'll take you at my leisure and when you're begging me for mercy, you'll finally understand who is the master here and who is the slave." He laughed wickedly and squeezed her with deliberate roughness.

Silver threw her arms around his neck and pressed herself against him, but she did not take up his teasing tone.

"Take me, Walker Gray's Son. But I will not beg for mercy." And she looked up at him gravely. "I will sing the Comanche LoveSong. And when I am even old and gray, you will still want me to warm your bed." Her eyes flashed a little. "You will never take more wives."

"Only if you promise. Even when we're old and gray and wrinkled."

"*Commar-pe* is good for the old ones as well," she informed him. Then she grinned. "Especially old and gray and wrinkled white eyes. Quohadie Teichas work till they die, but white eyes, they have very truly much time and nothing else to do."

Su-ua-te: That is all.